BREAKING THE RULES

THE DATING PLAYBOOK, BOOK: 2

MARIAH DIETZ

BREAKING THE RULES

Copyright © 2020 by Mariah Dietz

All rights reserved.

No part of this book may be reproduced in any form or by any electronic or mechanical means, including information storage and retrieval systems, without written permission from the author, except for the use of brief quotations in a book review.

Cover Design © Hang Le

❊ Created with Vellum

Learn More About Mariah

Website: www.mariahdietz.com

Also sign up for news, updates, and first glimpses with Mariah's newsletter:
Sign Up Now

Also follow Mariah on:

- Amazon
- Bookbub
- Facebook
- Goodreads

And join Mariah's readers group on Facebook: The Bossy Babes

For my Readers

1

RAEGAN

I expected peace.
After all, I'd just been forced to say a silent and rapid good-bye to those I loved, the chances I had and those I hadn't, and some that I'd just never taken. It seemed that if I were going to die, peace was a small return to never see the sunrise again over the Puget Sound, or taste freshly brewed coffee, or indulge in a great novel that keeps you up all night, or never to kiss Lincoln Beckett again.

My lungs burn as does the rest of my body. And everything aches like I've come down with an acute case of the flu. I'm painfully cold, and my head feels too light.

Nausea hits me like an eighteen-wheeler, and the swarm of panic and fear returns with a surge of adrenaline dictated by my body or maybe my mind—demanding I fight.

"Shhhh," a soft voice summons me, calming me, and then a gentle caress brushes my arm, a complete contradiction to the pain I feel everywhere. It's warm and soft, and for a moment, I wonder if this will be my last memory—my last *everything*.

I ball my hands into fists as I struggle to open my eyelids. Warm sunlight surrounds me, bathing me in a glow I feared I'd never see again, and though it burns my eyes, I can't force myself to look away.

There's a loud shudder, and then another sound that is similar to crying. I can't focus on it for very long, though, because the world has begun to spin, and my nausea is becoming stronger. I close my eyes to ward off everything—the pain, the fear, the discomfort. Going through this twice doesn't seem fair.

"Rae. Raegan. Rae, we're here, baby." Mom's voice is too muffled and bleary, but I know it's her just like I know I'm meant to be a cetologist, studying dolphins and whales, providing a voice for them. Like I know Poppy will always be my ride or die to the ends of the earth, and that my older brother, Paxton, is going to be in the NFL one day, and my older sister, Maggie, will win the Nobel Peace Prize for her determination to help others. Just like I know that Lincoln Beckett and his pirate smile stole my heart three years ago and just recently was willing to admit he harbors the muscle that beats for him.

Or did.

Or is?

A gentle rhythm plays against the back of my hand. It's soothing and warm and calls for me to open my eyes once more. Mom's dark hair is brushed back into a clip, and her face is red and blotchy, her lips dry.

"What were you thinking?" she asks, her lips trembling more with each word.

I try to talk, but my throat feels raw, and my jaw aches.

Tears spill from Mom's eyes, but she doesn't look away or even try to wipe them, likely because more quickly follow like tiny soldiers marching off to battle. "You can't talk," she says," her voice hoarse. "They had to put a ventilator in." Rounder tears slide down her cheeks, their pace increasing.

"Raegan?" The voice is a stranger's. I turn my attention to an older man with wiry white hair that's too long and unkempt. He's wearing green scrubs and a pair of glasses that are halfway down his nose, and he smells like tacos. "Nice to see you're awake. This is a great sign." He looks at Mom, and then behind him, I see Dad. Apart from when Maggie left for Nepal two years ago, I can't recall having ever seen my dad cry. Not even when Grams died did he cry in front of us. But, tears streak his face now, making the pain in my chest even greater.

"Your vitals are improving as well," the man with the white hair says, reviewing a set of screens I can barely make out over my shoulder. "All good news. The new doctor on shift is Dr. Grayson, and he should be in shortly. For now, it's just more rest. If you start to feel any pain, you can press this button," he says, lassoing a short cord around the hospital bed and sliding a piece of cold plastic against my palm.

I press it instantly, without hesitation, waiting for the medicine to seep in and numb me.

My eyes grow heavier, and the sounds become muted along with my emotions and fears, everything grows warmer, lulling me into a comfort I quickly succumb to.

Hours pass or maybe days. Maybe it's only minutes until I open my eyes again and focus on the blue balloon tied to the post of my bed. It's one of those giant Mylar balloons that remain inflated for long periods and written on it in rainbow script are the words 'Get Well.' It bobs against the air vent overhead, reminding me of watching something in the waves. Coldness has me trying to move my legs, wishing I could dig my feet under a blanket or between the cushions on the couch— anything that would offer some warmth. But, moving my feet is nearly impossible, my entire body sluggish and stiff. I close my eyes for several seconds in an attempt to appease the throbbing in my head, then open them again to get another look at my surroundings. Tubes and cords are everywhere, hooked to me and winding into a labyrinth that goes over my shoulder, beyond where I can see. Machines beep and echo; one reminds me of the sounds Grandpa makes when he snores. The doors are large, collapsible glass panels, covered with a curtain. In the chair beside my bed is Mom, her neck at an unnatural and painful angle that I'm sure she'll be regretting tomorrow. I mentally make a note to tell her to sleep at home tomorrow. Then, I focus my attention back on the balloon, watching it bob and weave as it transports me back into the ocean, slowly feeling the coldness fade as I hit the button to escape the aching again.

PAIN RETURNS with a hard threat and with it lots of noise. Voices and machines, the sound of wheels and metal. "Raegan!" Someone's calling my name again, and I debate answering. I don't want to endure more discomfort. I don't want to see the agony I brought to my parents.

"Raegan!" A new voice says my name, and though they're not technically yelling, the tone is assertive and too bossy for my liking.

"We need you to fight, girlfriend." Another foreign voice joins the chorus, bringing forth memories of the ocean: the utter blackness and the frigid temperatures that had felt like a thousand tiny needles stabbing into my flesh, puncturing my lungs and hope. I taste the bile in my throat, the burning sensation in my chest, the fear and frustrating certainty that I was trapped in the same manner I'd been trying to fight against since before I even knew how.

"Dammit," a terse voice calls out, defeat and peril hanging in the air like a thick fog. It forces a memory to bloom: the cold slice from each stroke as I swam through the dark water, the determination in my chest as I fought my desire to go back to be with him. *Lincoln*. His anger was evident as he'd yelled the same word. He'd likely felt the same defeat I had when I'd realized the fishing net—the one I dove into the Puget Sound for to free a dolphin named Blue—was wrapped and tangled around me, holding me prisoner several inches beneath the surface and stealing my tiny allotment of air.

Thoughts of Lincoln spread and multiply until every memory of the ocean is replaced by his startling brown eyes, sharp jaw, straight nose, and the short mane of hair I ran my fingers through when he explored my body for the first time. His laughter tickles my ears, and his fierce exterior tests my patience. With each thought, a new pain hits my chest and spreads until all I can think about is Lincoln, and all I can feel is torment.

"There we go, girlfriend. That's right. You stay here. All these people are here for you, baby. You don't get to leave that easily." It's the voice from earlier, velvet on my ears as she calls me girlfriend. I like the term of endearment. Like we're friends, though she doesn't know a thing about me.

I slowly crack my eyes open, regretting the decision instantly as a team of doctors and nurses hover over me.

"Hey, it's nice to meet you finally." It's the brusque voice this time, and though his words sound kind, his tone is still angry and rushed. His face is covered by a hospital mask, sparking an irrational fear I've had since I was a child—a fear consisting of waking up during surgery. I'd watched an episode of Dateline or Twenty-Twenty with my parents eons ago, during which they interviewed people who were traumatized by the very nightmare. That fear camouflaged itself and has remained in my memory, popping out at the most random and inopportune times, like now.

"Let's make sure we don't do that again, okay?" The emphasis on the word okay, the way he punctuated it brings out an accent that reveals he's far from home. I'm guessing New York, maybe Jersey?

The doctor brushes his fingers along the line of his brow, then lowers his surgical mask and rolls his shoulders. "Looks like we're not gonna need you guys," he says, turning his attention to a blonde woman standing next to a pushcart filled with supplies.

"You want me to leave the ones I've got on her there, just in case?" the blonde asks.

The doctor pulls in a deep breath through his nose. "Yeah. Probably should." He turns his blue-green eyes to me. "They're only a precaution because I like to have my bases covered. You keep your heart beating this time, yeah?"

My heart beating?

My vision is clumsy and clouded, the same heavy and constant cover of exhaustion urging me back to sleep, whispering promises of the discomfort fading if I just hit the little button encapsulated in my fist.

I slowly stretch my fingers, each of them sore and protesting the loss of the morphine drip. But I don't want it. Not anymore. I'd rather feel the pain that reminds me I'm somehow still alive.

I SPEND four days in the hospital.

Twenty-four hours after my heart stopped, they took out that awful tracheal tube that was down my throat. My throat had never been so sore, not even after my tonsils were removed when I was twelve. Ice chips and water were my saving grace. My first words were the request to remove the morphine. I was tired of its constant haze and still fearful of sleep. The doctor on call encouraged me to keep it, but that night, the

Northeastern doctor was on shift again. I learned his name was Dr. Grayson. He had straight black hair, a slightly bulbous nose, and olive skin. I asked him to remove the morphine, and surprisingly, he listened. My fourth and final night was spent on the general floor of the hospital, away from the constant checks and lights that consume the ICU. And this morning, they finally signed the discharge papers, stating I was free to go home despite my parents' concerns.

"What if she stops breathing again?" Mom asks.

"What if she starts going into cardiac arrest again?" Dad demands.

We're outside the doors of the ICU, visiting Dr. Grayson, the only doctor my parents seemingly trust, and who will likely be receiving handsome Christmas gifts from them this year for saving my life for the second time in a matter of days. They've decided his words are gospel, trusting him above the doctor who signed my discharge papers. I'm seated in a wheelchair—hospital policy they told me as they ordered I take a seat, dressed in the yoga pants and Brighton sweatshirt Mom had brought for me to wear.

Dr. Grayson flashes a gentle smile—one he never gave me while I was his patient. "She's doing great. Near drowning patients have a window of time where there are risks, and once you're past that, you're in the clear. Reagan's in the clear."

Mom places a tissue to her eyes. "You're positive?"

Dr. Grayson nods. "You know the signs if anything arises, but her vitals all look great, and she passed her tests with flying colors. Now, it's just a matter of gaining back some strength and healing."

I'm fairly positive I'm being wheeled out of the hospital with more injuries than I arrived with, namely due to the chest tube they pushed through my ribs and punctured my right lung with to drain the remains of the Pacific Ocean, I'd brought in here with me.

"I know it's been a rough week for you guys. But, I promise, we wouldn't let her go if there were any foreseen risks," Dr. Grayson concludes.

Maggie places her hand on my shoulder. It's an assurance to herself rather than me, though. Everyone keeps touching me. Mom slept in the hospital room with me last night with one hand on my stomach. She startled awake a half dozen times with a loud gasp, tearing her eyes to the monitors that were measuring my heart and lungs to ensure neither had taken a vacation. They hadn't. Instead, she was making them both work overtime. "Mom is so glad you lived because she's going to kill you now herself," Maggie says.

Laughter tickles my throat, but in its place comes an ugly and hoarse cough that makes me sound like I've been chain-smoking for the past fifty years.

"She sounds like she's still choking," Mom points out.

My cheeks redden with embarrassment and the labor of breathing as the coughing subsides, and I use another folded tissue I've replaced and kept in my palm as a constant for the past few days to wipe the small flecks of blood from my arm after covering my cough. It turns out, the tracheal tube scratched my throat, and coughing up blood is part of the healing process.

Gross, I know.

"It's perfectly normal. Her lungs endured a lot," Dr. Grayson assures her. "It's like a cold or the flu; the side-effects will take a little time to go away."

"I feel good, Mom. I want to go home." My voice still burns a little, but I don't admit that just like I refuse to admit the nightmares I've been having since the morphine stopped providing me the peaceful nothingness.

Mom turns to me. "You also wanted to dive into the ocean and look where that got us." She's a little mad—that might be the understatement of the century. I can't recall Mom ever being upset with me for this long. Poppy assures me it's normal, but it still comes with a truckload of guilt.

Dr. Grayson smiles. "I know this was really hard on you guys, but everything's going to be okay. Get home, get some rest, and some real food. In a week or two, she'll be as good as new."

My only reluctance with leaving is that it signifies the end of my time here, waiting for Lincoln to stop by. To show up with a cheesy balloon or nothing at all, I don't care. I just want to see him—need to see him. But, like nearly drowning, that isn't my choice to make.

2
LINCOLN

I live for game days.
    The anticipation.
    The adrenaline.
The focus.

The scent of leather when opening a fresh pair of cleats.

I've been playing football since I was seven and chills still race over my arms before a game.

Paxton, on the other hand, is a jittery fool who often sucks my enthusiasm away until he loses the contents of his stomach and then instantly calms the fuck down. He hasn't reached that point yet. We all have our routines—the same events and structures that lead us to prepare for a game. For me, game days start early with reps and transitions to sprints. After sprints, I run for two miles and then hit the showers and eat like a king. It's a double order of eggs benedict every single time, and then I study film until it's time to ice my shoulder and get my ankles taped. I don't hang out with others. I don't answer my phone. On game days, I become a solitary motherfucker.

I've played two games since Raegan nearly died. I didn't complete my routine for either fucking one.

I tried. Hell, I even managed to get certain parts of my routine, but somewhere amid my preparations, thoughts of her hit me like a linebacker, knocking the air out of me. Today, I didn't make it to my damn reps without thinking about her, my routine spoiled as Paxton shared with Arlo and me that they were releasing Raegan this morning. I hated the idea. She wasn't ready. I knew in my gut she wasn't ready, and that knowledge festered as I imagined the worst-case scenarios playing in my head like a highlights reel, again and again.

Coach Harris strides into the locker room, snapping as he makes a path to the center of the room. "All right. All right. All right. Are we ready for tonight?" he yells. The team erupts, sounding like a well-trained militia as we promise to beat them. "I said, are we ready for tonight?" Coach Harris yells again, his voice louder. The team responds with more force, more volume. Coach Harris grins around his large wad of gum. "I want to see hustle. I want to see intensity. I want to see you whoop their mother fucking asses!"

Everyone cheers while Pax and I remain silent. Pax is still and mute because he can't focus on anything but not barfing in front of coach. Me, I don't like this type of hype. It doesn't build me up or get me into the "zone" like it does others. I use that as my excuse to remain quiet, my jaw locked as thoughts of Raegan infiltrate my routine for the billionth time today.

Then Derek Jones leans into view, and my muscles grow rigid. Derek is a sophomore who transferred from Texas at the end of last year with a hunger for the spotlight that had me disliking him off the bat. And to add to that, he willingly threw two of our starting players under the bus by reporting them to Coach Harris for missing three mandatory weight-training sessions. Was it a coincidence that one of the two players who got benched was a wide receiver—the same position Derek plays? It sure as hell wasn't. We knew they were missing practice. They had a final to take, and practice was the only time they could meet with their teacher's assistant. And unlike Derek, both of them were actively working toward earning a degree, using football as their way of paying for college. That little act made my trust fall into the negative and my dislike soar. But what shot him straight into the loathing category was his interest in a girl, and like the players he had benched, I was confident he had an agenda. She wasn't just any girl, either, she was Paxton Lawson's—my best friend and our team captain's—little sister. Raegan. The same girl I've spent months avoiding because I don't do relationships and having an infatuation with my best friend's sister reminded me far too much of a Caesar and Pompeii relationship if something were to go sour like it inevitably always does. Yet, I set sail on the Rubicon before sense caught up with my ass.

Last week, Derek saved her from drowning.

Not me.

Hell, I didn't even manage to stop her.

No. I was stuck on a boat watching my world fall away from me because a stranger told us we'd make the situation worse by going in after her.

Every hour—every minute—my regret for listening grows stronger.

"Need a hand? Or a finger?" Arlo jabs Pax with a quick punch as Coach Harris concludes his spiel.

Paxton blows a slow stream of air through his mouth, then jogs toward the bathroom stalls.

"That's such a disgusting habit." Arlo cringes. "I don't understand. How can he just make himself sick?"

I shake my head. "I don't know, but it seems to work for him."

"Glad I don't have to deal with that."

I strive to turn off the channel in my brain that continually flips back to Raegan. "You're superstitious as all hell, dude. You've got your own bag of nuts." I eye his socks that are tinted brown because he's been wearing the same damn pair for five fucking years and has yet to wash them because he's afraid we'll lose if he does.

"Not everyone can be perfect like you." Arlo clasps my cheeks, pinching my face.

"Cute," Derek says, slowing as he passes in front of us.

"Does he know how badly I want to bash his face in every time he speaks?" Arlo asks, watching Derek walk away.

"No. His head's shoved up too far his ass to realize anything."

Pax appears with a sports drink in hand, sweat formed on his pale brow. He looks terrible, but he always does at this point.

"Ready?" I ask.

He nods before taking a long drink, and then the three of us go out toward the tunnel where the team is lining up, ready to take the field.

The dull ache in my shoulder and my evolving thoughts about Reagan are things I don't voice as we step into the lights, the last thing I want to reveal is weakness.

Coach Harris slaps me on the back; his hat pulled low over his eyes. "You ready, son?"

I flash a smile. "I'm always ready."

He chuckles, a large wad of gum visible between his teeth. Coach is always chewing gum, sometimes so hard I expect him to pop his jaw out of place. The man doesn't know how to remain still. Between chewing gum, snapping, and pacing, he's always moving. "I want to see your face on the highlights reel tonight on ESPN."

"You will."

He chuckles again. He loves my confidence—needs it to fuel his own.

I put my earbuds in and pull my helmet on. Coach pats my back again, firm enough to feel his touch through my pads, but gentler this time with more endearment. It might be because I'm his meal ticket, having brought Brighton more publicity in the past three years than they've had in over a decade, or possibly because I go to practice early and stay late, and all those hours together have accumulated and formed a bond between us that often has me looking to coach like another parent. A parent who doesn't have unrealistic expectations or a shadow of guilt each time he looks at me.

We stream out onto the field, passing by the cheerleaders who scream and shout a rhyme and wave flags as the crowd cheers raucously. We're anticipated to be a big contender this year, and announcers are already talking about us going undefeated. These types of news stories make Pax even sicker, but for me, they give me purpose.

Arlo is next to me, his arms raised in the air, feeding off the crowd, and then Quinton joins him, jumping in the air and doing what looks like a jig. He's a mountain of a linebacker, and like Arlo, he loves the pre-game. I focus on the music streaming through my earbuds to block out the chaos, and smile because that's what people want to see when they see the highlight reel tonight. They want to see The President smiling and being the cocky bastard who leads his team to another victory.

Coach snaps feverishly, the sound muted over the crowd. "Let's go, let's go, let's go!" He looks over us as we stand in formation. I pull my earbuds free and hand them and my phone to Benny, one of the assistant coaches who works exclusively with us wide receivers. He pockets them and nods before handing me a clean towel to tuck in. It's a dry night, but I still accept it because habits are as ingrained for me as they are for Arlo and Pax.

"Derek, you have strong side. Lincoln, you're the weak side, son." He looks between us as adrenaline swells in my chest t as I debate if *she's* watching me.

It's a ridiculous question. Few enjoy the game as much as Raegan, and Paxton is my insurance that she's watching. The reminder of that night creeps into my thoughts, recalling how she had looked me straight in the eye—straight into my heart—before jumping into the ocean. She didn't give me the chance to say one fucking thing. Not stop or don't or even good-bye. I was stuck in the midst of a silent battlefield that night, standing on the deck of the boat, searching for her while I felt myself dying in response. Derek was closer, and he didn't have Paxton and some crazy-ass lady holding him back, telling him he was going to scare the dolphins who were circling her body, making loud sounds as they chaotically moved and weaved through the water. Derek saved her, and in doing so, he spared what was left of my sanity. Unfortunately, she'd already taken nearly all of it, letting it fall to the bottom of the Puget Sound, where it sits, lost like a forgotten pirate ship.

3

RAEGAN

"Hey, are you feeling okay?" Poppy intercepts my route to class, her head dipped as she examines me.

An automatic 'yes' leaves my mouth out of habit. It's been a week since I went home from the hospital. I've been given a clean bill of health except for the cough that still steals my breath periodically, but even that, they assure me, will end soon.

"He still hasn't called?" She sees through my lie.

I breathe out a heavy sigh, watching my breath float in the cold air before shaking my head. "I was stupid enough to believe I meant something. That I might be different."

Poppy winces. "Something doesn't add up. It's too weird. He was going crazy. If Paxton hadn't been so blinded by his own fear, he would have realized Lincoln's got it bad for you. That doesn't just go away overnight." She's given too many empty assurances, and he's ignored me for too long for the words to provide any sort of ease or comfort.

"We could go out to a party. Track him down?"

My traitorous heart beats faster with hope. "If he's not responding to my calls or texts, do you really think he's going to talk to me in person?"

"I think you scared the shit out of him."

"I wasn't trying to."

There's something foreign about her expression, something that resembles doubt or possibly resentment that makes my heart thump louder and faster.

"You know I wasn't trying to actually drown myself, right?"

"I know. But, what would've happened if you'd died?" Her eyes rim red as she stares at me. "Did you even consider how we'd survive that? The guilt Lincoln would've lived with knowing he brought you out there, and Paxton for not having stopped you, and me on both of those fronts? Your parents, your sister, your grandpa?

"I get it. I know how much you love the ocean and the animals, and you reacted. But, Rae, you almost *died*." Her eyes turn glassy with unshed tears. "I want to hug you and throttle you every time I see you, and I'm terrified you'll try something crazy again."

A myriad of emotions push and pull at my heart, wanting to argue my independence and how that situation was the exception, not the standard, but guilt and shame silence me as I play out the past few weeks in a reverse role, with her jumping. Pax jumping. Lincoln jumping.

I release the unspoken words in a long breath and wrap my arms around Poppy. It takes her a couple of seconds to register my hug, and a couple more before she weakly wraps her arms around me, her breaths heavier and longer as she openly cries. "I don't know what I'd do without you," she says between tears, her voice raspy and uneven.

I hold her tighter, the pain in my side pinching, but it only encourages me to grasp harder. Pain reminds me I'm alive, and I no longer wish to avoid it.

When Poppy pulls away, her hands remain gripping my arms, bridging us. "I'm sorry. I know it's not fair to be mad at you. My mom says it's part of the grieving process, which doesn't really make sense because you're here, and even when they said you weren't breathing, I refused to believe you wouldn't make it, but..." she gasps, fresh tears rolling down her freckled cheeks. "I've never been so afraid. I spent the drive to the hospital thinking about everything we've done together, all the times you've been there for me, and it made me feel so stupid for being upset about Mike these past couple of months."

I shake my head. "*I'm* sorry. I'm so sorry."

She hugs me again; her grip is tighter. "You owe me some really good wrinkle cream for my birthday because I'm pretty sure you aged me like twenty years."

I laugh, nodding as we separate. "Deal."

"And Lincoln might just need to process for a bit. Or yell at you." She pauses. "Maybe both."

I fake another smile, nodding with understanding.

Poppy wipes at her cheeks with the heels of her hands. "I'm going to be late for class. Are you working tonight?"

I shake my head. "I'm off all week."

"Maybe we can catch up later? I'm working at my Mom's office until six, but I'll call you after."

"Sounds good."

She smiles, every bit of her expression familiar before she waves and turns, walking in the opposite direction of my next class. I debate skipping, lying, and saying I was too tired, or that I got dizzy, or one of the other hundred excuses at my disposal. Everyone is still looking at me like I'm going to keel over at any second—another consequence of nearly dying, I suppose. Not only is everyone upset with me on some level, but there's also zero trust between those I need it from most, and everyone's looking at me like I'm as fragile as an ancient glass ornament that's been cracked and will shatter at any moment.

I could grab some coffee and try to warm up—I've been permanently frozen since that fateful night. I could go home and spend the day with Maggie and the documentaries she loves. But, being absent will only make that crack they all see more prominent, so I hitch my bag higher on my shoulder and head in the direction of the science building.

I slide into my seat with only a few minutes to spare before class starts. The room is uncomfortably cold, so I leave my jacket on as I pull out my laptop, considering Poppy's advice. Could anger be what's keeping Lincoln from returning my messages?

"Hey."

I glance up, spotting a guy with short brown hair and light brown eyes. I stare at him, waiting for him to request to borrow something or ask if I have notes.

He swallows, blinking several times as he shifts his feet, kicking them out in front of his desk and crossing one over the other. "You're Raegan, right?"

I nod. "I'm Ben. That's Megan," he says, pointing to the girl with auburn hair and a quick smile behind him. "You're always quiet, so I just wanted to say hi. Introduce myself."

"And Megan," I point out.

He chuckles humorlessly, but his features are friendly. "We've been friends for like two years."

I nod again, reminded why I hate small talk and meeting new people so damn much. "It's nice to meet you both."

"You okay?" he asks. "You were gone."

I tuck my fingers into my coat. "Yeah. I just had a small accident."

"Oh, man. Like a car accident?" he asks.

"Um..." I glance at the door, wishing the professor would appear. "No. I got stuck in a fishing net while diving underwater."

The guy on the other side of Ben suddenly looks at me, as does the guy behind him, like my story warrants the attention I've diligently avoided.

"Holy shit. What happened? Did you, like, drown?" One of the onlookers asks.

"No, moron. Drown means to die."

I swallow the uncomfortable words from the other guy who I know as Bennet because he often answers questions or fires them off, causing us to release late on multiple occasions.

It feels like everyone's eyes are on me then, silent questions and judgment from a few. Their narrowed eyes and stitched brows are working to determine if I'm lying—if I'm looking for attention.

I'm not. Not from this crowd, at least. Not this type from anyone.

"How long were you stuck underwater?" Someone asks.

"Why were you underwater?"

"Isn't it, like, freezing?"

A girl giggles in the distance. "How did she get caught by a fishing net? Was she trying to pretend she was a mermaid?" More snickers and giggles.

"It was in the newspaper if any of you morons read or paid attention to anything." A guy pokes his head out from behind his laptop, a mess of dark and unruly hair as he combs over my sea of onlookers. "She was saving a dolphin, and you're a bitch." His attention stops at the girl who called me a mermaid.

The professor enters then, and the stranger doesn't move his gaze to meet mine as I silently debate if I'm grateful he stood up for me or if he's just opened the door for more punchlines.

Without work and with everyone being upset at me, I've spent far too much time with my homework, catching up for the classes I've missed as well as reading ahead. Any excuse to stay in my room has been welcomed. So, when the professor begins talking about something I've already studied and know, my thoughts drift freely, thinking about Poppy's words. I debate if Lincoln's anger will subside on its own or if we should try and find him at a party? I can't show up at his door and demand we talk because my brother lives with him. I could try texting him again. A call he might ignore, but it's tough to ignore the words in a text.

I tuck my things away as class ends, my thoughts volleying between my angry football god and the hurt I caused, and the pain he's returning in spades. My pen falls off the corner of my desk, and the sound of it hitting the floor is lost in the shuffle of others, but then someone reaches out and snags the pen, dropping it on my desk. I glance up to catch the same dark, disheveled hair, dark eyes, and clear skin that makes it appear like he doesn't spend much time in the sun. He's all edges and darkness with a grim smile that doesn't hit his eyes. Blake Matthews. That was the name he responded to when the professor called his name.

"Thanks," I say, depositing it into my bag.

He nods once and moves for the door.

I briefly debate telling Poppy about him. My best friend loves the broody type—don't we all, unfortunately?

I file him away as 'maybe' and head toward the offices.

Mom insisted Dad drive me today, and because she's still giving me the stink eye, I didn't question her, regardless of how badly I'd wanted to.

Mr. Webber, the dean of admissions, is in the hall, a full cup of coffee in his hands as he moves in the same direction as me. "Raegan," he says my name like he's relieved he remembers who I am. I've met him no less than a dozen times, but his job involves meeting thousands, so I can't necessarily blame him.

"Hi, Mr. Webber. How are you?"

"Fine. Fine." He nods, his beige sweater vest and blue tie contrasting. "How are you? I seem to recall you took a very ambitious class schedule this semester. Trying to make sure you don't have anyone questioning your admittance, huh?" He releases a dry chuckle, eyes under bushy and unkempt eyebrows turning my way.

"Something like that," I say.

"Well, this is Brighton. We pride ourselves on only accepting the brightest and most talented kids."

If my ego weren't already in tatters, he'd have just driven a hole the size of a large boat through it, leaving me to question a dozen different things.

"Have a nice day, Mr. Webber." My voice is curt, but my smile is too kind for him to fire back at me as I pause in front of my dad's door.

Mr. Webber's hips sway like he's debating stopping with me, but thankfully he continues farther down the hall to his own office.

I take a seat on the bench outside of Dad's office, grabbing my phone as I rehearse the words to say to Lincoln for the thousandth time.

Me: Can we talk?

My phone buzzes nearly instantly with a reply that has hope soaring, making me sit up straighter in my seat.

Lincoln: I don't know.

Me: I get that you're upset, and I've tried giving you your space, but I think we should talk about things.

Lincoln: I can't tonight. Tomorrow?

Me: Sure. Where do you want to meet?

Lincoln: I don't know.

There's a waltz going through my chest, one side is hope, and its partner is doubt, sashaying through me, twisting my heart and feelings until I'm convinced he'll cancel and then persuaded by the hope he'll come. Despite his absence and unanswered calls, he told me he wanted me. All of me. Something that serious doesn't change in a couple of weeks.

Me: We could grab something to eat or get coffee?

Lincoln: Whatever

Doubt takes the lead.

Me: 7 tomorrow at TidalWave Books. It's on Elmont.

I choose the bookstore because it's a large store that sells used books with few who appreciate its offerings, allowing us plenty of time and space to sort everything out.

Dad's door opens, and a girl slides through a brief opening, closing the door behind her. She glances at me, her eyes round as they tick around the hall, reminding me of a rabbit ready to dive under the nearest shrub.

A tight smile pulls her thin lips into a forced smile, and then she briskly passes me, her legs and arms both thin, almost bony in a dress that looks like something Poppy would try to convince me to wear to a party.

Lincoln: okay

Okay? *Okay?*

After two weeks of radio silence, his reply is *okay?*

I breathe out all the air I've been holding as hope takes a seat on my chest. My lungs pinch and my throat closes, causing me to cough again. I cough so hard that my face turns red, and my eyes water.

Slowly, my lungs remember they can work independently, pulling in shallow gasps as I lean back and place my hands over my head to open my lungs as Dr. Grayson had instructed.

Arlo appears, a water bottle in his hands. He sits next to me without an invitation, offering me the water. "You sound terrible."

"Only when I cough." I unscrew the lid and take a small drink.

"How often does that happen?"

I shrug. "Less often."

"Look at you, finding the silver lining." He pushes his knee against mine. "What are you doing up here?"

"Waiting for my dad. What are you doing?"

"Had to see my counselor about changing my major."

"To what?"

"Computer engineering." He reaches both hands in front of him, weaving his fingers together and stretching his arms. "I'm way more than just brawn, baby."

"And so humble."

Arlo laughs. "Humble is for those who fear failure. They don't want to tell people because they're unsure of themselves."

"I don't think that's the definition you'll find in the dictionary."

His knee connects with mine again. "Seriously, though, how are you feeling?"

"Better than I probably should."

"Is that your attempt at being humble? Because I'm not sure that was an answer."

My lips tip upward with a grin. Arlo stopped by the hospital on three different occasions, only missing the final day because the team had flown to California. "I feel fine, honestly."

"You aren't still sore?"

I shrug. "My side's a little sore still, but that's it."

"Your arm?" He glances at my sweatshirt covered arm like he can see the scar healing from where I'd cut my arm with the knife.

I pull up my sleeve, revealing the skin that they'd sewn back together. My stitches were removed on Friday, the tiny punctures from the thread created a Frankenstein appearance.

Arlo pulls his head back, mashing his lips together. "That looks like Halloween makeup."

"Doesn't it?"

"Your brother's still trying to figure out which asshole took pictures so he can kill them," Arlo tells me, instantly causing one of the images in question to fill my thoughts. I haven't asked a lot of questions, and Pax went crazy on Derek when he tried to visit the hospital, blaming him for the incident. My knowledge of the night has mostly been comprised of the article that made the back page of the local paper and its accompanying collage of haunting photos from that night. Few likely saw it, but those who matter most sadly did, facing an array of moments from that night I wish they didn't have to see.

"I may not try to stop him this time."

Arlo grins. "You shouldn't."

Dad's door opens, and he looks around the corner where we're seated. "I thought I heard voices. Arlo, how are you?" Dad moves forward, offering his hand to one of Paxton's closest friends and another fellow football player for Brighton. "You had a great game the other day."

He did. Arlo plays as a tight end, and Saturday, they used him as a receiver because California was a fast running team, making it necessary to get as many out onto the field as possible.

"Thanks, Dr. L." Arlo stands, taking his hand.

"You ready to go, kiddo?" Dad turns his attention to me. "I've got some stuff I need to take home, but if you're done with classes, we can jet."

"Jet? Is that what your generation used to say?" Arlo asks.

Laughter bubbles in my chest, making a quick exit that sends me into another coughing fit.

Dad watches me, and though I can't see him, I know worry and concern stain his thoughts. "Maybe we should get you checked out again?" he says as air once again finds its way back into my lungs, my chest heaving like I've sprinted a marathon.

I shake my head and take another drink of water. "They said this is normal."

"They also said patients who nearly drown could get acute respiratory distress syndrome, and you sound like you're dying each time you cough."

I maim him with a glare. "You saw the X-rays and the echocardiogram and every other test. I'm fine."

"You could be on one of those commercials to promote non-smoking," Dad continues.

"Only if I get to drive myself there."

He smiles, and it seems momentous. His ease with making a joke about the situation, giving me hope that he's allowing this to become a part of our past rather than an ongoing present.

4

RAEGAN

I didn't mean to show up forty-five minutes early, but the knowledge of seeing Lincoln has distracted me to the point I haven't been able to focus on anything successfully.

As though on cue, Lincoln's black truck parks beside me, and he slides out of the driver's seat, making chaos rise within me.

I push open my door, meeting him on the sidewalk. He stares at me, his eyes making a slow trek across my face and down my body. It isn't sexual. It's purely a necessity I'm realizing. Mom still does it each time I walk into the room, like she needs to verify I'm still here and okay. I shove my hands into the pockets of my sweatshirt, not rushing his assessment.

"How are you?" I ask when his eyes meet my shoulders on the second pass.

His eyes snap to mine, the familiar mask he wore for so long securely in place, making my heart beat too fast as that waltz starts over in my chest, spreading doubt as hope struggles to take the lead.

"I know you're upset—"

"The wedding's been postponed," he interrupts me. "A big case was assigned, and so they're delaying it for a month. You can still come if you want. I already checked, and that scientist you want to meet will be there."

Rain starts to descend, a scattering of small drops that quickly increases, the drops getting fatter and faster, soaking my hair and jeans. Yet, he doesn't make any attempt to move, and neither do I, the invisible cables I feel toward him securing me in place.

"I know you're mad at me. I get it. I upset you, and I'm sorry. It was never my intention to hurt you."

He shakes his head. "What did you think was going to happen? I hit my best friend in the face for you."

Another piece slides into the mostly empty puzzle of that night.

"This," he waves a hand between us. "This isn't me. I don't do relationships. I don't know how to be there for you when you look me straight in the eye and then try to kill yourself."

"That doesn't seem fair. I wasn't trying to kill myself."

He shakes off my words with a swift shake of his head. "I like being around you, but this isn't me. Relationships just aren't my thing," he repeats the sentiment like a rehearsed line.

My chest constricts, a sharp ache in the cavity where my heart belongs. "So, that's it? You went from all into pulling back because of one night?"

"This moment would have happened sooner or later."

"Better sooner, right? Borrowed time and all that?"

He glances up through his thick lashes. "I didn't even come to visit you in the hospital. Why aren't you mad at me?"

"Would it make this easier if I was?"

His jaw ticks as he raises his head, squaring his shoulders. "Doesn't that tell you something?"

"Yeah, that you're a coward."

He clenches his jaw, the muscle flexing as rain falls down his face in streaks he does not attempt to swipe away. "I have to meet Paxton at the gym."

For the second time in a matter of weeks, my heart struggles to continue beating on its own as I watch him walk back to his truck. He starts the engine, staring at me through the windshield as his wipers rid the rain. I turn away first, refusing to give him my tears when I've already given so much.

My teeth chatter as I get into my car, blasting the heat as I wrap my fingers around the steering wheel, a painful stiffness reminding me of seconds in the water as I tried to cut through the net. My forearm burns with a pain I know is solely in my head, reliving the memory and delivering the pain I never felt from the deep cut I inflicted on my own flesh.

My lungs ache as I pull in breaths, reminding myself I'm surrounded by oxygen, sweeping the memories to the recesses of my mind so I can focus on putting my car into gear and reversing before Lincoln can.

MAGGIE'S on the couch when I step through the front door, my hair and clothes still dripping. "You should change," she says. "It looks like you jumped back into the ocean. By the way, more flowers came." She points to a crystal vase filled with pink roses and white hydrangeas.

I unzip my coat, hanging it in the closet, my thoughts a wasteland of memories that has me feeling exhausted. "From Derek?"

"Who else?" she asks. "You should tell him it's starting to make this place look like a funeral home. We should start giving them to the neighbors or a senior center. There's nowhere even to put them."

Dozens of bouquets have arrived, filling every room in our house. Even Dad's office has been adorned with flowers.

"You want to order some pizza? Mom's still at work, and Dad's buried in his office." Maggie watches me.

Grandpa appears from the garage, a soda in his hand. He's been here every day since I was discharged. "You know I'm always up for pizza. Rae, you want some breadsticks?" Grandpa and Maggie are the only two people who haven't held a grudge. Maggie, because she lives by the motto of placing others before herself, and I think Grandpa's just clinging to relief.

"Sure," I say.

"Your study group was fast," Grandpa comments. "I didn't think you'd be back until late."

I shake my head. "I had the dates wrong."

He nods, accepting my lie. "You should get changed. Maggie hijacked the TV and has been watching the Harry Potter movies."

Grandpa read the Harry Potter books with me when I was eleven. Though he pretended not to be invested in the lives of the students filling Hogwarts, he never hesitated to grab the book we were on when I got home, and he never grumbled about staying late to finish another chapter.

"I'll be right down."

They watch me head up the stairs, because though they're not expressing anger, that hasn't stopped them from hovering.

I grab flannel pajamas with moose on them Mom had given me last year for Christmas, and shimmy out of my wet jeans and socks, discarding my dry shirt into my hamper before pulling on the warm clothes and tugging a pair of socks onto my constantly cold feet. I hang the wet garments over my shower and return to the living room where Maggie has the third movie ready. She pats the spot next to her, lifting the light blue throw she's cuddled under.

I sit so close our bodies brush, her heat seeping into my coldness, as she wraps an arm around my shoulder. It's a maternal move, a role she's filled on numerous occasions with our seven-year age gap.

"I got my new assignment." Her words are gentle, a slight lilt at the end like it's a question. Maggie is actively in the Peace Corps and was sent home after a potential threat cut her time in Nepal short. She was supposed to leave just days after my accident, but she requested emergency family leave, buying us a little more time.

"Where?"

"Nigeria."

"You'll be near the ocean."

Maggie slides her hand over mine, twining our fingers as she nods. "I can ask for more time."

My sister's been my sanity since returning home. She breathed life into me as well as a much-needed sense of clarity that I feel the loss of even with her current presence. "It won't make you leaving any easier."

"I know." She presses her lips together, her blue eyes reflecting the same pain I feel in my chest as I wonder how much I can endure in a short period.

"When?" Grandpa asks from his seat in the recliner, his voice gruff with emotions.

"Tuesday."

Six days.

The blink of an eye.

I grip her hand tighter, leaning into her as she hits play, and the classic and telling music fills the room as I cling to these moments with more force than I did the seconds before the world went dark.

MAGGIE'S impending departure keeps me from focusing on Lincoln as I spend Friday morning with her, setting up the Halloween decorations in the yard and throughout the house, reliving memories from a decade ago, as well as making new ones.

"What's going on with Lincoln?" Maggie asks as we sit down for lunch, bowls of reheated spaghetti steaming in front of us.

Her gaze is a gentle prod, reminding me she knows too much to try and deny my feelings toward him.

"He told me he's not the relationship type."

Maggie pauses, her lips wobbling. "I hope you called him on his bullshit."

"He's never dated anyone."

"He doesn't look at you like you're a booty call," she says, smothering her pasta noodles in parmesan cheese.

"Does it matter if he says he's not interested?"

Maggie lifts her gaze from where she's twirling noodles around her fork to me, her eyes wide and soft with compassion and thought. "I think guys sometimes get scared. I mean, look at Pax. Do you really think he's still with Candace because he's in love with her?"

I shake my head.

"No. Of course not. He's afraid that if he breaks up with her, he'll be alone. To him, that's terrifying. Lincoln's in the other camp where they're terrified to depend on someone, afraid that they might become vulnerable or get hurt by someone."

"I don't know," I tell her honestly. "Maybe? Or maybe he just realizes his time here is brief, and he wants to hold out for bigger and better things."

"If that were the case, he wouldn't have chosen Pax to be his best friend," she says, making me howl with laughter until I lose my breath with another coughing fit.

Maggie's gaze doesn't turn hard like Mom's does when these occur. Instead, she leans closer, rubbing a hand down my back as she reminds me to take small breaths.

"How long do you think Mom's going to give me the cold shoulder?" I ask her once I can pull in a full breath.

"You know Mom. She hates it when we get hurt, always has. I remember when you came home in the third grade with a black eye from that boy at the bus stop, and Mom literally lost her shit. She spent the entire night in their room, yelling at everyone in search of retribution. Hell, when I signed up for the Peace Corps, she wouldn't talk to me for a week. She was just forced to get over it because I was being sent to Nepal so soon.

"She has to work through it. She's already calmer. I didn't hear her sneak into your room last night to check on you."

I laugh around a bite of my spaghetti. Mom's been coming into my room at least twice each night, resting a hand on my chest for several seconds before she tiptoes back to the stairs and goes up to the third story where their room is.

I nod, hopeful Maggie is right. And then allow the silence that's been following me for weeks with hundreds of unsaid words hanging over us as we discuss the weather and politics and things that matter, just none of them nearly as much as her leaving.

LATER THAT DAY, I take Maggie to the aquarium. I haven't seen anyone since before my accident, and though they sent flowers and have sent text messages, I fear to see everyone. Will they be mad that I was irresponsible and offer the job opportunity to someone else who didn't make an impulsive decision that proved to be hazardous?

"I feel like I've corrupted you," Maggie tells me as I park.

"You have," I lie. In reality, I feel the weight of the past couple of weeks adding up and becoming this giant shadow, one I just need to evade for today.

Inside, we head to the break room, quickly finding Greta, the manager of the aquarium, tucked away in her small office, looking over some X-rays. I knock twice on her opened door.

"Rae!" She's out of her seat and coming toward me in a second, hugging me in the next. "Oh, I'm so glad to see you." She holds me at arm's length, examining me like so many have. "How are you feeling?"

"I feel great. Truly."

She exhales, like hearing this is a relief. "You know, it's a good thing the water was so cold that night. If it had been warmer, I fear what the outcome might have been."

She's right. The coldness that seemed to have soaked inside of me, causing me to remain continually freezing, is actually what I can thank for my life.

"How's Blue?" Lois has sent me several messages claiming he's doing well, but for some reason, I need to hear confirmation from Greta.

Greta blinks several times before waving a hand inches from her face, her eyes misting with tears. "I can't wait to see his reaction to you."

Her comment throws me off. My fear at her tears was so automatic, my own eyes clouded, expecting terrible news. My shoulders fall as my eyes close.

"Lois swears he saved you," Greta continues. "She said he got super upset, and all the dolphins were really vocal and then started diving into the water." She looks at me for confirmation.

I shake my head. "I honestly don't remember anything," I tell her.

A fleeting look of disappointment has her lips thinning. "It doesn't matter. Regardless, I bet Blue's going to go crazy when he sees you."

"I just hope he doesn't think I was involved in him getting hurt." I didn't even realize it was a fear until I say the words aloud.

Greta shakes her head adamantly. "No. Don't forget; dolphins are smart. He knew you were there to save him, just like he knew you were in trouble." She pulls me into another hug, this one not as tight, but longer, imparting something that feels almost like gratitude.

"Oh, Greta, I'm sorry," I say, glancing at Maggie, who's watching us with rapt attention, an outsider to this massive portion of my life. "This is my sister, Maggie."

Greta throws her arms open to hug her as well. "It's so great to meet you," she says.

Maggie smiles affectionately. "It's nice to meet you, too. It's great to see Rae has such a good support system here with so many that share the same love and passion."

"We plan to keep her as long as she'll stay," Greta says, assuring that niggling voice in my head that continues reprimanding my actions.

"When you're ready to come out, we're all interested to see how Blue reacts. Oh, and the best news, we saw all three orca pods this past week."

Anticipation makes my eyes grow wide. "Really?"

She nods, a reflection of excitement shining in her eyes. "And they all seemed to be in good health from what we could see."

"That's amazing. Maggie's leaving on Tuesday, so after that, I'll be back."

Greta smiles again. "Be sure to say hi to Joe. He's been worried about you, and I keep telling everyone to leave you alone so you can heal and come back to work."

We do. We stop and see Joe and several others, and each meeting is uncomfortable since I have to retell the same shortlist of my physical injuries as well as my even shorter list of memories. Yet somehow, when all is said and done, there's a sense of comfort in the process, and the fact they still see me the same as before. They fill me in on the new grant we were approved for that will allow us more funds toward the sea lions that continue to be killed along the coast by angry fishermen, who view them as competition to their livelihood.

We spend the afternoon at home with Grandpa and Camilla, watching Harry Potter four and five, eating a lasagna Camilla brought over with fresh French baguettes Grandpa baked that are still warm.

It's perfect, and I never want the day to end. Things are falling back into place, assurances giving me hope.

And then it all goes to hell with a single text.

Poppy: I just ran into Paxton. He invited us to go out tomorrow. No excuses. You owe me.

5

LINCOLN

If I were a betting man, I'd say the chick in front of me, pressing her body firmly against mine, has breasts as fake as the smile she's trying to pass on to me. I'll give her bonus points for attempting to appear genuine, though.

Her smile. Not her breasts.

Don't get me wrong; I have nothing against gummy bears. My grandma battled breast cancer when I was twelve and underwent a full mastectomy, followed by breast augmentation. No judging here. But, this chick wants people to notice them, and that's why her shirt is so low and thin, exposing the full form of her breasts. "Hey, President," she purrs. "How's school going?"

School is the last fucking thing on my mind as of late. Too many contesting thoughts have made classes exceptionally mundane as I work to focus my attention on two things: making sure my game is on point and forgetting about Raegan Lawson. Thankfully, the gym and the field seem to help like a medication, providing me an outlet that dims the temptation to pick up my phone and call her. But that's not what this girl or anyone else wants to hear. They want me to tell them that my year has been nothing short of perfection, my days filled with classes and my nights with football and workouts, and the girls who ask want to hear I noticed and remember them.

I also wish this alternate reality was real. But it's about as real as her breasts.

I smile. "It's been great. How has school been treating you?"

She leans forward, laughing though I haven't said anything to warrant humor.

Someone clears their throat, drawing my attention. It's Poppy. She stares at me, arms crossed over her chest. My knowledge of Poppy could fit on a notecard. She's Raegan's best friend. She has a really loud laugh. Her expressions expose her feelings at all times. And, like Raegan, she's a "good girl."

The stranger doesn't seem deterred, or if she is, her smile doesn't show it. She's confident. I like that.

Or I did.

The girl in front of me ignores Poppy, and the death glare she's shooting like daggers.

"What's up, Poppy," I ask.

"Let's get something to drink," Poppy says, reaching forward and snatching my hand. I don't fight her, lifting a hand to offer a dismissive wave to the girl's large breasts before turning my gaze forward. She leads us to the kitchen, which is mostly empty, papers taped across the fridge and cupboards warning people out of them.

Poppy stops and spins to face me, her green eyes bright with an intention that unleashes a bite of my unease that has barely been surface-deep as of late. "Why won't my best friend tell me what happened between you guys?"

"Probably because nothing happened."

She narrows her eyes, lifting a finger that she points at me. "That's bullshit. You care about her. I know. I've seen it."

I chuckle. "Are you part of my fan club, too?" It's a dick move, but I can't help myself. I've spent the past two weeks trying to convince myself of the opposite of everything she's claiming.

"You know she wasn't trying to hurt you, so why are you trying to hurt her?"

Something inside of me, a timer of sorts, seems to go off. "Because this entire situation proved how impossible it is for us to be together. Her brother's my best friend. My teammate. My fucking *captain*. What do you think will happen if he finds out? How do you think that will impact my game? My future?

"I couldn't go to the fucking hospital while he was there because I knew it would look too fucking obvious. And I couldn't call her because I knew he'd be there. Hell, I couldn't even send a fucking text because I knew their parents would probably see it because she was sleeping so damn much. And that had me realizing that this was only the beginning of sneaking around and lying to everyone."

Her stare is quizzical as she remains silent, allowing me to finish my laundry list of reasons that prove things between Raegan and I would end like most Ancient Roman stories: packed with betrayal and heartache.

"You were willing to take these risks just hours before the accident, so something obviously changed your mind."

"Her jumping." The admission leaves my mouth in two punctuated words, the defining moment where everything in my life seemed to tip from what could be to what is.

"You feel guilty because she jumped," Poppy says the words in a whisper like it's a revelation. A secret.

"Don't start with your psychobabble bullshit. I hear enough of that shit at home from Caleb." I shake my head, working to dislodge the words that keep breathing new embers into my chest, feeding a fire I keep working to smother because it makes me want to break every fucking wall in this house and the next.

"You should talk to her. She doesn't remember you being at the hospital at all."

Another burst of oxygen blows on the flame. "I wasn't."

She raises her eyebrows and puckers her lips like my words create a sour taste. "I saw you, you idiot. So did Maggie. We made friends with the night nurse, brought her some Chick-fil-A, and she was more than happy to tell us about your nightly visits." She tilts her chin, annoyance clear. "You should tell her. Even if you're too afraid to admit you like her as more than a friend, you should at least admit to her that you cared enough to be one when she needed you. She deserves that." She stares at me, daring me to insist I didn't show up again. I consider calling her bluff, but that could take us down pathways guaranteed to make this rage inside of me come barreling out.

Satisfied, she starts to turn around and then stops, her ruffled brow confirming she's about to deliver more upsetting news. "By the way, I thought you should know that Maggie leaves Tuesday. If you've learned anything about Raegan in the past month or so that you've been doing ... whatever ... you'll know that means something." She cocks a single brow with a challenge, then turns back toward the crowds and disappears.

I breathe out a long and heavy sigh. Alcohol feeds fire, yet even with this knowledge, I'm ripping the duct tape that holds the freezer door shut in an attempt to keep people from raiding their food, and dig for a bottle of alcohol. I find a half-empty bottle of whiskey that I grip by the neck and unscrew before bothering with closing the door.

I drink from the bottle like I'm at my first high school party, chugging the alcohol like I have something to prove. The heat of the drink plucks at the memories of Raegan, like Post-it notes torn from a wall. With each one, I'm forced to relive a memory of her smile, the humor that flashed in her eyes, the vulnerability she entrusted me with. I'm drunk on the memory of her when her voice filters through the past moments I'm burying myself in. She's less than ten feet away, dressed in long sleeves and jeans though like every party, it's uncomfortably hot in here. In front of her is a guy I don't recognize, passing her a glass that she accepts, but lowers. He says something to her, and she smiles, but her eyes wander, and I briefly consider if she's looking for me before I drop the mostly empty bottle to the counter and make my way over to where she's now laughing at something he's said.

Her eyes land on me, reading my pursuit. She lowers her brows and says something to the guy who turns to look at me as well. I stop in front of them, my shoulder connecting with his. It wasn't entirely intentional. It's been a while since I've drunk so much.

"Ben, this is Lincoln. Lincoln, Ben," Raegan introduces us with a wave of the red Solo cup still in her hand.

He nods, offering his hand to me.

I don't accept his handshake. I know I'd do something douchey like try to squeeze too hard, and I made a pact with myself a long time ago that I wouldn't be *that* asshole—especially when I contend for so many other asshole titles.

"Did you guys meet tonight?" I ask, looking between them.

"We have a class together." There's a warning in Raegan's tone that has me trying to focus on her.

"I'm not going to punch him, if that's what you're worried about," I tell her.

Ben blinks several times, trying to catch up to the maze of unspoken words. Luckily, Ben seems to be a smart guy and takes a straight shot of shut-the-fuck-up.

"We should go. I have to get up early. Ben, it was nice seeing you." Raegan sets that fucking cup I've been watching like a live grenade down and moves to my side where she takes my hand. It causes a chain reaction of conflicting emotions as the fire rages and then quakes at her touch. I follow her through the house and several feet out the front door before she stops and pivots to face me. She looks the way I want to remember her, the way I wish to think about her rather than of the lifeless person being Life Flighted by a helicopter we chased across town, dialing every hospital in an attempt to figure out where they were taking her. Those couple of hours it took until they had her registered and could confirm her location were utter hell—a hell that hasn't ended.

The wind blows, pulling her scent and hair toward me as I trace over each inch of her, searching for any sign of the accident again.

"I'm fine," she bites, standing a little straighter.

I'm about to fire back, match Raegan's attitude with my own, but before I can, a guy bumps into her, making her stumble. I reflexively reach out, balancing her as I pull her closer. The guy laughs, saying something to his friends who are nearby. He's not sober, but he's not drunk. He's just an asshole.

"Hey," I growl.

He looks at me and stops, his jaw going slack and his eyes wide. "You're the President."

"You just ran into my friend."

"What?" he asks, looking around and then at Raegan. "Oh, yeah. I didn't see you. I was just trying to—"

I grab the front of his shirt in my fist. I want to hit him. I've never wanted to punch someone so badly in my life. Yet, just as quickly as I pull my arm back, Reagan's reading my intentions and moving so I can't strike him without potentially hitting her as well.

I release my grip on his shirt and shove him backward, watching him stagger several feet. The contact provides only a sliver of the satisfaction I was seeking.

Raegan gasps, grabbing my hand again, her attention on the asshat. "I'm sorry. I'm *so* sorry," she says. I want to dispute her words, tell this asshole that I'm not even a little sorry for my actions, then prove the point by drilling my fist into his face.

But before I can react, Raegan's tugging me forward.

"What are you doing?" I ask.

"Taking you home. You're drunk."

"He ran into you."

She stops trying to pull me forward, her eyes connecting with mine. "That shouldn't matter to you, just like it shouldn't matter if I talk to some guy."

"There's a handbook for all these situations?"

"Yes. It's called common sense. Get some."

"I didn't do or say anything." My voice is exasperated. "I came over and said hello."

"You wouldn't even shake his hand. You looked like a complete asshole."

"Who cares? I'm never going to see the guy again."

"You can't treat people like they're disposable. He matters, and that guy you shoved matters."

I tear my hand free. "Oh, God. Stop. Please." I place both of my hands on my head. I can't accept a speech right now about ethics or morals, not when my entire life has been twisted and turned upside down over the last couple of months.

She huffs, folding her arms over her chest. "You need to go home. You're going to do something stupid and have to pay for it on the field."

"Doesn't your handbook tell you not to care?"

Raegan narrows her eyes, glaring at me.

"What?"

She shakes her head. "Nothing. Let's go."

"After all this, you're still fucking filtering yourself."

Her nostrils flare, and her lips flatten. "I can't believe I never recognized how big of an asshole you are."

I hold her stare, a thousand words fighting to be strung together in offerings of excuses and blame, promises and lies. "Why can't I just be your friend?" I ask her.

She winces like the words are an assault. "Because I don't want to be your friend."

She doesn't say why, and I don't ask. Neither of us is ready to cross that bridge.

"Just get in my car. Let me take you home."

"That sounds an awful lot like something a friend would do." I bait her.

"Will you just walk?"

I remain rooted in place, her hair blowing across her face. She reaches up to slide the loose strands behind one ear, the edge of a cut a stark contrast against her light skin. Reason doesn't have a voice. I'm not sure reason even has thoughts because before I realize what I'm doing, I'm grasping her arm and pulling her shirt up so I can see the entirety of the cut that had been covered each time I'd seen her in the hospital. I had no idea what caused it, but I sure as shit didn't except a wound of this size to be hiding beneath.

Her jaw is set as I look to her for answers. "It's fine."

I trace over the wound again with my eyes. "Will you stop telling me it's all fucking fine." My voice is quiet, because the words in my head are a plea, though, to my ears, it sounds like a demand.

"It happened when I was cutting the net."

I empty my lungs in a long breath, pull her forward so her chest presses against mine, and wind one arm around her shoulders and the other around her waist. Her arms go around me, and though her grip is loose, she doesn't move away. I hold her for several seconds, breathing her in as I memorize the rhythm of her heart once again. It's a tune I need to hear nearly as badly as I need to feel her—confirm her presence when her ghost has been my constant companion for the past couple of weeks.

"I need my truck. I've got practice in the morning."

Raegan takes a step back as my arms slip free. She holds a hand out to me, waiting for my keys.

"You got to be reckless. It's my turn."

She shoves me, both hands against my chest with a surprising amount of strength that sends me backward several steps.

"Don't. I didn't do it to hurt you." She tries to glare at me, but her vulnerability is fracturing her anger. "You have no idea." She shakes her head and starts to turn, but I catch her arm, forcing her to face me, knowing at the very least she owes me this truth as we hash out the broken and fractured details through a dozen different conversations that all rotate around the same single issue.

"What? What do I have no idea about?"

"Let's go."

I release my grip, taking a step closer to her. "Tell me."

She squeezes her eyes shut and then slowly shakes her head. "I... No."

"You didn't even look back."

"I couldn't," she fires. "I couldn't talk to you because if I had, I wouldn't have jumped, and then I'd have to live with myself knowing I let him die. I know that you guys think he's just a dolphin, but it didn't seem fair that his life was so inconsequential. Not when I've stood back and watched for so long and could finally make a difference." Her chest sinks as she takes in a ragged breath. "I thought of you every single second. I fought for you. I cut off the damn drugs in the hospital because I was terrified I'd never see you again."

I lose myself in her words, in her truths, realizing for the first time, her guilt might rival my own.

"I don't trust myself around you," I admit. Her blue eyes search mine, warmth setting in as she misinterprets my meaning. "I don't trust you."

Her lips part like I've knocked the air out of her chest. "That's the truth you want to exchange?"

"It's the only one that matters."

She turns, stalking toward the road, pulling me along behind her without a single touch. She seems to realize she doesn't need my keys to drive my truck, going to the driver's side door and opening it once I'm close enough that the fob reads, freeing the lock.

Reagan pauses to take her cell phone out, her fingers racing across the screen for several seconds before she climbs inside and moves the seat forward. She sets her purse down, and a blue jewelry box falls open at her feet.

I cringe, waiting for her to ask me about it.

She leans forward to collect it, her eyes tracing over the gold chain and pearl pendant that's been sitting in my truck for months. Then, without a word, she fishes for the lid and puts it back on before slipping it into the cup holder and starting the engine.

We ride in silence, her confession swarming my thoughts until we stop in front of the house I share with Pax, Arlo, and Caleb.

The silence is magnified as she cuts the engine, but before it can cross into uncomfortable, she swings her door open and hops out. The second her feet connect with the ground, she starts coughing. It's a guttural sound that has her bending at the waist.

I cross the front of the truck and place a hand on her shoulder, sure she's going to pass out. Her lips form a small 'O,' and the coughing slows as she takes short breaths, her chest rising and falling in quick bursts as she reaches her hands above her head. She opens her eyes, looking at me with regret and shame before she closes them again, taking measured breaths as her skin fades from red.

"What was that all about?"

"Another product of my decision."

A car pulls into the driveway, the headlights so bright we both have to lift a hand to shield our eyes. She slowly takes another deep breath, as though testing that she can, then she takes out her phone, revealing the Lyft app. "There's my ride."

"You just coughed up a lung. You should stay. Sit down."

"I'm fine," she says. "If you'd been around, you'd realize it sounds way better than it did."

She twists the dagger by turning away, disappearing into the dark car.

Once again, I don't stop her.

6

RAEGAN

Ag·o·ny
/ˈagənē/

noun
Agony: Extreme mental or physical suffering.
Synonyms: Saying good-bye.

I pull my sweatshirt sleeves down, gripping the balled excess fabric I've repeatedly used as a tissue. Regardless of knowing this moment was coming, it hasn't made it any easier to accept. Maggie's blotchy cheeks and red nose aren't helping either, the desire to comfort her warring with my own emotions that have been spilling down my face as I fear for lost time, her safety, and a tinge of selfishness about who I'll talk to and confide in.

I wasn't even supposed to see her, and yet the time I wish to continue feels stolen. Invisible threads of fear and unshed tears wrap around my larynx, making my throat so tight it aches. It's a miracle I'm not choking on another coughing fit.

Dad pulls into the parking lot of the airport. It's too soon. The thirty-minute drive felt like two seconds. My mouth grows hot, my eyes heavy with tears that blur my vision, and the lump in my throat becomes impossibly bigger. Maggie doesn't move from her seat beside me in the back to unlatch her seat belt, pressing her lips together in a firm line though her chin shakes.

Mom gets out first. She's been crying all morning, and I know it's only going to get worse. Paxton and Dad follow, going around to the trunk to start unloading the single suitcase and carry-on that Maggie's taking with her for the next year. I try to swallow—attempt to gain some bit of composure, so Maggie doesn't feel sadder or gather any doubts in these last few hours. She turns to me, her eyes swimming with unshed tears. She lifts her hands, gripping both sides of my face before the thin veil of self-control she was holding onto falls with a torrent of tears and a guttural sound that rips my heart back into my throat. I can't breathe because if I do, I'm going to fall apart at the seams.

I focus on the coolness of her touch against my hot and puffy cheeks, on my parents talking at the back of the car, discussing what time Maggie will be landing and the weather reports for her impending flight.

"You're going to kick ass at college." She takes a deep breath, her fingers pressing into my cheeks. "I love you, and I am only a phone call away if you need anything. *Anything* at all, okay?" Her stare is more familiar than my reflection, and it's filled with a thousand words and memories that seize my maturity and crush my heart. Maggie pulls me closer, holding me as I wrap my arms around her. Her shoulders bob, closely followed by her cries, the difficulty to breathe and find composure is again lost.

After several long minutes, I pull back, wiping at my dampened cheeks with the wad of sweatshirt still balled in my hands. "Promise you'll be safe and won't try to fight every battle on your own?"

She hiccups, using the box of tissues she'd packed to dry her face. "If you promise not to jump into the ocean alone." Another tear falls, but she swipes it away. "I want to hear about your boy journal. Bad first dates and epic kisses that turn you inside out." She nudges me. "But, don't give up on Lincoln. Not yet."

Currently, boys are in the very back of my thoughts, but I stick my pinky out anyways because I'll gladly make up stories about guys if she sticks to her end of the bargain.

Dad opens Maggie's door. "Sorry, kiddos, but this plane is going to leave with or without you."

Tears tumble faster, spilling down my cheeks

Maggie nods a couple of times, and then climbs out of the car, grabbing her purse and a small bag Mom and I arranged with some of her favorite things for the long flight.

Grandpa and Camilla join us as we walk into the airport, where Paxton and Grandpa work to exchange bad jokes to lighten the mood as Maggie checks her bag. We take the short path to the security checkpoint, and I have to turn away as my family professes their love for one another because it hurts too badly to watch.

Pax swallows me in a hug as Maggie disappears past security. He's been aloof and absent lately, and I think much of it has been because, like me, he's feeling too much. He and Candace broke up again, and between my accident and the impending date of Maggie leaving and his football schedule, I can feel his mental exhaustion with just a glance. His chest falls with a heavy sigh. "I'm sorry I've been a dick."

My voice is too garbled to respond, so I hug him closer, reliant on his comfort and support.

"Why don't we head home? Order some Chinese food before Paxton has to leave for practice." Mom rubs a hand across my shoulders, and the gesture makes me cry harder. While my mom's hovered and fussed over every aspect of my life over the past couple of weeks, she's been absent in all the ways that have mattered, never talking to me about anything other than how I'm feeling and where I'm going.

Paxton's breathing begins to shudder, and his arms wrap even tighter around my shoulders. He holds me until the pain in my chest stops threatening to destroy me, long enough that the tears dry in sticky paths down my cheeks, making my skin feel tight.

"Can I borrow your car?" I ask Pax.

"I'll take you wherever you want to go."

I shake my head. "I just need some time."

His jaw flexes when I finally look high enough to meet his gaze. "Rae..."

"Please?" I ask, cutting him off.

He digs into his pocket, dropping the small wad of keys into my palm.

"I'll be home soon," I tell no one in particular, and then I set across the bright white tiles of the SeaTac airport, heading toward the parking lot.

Paxton drives a manual, allowing me to shift and punch the clutch and gas pedals, to feel the gas inch higher with my speed.

I drive until I reach the marina, parking and turning off the car, but I don't move. I remain in the car, my brother's cologne so strong I have to roll the window down.

I stare out across the gravel lot, my eyes tight with the loss of so many tears, and my head throbbing with each beat of my heart. Outside, summer hangs on by a thread, the afternoon sun surprisingly warm in its direct path, beckoning me to roll the window down farther. Lacey clouds rove across the sky like they're late for an important event, a cool breeze tugging them to go faster, tickling my neck with the promise of autumn.

My phone beeps with a message that I glance down to read.

Poppy: You okay? I got some Oreos and all the Drew Barrymore movies.

Thoughts of Maggie and I binging the Harry Potter series while feasting on junk food and copious amounts of Dr. Pepper has my chest shuddering.

Poppy: I love you, Rae. I'm here for you.

I close my eyes, leaning my head back as tears stream down my temples. I know Poppy would be here for me, and part of me wants to reach out and rely on that knowledge—hole up in my room where we've spent countless nights lost in thoughts and dreams, heartaches and crushes, homework and ambitions. Yet, those four walls seem like a prison after the past couple of weeks.

The crunch of gravel growing closer has me sitting up, turning to discover Lincoln, his truck parked behind me.

"What are you doing?"

"Looking for you."

"Why?"

"Because you need a friend after today. And probably some booze."

I close my eyes to make rejecting him easier. "We're not friends."

He places both elbows on the opened window and squats so our faces are level. "I'm not convinced."

I pull in a breath and slowly open my eyes. "I'm in a shit mood. I'm not going to be good company." I swipe at the damp trails across my face, keeping my attention directed anywhere but on Lincoln.

Out of the corner of my eye, I see him shake his head. "I didn't come here for you to put me in a better mood, Lawson."

I roll my eyes as I turn to face him. He called me Lawson for well over a month at the beginning of the school year—up until he kissed me. It seems like a tedious measure to go back to since he's already stuck his tongue in my mouth as well as down there.

He chuckles. "Raegan," he says, as though he can read my thoughts. "Come on. Let's take a walk."

I shake my head. "I don't … I didn't mean to come here. I just couldn't think of anywhere else I could go."

Lincoln opens the car door, extending a hand toward me. This situation is on par with taking another shot to cure a hangover. Instead, I'm trying to aid one heartbreak with another.

I grab Paxton's keys, and against my better judgment, take his hand.

"Your hands are always freezing," he says.

"It's been worse since the accident."

His brows lower. "You think you just notice it more?"

I shrug. "Maybe. But I feel cold now. Constantly." I shove my free hand into the fleece-lined pocket of my jacket. "It's like the ocean changed my body temperature." His skin, in contrast, feels hot against my chilled fingers.

"Nigeria will be warm."

I nod. "Maggie will like that. She loves the sun."

We walk along a path I've only taken once because it's long, windy, and unkempt, leading to a shore covered in rocks and pebbles and little sand. I don't complain, though, because I have no desire to walk to the end of the pier.

"How'd you know I was going to be here?" I ask, glancing over at him as he pauses in front of a long piece of driftwood blocking our path. He releases my hand and climbs over it, reaching back for me. I don't need his help to balance or get myself over. It's not a very big log, and before Mom and Dad spent eighty-plus hours a week working, we spent most of our weekends with the woods as our classroom, climbing and exploring all of nature's secrets. Still, I take his help in scaling the log.

"What was your childhood like?" he asks, like I didn't just ask a question.

"What?"

Lincoln dips his chin and raises his shoulders. "I didn't know you guys when you were younger."

"It was good. I mean..." I shrug. "It was normal."

He chuckles softly. "Your family isn't normal. They like each other. You guys don't fight and only see each other on Christmas."

"We fight, we're just quick to forgive ... usually." I think of Mom again and how each day, her anger surprises me. Lincoln stares at me, refusing to accept such a simple response.

"Supposedly, Maggie was upset when my parents were pregnant with me. Paxton didn't sleep and stole all her toys. Plus, they say he was a biter. She was afraid I was going to be a menace, so she refused to acknowledge me until I was nearly two."

Lincoln's mouth parts with surprise, his brow rising. "No. No way." He smiles, weaving us around a large puddle in the middle of the path. His jeans are clean and look new, as do his black tennis shoes.

"It's going to get muddier. Maybe we should turn back. You're going to ruin your clothes."

He glances from his attire to my own. My jeans are comfortably worn, and I'd put on my old tennis shoes that are stained, and one has a hole in the side from excessive wear because while I love eyeliner and fashion, I hate shopping for shoes and only own a handful of pairs. These are still my favorite.

"I'm not worried about it," he says, tugging me forward. "She really didn't pay attention to you until you were two?"

I nod. "Well, almost two."

"What changed her mind?"

"Dad said I refused to let her ignore me." I smirk. "My first word was Maggie."

Lincoln glances at me. "You're not an easy person to ignore."

"Yet, you've both proven it's achievable." I throw the words out, surprised I don't regret them though it feels like I should. "Our childhood was good. I mean, we had parents who cared for us, family dinners every night, an annual vacation to the Oregon coast. But, it was definitely different than now. My parents never had much money, which is probably the biggest difference. Dad also seems happier now. Like he worked so long to be something more and better, and he finally feels like he achieved that."

"I think guys are sometimes worse at that."

"At trying to be the best?"

He grins, but it doesn't reach his eyes. "Just at being present."

"What was your childhood like?"

Lincoln smirks. "You ask that like I'm done. The only thing I learned out of that was Maggie ignored you for two years. Paxton being a pain in the ass doesn't surprise me in the least."

"I don't have anything more to tell."

"Have you always lived in that house?"

The path narrows, and Lincoln slows, forcing me to lead the way. "No. We moved in when I was eight. My grandma on my dad's side passed, and she left it for him. We wouldn't have been able to afford to live in Seattle otherwise."

"What made you love football?"

"Grandpa." I move close to one edge so I can look over my shoulder at Lincoln to make this feel more like a conversation. "He used to spend a ton of time over at the house. My parents met shortly after college, and both their families lived here, so in some ways, I think regardless of the house, we would've stayed nearby. Before they got the house, we lived with my mom's dad, our grandpa, Cole, who you sometimes see. And once we moved, he'd come over every day while Mom and Dad went to work and school to watch us. He used to watch football all the time. Pro, college, even high school if it was on. He'd explain all the routes and plays to us, and I liked listening."

"It paid off. I'm pretty sure you know more about football than most of our team."

"Your turn."

He pauses, reluctance flashing in his eyes before he nods. "My childhood was ... brief," he says.

"Why?"

"I was an only child, and my dad, like yours, worked a lot. He didn't have much time to focus on me, and when he did, he'd get annoyed. He's not a kid person. He doesn't like cartoons or jokes or being outdoors—all the things kids love. So, when I was seven, I went to boarding school, where I learned how to become an adult pretty damn quickly."

I think of the mask he wears, the way he hides his thoughts and feelings about nearly everything. How I have mistaken what is likely a taught mechanism for broodiness. "But you learned the staples? Camping? Riding a bike? Making mud pies?" I steal another glance before ducking below the thick branches of a pine tree.

A smile graces his lips before he bends in half to clear the same branches. "I went camping with you guys. Riding a bike, yes. Mud pies, no."

"What about your mom?"

"My parents divorced when I was young, and she moved a couple of hours south. I'd see her sometimes on weekends when I was home and holidays, but she had to work a lot, and my boarding school was in Rhode Island."

"Rhode Island?"

He nods. "Most boarding schools are only for ninth grade and up. This one was for elementary."

"I'm sorry."

"For what? I didn't have a bad childhood. I had a good education and have known I'll be able to walk into a well-paying job since before I knew what that even meant. Trust me, you shouldn't feel sorry for me."

My thoughts stray to the idea of having grown up away from my parents, of not having pancakes on Sundays, football and Grandpa, of missing out on scraped knees and catching snowflakes on my tongue.

"It had to be difficult, though. I mean, you left your family, then you left your friends... You've had to leave everyone you've ever known repeatedly." The path widens, allowing us to walk side by side again and for me to look at him without it being so obvious.

Lincoln glances at me, his hands loose at his sides. "You think that's why I don't date?" he responds, seemingly reading my thoughts. It's eerie how he can understand words I've barely constructed together mentally, and times like this, it can be both a relief and an annoyance. I want to know as much as I don't.

"It would be hard to get close to someone," I say.

"I moved back here when I was fifteen for high school. I've only moved two times. Plenty of people move more than that."

"Are you saying I'm wrong?"

His dark gaze flashes to mine again. "Are you asking if I have abandonment issues?" He isn't angry, but he doesn't seem sarcastic either. Surprisingly, he seems completely calm and contemplative as he moves around another puddle. "I don't know. Maybe. Probably."

I try channeling Poppy, thinking about the right thing to say. How to comfort him and ask more questions at the same time.

"But, I don't date because it all seemed so contrived. So juvenile. I mean, look at your brother and Candace. They stay together because they're afraid to be alone, yet they don't even like each other. What's the point?"

"Maggie thinks Pax is afraid to be alone, too."

"He is."

"Maybe. I don't know. You should have seen Poppy with Mike. They never acted like they were obligated to be together. As close as she and I are, she was different with him, more vulnerable, more open, like she entrusted him with those parts of her that were difficult for her to expose to others—even herself. She was sillier with him, too. Like, giggly and goofy. And he was even worse." I chuckle at the memory of his expression each day when they parted for class, and he acted physically pained by it.

"But it didn't last."

"Maybe not all loves are supposed to? Maybe some are meant to end, teaching us lessons about ourselves and life."

"Do you think Poppy would agree with that when she's still recovering months later?" he asks.

"Poppy recovered, she's just afraid to move forward because it means Mike is officially in the past. She likes the idea of dating around because she gets the fun side of relationships without all the heavy stuff like sharing imperfections and fears and learning they have weaknesses, too. Because once you start learning those things—those details that make them who they are—the other innately starts to feel those things as well, like the person is an extension of their own emotions and feelings."

"The fun side being sex?"

"That and the excitement. Flirting, innuendos," I shrug. "Making out and dirty secrets."

He snickers. "Weren't you going to date around this year?"

I avoid looking at him as the path starts to decline. "Yeah, but I'd forgotten how exhausting it is to make small talk for any length of time."

He chuckles. "Bullshit." His tone is easy and light, but he's still calling me out regardless, his gaze confirming the fact.

"I planned to date around to get over you. But, that's not necessary anymore."

"I'm that forgettable?"

I try to think of something sharp and cunning to say—something that won't remind either of us that his voice calling to me that night may be the very reason I'm still here. "There's a horde of girls who will happily inflate your ego—I'm pretty sure their names are all in your phone. Start with the A's, and I'm sure by the time you reach the B's, you'll be like, Raegan who?" I smile, though it feels as clumsy and wrong as walking in a pair of shoes several sizes too large.

7

LINCOLN

This trail should have been closed. It's a broken leg in the making. Yet, I keep guiding her forward, concerned she'll stop talking to me like this—like there isn't a landfill of resentment and secrets between us because each time she creeps deeper into my life, the harder and faster I close the next door.

Her admission sits heavy on my thoughts, a reminder that Raegan's had feelings for me, ones she fought against rather than for. The knowledge is a double-edged sword that I can't manage to sheath.

"I wasn't lying when I told you that you deserve someone better than me. You need someone who can trust you and see your best sides without constantly thinking those are the things that might drive you apart and hurt them the most."

Raegan's steps falter, one foot sliding against the loose gravel covering the path. I reach for her, one hand on her waist, the other on her shoulder. Her blue eyes are bright and round, her body rigid as she recovers from her near fall, then she moves forward, her steps purposeful and careful.

"You can't say things like that," she says, her back to me.

"It's true."

She turns, her eyes downturned just like her mouth. "Those risks are mine to take, and you're making the decisions; therefore, I don't believe you. Every time you give me an excuse and say you're not good enough, it feels like you're reminding me that *I'm* not good enough."

"Don't you understand? I've been trying to tell you you're too good for me since the beginning, from the first time I told you to stop me from kissing you because I knew then I couldn't stay away from you. I'm selfish with you, and my trying to be away from you is the best chance at saving you."

"Saving me from what?"

I run a hand over my hair, my regret growing with each truth she uncovers. "Me."

Her blue eyes drift over my face, a quantifiable pain in her gaze that appears equivalent with the one in my chest. "I don't know what that even means. You say that like you're some kind of bad person."

"I've seen what happens when things end badly, and I don't want that. Not with you. Not *for* you."

"Why does it have to end badly?"

"Because it always does."

"It doesn't have to."

"But, it's a gamble."

"Everything's a gamble." She rubs a hand across her forehead, brushing the stray hairs the wind has blown free once again. "Why are you even here?"

"I didn't know you were going to be here," I tell her, the admission slipping through my lips before I can consider if I'll only be hurting her more. She turns, her blue eyes patient and curious as she studies me, waiting for my honesty to match hers.

I clear my throat. "Lately, I've been coming here, thinking about that night, and how I could have changed the outcome. If I'd jumped in after you rather than waiting long enough for Pax and that lady to stop me. I consider if the boat hadn't worked. If we'd have just let the cops come and arrest them for being shitheads instead of saving their sorry asses."

"Does it help?"

I shake my head.

"I can't change the past."

My will bends with each second that I'm close to her, and this is no exception.

Laughter approaching draws our attention back to the trail where three teenage boys are walking toward us, the scent of pot greeting us.

"Hey!" One of them yells. "Nice weather, right?"

Raegan glances at me, a gentle smirk tugging at her lips as she reads my annoyance. "Yeah. Is the trail pretty bad ahead?"

"No. Not too bad. There's another tree up a ways, but if you guys made it this far, you won't have any problem." The guy's hair is practically in his eyes, his stocky build looking wider with baggy jeans and coat.

"Cool. Thanks."

"Yeah. They said you can sometimes see whales, but we didn't see anything." A blond with glasses says.

"You have to be really patient or really lucky with them," Rae explains.

The dark-haired guy laughs. "Apparently, we're neither."

From the side, I see Rae smile before moving to the side as they get close enough to pass. "Have a good one."

"You too!"

Rae continues walking, our conversation seemingly over.

"What was your introduction to football?" she asks after a few moments of silence except for the squawk of several seagulls flying overhead.

"It wasn't actually supposed to last," I tell her. "I only signed up because my dad hated football and forbid me to play."

Her eyebrows rise as she smiles. The expression is unfiltered and automatic, like much of her personality is. She's genuine on a level that most aren't, and sometimes it's that side of her that scares me most because I find myself looking at her reaction to things rather than how others are trying to respond.

"And you decided to stick with it to spite him?"

"That was only a perk. Turned out, I loved the game."

Her full lips pull into a taunting smirk. "I've always liked things I excelled at, too. I'm sure prodigy level is even better."

"Prodigy," I scoff. "It's taken years of my life in a gym to do half of the shit I can."

"Liar." She stares ahead, the breeze pulling at her hair.

I scoff again. "What's that supposed to mean?"

"Being in a gym can strengthen and heighten your skills, but you have a talent that can't be taught. You move like you have skates on your feet. It's crazy."

Her smile makes my chest feel both lighter and heavier, a conflicting and irrational sensation that leaves me light-headed.

Then my phone rings. Coach Harris.

"You can get that," she says.

"It's Coach."

She nods, understanding the importance of this call. "Hey, Coach."

"President, we've got something in the works that I need you and Lawson to come in and see. I think we've got a good work around for San Fran's defense. Where are you?"

"I can be there in an hour."

"Good. Get here." He hangs up.

Raegan rocks forward on her toes, then changes direction, leading the way back up the trail.

The crunch of gravel beneath our feet and the distant call of birds are the only sounds for several minutes as we work to navigate ourselves back to the parking lot—back to the same familiar territory where she's Paxton's sister and the lines that divide us are clear and concise.

8

RAEGAN

"Raegan!"

I stop, hitching my bag a bit higher as it starts to slide under the weight of my book. Derek eats up the space between us with a few quick strides. "Hey," he says, looking me in the eye rather than taking me all in, looking for broken pieces like everyone else does. "How are you?"

I smile, and though it's more out of appreciation for being treated normal, it grows when his lips turn north. "I'm well. How are you?"

His smile slips. He's tried calling me at least a dozen times and has texted even more. The calls went unanswered, but I'd replied to several of the texts, assuring him there were no hard feelings because although he was a contributing reason to the accident if he hadn't been out there, I may not have survived.

"Doing twenty to life currently for guilt," he says, placing an open palm across his chest.

"You shouldn't. You helped save me that night. Besides, you've sent so many flowers over my house is starting to look like it's a flower shop."

His caramel-brown eyes spark with a brightness of hope that makes me nearly regret admitting the fact. "I'm glad you've been getting them. I've been sick over everything. I keep thinking about that night and how we weren't even supposed to go out, and how if we had just gone to that party, none of this ever would have happened."

I know how dangerous those 'what-if' thoughts are, having lived through two solid weeks of them myself. "We all make mistakes."

He scoffs. "Except mine nearly killed you." Regret sits heavily on his slumped shoulders.

"You didn't make me jump."

"No, I just stacked the logs and lit the match." He sighs. "And, Paxton hates me."

"He'll ease up. A lot has happened lately. He just needs a little time."

Derek licks his lips. "I don't know. He's asked the coach to bench me and start Matthews."

Awkwardness makes the air stagnant as my guilt mixes with his, creating a tonic that makes this entire situation taste even more bitter. "I'm sorry. I can talk to him."

He shakes his head. "It's not your job to clean up my messes. I don't want you to compromise your relationship with him. I probably deserve to be benched anyways."

Lincoln and Pax have often accused Derek of showboating and disregarding the team as a whole, blaming him for not working harder to make peace with the guys. At times like this, it's difficult for me to imagine that when his humbleness seems greater than Lincoln and Paxton's combined. "It won't," I assure him.

Derek wipes his hand across his chest covered in a sweatshirt that the puffy jacket he's wearing reveals. "I didn't want to catch up with you to talk about Paxton. I just wanted to see how you're doing and see if maybe when you're feeling a little better, we could hang out again. I'd like to spend an evening groveling and begging while taking you up to the Space Needle."

My stomach feels like I've eaten an entire packet of the pop rocks my mom used to fill our Easter baskets with and chased it with a can of soda. Aside from prom, I haven't been on a formal date, and I've painted the picture in my head so many times in the past couple of months. Except on those dreams, my date had dark hair and darker eyes, and a mask he only removes for me.

"I know you have classes and stuff you've got to catch up with, but maybe in a couple of weeks?"

I nod, the gesture more of a reaction than a response.

His smile is kind, easy. "By the way, I need you to tell me which flowers have been your favorite."

"You have to stop sending me flowers. You've spent a fortune on them."

He shrugs, like kids who I went to high school sometimes did when the cost of something would come up. He's never known life without lavish nonessentials.

"After what you went through, you deserve to be spoiled." He takes a measured step back. "I'll see you later."

My thoughts spin as I watch him walk in the opposite direction of where I'm headed, wondering if there's a reason he keeps appearing in my life when I'm hurting.

I LEAN BACK on Poppy's bed, flipping through the textbook I'm supposed to be reading. She's dialed up the hovering since Maggie left, inviting me over and making plans to hang out nearly daily, switching her schedule around with hours she picks up from her mom to align with my more chaotic schedule.

"Are you hungry?"

I shake my head.

"Want something to drink?"

I glance up from the black and white print. "Do *you* want to get something to drink?"

Poppy leans forward in her desk chair, her elbows propped on her knees. "You haven't volunteered to go out on the Sound."

I stare at her, waiting for her to ask the question she's been hinting at for a week now.

"Are you afraid?"

I shake my head. "No. I've just been busy. Plus, I'm trying to give my mom a little break. I know she'll be a wreck when I go out again."

Poppy nods, accepting my answer. "You know, I was talking to Michelle, that girl in my English Lit class, and she rents an apartment over on Fifth. She said the apartments are huge and quiet, and they have a gym and an indoor pool. I know we talked about waiting until next year, but what do you think about looking at them? Maybe we do it this year."

All along, we'd planned to move out during the summer. It was our plan since freshman year of high school. We knew we would go to Brighton together, knew we'd live together off-campus. We knew Poppy would grocery shop because I hate it, and I'd cook because she burns everything. But, then her mom started talking to us about how our schedules would change and, there would be new pressures and expectations we wouldn't be prepared for and how we both had the advantage of living at home where we had zero expenses, food, and enough independence that much of the time it feels like we do live alone, specifically in my case, less so for Poppy who's little brother, Dylan, is often around.

"I think they were more worried about us staying out and partying and having boys over than they were about our feeling overwhelmed."

I chuckle. "You just now realized that?"

"You have to admit, they made the idea of living at home make sense."

My laughter settles as I shrug. Most of the time, it feels like I live alone, anyways. Maggie being home had changed that, and my accident propelled it, but things have quickly slipped back into their normal ways, my parents working too much, and Dad escaping to the gym. "I'm game if you are."

"What do I say about Dylan?" she asks.

I know it's not her job to babysit Dylan or please her mom, Poppy knows it as well, but disappointing our parents is something we both work to avoid. "Maybe it would encourage her to work less?"

"Maybe." She looks wistful, and for a moment, I remember us when we were both eleven. By that age, Poppy made her own breakfast, caught the bus, and returned home, where she proactively did her homework and did a slew of chores including laundry, vacuuming, starting dinner, and a dozen other tasks, all of which Dylan has been shielded from. It's a subject we don't discuss because when broached, Poppy turns defensive.

"Are we going to talk about Lincoln?" Poppy asks, her eyes turning sharp as she looks at me.

"Only if we have to."

"He went to the marina because he knew you'd be there."

"He also confirmed we're friends."

"Friends don't make out with friends."

"I saw Derek today," I tell her, switching chapters in this book I'd prefer to shelve for now.

"What? What did he say? When? Where?" She shoots off the questions, leaning closer to me.

"At school. He asked me out."

Poppy blinks in long, exaggerated movements. "He did not!"

I shrug. "He was nice about it."

"You aren't seriously considering it, are you?"

My shoulders bob again. "I don't know."

"Raegan, he nearly killed you."

"I nearly killed myself. He saved me."

"Paxton will lose his shit."

I sigh, knowing she's right. "But, don't you think it would make everything easier if I just tried to like someone else?"

"You've been there. Done that. You left the date with Derek with Lincoln and then proceeded to make out with him. Twice."

I flinch. "That was before."

"Before what?"

"Before I realized things would never work between us."

Poppy breathes out a long breath through her nose and sits back in her seat, crossing her legs. "I'm still team Lincoln."

"Good luck with that."

"If you're not going to pursue things with Lincoln—which I still think you should, for the record, but if you're not—I think we should cross off Derek. It's too messy. Too much baggage. Besides, he was a rebound. Let's be honest."

It's my turn to sigh as I close my textbook. "You're probably right."

"I'm definitely right."

"What about you? How are things with Chase?"

A smile smooths her brow. "He's been blowing up my phone lately."

I try to hide my envy with a smile. "See? I knew he liked you."

"He still hasn't asked me out, though."

"Tell him you won't give away the cream unless he buys the cow."

"I hate that saying,"

My grin widens. "I know. That's why I said it."

"I think at the next party we attend, I might flirt with someone else. See if I can make him jealous."

"That's a textbook bad idea," I warn her.

"Definitely. But this is just for fun."

"One day, I have a feeling we're all going to be in a book you write: social experiments conducted by Poppy Anderson."

She grins. "I'll give you all pseudonyms, don't worry."

I pretend to wipe my brow as I stand, gathering my things into a pile as I hear her front door open, followed by the loud barks from their dog Cooper, confirming Poppy's mom is home.

"You can stay," she says.

I shake my head. "I need to go do some laundry."

Poppy stands. "You sure?"

I nod, her concern and love for me makes me smile. "Yeah, but we can do breakfast in the morning. Your first class is at eleven, and I don't have anything until one."

"Yes. I'm so in. Frank's at eight?"

"Nine," I counter.

"It's always busy on Thursdays. I'll be late for class."

"Fine. Eight-thirty," I concede.

She walks me downstairs, passing by her mom, who's dressed in a khaki pantsuit with an orange top, her hair and makeup in clean lines. "Hi, girls."

We chime our hellos, Poppy stopping to pet Cooper as I slide on my coat. "See you tomorrow. Bye, Miss Anderson."

She smiles. It's the only part of her that I can see in Poppy. Everything else about her is icy and intense, almost harsh.

I walk down their long driveway to where I parked on the street, my muscles tightly bunched as the cold seeps in. I'm lost in thoughts of Lincoln and Derek, and the possibility of moving out and what my parents will say when the thoughts scatter upon the sight of a paper crane tucked into my windshield wiper.

I swallow, my steps coming to a stop as I glance around, the small hairs on my arms standing erect as concern swirls with the chilly night. The high-end neighborhood Poppy lives in has immaculate yard after immaculate yard, each house shining bright with numerous porch lights, cars neatly tucked away in their garages. Nothing is amiss, and I don't know if that is more assuring or concerning as I hastily grab the crane and climb into the driver's seat, dropping it to my passenger seat. My car has turned freezing in the hours I stayed at Poppy's, my steering wheel stinging my fingers. My impatience urges me to bear through it, but the cold makes my muscles ache, and the edges of my thoughts turn even darker than the night sky. I blast the heat and set it to defrost as my windows start to fog, rubbing my hands together in search of warmth.

I stare at the crane for several seconds. It seems like a lifetime ago that Maggie opened them and revealed the ugly words that were masked within the intricate folds.

I think of my conversation with Derek today, trying to recall the faces of those who passed by us. I can't remember any of them, though.

I carefully unfold the paper, catching glimpses of the angry letters.

> *You jumped into an ocean, proving to be the martyr we all knew you were. It's too bad you lived because your miserable existence plagues my days and destroys my nights. Why does he care for you the way he does? Why does he always put you first? You take, and you take, and you take, and you don't even recognize everything he gives up, all for you. Why couldn't you just have died?*

I SWALLOW, tracing over the same handwriting that slants down to the right hand corner of the sheet. The heater is finally blowing warm air, but I feel even colder as the words settle into my thoughts.

The outside lights from Poppy's house flip on, cueing it's my time to leave before she comes out to see if I'm okay. I shove the note into my middle console and pull forward.

My thoughts are on the opposite side of the world, in a tiny town in Nigeria with Maggie, as I silently move into the kitchen, wondering what she'd think of this letter. She'd say I needed to tell our parents and Paxton and be smart about this.

I sigh, running through the plausible conversation in my head. How my dad would get his sister the police officer involved. How each of my actions would need to be accounted for again. It's daunting and promises to accomplish the opposite of what I've been trying so damn hard to achieve, which is to provide some assurance to my family. I consider ways to mitigate their concerns as I set my bag down and flip on the lights.

For the most part, I feel the same as I did before the accident, but my appetite still hasn't returned. I'm sure it's because I wasn't able to eat for several days due to the tracheal tube, but since the hospital, I've craved hot chocolate. I fill the blue kettle that sets on our stovetop and set the burner to high.

A noise catches my attention. The sound of voices, making me listen more carefully. I follow the sounds down the hall to Dad's closed office door. This morning he'd told Mom he couldn't attend a dinner she's at because he had something at Brighton. I move to open the door, but it's locked.

My father's voice ceases, and then footsteps and rushed words tickle my ears. I take a step back, working to gather the contents of the situation. Could it be a robber? Might someone have broken in and is looking for something? Was that my dad's voice?

I take several steps back, my heart pounding in my chest as I realize I might have leaped back into the arms of danger without even having realized it.

The door creaks open before I finish organizing the facts, my dad's face a shadow as a light behind him clicks off.

A gust of air falls from my lips as I grip the wall for balance

"Raegan?" His tone paints confusion, albeit a quiet and marginal amount of relief.

"Dad?" I ask in the same shade of confusion. "What are you doing?"

"I thought you were going to Poppy's?" he counters, the scent of wine rolling off his breath, staining his teeth and lips.

"I was. I did. I just got home."

"You said you were going to be home late?" The sound of something falling pulls his attention back into the room before I can answer him. He starts to close the door, but I move my foot first, my palm connecting with the door, pushing it wide. Dad's reaction is too slow, and while I'd like to blame it entirely on the wine he's consumed, I quickly realize another distraction held his attention.

A woman—no, she's a girl—is sitting at Dad's desk, wearing a white dress shirt that I suspect is his, multiple buttons popped open. Her hair is dark, her lips bright pink. I can't see if she's wearing pants or even underwear, but at this point, I'm not sure it matters.

"Raegan," he orders, grabbing me by the elbow and shoving me back into the hallway with a roughness I've never associated with him. I stumble, my shock still working to decipher what I just saw.

"What are you doing?" I demand as I jerk my arm free.

"It's not what you think."

Tears burn in my eyes, an army of traitors prepared to expose my sheltered life where things like this weren't even fathomable. Traitors he trained and assembled by loving my mom and us so wholly and entirely that doubt never even entered the confines of our house. For repeatedly assuring us that we were happy. "You're having an affair?"

"Your mom and I—"

"No. This is *you*. This is all *you*," I tell him, pointing a finger in the direction of his desk chair.

"It was a mistake," he rushes to say the words, his eyes heavy with sadness, and what I hope is regret and guilt. "This..." he exhales slowly, his brows bunched with emotions that under any other circumstance I'd be rushing to ease—emotions I want to soothe out of habit and a love I've harbored for this man for my entire life. My stomach rolls with the reality of the situation, and I take a step back, so I don't touch him.

"It was a mistake," he says.

"A mistake is when you call me Maggie. A mistake is when you forget your coat when you go outside in the rain. That—" I point to the door. "*She* is *way* more than a mistake."

He shakes his head in rapid little bursts. "No. No. Rae, I can fix this."

"Fix this? How? With what?"

He reaches for me, gripping one of my hands in his. His skin is sticky and slick, making me shudder before I pull free, trying to ignore the scent of cherries that stains my skin where he touched me. "Please. Don't tell anyone. Let me make this right. I swear, I will."

I shake my head, hating the look of desperation in his eyes so much I can't look at him. "That's not fair. You're asking me to lie to them."

"I'm begging you not to break our family up. Don't hurt them when it's unnecessary. I'll fix this. I'll be better. I'll stop."

"More lies aren't going to fix this."

His demeanor flips like a switch. Anger flattens his brow and curls his lip as he raises a hand like he's going to slap me. Self-preservation and fear are what has me taking several steps back, while my pride wants to move closer and dare him to do it.

His hand falls as fast as it had risen, another immediate change as he steps back as well, his eyes wide as he shakes his head. "I wasn't going to hit you. Rae, I'd never hit you." The two truths war in my head. He was ready to strike me—wanted to hit me, yet I've never feared my dad hitting me, even on the few occasions I probably did justify being spanked, he barely even raised his voice. No, Dad was never an aggressor or a yeller. Instead, his shoulders would drawback, and his whole face would turn several shades of red like an old cartoon character, except steam would pour from their ears, and his steam poured in the form of harsh words that were spoken in a tone that always made me listen.

"Rae," he says my name softer, gentler, his face still unrecognizable with flashes of guilt and a plea that are nothing like the proud and loving father I know. He takes another step closer to me, and I match it in distance with two backward.

"Please. Talk to me."

"I can't. I don't believe you. Everything you've ever said to me feels like a lie."

A rush of emotions hits him again, requiring my full attention as I work to recognize them: anger, hurt, accusation, sadness, offense, and fear are the descriptions popping into my head.

"You'll destroy our family if you tell anyone. Let me fix this. It will never happen again, I swear."

I turn on my heel, unable to give him my word and refusing to grant him the knowledge of how terrified I was. I didn't want to plead with him to be honest and face his infidelity because, at this point, the last thing he deserved was my own truth. I stop before reaching the kitchen where the tea kettle is whistling. He follows me, saying my name in another angry tone I don't recognize. I twist to face him with the realization that while he doesn't deserve it, Mom certainly does. "You can't lie about this. You can't pretend it didn't happen. You had an affair. In our house. What were you thinking?"

"She took advantage of me," desperation rounds his eyes and rushes his words. "She knows I've been lonely."

"Lonely?" I spit the word.

"You're too young to understand. Just because two people are married, it doesn't mean they can't feel lonely and detached."

"Then you go to counseling. You talk. You go on a trip together and work on things. You don't get a girlfriend."

"Shhhhh!" His brows squeeze together, another flash of irritation marring his features. His graying beard and graying hair that's thinning on top and along his tall forehead are only details that make him look his age. A few weeks ago, I thought it was unbelievable for a man who was six years my senior to flirt with me. A thirty-year age gap makes my stomach heave.

"You owe Mom the truth."

He nods. "I will. I'll tell her the truth. But let me do it. Let me explain it, so she understands."

I shake my head in tight little jerks. "She doesn't owe you understanding."

"Why are you trying to ruin our family? Do you understand the backlash of this situation? I'd lose my job. You'd lose your acceptance to Brighton. Paxton would lose his scholarship. We wouldn't be able to afford this house or things like your boating lessons and the ability to support you once you graduate with a degree you can't use. I'm not asking you to save me, I'm asking you to save yourself. Save your mom who everyone will whisper and talk about behind her back, and Paxton who will be in the news because of his parents, and they'll forget all about his football career. You'll ruin it. You'll ruin it all. After everything you caused in the past few weeks, this is the least you owe me. The least you owe them."

I always knew fear was the ugliest of emotions. I just never expected it would be my dad who confirmed this fact. I turn on my heel, flipping off the burner, and head upstairs. I pace the length of my room, thinking about things that don't matter. I wonder about who she is and how old she is. If she knows who my dad is and if I've met her before. I question her intentions and motivation. Why she'd be interested in someone like my dad who has three kids, a wife, and a growing stomach and shrinking hairline.

And if my dad, the seemingly smart, caring, doting husband isn't capable of being faithful, is anyone?

Tears blur my vision as my thoughts veer to Lincoln. Of the sentiment he'd shared, assuring me that things always end badly.

My body feels worn and tired, my emotions the aftermath of a tsunami. I trade my clothes for a pair of pajamas and climb into bed, soaking my pillowcase with all the words I can't say and don't understand that come out in the form of a million tears.

9

LINCOLN

I wait outside of the building where I know Raegan will be coming tonight for her Statistics Class, my thoughts still in my last class where I listened to Professor Adams blame Tiberius for his shortcomings that ultimately failed Rome as the second Emperor, listing off facts like his tyrannical ways and frequent absences to the island of Capri. However, Professor Adams neglected to mention how Augustus, his adopted father, had ordered for Tiberius and his first wife to divorce so that Augustus could marry her. How his family pledged allegiance in accordance with Caesar and then became victims when that relationship soured. Forced to become proud and powerful out of self-preservation and a lack of allies and trust.

I'm nothing like him, and yet there are aspects I can clumsily align with my own life that leaves me feeling sympathetic as my thoughts wander down footpaths of my past, back when I was ten and caught the flu and spent three days with a hired nurse before being hospitalized. I could take care of myself, but I couldn't sign my own release papers, and my parents weren't there to do it, so the headmaster had to come and do it. I think of the holidays I came home and Gloria, our housekeeper and my nanny, would be the only one to meet me at the airport.

Those thoughts and their potential effects disperse the second I see

Raegan. I'm here to invite her to a party that is a prelude to my father's wedding. I could easily have texted her the details, but I haven't seen her in three weeks. Halloween came and went, and I haven't seen her at any of the parties, not at the house, not even at her home for the last team dinner that was catered with trays of Italian food. I know I'm being an asshole by seeking her out when she's doing a diligent job of ignoring me and moving on. I should let her, encourage the fact by maintaining this absence. I've spent more time in the gym in the past three weeks than I have in months, pushing myself, demanding more from my teammates, working on plays with Coach Harris and our offensive director Coach Harold, eating, sleeping, and breathing football to keep my thoughts from wandering to her.

As she gets closer, I realize Raegan's distracted, her arms folded over her chest, and her eyes vacant.

I step away from the overhang, walking straight toward her, and still, she doesn't seem to notice me. "Raegan," I call her name.

Her blue gaze meets mine, then slides over my shoulder as she stops. "Hey."

Something is missing. Something I can feel on a visceral level like I could that night she dove underwater and the others kept saying she'd be back any second, but I knew she wouldn't. "What's wrong?"

Her eyes flash to mine and then away as she opens her mouth and then closes it. "Nothing." She shakes her head, rolling her lips together. "Nothing," she says again.

"Bullshit."

Raegan snickers, but it's gone just as quickly as it formed. "I need to get to class."

I glance at the brick building behind me, knowing she has at least fifteen minutes to get to the second floor, but, I don't argue this fact. In the past couple of months, I've lost touch with her on so many levels, unaware of how her classes are going, if she was in the majority who complained about the early first snow or the minority who celebrated it. I have no idea if she dressed up for Halloween or if she's been seeing anyone. "There's a party this weekend. Our game is on Friday, and Saturday night, my dad and his fiancé are having a second engagement party of sorts." I shrug. "She's worried people think something happened because the wedding was delayed. I checked, and Dr. Swanson is going to be there. I thought you might want the chance to come meet him."

She rubs her hand across her forehead. "I don't know."

"You don't know?"

She swallows, looking away. "Maybe."

I blink away my disbelief, trying to catch up to her dismissive tone. "Did I miss something?"

"I need to get to class," she says again. "I'll text you." Without a second look, she disappears inside.

It's better this way.

She's making it easier, so why in the hell am I following her inside and up half a level of stairs?

"Rae."

She turns, her surprise greater than my own as she moves to the wall so someone can get by, her eyes soft and yet tentative as she works her way across my face, looking for a reason.

"What's going on?"

"It's nothing. I'm just tired."

She looks tired. Scratch that, she looks exhausted.

"Blow off class. Let's grab some food. Catch up."

Her brow creases. "No. I can't."

"Yes, you can. Statistics is a Netflixer. Get the notes from someone."

"Because now is convenient for you?" Her voice is soft, a twist of sarcasm that doesn't dilute her honesty.

"Okay, then when?"

She shakes her head. "Why are you doing this?"

"We're friends."

Her eyes fall back in her head as she laughs, but it's too dry, and her eyes don't close like they do when she's genuinely laughing. "I'll go on Saturday, okay?"

"This has nothing to do with Saturday. I didn't come in here to beg you to go. If you don't want to, then don't. I was doing you a favor because I thought you wanted to meet him."

It's like everything in her falls, her shoulders, her gaze, even her pride slips, making me regret the words I'd fired like a missile to ensure it wasn't my pride that left this war with a wound. Instead, I'm leaving with it mangled as she nods, as though she understands.

"I don't know," she says. "I don't know if I need to waste his time because I'm not sure about cetology anymore."

Whiplash. That's the only word I can think of to describe the one-eighty of my thoughts and emotions. "What are you talking about?"

Her eyes are windows with drapes that are always left open, telling me exactly what she's feeling and thinking. While I can't always know why she's upset or bothered or amused, I can feel her emotions like they're my own, and as I stare in her eyes, I lose that sense. She continues looking at me, her eyes wide with a silent plea like she wants me to understand just as badly. A sad smile paints her lips, and her eyes slowly fall shut. "I really do need to go. I'll see you."

Her black tennis shoes squeak on the stairs, carrying my thoughts higher before veering to the right.

I drop my head back, debating my options while seeking my own reasons. I slap a hand against the wall, my anger so great it needs an outlet before it leads me back up those stairs. A girl jumps and cries out with surprise, then giggles as she leans into a friend.

Poppy.

Poppy will know.

But I don't have Poppy's number or know where in the hell she lives, so instead, I'm left with my unfavorable alternative: Paxton.

He's been alternating his nights with strangers and the gym to keep his thoughts off of Candace, who recently started dating and plastering shit all over her social media pages to ensure Pax saw. I told him just to block her, but I think he's becoming addicted to the pain and the excuses it allows.

Me: You at the gym?

I step outside of the building. The skies are clear tonight, a coldness sweeping over the campus, making everyone hustle to their next location.

Paxton: OMW now. You in?

Me: Yeah.

The gym is nearly empty. There are periods where it gets too busy, the beginning of the school year, after the holidays, the start of a new sport's season. I prefer these lulls when everyone has forgotten their goals, and I can navigate freely through the space.

"Hey," Pax says, racking his weights.

"Arms tonight?"

He nods. "You?"

"I was going to run."

Lincoln nods. "Derek's been working on his speed."

"Fuck Derek."

Pax chuckles, lying back on the bench press. "Just wanted to throw it out there in case you needed some motivation tonight."

"Hey, so, I ran into Raegan today."

"Oh, yeah?"

"You know how she's going to my Dad's wedding so she can meet that scientist guy she was geeking out about?"

Pax expels a breath as he lifts the weight. "Yeah?"

"She said she's not sure she wants to meet him anymore. Said she'd be wasting his time because she doesn't know she wants to do cetology anymore."

The bar clangs as Paxton racks it again, sitting up so he can see me. "What?"

"She seemed off."

Pax's brow lowers as he shakes his head. "I've barely seen her lately. Hell, I've barely even heard from her." He blows out another breath. "Did she say why?"

I shake my head. "We only talked for a minute. She had a class."

Pax lifts a shoulder. "She's probably just tripping out because finals are coming up. She's always hated tests." He lies back. "Dude, you should have seen the girl I banged last night. She was seriously hot, and she kept asking for things. I felt like I was starring in a porno."

I don't know what I'd hoped for or expected, but it wasn't this easy blow off. I needed a reaction. For him to demand we talk to her and find out what in the hell is going on. To laugh and tell a tale about times she's done this previously.

I dial up the speed and the incline. "She didn't have her phone propped up, did she?"

He laughs between labored breaths. "Phones always go in a drawer. I'm not about to take that risk." He continues telling me about something, random words dropping into my consciousness to confirm he's still talking about having sex as my thoughts wander to Rae, working to recognize her demeanor.

10

RAEGAN

It's still dark as I pull into the parking lot at the marina, the sky blooming with light shades of orange and blue, making the bottoms of the clouds appear like they're glowing and the tops to look bulky and black. My heart beats unevenly in my chest as I grab my jacket from the passenger seat and open my car door. There are only two other cars here, Lois and Joe. They're always here early when we go out, and today is no different. I wait a few minutes, allowing the heat from my car to soak into my body before I grab my heavy winter coat and hat and step out. I thread my arms through my jacket and zip it before pulling on my beanie and fishing my gloves from my pocket. The yard was frosted this morning, promising a freezing game tonight for Brighton's football team.

I pull in a deep breath and slowly trudge forward, each step heavier than the last as I eye the ocean, feeling each wave lap at my neck, my chest, my face. They go higher the farther I get until it's stealing my breath and drowning me. This is the first time I've been back since Maggie left, and the first time I've agreed to go out onto the Sound with the team of scientists.

I pause, my chest tight and my muscles even tighter. I reach for my phone to send a quick opt-out to Joe—another opt-out.

"Raegan?"

I turn, surprise nearly tripping me as Lois emerges from her car, wrestling her full-length coat and scarf. She slams her car door and hustles toward me. "It's so good to see you. We've missed you."

I consider one of the dozens of excuses I've made since being discharged for not coming out, ready to relay one to her, but then she's hugging me, her lips pressed to my temple in a gesture that feels so maternal and loving I nearly weep. Mom's still short with me, and I have no idea if it's still due to my accident or if Dad has told her. Lately, it feels like I don't know anything, and it's left me with this sense of purgatory that has me begging for Hell so that I can get out of this stage. "How are you?" She holds me for another long minute before pulling back, her eyes searching my face, waiting for an answer—a real response rather than a fake one.

My eyes blur with tears that I quickly blink away. "I don't know if I'm ready to get back out there."

Lois nods, one hand still on my arm. "That's understandable. You went through a lot."

I'm freezing and yet too warm, regretting my timing and for running into someone I know when this moment—this decision—feels so personal. Though her sympathy and compassion are both a hundred percent authentic, I feel judged. Judgment for allowing fear to dictate my life, for taking someone else's opportunity when every single volunteer at the aquarium would eagerly jump at this chance, for failing to be out there, studying the animals who I know still need advocacy from others—others like me who are willing and capable of doing it. If only she knew I have the opportunity to meet Dr. Swanson, a hero for those of us who follow his work.

"We understand, Raegan. We don't expect you to get back out there."

Expectation.

The word gets trapped in my thoughts, memories of earlier this fall when I confessed to Lincoln how many expectations I feel others have for me while others lack them entirely. In a matter of weeks, I went from having a complete setlist of expectations to a single one: keeping a secret for my father, a secret I selfishly wish I didn't know because when I think about it for too long, I feel ill and everything seems like a lie.

"Give it some time." She brushes the hair from my forehead, tucking it under the edge of my beanie. "There's no rush."

I nod. "I'm sorry."

Lois shakes her head. "Don't apologize. You have nothing to apologize for. Rest—mentally and physically. And when you're ready, we'll be here." Her gaze is steady and sure, nearly impossible to hold because shame is creeping up my spine, using my body like a marionette.

I turn back to my car, distance relaxing my muscles as tears fall down my cheeks, each one chasing the last.

Mom's car is in the driveway when I return home. It's early enough, I'm surprised to see her car out of the garage.

I find her in the living room, her knitting needles in hand. She glances up from where she's reading through a book propped in front of her, to me. "You're back early."

I don't try to make a lie, knowing it won't help the situation. Plus, the knitting is a guaranteed sign something is already taking up residence in her thoughts. "What are you doing? It's Friday." Usually at this point, she's in the shower, getting ready for school.

"Teachers have a prep day. I decided to stay at home. I need a break from that place and the constant stream of complaints." Mom sets the needles down and pulls off the glasses she began wearing a couple of years ago for reading. "I can't remember how to do this," she says. "I thought it would be like learning to ride a bike."

I kick off my shoes and set my coat down. "Yeah, well, you never really got to the stage where you removed your training wheels." I move into the living room, grabbing the throw off the back of the couch and sitting on the adjacent couch.

"Hey," she says, pointing one of the knitting needles at me. "I've successfully knitted four blankets, thank you."

I raise both palms in surrender. "You're right, knitting master. Move forth and conquer."

The ghost of a smile makes her eyes shine.

"Who are you knitting a blanket for?"

"Candace."

"What?" I balk. "I thought they were broken up?"

She laughs. "They are. Five weeks now."

"Don't jinx it," I warn her.

Mom sets her needles down again. "I was going to make you a new blanket. That one I made you is starting to fray."

"I still like it." The light pink blanket has sat at the end of my bed since she gave it to me.

She picks up her glasses, sliding them back into place before gripping the needles, and reviewing the book again. This is the longest exchange we've shared over the past several weeks, and I'm pretty sure this is her subtle way of giving me her proverbial cold shoulder again.

"Mom," I say, reaching forward and laying the book face down on the coffee table. "Can we talk?"

She glances at me, her nostrils flaring as her face tinges several shades of red. "Mom," I repeat her name, this time gentler. "Talk to me." My thoughts race in an attempt to understand her reaction. Did Dad tell her? Does she know? Is that why she's home?

"I feel like I failed you. Like I keep failing you."

"What? Mom, what are you talking about?" I kneel in front of her, gripping her hands in my much colder ones.

"I'm supposed to protect you. You're my baby, and I couldn't do anything." Her chin quivers and my eyes cloud with tears. It's an automatic response to seeing her upset, a reaction I see from her so rarely.

"It wasn't your fault."

"I want to forbid you from working at the aquarium and ground you so you can't leave the house anymore. I want to keep you in your room where I know you're safe." She sniffs, working to control her emotions. "I know I can't. I know you're nearly nineteen, and you need to experience the world, but God, Rae, you scared the hell out of me. I was so worried you were going to leave my world, and I don't know what I'd do if that ever happened. I don't think I could live if something ever happened to one of you." Her chin shakes violently this time as tears streak her cheeks.

I lick my lips that have gone dry with the cold weather, tasting the salt from my tears. "I hate that you're mad at me," I tell her. "I hate that we're not talking."

She nods. "I do, too. I've never been so mad at you. When your heart stopped, I swore to God I'd do anything to have you back, and then when they gave me the all-clear, I was so angry with you, and I've been trying to get past it, Rae. I swear I have. I just don't know how. I keep thinking about what my life would be like without you, how empty I'd feel, and it makes me angry all over again."

"Poppy says that's normal. That it's part of the grieving experience, and I can take it, Mom. I can take your anger, as long as you promise me you won't hate me forever."

"Hate you?" She releases a sob. "Oh, Rae, I could never hate you. I don't even hate you for jumping into that stupid ocean. I know you did what you thought was right. I just hate that it happened. I hate the reminder that I can't protect you because that's all I've ever wanted to do. I just want you to be safe." She hugs me, her hair falling across my face, sticking to my tears. "I could never hate you."

Her scent soothes me, bringing a lifetime of memories that are filled with laughter and warmth. We hold one another for several long minutes, only pulling away from each other when the front door opens, and Pax yells, "Knock, knock!"

He stops, his fist still raised midair. Lincoln's behind him, two drink trays in his hands that he lowers several inches as he steps forward, his eyes moving with a silent urgency as he takes in me and then Mom, our tear-stained faces and blotchy cheeks.

"We're okay," I tell them, sitting back on my feet and wiping my cheeks with my fingers.

"You have a strange definition of okay," Pax says, still unmoving.

I release an uncomfortable laugh that is only partially fabricated, swiping at a stray tear.

Lincoln hangs back, his jaw clenched as he stares at me.

I release a breath that's considerably less shaky and stand. "What are you guys doing?"

Pax lifts a DVD case and a bag. "I came to bribe you with doughnuts in exchange for watching some tape."

I've barely seen Pax. I don't know how to be around anyone right now with the secret I'm holding because I feel like a grenade with the pin pulled, ready to tell someone at any moment. I wanted to tell Lois this morning in the parking lot. I've wanted to tell Mom a dozen times, Poppy and Pax, too. I even wanted to tell Lincoln when I saw him earlier this week, and he read the distress on my face.

"You're lucky. She wasn't supposed to be home," Mom says, righting her glasses and turning her attention back to the book once more.

"You ditching class?" Paxton asks.

"At this hour?" Mom asks. "Come on, you know your sister. There's only one thing that gets her out of bed before nine, and it's not school."

Pax's gaze turns critical. "You didn't go out onto the Sound?"

"I didn't sleep well and have had a headache all morning." It's a half-truth. I didn't sleep well, but my headache didn't start until the tears did.

Pax's brow lowers. "I didn't think anything could keep you off the water." Beside him, Lincoln has a matching look of doubt—one I'm sure I created after giving such a vague and uncertain response regarding his invitation to his dad's engagement party.

"Everything else good? Classes?" He moves forward, sliding his shoes off.

I nod. "Yup."

Pax's eyes cut to me again as he rights a sock from slipping down his foot. My short answers are constructing an entire kingdom of doubt, and I know it, but I don't know how to stop them. Lying has never been my forte. "It's getting cold out."

"I had to turn the heater on," Mom says.

"Finally," I add.

She laughs. "You're the one always pressuring us to reduce our carbon footprints."

"I was starting to see my breath in the house. I was considering bringing the firepit into my room so I wouldn't get frostbite."

She tips her head back, laughing—a real laugh. The first I've heard in weeks from her. It feels both vast and relieving, giving me hope that with our brief exchange, we can hopefully move forward, and this time will wane, allowing us to return to a normal rhythm.

Pax sets the box of doughnuts beside Mom's knitting book and puts the disc into the DVD player before sitting next to Mom. "Where's Dad?"

"He left for the gym. Basketball, I think."

I consider if that's where he really went. If he's actually been going this entire time or if it's been a façade. I think of the facial hair he started to grow, how he suddenly started to care about his weight. We'd attributed it to him getting older, but now I doubt each of his actions and stories.

"He's really getting after it. I'm proud of him." Pax sits back, crossing a foot over his knee.

Lincoln sets the two drink trays on the coffee table as well.

"We stopped by your work to get drinks," Pax says, "And they gave them to us for free."

"You should've asked for muffins."

Pax laughs. "Right?"

Lincoln takes two of the drinks, handing one to Mom and the other to me, his gaze connecting with mine like a magnet, taking a silent inventory of my thoughts.

I avoid his inquisition, looking around the living room for possible places he can sit that don't include next to me. He doesn't choose any of the alternatives, sitting so close I know my sweatshirt's going to be stained with his scent. I wet my lips that still feel dry and sticky from my tears. His gaze drops to my mouth, staring for several seconds before reaching for his phone and grabbing the cup marked with his name.

My heart races, struggling to decide if this is awful or incredible.

I take a drink, hoping the caffeine eases the headache that's due to the burst of emotions.

"Have you seen Arizona play this year?" Pax asks.

"Yes," my answer is rushed. "Yeah, I've watched a couple of their games. They're a strong offensive team," I say, watching as Mom resumes looping the yarn around her knitting needles. "Their defense isn't great, which is why so many of their games have both teams scoring so much."

"Two of our defensive linemen are down with injuries, so we need to capitalize on our offense, knowing we likely won't be able to shut them down offensively."

Arizona isn't a strong team like they have been in years past, but each game seems to be a greater feat as each win brings Brighton closer to an undefeated season and a bigger spotlight to the team. Though I could likely summarize the basics of their defense without watching the game, I take advantage of the feeling of being needed—an expectation I understand and can deliver on. I cross my legs, leaning farther from Lincoln as the barrier between us thins to nothing. His arm is against mine, his hip pressing against mine, his fingers running along his phone, taunting me to look and see what he's doing.

I don't. Self-preservation doesn't allow it.

"They're slow," Paxton says after a few minutes.

Lincoln spreads his legs wider, invading what's left of my space and my sanity. I stand, setting my coffee down. "I need to grab Chapstick. My lips are so dry they're ready to bleed." I move to the stairs before adding, "You'll still need to watch out for their cornerback. I've seen games where he's had several sacks when the offensive lineman can't keep him back, but he doesn't like contact. If they take a few hard hits from him, he'll stop."

"Got it," Pax says, skipping forward on the disc.

I nod before heading toward the stairs, taking each of them a bit faster as I create some much-needed space.

I grimace, catching my reflection in the full-length mirror beside my closet. My outfit was chosen for comfort and warmth this morning, my hair pulled back into a simple ponytail and makeup forgotten. Before I can exchange my baggy fleece sweatshirt with something that makes me look less like a bag lady, Lincoln appears in my doorway, hovering at the entrance.

"What are you doing?" I ask, my tone lacking the defense it should have.

"A package is going to arrive in the morning. Open it."

His order sounds like a line out of a spy movie. "What?"

"You're going to the party tomorrow. You're meeting Dr. Swanson."

My eyebrows knit. "Are you crazy?"

"The idea of you missing this opportunity is crazy. Get out of your head, Lawson. It starts at six. I'll be here to pick you up at five-thirty."

He has no idea how much I wish I could get out of my own thoughts and steer them far away from him. "This isn't a decision you get to make."

"Too late. I already have."

11

RAEGAN

"I'm starving," Poppy grumbles, sliding into the seat beside me. She pushes her dark-red hair back, revealing a gold stud earring. Her cheeks are rosy from the cold weather, her makeup flawless. You'd never know she rushed to get here on time.

"I got you nachos with extra cheese, a hot dog with extra mustard and relish, popcorn with extra butter, and doughnuts." I grab the bags of food from between my feet.

Her grin is broad as she scrunches her nose. "You make me sound so extra."

"You are," I tell her.

She laughs. "I am," she agrees, digging into the bag. "Now that you've made me dinner, tell me about your day, dear."

"Wonderful, darling. I ironed the sheets and your jeans, so they have that crease you love so much right down the front."

"Fantastic," she says, her voice enthusiastic, keeping up the act. "And how were the children?"

"Little Susie was perfect, but Charlie was a handful."

"Charlie?" Poppy's eyes narrow, and then she shakes her head. "You'd never name your son Charlie."

"But, I'd name my daughter Susie?"

She lifts a shoulder. "Well, I picture you with one son, so Susie was purely fictional."

"Obviously."

Poppy nods, squirting the toppings on her hot dog. "Remind me why I thought taking political science was a good idea."

"You love that class."

"But," she says, raising a finger, a mustard packet pinned to her palm with her other fingers. "I can't stand my professor. He's so douchey, and his T.A. is even worse. Every time he talks, I have the urge to kick him in the ball sack." Poppy is rarely so direct, and the idea of her doing this has me cracking up. "I'm serious."

"If we were in reverse roles, you know you'd be giving me some psych talk about how I was displacing attraction for aggression."

"Oh, no. Zero attraction. *Zero.* You'd hate him. He's a sexist pain in the ass who constantly smirks. Literally, *always* smirking."

"Lincoln and Pax came by today," I tell her.

"And you let me lead with my complaints about douchebag?"

I grin, and she elbows me. "What happened?" She takes a big bite of her hot dog.

"Apparently, his dad is having a pre-wedding party tomorrow, and a marine biologist who studies orcas is going to be there, and he invited me so I could get the chance to meet him."

She licks the mustard from her lip, her eyes wide as she chews her food. "And you're going, right?" she asks.

"I don't know."

"Don't make me force you to go. I'll do it." She takes another bite, making her threat even less invasive.

"I don't even know Lincoln's dad. I'm worried I'll come across as rude if I use his party as an opportunity to climb a social ladder."

Poppy shakes her head, covering her mouth with her hand because she's too impatient to finish chewing. "You're going to put on a cute dress, do your hair, and go woo everyone."

"Woo them?"

She drops her chin. "Yes, woo them. Dazzle them. Impress them. Show them exactly who Raegan Eileen Lawson is." Her tone is direct, her stare an order. "Do this, Rae. Go."

I reach into one of the bags of food that's now balanced on her lap, digging to the bottom for the package of Skittles. My best friend may not be quite so encouraging if she knew I was asking her because I needed her to push me—was counting on the fact. Then again, she probably would. She'd just start pulling down these smoke screens I've been hanging like art in a dark hallway, distracting from the cold darkness that is actually there.

"I'll help do your makeup. What time?"

"I have to be ready by five-thirty."

She nods. "We should do your nails. Do you know what you're going to wear?"

I feel my heart beating in my stomach. "I have no idea. I don't know how fancy it is."

"I'm guessing *fancy*."

I expel a deep breath, but before my mind can start panicking, Poppy's gripping my hand. "It's going to be so busy. I doubt you'll have to do much except smile. Just find this doctor guy, flash that killer smile that makes people bend to your will, and boom. Done."

"What smile? This one?" I scrunch my nose and stick out my tongue.

Poppy rolls her eyes.

"Or is it this one?" I pull on my ears and cross my eyes.

She puts her hand on my face, pushing me back into my seat. "Thank God, the game's about to start."

Laughter again finds its way out of me, making me feel lighter and happier than I have since before Maggie left.

"Rae!" Mom yells from downstairs. "I'm leaving!"

I pry one eye open to look at the alarm clock. It's barely after ten. I close my eyes, lying back and snuggling deeper into my blankets. Last night another crane was on my windshield, this one like the others, filled with angry words that kept me up, questioning too much.

"Rae!" Mom yells again, this time louder, echoed by the hallway. "Did you hear me call for you?"

"I didn't realize you were expecting a response." I sit up again, wiping the sleep from my eyes. Most days, my parents come and go without telling me. Perhaps it's because Grandpa watched me from a young age, and then Maggie and Pax shared the task, and before this pattern was established, I was already capable of taking care of myself.

The door opens, light from the hallway pouring in before Mom flips on the light in the corner. "This came for you." She drops a large box at the end of my bed. "Did you order something?"

I squint, my eyes struggling to adjust to the light. I have no idea what's in the box, but I nod, recalling Lincoln telling me something would be arriving today. "Yeah. It's just something for school," I tell her. "Where are you going?"

"I'm meeting a few people this morning to discuss the current superintendent retiring." The superintendent role has been my mom's ultimate goal for as long as I can remember.

"Really? It's becoming available?"

Mom sits next to the box, her red manicured nails grazing the top. "It wasn't planned. His wife is sick, and she requires a lot of extra help. It's a sad situation." Her gaze is unfocussed with thought as silence comfortably settles, allowing me to notice how tight her jaw is.

The edge of that hammer that has been waiting to fall comes into view. My gut twists as I wonder if this is it, if she now knows Dad's secret. "Are you okay?"

She blinks a few times before meeting my gaze. "Yeah. I just always thought if I got the opportunity to work in the role of superintendent, I'd do it for a public school where I could do the most good." She rolls her eyes, chuckling at herself. "I'm getting way ahead of myself. I'm not even sure this is a job offer. They might just be asking for my professional opinions. Plus, why am I complaining? This would still be a huge honor."

I nod, reaching forward, resting my hand on one of hers. She smiles, her eyes which are greener than blue focus on mine. "You okay? You seem a little jumpy?"

I shake my head. "No. I'm fine." I smile to assure her.

Her smile grows wider. "Do I look okay?" She sighs as she stands, spinning in a circle. "I was doing so good, and my pants were starting to feel baggy, and now they all feel tight." She pulls the navy-blue blazer tighter as though to cover her body.

"You look beautiful, Mom."

"I don't look like I have six chins?" She lifts her chin higher.

"No. Right now, you don't even have one."

She laughs. "It's probably going to be a long day. I'll be home late. Do you have any plans?"

"I'm going to a party tonight."

"With Poppy?"

I nod because it's easier to lie than explain it's for Lincoln's dad and explain it's not a date. Or how I'm hoping to impress a scientist who leads an independently funded team here in the Pacific Northwest who studies orcas, a dream of mine.

"Be careful, okay?"

"You be careful," I tell her.

She exhales deeply, glancing at the ornate mirror beside my closet. "There's coffee downstairs and some of those banana muffins Camilla made." She walks to my door before turning around. "And, Rae?"

I'm already looking at her, trying to understand her apparent nerves when Mom so rarely has any when it comes to her work. Mom has worked tirelessly to earn her position, and though she frets over tough decisions, she has a nearly unmatched confidence.

"I'm sorry for being so distant lately. I appreciate you talking to me, and I love you."

"Love you, Mom."

I eye the box as Mom disappears. It's massive—the size that, if found under a Christmas tree, would have anyone itching with anticipation. I climb out of bed, ignoring the cold that attacks my bare flesh as I cross to my desk to retrieve a pair of scissors. Careful to not slice too deeply, I cut the tape and pull back the flaps, revealing a mass of tissue paper that crinkles and creases under the slightest pressure. I set the scissors down, using both hands to peel back the layers until cool, sleek fabric is revealed. It's a pale, blush pink, a color I generally avoid because of my light complexion. With gentle fingers, I lift it out of the box, revealing a floor-length dress, the bodice a deeper shade of pink, embroidered with intricately patterned beads sewn to the floor in a darker shade. The pale pink is a train attached to the back of the sleeveless dress that is the most beautiful and heaviest piece of clothing I've ever held. I stare at the shimmering beads, the rich gloss of the fabrics, the sleek lines—it's stunning, something out of a fairytale.

I grab my phone, thinking of what to say, how to thank Lincoln for a dress that likely cost a small fortune. I consider how much Poppy is going to freak out, and how I feel overdressed just looking at the gorgeous piece.

Coffee.

Coffee will help. Coffee always helps. I drape the dress across my bed to prevent any wrinkles and head downstairs to the kitchen. I grab my favorite mug, an extra-large one that is big enough to hold a bowl of soup, and bright shades of orange like the sun. I'm stirring in creamer when Dad comes in, wearing jeans, a dark green sweater, and a focused expression as he silently reaches for his keys, stopping when he notices me. Guilt prevents him from looking me in the eye. "Morning." His voice is gruff as he fixes the sleeve of his sweater tucked into his watch—a gift from Mom.

"Where are you going?"

"Work."

I stare at him. "You aren't still seeing her, are you?"

"Who?"

"Who? There's more than one?"

"What are you talking about?"

I stare at him, shaking my head. "Your teenage girlfriend."

His eyes turn hard. "That was a misunderstanding. Nothing happened."

"You remember I saw you, right?"

"Nothing happened," he repeats.

"Are you kidding me? That's the story you're sticking to?"

"Dammit, Raegan." He slams his hand against the counter, the granite barely making a sound. "This isn't any of your goddamn business."

"But it is Mom's business. You need to tell her. They might be giving her the opportunity to be superintendent, and if this comes out, it could ruin her chances. You owe it to her to be prepared."

His scowl makes him a stranger. "Forget about that night. Forget what you think you saw. Forget all of it." He grabs his keys and turns on his heel, ending the conversation as he breezes through the house and slams the garage door behind him.

I wrap my hands around my coffee cup, the warmth seeping into my icy fingers, my emotions numb as I try to process his words. Could I have been wrong? Was he not having an affair? My dad is smart. If he were having an affair, he certainly wouldn't bring the girl home where his chances of being caught would go up ten-fold, right? Did I misread the entire situation? But if I did, why didn't he clarify who she was? Why did he get so defensive? Why has he been sneaking around? The questions continue to mount, making my thoughts far too heavy. I set my forehead against the counter, soaking in the coolness from the granite.

Am I just avoiding the truth?

My phone buzzes beside me, and I'm reluctant to look at it until it sounds again, and then again.

Poppy: Did you find something to wear?

Poppy: Do we need to go shopping?

Poppy: You better not be sleeping!!!!

I pull in a deep breath and sit up.

Me: Got the dress.

Me: Going to shower now. You can come over anytime.

Poppy: Need me to stop and get anything?

"Just answers," I say to the empty kitchen as I type out a quick 'no.'

I scroll to Lincoln, my cheek still resting against the counter, breaking every rule of good posture.

Me: The dress is beautiful. Thank you.

It's a gross understatement for both the dress and my feelings, but I still feel like I'm tiptoeing around Lincoln, uncertain about where we both stand.

POPPY ARRIVES while I'm blow drying my hair. I answer the door in a towel, and she lifts cups of coffee from Beam Me Up, where I work. "Nate was working. He says hi."

"Don't freak out, okay?"

She cocks a brow. "You can't start a sentence like that. It builds my anticipation, and then I'm either disappointed or primed to freak out."

I tilt my head, indicating for her to follow me.

"Are your parents home?" she whispers.

I shake my head.

"Then, why can't you just tell me."

"Because I need to show you." I grip my towel in one hand, and her arm in the other since her hands are still full with the coffees.

"You didn't kidnap Candace and hide her in your closet, did you?"

"You should've suggested that two years ago."

"I did. You told me it was illegal."

I laugh, pushing my bedroom door fully open. Poppy stops, her eyes roving over the stunning dress before bouncing to me. "If you tell me he sent that, I'm going to freak out."

"You should probably set the coffees down."

"Oh. My. God!" She turns, setting both cups on my desk. "Did you know?"

I shake my head. "I never wear pink."

She chuckles. "It's gorgeous." She wipes her hands across her torn jeans before approaching my bed and running a hand down the fabric before she checks the size, just as I had to ensure it's going to fit. "I'm so Team Lincoln after this, Raegan!" Her eyes jump to mine. "This is the most romantic thing ever."

"Is it? Am I channeling Maggie as I question if he thought I wouldn't look nice enough if left to my own devices?"

Poppy shakes her head. "Push those thoughts out of your head and out the window, down the street, and into the ocean because you're so wrong. That is not Lincoln, and you know it. This was his way of telling you he wants you to go. His way of telling you he thinks you're as gorgeous as this dress. His way of being romantic."

I release the air that keeps getting stuck in my throat. "You're freaking out a little."

"Oh no, I'm freaking out a lot. I'm just trying to keep it together, so you don't get nervous."

"This is a lot fancier than I imagined in my head."

She grins. "He's going to be wearing a tux."

My heart races erratically, a mess of conflicting thoughts and emotions, making this moment far more bitter than it ought to be.

"Finish blow-drying your hair. We have nail appointments in an hour. You're going to look so good, this doctor you're trying to impress is going to be recruiting you on the spot. We won't even cover what Lincoln's reaction is going to be."

12

LINCOLN

I park in Raegan's driveway, the button of my dress shirt pinching at my neck. I leave my keys in the console, passing by a colorful metal turkey in the flowerbed, my determination to make this night a success with her introduction to Dr. Swanson, making my steps light as I climb the porch and ring the doorbell.

I rock back on the heels of my dress shoes that, like my shirt, feel too tight.

The front door opens, and my thoughts come to an abrupt stop. My breaths stop, my heart stops—time fucking stops—allowing me this moment to study and admire Raegan. Her high cheekbones, bold eyes and long lashes, and her perfect lips that are stained red. Her neck is bare, drawing my attention to her collarbone, the line of the dress tastefully hinting at her cleavage. Then she smiles, and it's nervous and hopeful and so goddamn perfect I want to tell her to forget about the party and about the reasons we should be avoiding each other and focus on all the ways I can make her feel good, all the ways I'll pledge myself to her pleasure and happiness.

She remains on the other side of the door, glancing down at the dress before looking at me. "I don't think I've ever been this dressed up," she says. "Also, I can't stand next to any candles tonight. I'm fairly certain the bottle of hairspray Poppy put in my hair makes me super flammable." She lifts an arm, but stops, like she wants to touch her hair, but thinks better of it. The sleeveless dress has deep cut lines, exposing only the hint of where her breast swells from her side, and fuck if that image doesn't feel like the most erotic thing in my life.

"This dress doesn't do you justice."

She closes her eyes, unwilling to accept my compliment, or skeptical of my honesty. My heart pounds in my chest, the obligation to go, and the desire to stay warring within me—allies to enemies. I step closer. "You look amazing."

"You don't look so bad yourself," she says, reaching for her purse and a slip of fabric that looks nearly gold, which she wraps around her shoulders.

It takes everything inside of me to let her step out onto the porch rather than invite myself inside and forget about the damn charade of an engagement party.

I offer my arm, and she slips her hand through, her grip light as she gathers her dress with her free hand. She keeps her chin forward as we take the steps, the air miraculously dry so we don't have to contend with umbrellas or puddles.

"How's your shoulder?" she asks, glancing at me. Her eyes shine in the darkness, patient as they remain on me like I'm capable of casual conversation while she's on my arm, her lips a breath away. She grins. "Your reaction is confirming I spend too much time in jeans and sweatpants."

I stop at the passenger side of my truck, opening the door. "I like you in jeans and sweatpants."

She laughs, shaking her head like she doesn't believe me. Then she gathers her dress again, eyeing my truck before turning back to me. "Can you close your eyes? I'm not sure this is going to be my most graceful moment. I feel like I'm going to flash the entire neighborhood."

"If there's a chance of seeing your underwear, there's no way I'm looking away."

She cocks her eyebrow, her lips pursing as determination flattens her brow. She grips the fabric in one hand and raises a foot, balancing it on my truck, exposing a high heel and her bare leg up to her thigh.

Fuck me.

I reach for her to help, but she climbs in, settling into the seat before slowly lowering the dress back into place and flashing a confident smile that radiates to her eyes, stealing my breath. I close the door, my mind taunting me with memories and thoughts and possibilities of what could have been. I imagine her looking at me like that had I not played the friend card and set up every fucking barrier in my arsenal to stop her from continuing to slide into every aspect of my life, making me want her in each part of my day and routine.

I climb into the driver's side seat and turn the heat higher. "I'm worried about you freezing tonight."

Her laughter dances across the cab, playing a tune across my heart that makes it pinch with unease. "I might just hide out in here during the party. You guys can eat and mingle, and I'll take a nap." She leans back, resting her cheek against the seat and closing her eyes as though testing the possibility.

"You've made it this far, Lawson. Don't make me carry you in there."

Her eyes remain shut, but her lips curl into a smile.

"You gonna tell me what that comment was about the other night?"

That has her eyes popping wide, her lips falling into a straight line. "Which comment?"

"About giving up cetology."

"I was enjoying the playful banter. Can we go back to sarcasm?"

"Have you been back out on the water?" The stoplight turns red, earning me the time to set my full attention on her, reading all the words she rarely says.

She sucks in a breath but holds my stare. "Not yet."

Her answer is a bruised rib, painful each time I breathe. "Why not?"

"Because my life went from expectations to consequences in the blink of an eye." She shrugs, her gaze volleying to the streetlight. "And I'm still dealing with them."

"Paxton said they gave you the green light. That you're fine."

Her eyes strike me like a slap. Accusation apparent as her lips purse and relax and then purse again, fighting to say things or maybe fighting to hold them back.

I want her to say it. Want to hear her accuse me of being a shitty person and a shittier friend by not knowing this information first hand, but rather through Pax.

She doesn't.

"You can't let that night change the entire course of your life," I tell her.

"I'm not. It's not just about me."

I shake my head. "What does that even mean?"

She smiles. It's a veil, though. A distraction. "No one's asking or telling me what to do. I just had a wakeup call, that's all."

Last year when I hurt my shoulder, the team's trainer was insistent on talking to me each day while doing stretches, knowing that athletes face a plethora of issues after an injury, things like isolation, lack of motivation, anger, sleep disturbance, and more.

"It's not a big deal," she says.

"Yeah, it's just your life and shit."

She passes another glare, this one filled with frustration. "I'm here, aren't I?"

"Are you? Are you ready to do this? Because when I told you my dad wants me to drop football, you flew off the handle telling me that was crazy, and here you are, talking about giving up your passion, and you won't even tell me why the fuck you'd consider it."

A horn blares from behind us, bringing my attention to the green light ahead, connecting a memory to the last time I'd stopped at a red light with Raegan that ended in my windows steaming up and me professing my intentions for her—naked and undone. This conversation is a separate dimension entirely, yet I feel the same hesitance to move forward, fearing, like then, the moment will end.

"You have a talent. An unmatched and uncharted talent. I have a curiosity and obsession for learning about orcas and other dolphins that will be difficult to find a job in and may never even allow me to use my degree in the way I want to. Our situations are polar opposites."

The car honks again and then pulls around us, speeding off.

"So, this all comes down to money?"

"It's complicated."

"Then uncomplicate it because right now, it sounds like you're saying you want to give this up because it's going to be tough, and then you want to tell me I should keep going. You can't preach shit that you won't follow."

"Why are we fighting over this? We're going. I'm talking to this guy, and I already know he's going to blow me off because the second I mention volunteering for the aquarium, he's going to write me off completely and blacklist me."

"Don't let him."

A cry of frustration leaves her. "Will you just drive?"

"What are you going to say to him?"

"What?"

"What are you going to say to help make you stand out?"

Defiance shines in her eyes.

"You can't go in there thinking he's just going to notice you and want to hear your life story. These people will eat you alive."

"I've been smiling and holding casual and meaningless conversations since I was ten. I think I've got it covered."

"Tell me what you're going to say to him. How are you going to introduce yourself?" I demand.

"I don't even know when or where I'll run into him."

I shake my head. "This is your purpose of the night. You don't wait around and see if you can bump into him, you make it a point. You're seeking him out like he's the quarterback, and you're a defensive linebacker."

"Why are you pushing this so much? It doesn't even impact you."

"Because I still have a shitload of expectations for you."

Her shoulders sag, falling against the seat as her chest falls with another breath, as though my words have found some small bit of peace inside of her. I get it. I understand the need to have a focus to feel ease.

I slowly release the brake, our conversation turning into silence as we make the drive to my Dad's.

A parking attendant dressed in a white jacket waves us forward when I pull into the driveway. Raegan dips her head in an attempt to see the house as we drive forward, following to the next attendant who directs us to a makeshift parking lot to the right of the house.

"This is where you grew up?" she asks.

"I wasn't here much, but this was the address on my file." I put the truck in park and turn off the engine, silence enveloping us as she glances at the house again and then me like she's attempting to picture me here. I'm tempted to ask her what that image looks like, but she frees her seat belt and moves to open her door.

"Hang on," I tell her, hopping down and making my way around to her. This view is even better, her legs are both revealed, her heels showing off her toned calves.

Rae smirks when I meet her eyes. "I never pictured you being a leg man."

"I'm not." Tonight, I'm pretty sure I'm a shoulders man. Or maybe a neck man, I think, gazing over her exposed skin.

She scoots forward in her seat, and I grip her waist, lifting her down to the graveled ground. She makes a sound in the back of her throat, a gasp of surprise as her free hand grips my shoulder.

"Ready?" I ask.

She shakes her head. "Not really." But she's already walking forward.

I grin, stepping beside her, my hand at her back. "You've got this, Kerosene."

She glances at me, shock rounding her eyes and slowing her steps. I have little doubt that she's reliving the night I told her I was willing to take the risk—prepared to get burned as long as I had my chance with her. I consider telling her I was burned. That I still have the embers she left behind, ones that grow into a flame and spreads when she's gone and are insistent when she's near—a constant distraction.

"This place is the size of a museum," she says as we reach the stone steps, her head back, trying to take in the house before turning to look over her shoulder. "The front rose garden is bigger than my neighborhood."

"Don't get distracted."

"Trying," she says quietly, moving her attention to the front doors that are propped open, a woman wearing a silver dress clutches an opened leather book, smiling as we get closer.

"Good evening, Mr. Beckett," she says, nodding.

Rae turns her attention to me, but before she can say anything, we step inside and are greeted by another member of the wedding planning party who offers to take Raegan's purse and shawl.

"I need to know the rules," Rae whispers, watching her things slip away behind a curtain.

"The rules?"

"Expectations," she says, flipping her hands in short, panicky bursts. "This is beyond fancy. She called you Mr. Beckett."

"Breathe, Lawson." I take her hand, threading it through my arm.

She pauses, taking in the large entryway, the impressive staircase, the immense white walls, and white tiled floors. "I'm pretty sure you're supposed to call me Ms. Lawson tonight."

I grin. "You know how I feel about rules."

Her eyes dance across the space as she follows me to the living room where over a hundred people are gathered, crystal glasses filled with champagne in their hands, while a string quartet plays in the corner.

"It started with an f. Was it follow them? Finish them?" she teases.

"Lincoln!" Carol, my dad's fiancé, appears, wearing an ivory dress that falls to the floor and a tiara tucked into her dark hair. She leans forward, kissing my cheek. "You're going to need to find your dad. He thought for sure you'd be late." She turns her smile to Raegan. "You must be Raegan."

I brush my hand along her back, a gentle pressure in hopes of reminding her I'm swimming with her tonight among these sharks. Rae smiles, a natural and practiced reaction as she offers her hand. "It's so nice to meet you."

Carol takes her hand but looks at me. "Isn't she adorable."

There are a thousand words one could use to describe Raegan Lawson, and adorable is near the bottom. Sexy, desirable, stunning, but adorable is a term one applies to a dog they see on a commercial—or a child who isn't in the midst of a screaming fit—and a gross understatement to Raegan's beauty.

"Look who the cat dragged in," Dad says, appearing in a black tux complete with a black shirt and freshly dyed dark hair to cover his grays, but failing to mask his age. He shakes my hand, his other patting my shoulder before looking at Raegan. He offers his hand, an appreciative smile tugging at his charm. It's apparent with the way he tilts his head and uses both hands to shake hers. "I'm terribly sorry, but I don't believe we've met. I'm Noah." He's playing casual, which makes me bristle with unease. The only times my dad is this relaxed is when he's either flirting, or he's impressed. He doesn't know enough about her to understand how impressive she is, which leads me to the initial. I stare at him, my eyes narrowed with a silent threat that I know he reads as he gingerly takes a step back, closer to Carol.

"Raegan," she says.

"What a beautiful name for such a beautiful girl." He shakes her hand too long, but she doesn't seem to mind, smiling, and meeting his gaze. "How do you guys know each other?"

"I've known Raegan for several years. She also attends Brighton. She's in their marine biology program. Her father's the dean of business there. Do you remember Dr. Lawson?"

Dad pulls his chin back, his brows rising with surprise and pride as I give him the brief biography I know will put her in his good graces and help with the opportunity of introducing Rae to Dr. Swanson.

"I had no idea Dr. Lawson was hiding such a beautiful daughter." Dad smiles at her again, his gaze appreciative.

"Well, he's full of surprises," Rae's bright smile hides the fact her tone borders on contempt, but I catch the notes, staring at her to decipher the words.

"I was planning to introduce Raegan to Dr. Swanson tonight since they both share a passion for marine biology."

Carol frowns. "Oh, I'm sorry. He's not coming tonight."

I shake my head, knowing she's wrong. Carol has familiarized herself with most people in my father's life—to a startling degree. However, with everything she's been doing to get the wedding moved and planning this event, I'm sure she's wrong. Hell, I'm positive because I personally contacted the wedding planner to confirm the fact. "No. He'll be here."

Carol shakes her head, her brow not creasing like it should as her eyes widen. "He had to cancel. Influenza. It's that time of year, unfortunately." She sighs quietly, looking at Dad. "I hope it doesn't impact our wedding."

Dad dismisses her concern, turning his attention to Raegan. "I'm sorry it didn't work out. You know, he'll be at the wedding. So, as long as my son stays in line, hopefully, you'll be able to join us and meet him then."

I swear Raegan's shoulders fall, but it's difficult to decipher if it's disappointment or relief as she flashes a fresh smile. "That's no problem. He's such an accomplished and ambitious individual that even though I was looking forward to the opportunity to meet him, I have to admit, I was a bit nervous."

Dad leans back like her disappointment is a personal burden. He's smitten with her, and he doesn't even know she's smart and funny, and has more wit than most. That her heart seems three times larger than average.

13

RAEGAN

Aside from the trip we took as a family to Italy when I was a freshman in high school, and we toured The Vatican, I can't think of a time I've seen a place so fancy and grand. It doesn't seem possible that this is merely a house, let alone for just two people. I stare at the far wall, the line of paintings that interrupt the stark white lines of the house.

"You're staring," Lincoln whispers.

I startle, looking at him with an apology in my eyes. I want to ask him a dozen questions, but I know none of them are appropriate nor any of my business.

"Want to get a drink?" he asks.

I nod, wishing I still had my purse so that I had something to busy my hands with as I follow Lincoln farther into the space, moving toward the large kitchen that is all gold and white, peppered with minimal teal decorations. A bar is set up near the island, which is piled with gifts.

"Bourbon. Straight, and a vodka cranberry with a splash of orange juice."

The bartender nods to Lincoln's order.

"I didn't age three years in the past two months," I whisper.

He shrugs. "Tell everyone its cranberry juice if you want." His mask of indifference is firmly in place tonight, making this dress and party and rows of beautiful artwork seem like a tragic chore.

Our drinks are served in heavy crystal glasses, poured with a heavy hand so they're too full. Lincoln tips for the drinks and returns his hand to my back, guiding me a few feet forward, closer to the fireplace with a hearth so large five people could fit inside. I cradle my drink, terrified it might spill on the dress and mar its perfection, while looking at the guests milling around. Every person here looks dressed to go to a red-carpet event, pristine in every way. I wonder if the wedding will be fancier? If that's even possible?

Lincoln's dad and future stepmom are shaking hands with an elderly couple. Neither of them appears surprised to see that Carol is several years younger—young enough, she looks capable of being his daughter. That thought propels my mind to the girl in my dad's office. Noah's hand is on her shoulder, but his gaze rarely falls on her. What brought them together? What intrigued my dad to have an affair?

Lonely. That's the word he'd used in the way of explanation.

Is that why Lincoln's dad has been married so many times?

"How come you didn't tell me tomorrow was your birthday?" Lincoln asks, interrupting my thoughts.

I stare at him a moment, waiting for sense to catch up, for realization to dawn. His stare doesn't ease. "We're not exactly chit-chatting," I tell him.

He finishes his drink, his strong jaw tipping up, enunciating the cords of muscles in his neck and the hard plane of his chin. I once thought shirtless Lincoln was the most beautiful thing I'd ever seen, but tuxedo Lincoln is making a run for the title. "You're not going to tell me what's going on, are you?"

"With what?"

His eyebrows check me, the silent, *you know what*, clear and intentional. Even with his mask back up, I've started to know him and see past the mask by the way he answers, and the way he doesn't, which is sometimes even louder. I know by the hardness of his jaw, the flex of his fingers, the tilt of his head, the tone of his voice—I'm learning all of his details and each of their meanings.

But he has no idea how broad this question is. I could easily list the things bothering me, including Maggie being gone, school becoming increasingly challenging, how I feel lost attempting to navigate my future. I could finally tell someone, admit that my dad is having an affair and has exposed distant and cold sides of himself that seem neither familiar nor warranted. Or admit that my mom is going to be crushed when she learns the truth, and how I feel obligated to be the one to tell her, and increasingly terrified as I continue dragging this mammoth of a lie. Or I could tell him how worried I am about Paxton, who has seemingly checked out of reality. Perhaps, I reveal how I'm risking my potential job offer with the aquarium as well as my future as a cetologist by continuing to fear the ocean. Then, I stare at him, realizing how him ignoring me has cast more doubt on myself than I ever thought possible, and how ashamed I am to admit the fact.

I shake my head. "Not tonight. Tonight, I just want to pretend."

"Pretend what?"

"That everything is easy."

He grins. "This is not the place to do that. Have you looked around?"

"This house is unreal," I admit. "I'm pretty sure my entire neighborhood could fit on the bottom floor."

He ignores my comment. "What are you doing for your birthday?"

"I was going to check out a brothel downtown, and then maybe get drunk on some Everclear."

His patience is thin tonight, unimpressed by my growing desire to fictionalize everything. "It doesn't matter." I shrug. "I have class on Monday morning, and birthdays have never really been my thing."

"Not your thing?"

"I feel like birthdays are reminders that nothing stays the same."

"Is that a bad thing?" He raises a single brow, his dark eyes misleading as he stares at me. "Most things aren't made to last forever."

Unfortunately, it feels as though life is giving me a harsh reality check of that same lesson. "Do guys everywhere listen to a podcast or something that shares that same sentiment? One that cleanses your conscious, so that when you get bored or tired of the person in your life, you can make up some one-liners that make it all sound nice and easy?"

"What?" His brows lower, his eyes boring into mine, working to find a foothold that will allow him into my thoughts. I shut him out by closing my eyes and taking a long drink that also helps prevent more bitter words from spilling out of my mouth. I wish I had a watch on, or that there was a clock visible so I could gauge how long I'll be obligated to stay.

I open my eyes and take a second pull when an older petite woman with hair the shade of midnight, wearing a royal blue dress and matching jacket approaches, her smile growing with every step. She barely slows as she wraps Lincoln in a hug. She's so small, her head rests against his chest. His face is soft, a variety of a smile splayed across his lips that I've never seen.

"Where have you been? It's been at least a month since you've been home." She pulls back and looks at me, her gaze critical and yet kind. "My name's Gloria. It's nice to meet you."

"I'm Raegan."

She laughs. It's soft and warm. "Oh, I know." Then she hugs me like we're old friends, her grip secure. "I like her. I like she doesn't expect to be known," Gloria says, turning to Lincoln, and for the second time tonight, I feel like a contestant on a game show as people talk in front of me like I'm not here. I might care more about this if I weren't so distracted by the fact this is the second person in Lincoln's life who knows about me. Knows my name and possibly more. Do they assume we're dating? That we're friends?

"She's fucking kerosene," Lincoln says, taking another drink from his crystal tumbler.

I frown, but Gloria's frown is greater, smacking his chest with the back of her hand. "You talk like you were raised by wild dogs."

He grins. "Only one." He winks.

I have no idea if she's his grandma or aunt, or how she fits into his life, only that she does.

She hauls off and hits him again, but it's softer, and her lips fight a smile that she loses the battle to, breaking into laughter. "Come on. Let's have some dinner before they serve the meal."

I blink at the contradiction of words. I'm terrified to stain this dress, and I'm not sure how I'm going to sit down without several feet of clearance, but I'm still intrigued to see what kind of food they serve, certain my foodie of a best friend is going to be interested to hear all the details.

Lincoln's hand returns to the small of my back. "We'll be right behind you. I was going to take Raegan on a quick tour. She has a thing for the Renaissance period. I was going to show her dad's collection."

I don't. I'm not even certain I could name a piece of artwork done during the Renaissance, apart from works done by Leonardo da Vinci and Michelangelo.

Gloria nods. "Don't take too long."

As she disappears across the room, Lincoln turns to me, his hand at my waist. "Why can't you just tell me you're mad at me?"

"I'm not." It's a half-lie. Tonight, I'm fairly positive my anger is solely aimed at my father, and while it seemed at bay for several hours while I was distracted getting ready for tonight, his words seemed to pull the cover off entirely.

"Bullshit," he growls the word, leading us back toward the front door, dropping our empty glasses on a small table dressed in white linens before continuing straight for the elaborate staircase that is wide enough for four people to go up at once.

"You ordered the same drink for me that Maggie ordered," I say, a note of question in my tone because I'm curious if he knew and how, but more terrified to ask.

"You said you liked it."

"I did?"

He nods. "Paxton had asked what you were drinking, and you told him. Told him you liked it. If you don't like this one, we'll get something else."

"No, I do. I just didn't know you knew…" I leave the trailed off sentence, though I hate them because my words—like my thoughts—are floundering.

His jaw tics, his dark eyes narrowed as he sifts through my thoughts with a penetrating and invasive stare. I question what he finds? What might be revealed tonight when I feel so raw and bare?

"Because you're pretending tonight?"

I shake my head. "What?"

"If you haven't realized how well I know you, then you've been pretending for a while."

His words feel cruel, opening that hollow spot in my heart that I've been working so hard to avoid, ignore, and fill with every other distraction available. Now is not the time to start wandering down this one-way tunnel guaranteed to leave me questioning too much and hoping for more.

I have no idea where we're going or why I'm following him, our steps the only sound as the party noise fades with the second floor coming into view. A voice in the back of my thoughts reminds me this is a bad idea. That only private things and secrets will happen this far from the others, and right now, I don't wish to partake in either, but my traitorous heart continues, standing closer with the slightest squeeze from his fingers.

The upstairs is more of the same cold white tiles and white walls, bright lights, and minimal furniture, opening up to another fireplace, this one of white marble with two white leather couches set in front of it, the mantle blank. Large columns hang near each entrance as we pass a large room housing a blue-felted billiards table.

"Who's Gloria?" I ask.

"My dad hired her shortly after marrying my mom. My parents came from very different worlds, and I think he wanted to protect her from the reality of his world for as long as possible, so he hired Gloria. She helped prepare dinners when Dad invited partners over, and she helped Mom shop for scheduled trips and parties." He watches me as though expecting me to react to his words. I'm not sure which reaction he's expecting and can't offer one because it's difficult for me to fathom this lifestyle, even tonight, when I'm stuck in the pages of fiction.

"Then, when I was born, she helped take care of me." He shrugs. "Not exactly a nanny because my mom was always here with me, but, sort of in that way, helping when they were out, watching me if my mom wasn't feeling well, and later when she started meeting with counselors and lawyers leading up to their divorce." He pulls in another breath, his chest rising as he shoves his hands into his pockets, a contradiction of strength with his broad shoulders and stacks of muscles to the story of the little boy he's telling me about. "She's not blood, but she's family all the same."

We pass a wall of windows reminding me of an airport terminal as they go from floor to ceiling and are the first without heavy draperies blocking the view. I pause in front of one, the pane of glass a mirror because the sun has been set for a couple of hours, yet I know exactly what this view would be if it were light.

"You have a view of the Sound."

"When I was a kid, I used to come up here and watch your orcas."

Hearing this makes my heart swell. A tie forms between us, one I have little doubt is made from fabrication and hope, knowing that just because he watched them doesn't mean we share anything but a disconnected past. Still, a peacefulness seeps into my thoughts, picturing Lincoln as a boy, sitting for hours like orcas often require.

I glance at his reflection in the window before turning to face him. "I can't picture you as a kid," I admit.

His lips quirk with a smile. "That's a good thing."

I laugh outright, the feeling so freeing I cling to it, stretching the moment when Lincoln chuckles along with me.

"Come here." He continues, and I hurry to catch up with him, debating why if one has an art collection, they'd tuck it this far away. Lincoln opens a door that breaks a suction, and I can feel the temperature change as we pass through the threshold, a series of lights flipping on with our steps. It's a large square room without a single window of glass that looks out to a hallway and dozens of pictures that offer to take me into other worlds made of brush strokes and paint. Each wall seems to represent a different style of art, ones I don't know their names of only their differences. Cartoonish figures with bright colors and straight lines beside images of paint that explode across the canvas in blobs and shapes that feel as messy as my emotions and thoughts, and then landscapes and portraits complete the space.

"This is amazing," I say, stepping closer to see better.

"My dad thinks he likes Picasso and his style," Lincoln says, stepping closer to me. "But he keeps buying ones that reflect the styles of Warhol and da Vinci."

"Why?"

Lincoln stares at me, an answer reflecting in his eyes, but before he voices it, he steps away, walking to the far wall, filled with extravagant and simplistic images of scenery. "Because my mom liked them." He turns, moving his gaze across each wall. "This room is a reflection of them and the realities of how they couldn't be together, just like these paintings."

"But, he still collects the works she loved?" It's a question or maybe a point I'm not brave enough to add a period to.

"Just because people don't last forever doesn't mean the feelings don't."

"Your dad still cares for your mom?"

Lincoln's gaze cuts to me. "He's been in love with her since he was twenty, leaving a string of divorces and bad decisions to prove the point."

"What happened? Why'd they get divorced?"

"It wasn't one thing, but years of being chosen second. Dad thought if he invested all of his time early with work, he'd make enough money so he could retire, and they'd never need for anything. So, he worked all the time. He ensured she was comfortable—buying this house, getting her anything she ever wanted, the art..." He takes a couple of steps toward the paintings covered in shapes and colors. "But, she didn't care about any of this stuff. She didn't like parties like this or vacations where other people unpacked her bags. She didn't want second houses or a room created to house art."

I watch him, striving to understand what he's telling me, trying to decipher if he's simply opening up to me as a friend or trying to give me insight to a place deeper than friendship. Or if he's exchanging another truth, this one greater in hopes that I'll reveal something equally significant in my life.

"She wanted to be his top priority, at least part of the time, and no matter how hard he tried, he couldn't. My dad fell in love with success before he'd met her, and that love, while it was rivaled, was always his first choice. He'd miss dinners, birthdays, anniversaries, and the times he'd been there physically, he was still mentally absent."

"Are you telling me this because you think I want to be a top priority?" The question somehow slips through every filter and line of defense. I regret it instantly because I know I'm not prepared for the answer—not tonight.

"Everyone wants to be first. It's human nature."

I should be focusing on him and me, clarifying his points and laying out all the pieces in the playbook, so I don't get hit again, but I'm too busy trying to ascertain my parents' relationship, thinking of years they both invested into their individual dreams, how they often tag-teamed parenting and other tasks because there was never enough time and always too many responsibilities.

"We should go. Gloria's going to bitch us out for taking so long." He walks back toward me, allowing me the space to see his entire form in the tux, the ease of his muscles paired with sleek style that makes my heart trip over itself.

My confessions line up, ready to tell him I selfishly want to be his first priority as well as his last, my fears, my concerns, the threats that keep me up at night, the fragility of my hopes and how they shatter a little more with each day.

"I'm sorry about your parents."

His chin tilts as his steps slow. "I'm not. If they hadn't divorced, there's a chance my life would have played out entirely different." His soulful eyes meet mine. "I may never have tried football, and Gloria likely wouldn't have stayed with us. I'd probably be attending school on the East Coast, and then I'd never have met Paxton. I'd never know you."

14

LINCOLN

My bedroom is down the hall. I can see the door as we leave the art gallery—a space that is neglected and sadly underused like much of the house. I consider taking Raegan there under the guise of allowing her another step into my life when in reality, I want to kiss her until she can't remember how to breathe, until she doesn't remember pain, until she forgets about everything since her accident.

"How long have your dad and Carol been together?"

I shrug. "Eighteen months, maybe?"

She blinks away the shock, making me chuckle. "Did you miss the part about me telling you she's his sixth wife?"

"That has to be hard—having people come in and out of your life."

"I barely knew most of them."

She nods, her gaze falling like an acceptance. Maybe she assumes I'm the same, and it's a valid concern, one I've housed for most of my life. My dad's drive, determination, and focus are all things to be coveted and admired. Still, there's nothing about personal relationships he excels at, leaving a long path of destruction that leads farther back than my mom. I offer my arm again, waiting until she takes it before leading her back to the stairs.

Raegan stops, her fingers tugging gently at my arm. Indecision is apparent as her lips open and then close before she takes in a deep breath, the anticipation is like facing off with a cornerback knowing I might get leveled as I consider what thought is being mulled over in that head of hers.

"I've never been afraid of the water. Even when I was little and we'd read ghost stories about the Kraken and sirens, basilisks, and bloodthirsty great whites, I was never afraid. I've been swimming in the ocean and defying hypothermia for as long as I can remember. And now I can't even look at the ocean without remembering that night. I know I'm safe. I know what went wrong and how to ensure it doesn't happen again, and yet, I still can't convince myself to go out there. I haven't been out since that night, and I don't know that I want to. And the reality of it is, I may never be able to make this into a career. I might be wasting this opportunity I have at an education, earning a degree I'll never be able to use. What if I can't afford to take care of myself? I don't want to depend on anyone else. I don't want someone to feel responsible for me."

"Trust me; no one is going to feel responsible for you. Not like that. They're going to be proud of you for following your passions, for loving something bigger than a paycheck and a title. They won't be keeping tally of how much you're making in dollars—trust me, money only gets you so far. My dad is the poster child for that sentiment. The person who sticks with you at your darkest, the one who remains on your side when everyone else gives up, the one who doesn't lose faith—that's worth more than any sum of money."

She slowly brings her gaze to meet mine, her bottom eyelids tinged in red like she's going to cry. "Does that really happen, though? Or do people just make excuses and want more—want better and move on?"

My chest expands as something similar to a traffic jam occurs, my words twisting with the reality she paints.

"We should go," she says, her hand slipping from my arm. She gathers her dress and starts down the stairs.

When we hit the first floor, I place a hand on her back, steering her in the opposite direction of the party. "She'll be in the kitchen."

"Isn't the kitchen that way?" she asks, pointing behind us.

"That one's only used for caterers and parties like this."

"You guys have two kitchens?" Her eyes grow round. "You must feel like you're slumming it when you come over."

I grin but can't respond because Gloria's halfway to us, her hands thrown up in the air. "If you miss the entire party and are here, you know your dad is going to be upset."

"He liked Reagan. I'll just tell him she was a big fan of his art choices. He won't even blink. Plus, he's got a party to impress."

Gloria's brow ruffles with thick lines that weren't there when she got on the floor and played Matchbox cars with me. "You know he's going to want to show you off. With your schooling and this season going well, he'll want to make sure everyone knows."

Raegan glances at me, curiosity and recognition hollowing her cheeks.

"Come on, let's get some food. They're serving oysters, and I know you won't eat those, and then you'll be hungry and won't play nice," Gloria says, leading us farther into the kitchen.

"You make me sound like I'm five. I'm pretty sure I'll survive and still manage to share and play nice on the playground."

Raegan's lips twitch. "I'm not sure I can, though. I don't like oysters, and I haven't eaten all day in fear of not fitting into this dress."

Gloria appraises her with a look of adoration, then places a hand on her arm and guides her into the informal dining room where three plates are drowning in pasta with a red marinara and white cream sauce, slices of garlic bread stacked in a bowl, and an opened bottle of wine.

Raegan doesn't seem deterred by the circumstances—uneasy by the idea of sitting with just Gloria and me.

"We just need water, silverware, and napkins," Gloria says.

"I'll get the water," Rae volunteers.

Gloria shakes her head. "You're our guest."

But Raegan starts opening cupboards, finding the glasses on her first try. "Thank you for making dinner for us," she says.

Gloria turns, silverware and napkins stuffed into her fist—the look of adoration she had seconds ago has grown tenfold. She's a sucker for manners and an absolute goner for genuine. "You're very welcome. Now, tell me, how did you guys meet?"

"Through my brother," Rae says. "They play football together."

"So, you guys were friends first?" Gloria looks even more surprised.

"We're still friends," Rae says. "Only friends."

Gloria's shoulders pull back like she's been shocked, her gaze turning to me for confirmation.

"She's Paxton's little sister."

Gloria's eyes round, and she swallows because while Rae is nearing perfection in her eyes, Gloria also has a strong value system, and she's been telling me since I was a kid not to shit where I eat. She knows my success on the field relies heavily on the quarterback who currently trusts and likes me. Raegan fills the glasses, her back to us as Gloria grapples with her thoughts.

I fill the wine glasses, passing Gloria one as she takes a seat. She accepts it, taking a long drink before turning her attention back to Raegan. "I didn't realize that. But, you're here together?"

"Lincoln invited me so I'd have the opportunity to meet a marine biologist who works locally."

Gloria's eyes are sharp as she attempts to decipher this riddle, her gaze turning from Raegan to me and back again before she takes another large drink of wine. "And your boyfriend didn't mind you coming?"

Raegan's eyebrows raise as she makes her way to the table, holding all three glasses. A soft smile sweeps the frown from her face. "I don't have a boyfriend. To be honest, I don't have any desire to be in a relationship. I have too much going on." She places the glasses in front of each table setting, her eyes illuminated with a heavy stream of thoughts that erase the chance of her maintaining her smile.

I did that.

I created that doubt.

My chest feels like an opened flame, the burn so strong it curdles my blood and singes my thoughts.

"Well, I have a feeling someone is going to be trying to convince you otherwise," Gloria says, draping her napkin across her lap. "You're a beautiful woman, and you seem to have a good head on you. I imagine the guys have already begun lining up."

Raegan's smile is curated. I know because I've seen this same expression before, used when she was introduced to a girl at the piano bar for the third time, and when I crashed their sibling's breakfast. "I was telling

Lincoln I have a hard time imagining him as a kid. Are there pictures around the house?"

Gloria's smile, however, is entirely wholesome as she quickly scoots her chair back from the table. "Yes!"

I turn my gaze to Raegan. Humor makes her lips twitch. "You've seen pictures of me. This only seems fair."

"I met you when you were fifteen. You *were* a kid."

"More reasons this is fair."

"You'll likely get more questions about us from others at the party," I tell her. "I can answer them so you don't feel like you're put on the spot."

"Did I not clarify well enough that we're only friends? Do you prefer the term acquaintances?"

"That's not what I meant," I quickly say, shaking my head.

"Better yet, I can just tell them you hired me." Her eyes are hard, empty.

Before I can say anything else, Gloria returns with a picture album and a conspiratorial smile. It starts to slip as she looks between us, Rae taking too long of a drink from her wine glass, me tugging on the tie that feels like a fucking noose. Gloria takes her seat, setting the album on the table, and opening it to the front page. It's an old album with cellophane pages that crinkle as she flips the cover open, revealing a set of pictures of me as an infant, sans diaper. Gloria chuckles. "He hated clothes as a child, so prepare yourself."

"Jesus Christ. No. Out of the millions of photos in this house, you brought these?"

"So many are of you posing. These show you—the *real* you."

I groan. "That's a bunch of bullshit."

Gloria smacks my bicep. "Maybe, but with your mouth and how little you've come around, I think this makes us even."

Rae smiles, her wine glass still in hand. Her nails are painted a light nude color that is neither pink nor white, that like Rae is feminine and beautiful.

The next page exposes my life when it was what others perceive as perfect: my mom and dad hugging, me in the middle. I have few doubts that when the camera was put away, they tore into each other, fighting about things that never mattered to either of them because they were both too afraid to discuss their true feelings.

Raegan scans the pictures and then me. "You look like your mom," she says.

Gloria nods. "I always say the same."

She does, but Dad and his family were always quick to correct her that I looked like a Beckett.

"Do you look like your parents?" Gloria asks.

"A little."

"Not really," I interject. "Except her eyes are similar to her mom's, and when she focusses really hard, she looks a little like her dad. Her brother and sister have some similarities, but even those are pretty damn thin."

Raegan stares at me like she's surprised by my assessment.

Gloria smiles, it's smug like she knows a secret as she flips another page, more pictures of me naked, these ones of me in a bath, my stomach round. "He was a happy baby," Gloria says, flipping several pages to reveal pictures from times I have memories of. I'm six, on vacation to Disneyland. My arms loaded with stuffed animals and toys that my parents bought each time they fought and offered a new gift to repay their guilt. A close up of me sitting on Mom's lap, laughing—a candid shot—one of my favorites because although I remember the fights that broke out like thunderstorms, hitting everything in the house and leaving everyone with a darkness, there were plenty of light moments. Moments when the sun was our guide, and Mom and I would spend entire afternoons together, building forts in the living room and racing around the backyard.

"Do you remember this?" Gloria asks, pointing at a picture of me in a canoe, a paddle in my hands. "You said you were going to go out and see the whales. You were determined."

Rae closes her eyes, finishing the rest of her wine in one drink.

15

RAEGAN

Lincoln's truck is freezing as I settle into the seat, his jacket around my shoulders as I try to right the skirt of my dress so it doesn't get closed in the door, the scent of his cologne making me dizzy.

Lincoln climbs into the driver's side, starting the truck and hitting a sequence of buttons and dials to turn up the heat. "You should have waited and let me get the truck warmed."

I shake my head. "I'm fine." My muscles ache, but I won't admit that because there's no way I was going to stay inside alone. Too many were watching me with curiosity, waiting for a moment to step in and ask their questions about who I am and how I fit. Admitting I don't was guaranteed to be an uncomfortable conversation.

We wait for two cars in front of us to back up, silence ballooning as my ears ring from the new quietness, a stark contrast to the music and conversation inside.

"Was it what you expected?" He loosens his tie, freeing the top button of his dress shirt, making me stare too long.

"I didn't have any expectations. I know little about your past and your family."

"But, you know me."

"Sometimes, I think I do."

He frees another button, then moves to his wrists—bone and skin and muscle that somehow look erotic as he rolls up his shirtsleeve. "You do," he insists.

"Why are you doing this again?"

His eyes balance on mine, his fingers paused from where they're rolling his other sleeve. "Doing what?"

"Playing mind games. Why did you order me this dress? Why are you still telling me things like I know you and that you know me? And staring at my mouth like you're about to kiss me? I can't do this. I can't keep being around you because you're drowning me."

He twists so he's facing me, invading the cab of the truck though he doesn't lean forward. "That's because I've never known how to be your friend. The more I learned about you, the greater my interest became, so it was easier just to avoid you."

"Then, avoid me."

His opened palm slams against the steering wheel. "I can't."

Tears burn in my eyes, realizing the level of toxic this is guaranteed to spill into my life—how this conversation is promised to haunt my thoughts and dreams for weeks—months—to come. How long I'm going to debate all the words I should be saying, the questions I should be asking.

Anger steadies my voice. "You already made your decision, and so have I. I'm done. I don't want to stay on this merry-go-round anymore. I can't."

"We've already said this. Been here, but this doesn't shake off. Now, I try to be away from you, and I find myself making excuses to see you because I can't think of anything else."

"We're no better than Candace and Paxton, hurting each other and then coming back together because we're both afraid to move on."

Lincoln shakes his head in tight jerks, his jaw flexing. "We're nothing like them. Fear isn't what keeps pushing me back to you. Fear is what keeps me pulling away."

My thoughts and heart feel too big, filled with too many emotions that have erupted into a civil war where both sides are guaranteed to lose. "Until tomorrow, when you're back to having a hundred women fawn over you and next week's game is your number one priority."

"You want this. I know you want me, too."

As badly as I want to deny this, I don't because he's right. I've been trying to forget that for nearly three years, but it doesn't negate the fact. But, this wasn't enough two weeks ago or a month ago or even yesterday, and I have zero doubts it won't be again tomorrow or in two weeks or a month. "I just need some space right now."

"Raegan," he says my name, drawing my gaze back to his, recognizing the torrent of words he keeps locked away.

Before he can say anything, I shake my head. "I just want to go home."

Lincoln doesn't race home like he had the night he drove me home after mini-golf when anger and lust made the air thick and impenetrable. Instead, he follows the speed limit, silent questions volleying between us as we both avoid looking at the other as the silence spreads like a virus, infecting each memory of the night so that I'm regretting ever having agreed to come.

When he pulls up to my house, the windows are dark, only the porch light is on. I lean forward, removing his jacket.

"Keep it," he says.

"No, I'm fine."

He waves my words off. "I'll get it later."

"It's your tux."

His eyes narrow. "Why do you always argue?"

Indignation leaves me glaring at him, an entire arsenal of anger equipping my words.

He rubs his jaw, releasing a short breath. "Please." He meets my glare, a white flag. "Take it. It's freezing outside. You can give it to Paxton the next time you see him."

His words echo in that hallway carved into my heart, the one I've worked dutifully to avoid, and makes me regret all of my angry words and claims of not wanting him. I want to plead with him to forget everything about tonight except the feelings he has for me. Then, the front door opens, and my dad appears, still dressed in jeans and a sweatshirt, keys in his hand, and my breath falls out in a shaky and shallow puff.

"What?" Lincoln asks, his brow drawn as concern paints his voice.

"I'm sorry," I tell him. "I'm sorry to leave the night like this. I just don't know how to do this anymore." Tears make my eyes feel as weighted as my heart as I take in his rumpled tie and exposed skin, filing this memory away in a locked space where I vow to remember the perfection of Lincoln Beckett.

He exits his side of the truck before I can ask him not to. I never did mention this event to my parents, so I have no idea what my dad's thinking as Lincoln pulls open my door, a gust of the autumn air rifling through my hair. I stare at my dad, our shared knowledge feeling somehow more substantial as I see him sneaking around for the second time today. I debate how often he slips away when I'm not here to know any different—how long he's been doing this when I was. He takes two steps before lowering his head just enough to convey a silent reminder that this isn't my secret to tell, that my telling could only make this situation worse—if that's even possible.

"Hey, Mr. Lawson. You're out late." Lincoln calls, glancing over one shoulder before shifting his gaze forward as he extends his hands to help me.

I consider jumping. Testing the boundaries to see if he'd catch me—catch my body, my feelings, my heart, and this sinking feeling in my chest.

"Did you guys have a good night?" Dad asks, taking steps toward his car that he must have left out of the garage because the garage is below their bedroom, and he'd wake Mom opening the door. The realization has my stomach twisting further.

Lincoln's brow furrows as he tears his stare from me to my dad. "Yeah, thanks. Your daughter stole the evening. I think the entire party was talking about how smart and beautiful she is."

"Good. I'm glad to hear it. Well, listen, I forgot something at the office that I'm going to need tomorrow, so I'm going to make a quick run to the campus. Raegan, I'll see you tomorrow. Lincoln, hopefully, I'll see you soon." His phone makes a near-silent beep as he approaches his car, slipping into the driver's seat without a second glance.

"What's going on?" Lincoln asks.

I sigh, realizing it's time to get out of his truck and end this fictional night that went so offbeat. "A reminder of your words. Nothing lasts forever, right?"

He tips his chin forward, a silent sequence of questions to verify my words.

I shake my head, refusing to open this wound, not in front of him when I know tears are going to accompany the story. I slide forward, testing my theory. Lincoln accepts my weight without flinching, lowering me slowly to the driveway, but he doesn't get the chance to catch the rest because right now I feel hollow and empty as I stare at him, realizing just how bad it would wreck me if I were in my mom's shoes. How impossible it would feel to breathe or function if I gave him my heart, and he refused it or later chose to give it back.

I walk to my porch with Lincoln shadowing me to the door.

"Is something going on? Is something wrong?"

I can't meet his eyes because I know he'd see the answer, regardless of my words. Instead, I shrug out of his jacket, missing the warmth and scent as soon as it leaves my shoulders. "This will be easier if we just cut ties. Stop trying to be friends. Stop worrying about hurt feelings. If you want to date someone, you should."

Lincoln narrows his eyes but doesn't say anything, making the moment almost feel like it didn't happen, like there's an option for an alternate ending to this night. He takes his jacket, folding it over one arm, then leans so close I feel unsteady. His lips graze my temple in a chaste kiss that conveys less than his silence. He slips a small, sleek box from his pocket and into my hand. "Happy birthday, Kerosene." His voice floats over my skin, paralyzing me as I watch him descend the porch and the driveway, taking what's left of my strength with him.

Inside, I lean against the closed front door, tears coursing down my cheeks, clutching the box. I always swore I'd never be involved in a relationship with mind games—would wait for a guy who treated me like a queen, and here I had the dress, the ball, the invitation, and I rebuked it all. Maybe I was right, maybe I was wrong. Borrowed time is better than no time. It's a fact I've learned too well, yet, the realization that the end is inevitable makes my heart feel bruised in the most painful way.

My phone rings with a text that has me digging through my small purse.

Poppy: Happy birthday!!!!!

Poppy: I'm anxiously awaiting ALL the details from tonight. But, as a heads up, we're going out tomorrow. I talked to Pax, and we already decided you need to get out. I love you! XO

Me: Like, out to dinner?

Poppy: Negative.

Poppy: How was tonight?

Me: I think we ended things. Like done. Over. The end.

Poppy: What happened??!?!?

Me: Reality.

Poppy: The non-vague answer?

Me: I don't know. I think it was me. I think I made the decision.

Poppy: Are you okay?

I sniffle, wiping at my dampened cheeks.

Me: It's for the better. This year was supposed to be about getting over him, and I've spent most of it obsessing over him.

Poppy: You want me to come over?

Me: I'm exhausted. I'm going to bed, but I'll text you in the morning.

Poppy: Breakfast?

Me: Lunch. I'm sleeping in. It's my birthday.

Poppy: You're sure? I can be there in 10 minutes.

Me: I'm already in my pajamas with one eye closed.

Poppy: I love you.

Me: XO

I climb the stairs slowly, flipping on the lights in my room and placing the small box near my bed. Standing in front of the mirror, I marvel at the dress one final time before exchanging it for flannel pajamas. I hang the gown in my closet, tucking the heels I'd worn with it away. Then, I head to my bathroom where I free each bobby pin from my hair, wash my face, and brush my teeth. My steps back to my room are slower, paced by my hesitation to open Lincoln's gift.

I consider placing it in my desk drawer and waiting until tomorrow to open it, but I know I'd never be able to sleep if I did. I take a seat at the edge of my bed and cradle the box in my hands like it's breakable. Is it the necklace I'd seen in his truck?

The box creaks as I open it, and shining back at me is a silver necklace with a dolphin and whale pendant, a diamond between the two animals who share my love.

16

LINCOLN

"You assholes ready?" Pax asks, stepping into the kitchen where Arlo and I are already a beer in. "Why are you eating? We're going to dinner."

"We've been waiting for you, Princess. We got hungry." Arlo says, grabbing another pizza roll from the sheet tray we'd heated up.

Pax nabs two, shoving one into his mouth. "Poppy texted. She said she's getting Rae drunk tonight." He chews the second pizza roll as Arlo cheers. "She thinks Rae hasn't been herself lately. Have you guys noticed anything?"

Arlo shrugs. "Man, I feel like I've barely seen her."

Pax looks at Caleb, who shrugs as well. "I haven't seen her much, either. I texted her this morning, and she responded, but that's it."

He turns his inquiring gaze to me. "You guys had that thing last night. Did she seem okay?"

I give a short jerk of my head, working to read his response, and if he—like me—assumes it might be connected to myself. "Something's bothering her, but she didn't mention what."

Pax nods in return, like he's hearing my words and is trying to process them. He grabs a couple more pizza rolls. "Maybe she just needs to blow off some steam. It's been a shitty fall."

In our circle, blowing off steam consists of drinking until we can't think about what's bothering us, and then finding someone to distract us from caring. All day, I've struggled to keep from reaching out to Raegan. Working to uphold my end of this bargain feels like I've been asked to peel my skin off as I check my phone for messages from her that never come.

"If they both get shit-faced, I'll probably bring them back here so they don't have to deal with my parents. You guys care if they hole up in the living room?"

"You remember the last time Poppy got drunk, right?" Caleb asks.

"Oh, you mean when she took a piss in the alley?" Arlo asks.

Caleb laughs, nodding his head. "Before telling everyone how much she loved them over and over and over again."

"She does get nuts," Pax says.

"Have we seen Rae drunk?" Arlo asks the question I'm considering as I flip through a series of memories.

Pax shakes his head. "I think the closest she's come to being drunk with us was when we stayed at the house last fall when my parents were out of town, and we played quarters."

I snap. "Yes. She was singing all those pop songs."

Paxton laughs. "Yup."

We divide into two cars, me taking my truck and Caleb driving his Tahoe out to the Mexican restaurant where Rae celebrates her birthday each year.

I can't worry about her reaction to me coming because I spent most of last night and all of today thinking about how and why we let things get so fucked up, and right now, I'm ready to lay all my cards out, company be damned. Let them know. Let everyone know. Maybe it will be easier to admit that I'm tired of staying away from her, that I hate the idea of not seeing her smile and being the one who she communicates in silent glances with. How I'm tired of feeling so damn undone when she's gone, and how badly I want to feel her beside me through the bad and good, the terrible and fucking amazing—I want her there for all of them.

Arlo stretches out beside me. "Practice is going to fucking suck this week," he says. "Coach won't shut up about Utah's fucking defense."

I've been channeling my inner frustrations at the gym, so additional practices don't phase me. I welcome the idea of a challenge right now. "Probably," I answer.

"You think Rae Rae's cool? I saw her a couple of weeks ago, and she did seem different. She kind of blew me off, though, saying she was tired."

I shake my head. "I don't know."

"How'd I get stuck in the car with you? You're like sitting next to a brick wall," Arlo says.

"Thankfully, it's a short drive. Soon, you can talk everyone else's ear off."

He pulls in a breath and shifts. Silence makes him uneasy, like being in his own head for too long makes him lose his sanity.

"I saw the hottest chick last night," Arlo continues. "She works at that drugstore off Halsley."

"Don't tell me you hit on her while you were picking up condoms."

He laughs. "Gum, asshole. I was out of gum for practice this week. But I should have picked up some condoms, that way, she'd know I'm an extra-large."

"Yeah, if she were smart, she'd ask you to prove it before you had the chance to flip off the lights."

"Oh, she could because I'm a shower, not a grower. I'm always prepped and ready." He grabs himself.

"If you whip out your junk, your shit's going to be on the yard in the morning."

Arlo laughs. "You think Poppy's hot?"

"Poppy?"

"Yeah, you know, Reagan's friend." He draws out the syllables.

"I know who you're talking about, asswipe. I'm just trying to figure out why you're asking me."

He shrugs. "I don't know."

"You can't fuck around with her. She's Rae's best friend."

"I didn't say I was."

"But you're asking about her."

He draws his shoulders up. "I think she's kind of hot."

"I'm pretty sure she likes that rugby guy."

Arlo nods. "I don't mean to necessarily date *her*, I just sometimes wonder if I want to have someone around like that, you know?"

"Someone like Poppy?"

"Someone who isn't just with me to have a good time or brag to their friends. Someone who doesn't want to just party all the time."

I steal a glance at Arlo, the guy who seemed to have an allergy to the mere thought of a relationship since I've known him, rarely hanging out with the same girl twice. "What's got you thinking about this?"

"My brother called to tell me he's getting engaged."

"Yeah?"

Arlo nods. "They've been dating for like two years. I don't know, it all just seems so boring and mundane when you think about it, but at the same time, there's something that kind of makes me kind of curious about it. To let your guard down and talk about real shit and things that actually matter. To have someone who actually cares about more than a winning record." He taps a beat on my dashboard. "For a while, I thought you had something going with Raegan. You guys were hanging out all the time for a little while there."

I cut my gaze to him again, attempting to read if there's a question or insinuation behind his comment.

"Wait," he says, his eyebrows jumping. "No shit?"

I shake my head. "It's nothing."

"You like her."

"It may not matter."

"Because you realize Paxton will rip your scrotum out if you even consider it?"

"Because I pissed her off."

"What'd you do?"

"Fucked up."

Arlo chuckles. "You're serious? You like her? Have you talked to Paxton?"

I shake my head once.

"He's going to lose his shit. You don't exactly have the reputation of being a choir boy." He blows out a sigh, like he's watching this situation play out in his mind. "Shit, that's why you haven't gone home with anybody. How long has this been going on? Did you guys…?"

"Mind your own fucking business."

"That's a no. Why? Don't tell me she's waiting for marriage. Wait, you guys have done something. Tell me, is she wild? Quiet? Loud?"

I maim him with a glare.

"Too much?" he asks.

"You passed that marker when you asked about her."

"Shit, dude. You really do *like* her." He rubs his palms together. "That should make this night interesting."

"Keep your mouth shut."

"Oh, no. I'll let you drive this runaway train all by yourself."

We pull into the restaurant, Arlo verbalizing his expected outcomes for the night. I'm a hairbreadth from breaking his nose as we step inside where a hostess greets us with a wide, toothy smile.

"Forget what I said about relationships," Arlo says, stepping forward to flirt with the girl.

"Lincoln!"

I turn, catching sight of Poppy in the distance, waving at us. Paxton and Caleb push the door open behind us, talking about a video game. Poppy appears, her red hair pin-straight, smiling as she peeks behind her. "Okay, just so you guys know, your mom invited a ton of people, and Rae's in a really weird mood. We definitely need to get her drunk tonight. Let her just have fun. I'm happy to be her DD, but you guys have to lay off on the bodyguard crap because she might actually haul off and punch one of you tonight."

Paxton chuckles. "Arlo, I'll give you a twenty if you can piss her off enough that she hits you."

Poppy scowls. "Don't."

"I'll be the DD. You should party with her. She'll have more fun," Pax offers.

Poppy flashes a grin. "Also, if you guys mention Chase tonight, I'll punch you. Fair warning."

"Need us to kick his ass?" Arlo asks.

"I need you to pretend it never happened. But, thanks." She waves us forward, leading us into an area portioned off from the rest of the restaurant where tables are set up in rows with people I don't know. I wasn't even aware today was her birthday until yesterday when Paxton mentioned attending dinner tonight. I wonder if this was how she'd felt last night at the party, if being an outsider made each set of eyes feel like a judgment. None of them know me, and yet half will heckle me, and the other half worships me. Everyone loves a winner unless they aren't that winner, and then they like to take to social media with snarky remarks.

A couple of girls whisper and point, but I don't stop on them, searching for Raegan until I find her sitting beside her grandpa and Camilla. The rest of the table is empty except for Poppy, who makes her way to the seat on her other side.

"Rae Rae!" Arlo yells, drawing the attention from the few who weren't looking at us. "Happy birthday!"

She glances up, a gentle laugh playing on her lips as she watches the four of us make our way to her table, her gaze continuing past me too quickly.

"Happy Birthday, you pain in the ass," Pax says, reaching her first and pulling her out of her chair and into a hug. "Are you feeling old?"

"I already asked her that," their Grandpa Cole says. "She flipped me off."

She's grinning as Paxton releases her. "That was because you gave me dead roses."

"Nineteen of them," he says proudly. "I had to buy them a couple of weeks ago, make sure they'd be nice and crispy for your birthday."

"You're morbid," she says.

"Others call it thoughtful," he says with a smile.

"I call it being a pain." Raegan gives him a glance that spells humor and intention that leaves him chuckling before Arlo snatches her into an aggressive and brief hug. He says nothing before shoving her directly at me like we're in the fucking third grade. Douchebag.

She stumbles into my chest with a quiet grunt, our hands gripping each other for support. "Are you high?" she asks him, righting herself.

"My bad," Arlo says. "It's all those extra practices. I don't know my own strength." He flexes his biceps.

"And humble, too." Raegan shakes her head, finally turning to acknowledge me, her hand still gripping my forearm for support. Her perfume is light and citrusy, reminding me of spring breaks from my childhood when we'd go visit my Mom's parents in Arizona once they became snowbirds and spent half the year in a mobile home park. They had three orange trees in their backyard that bloomed in the spring, the scent rich and sweet.

"Happy birthday," I tell her.

Raegan smiles, her actions slow as she leans forward to hug me. In all the time I've known her, I can't recall ever holding her like this, studying the way her body aligns with mine so seamlessly, even with the completely platonic gesture.

We move to greet Cole and his wife, Camilla.

"If you guys are team Poppy tonight, we're not friends." She moves to Caleb, who gives her an awkward one-armed hug.

"What's team Poppy?" Cole asks.

Rae turns around. "You don't want to know."

"We used to spend every one of her birthdays going to the aquarium and then to pick up ice cream," he says, his smile crooked as he watches her, his thoughts bouncing between the present and past of this date. It's evident in the way his eyes crinkle, and his smile stretches with fondness. If an artist could capture his expression now, it would be deserving of art museums across the world because there are a million emotions so blatant and evident in this single look.

Raegan's smile is radiant. "I'll take you for ice cream and blow off all these people."

Cole grins like he knows this as a fact. "You should go out with your friends. We can go get ice cream this week."

I think of her telling me how birthdays bring change and wonder if it's this tradition, in particular, she'd been referring to?

"Where's Mom?" Paxton asks.

Raegan shrugs, her gaze skipping across the room. "I have no idea."

"Dad?"

She shakes her head. "He was here, but I don't know where he went." There's the whisper of an expression, one she silences by a louder, more obvious smile. "You guys can sit wherever you want. I don't think I know that half of the room," she says, glancing at the farthest tables from us filled with people somewhere between or near our ages. "I think I even saw some cheerleaders come, which I'm blaming you for." She moves her gaze to Paxton. "Thanks for that."

"I told them we were going to a party. I didn't invite them to dinner."

Her eyebrows lift with a silent *bullshit*, which has him grinning. "You're popular, what can I say?"

"Sorry I'm late!" Mrs. Lawson says, swiping at some loose hairs, the act so similar to Raegan when she gets flustered.

"You okay?" Cole asks. "Is Cal with you?"

Mrs. Lawson nods. "I'm fine, Dad. I was just out in the parking lot on a call with several board members. He's not with me. He said he had to work late and would meet me here." She looks around like she's going to find him.

"Was your call about the job?" Raegan asks.

Mrs. Lawson nods. "Yes, but we're not talking about that right now. I've barely seen you today, and you somehow lied on your birth certificate in an attempt to say you're nineteen today." She looks at their grandpa. "She's only ten, right?"

He smiles. "I thought she was turning five today."

Mrs. Lawson laughs, sadness preventing it from sounding sincere. "Let's sit. Tell me about your day."

Whether she sees them or not anymore, the outline of expectations is still present—I recognize them from the ones that hang over my head: the forced independence, the obligation to be happy, to be present.

"I'll be back. I'm going to say hi to the cheerleaders." Paxton's eyebrows dance before he turns, scanning the room again.

"You in, Caleb?" Arlo asks, already following after Pax.

Caleb shakes his head. "I'm good." He takes a seat across from Cole, and I pull out the one next to him, across from where Rae's seated. She glances at me, her brow creased with confusion.

"Should we order for Cal?" Cole asks, lifting his menu as he slings an arm around the back of Raegan's chair.

Raegan looks at her mom as she moves to the other side of the table and takes a seat. "Probably. He said he'd be here by now. I don't know what's keeping him." She checks her phone as Poppy sits beside me, with what I'm fairly certain is hope shining in her gaze.

"Nice seeing you here," Poppy says.

"Is there a plan beyond alcohol?" I ask quietly.

Poppy shakes her head. "We swore we were going to act our age and be stupid and make dumb mistakes, and tonight my goal is to carry that plan out." She grabs her napkin, folding it into her lap. "Something's bothering her, and she won't tell me what it is. I'm hoping if I can get a few drinks into her, she'll spill."

17

RAEGAN

Lincoln sits across from me, his hair disheveled, and his dark eyes watching the room like he often does. I wonder if it's because of playing football and needing to read the intentions of so many, or if this habit is what makes him so good at football.

I ignore him through dinner, through stories of birthdays past and of school. I don't even look at him when Mom asks him about school and football. Even when Paxton and Arlo finally return to the table, I keep my attention close, listening to Camilla tell me about an event she's hosting at their church, feigning interest in the tea options she's debating. I ignore him as Mom apologizes for Dad's absence, and Grandpa contemplates aloud where he might have gone, and the thirty minutes we wait after the tables have been cleared in case Dad shows up.

"Is this where I tell you not to do anything I wouldn't do?" Mom asks, hugging me as she signs for the bill after arguing with Grandpa over it.

"Yup," Paxton says, wrapping me in a headlock. "And then, she's going to nod and proceed to fill her night with poor decisions. Luckily, you have the best child in the world—" he points a finger at himself, "—and I'll be watching out for her."

Grandpa chuckles, and Mom smiles as I pop him with my elbow.

"You guys have fun and be safe," Mom says. "If you guys need a ride home, call me. I'd rather come and pick you up then have you drive if you're going to be drinking."

"That's why we brought Caleb," Pax says, flashing a smile to his oldest friend to convey his joke.

"Love you, Mom," I say before turning to Grandpa and Camilla. Grandpa has a toothpick between his teeth, a habit he procured after he stopped smoking a decade ago. Camilla is clutching her purse, watching as several get rowdier as time dwindles on.

"Be safe," she tells me, pressing her cold lips to my cheek.

"Love you guys. Thanks for coming."

"Don't forget you owe me ice cream," Grandpa says, his hug tight and unforgiving, just like the love we share for each other.

Mom grabs her purse and jacket so she can follow them out. Mom claims she looks like her mother did, but I see Grandpa in her every time she laughs and anytime she talks with her hands, which is always. Grandpa places a hand on Camilla's shoulders and another on Mom's arm, leading them toward the exit. He looks back and waves a final time as they reach the door.

"Okay. Party plan, step one, complete," Poppy says, reaching for her purse. "Now, on to the fun stuff." She digs into her large purse, pulling out a reusable water bottle with a bow around the top. "Happy birthday."

It's so full, the liquid hardly sloshes as she passes it to me. "You're not funny," I tell her.

Poppy tinkers a laugh. "It's alcohol in a reusable water bottle. This spells Raegan."

Paxton chuckles outright. "That's awesome."

"It is, and if she drinks a quarter of it before we arrive at the party, she will be nice and tipsy and ready to have fun. Because fun is good, and we're hot and nineteen, and we deserve to have a good time."

We went to lunch this afternoon, where Poppy confessed that Chase has been dating multiple girls and that while she wanted to be okay with it, she wasn't. And she was less okay with it because he'd lied about nearly everything. Currently, my thoughts are like a shaken bottle of soda, the pressure so great, I don't know how to remove the lid without making a massive mess. So, I turn it off. I turn off the indecision, the fears, the disappointment—all of it and take a long pull from the bottle, my eyes and throat burning as the liquid washes down my throat.

I wince. "Is that straight alcohol?"

"I added some pop."

I shake my head. "Not enough. If I drink a quarter of that, I'll be so drunk I won't know you from Paxton."

She giggles. "Let's test that theory."

I screw the lid back on. "Let's not."

"Hey," Derek says, his smile hesitant as he looks at us. "Sorry I'm late. My study group lasted longer than I thought."

I wait for emotions to bloom—for the distraction of butterfly wings to make my stomach and chest feel too small—for absolutely anything to spark as I stare at Derek.

Paxton folds his arms across his chest, his anger is evident. My accident created a geyser between the two, and though he claims it's always been there, it's definitely more pronounced now.

"Don't worry about it," I tell him. "We're just leaving for a party Poppy wants to go to."

Poppy exhales deeply, her gaze scattered as she works to realign the evening with this slight wrench I've thrown into the plans. "This night is all about us having fun. No focusing on school or work or boys," she glances at the guys before returning her green eyes to me, another heavy sigh. "So many things we've planned for this year have gone awry, but we're sticking to *this* plan. We're going to drink too much, flirt even more, and we're not taking a single regret home with us." She gives me a challenging stare.

I glance at Derek's smile, and then at the others, flinching when I meet Lincoln's questioning stare. "We'll meet you guys there," I say, taking Poppy's arm.

We make it to the hostess desk when someone catches my arm. Lincoln is behind me, his eyebrows lowered, his eyes darker than I've seen them with a storm brewing that he's clearly ready to unleash on me. "You invited Derek, and you didn't invite me?" The defiance in his eyes and the tilt of his jaw erase the vulnerability lacing his question.

"Let me guess, now you care?"

Poppy slides her arm from mine. "You guys should probably take this somewhere else. There's a lot of people around."

"I don't have anything to say." I shake my head, confirming the point as I look for Poppy to bail me out of this.

"We're in party mode. Maybe you guys can have this fight tomorrow?" she suggests.

Lincoln's jaw flexes. "I'll drive her. We'll meet you there."

Poppy winces, her association and ties to my fictionalized hopes for us keeping her from saying no. "It's her birthday. Don't make me regret agreeing to this."

Lincoln doesn't say anything, using too much force as he pushes the door open, leaving me to follow him.

He's silent as he stalks toward his truck, something I realize tonight is grossly understated to his family's means after seeing his house last night. He waits at his passenger door, holding it open in what feels like the gate to a trap. Against my better judgment, I climb inside and fasten my seatbelt, fighting the impulse to pull in deep breaths of his scent and relax when I know I need to have all of my defenses up and prepared.

He starts the truck and leaves the parking lot without exchanging a word or even a glance.

"Are we really going to do this again?" I ask.

"No. I'm fucking exhausted by whatever in the hell this shit is. I don't want to keep dancing around things and pretending everything's fine between us."

"Then let's stop. You were right. This entire situation is just going to blow up in our faces, and it's not a matter of if but when. You're going to leave. You're going to be drafted next year, and I'm going to be a sophomore still trying to figure out stupid statistics. This preserves your time here, your relationship with Paxton, and my sanity. So, let's just call this what it is, an infatuation because we both know we shouldn't cross the line. We both know it—we've known it all along."

"What happened to borrowed time and all that bullshit?"

"Reality." My answer is slapped with finality as my voice comes out balanced and clear, far from anger or bitterness, striving for indifference because it's the only way to turn off my feelings toward him.

"So that's where you want to draw the line? We're strangers now?"

"I'm pretty sure we've always been strangers. I don't know anything about you. I don't have any idea what your favorite color is or your favorite movie or your greatest pet peeve. I don't know anything about your mom and nearly as little about your dad. I didn't even know about Gloria until you introduced me to her. You keep everyone out, and I tried to get in, and every time I learned something about you, it just has me realizing how little I really do know."

"Who cares about that shit? That is my past. It doesn't define me—it's not who I am."

"It shapes you, though. It's a part of you, and if you can't let anyone see those parts and let them in, they're never going to be in your life as anything other than an infatuation because they're never going to know you."

He pulls to a stop at an address where cars spill onto the streets, a house lit up, surrounded by giant evergreens, his attention still directed out the windshield. "So, you're just going to fuck Derek?"

I stare at him, hearing the anger vibrate off each syllable as they play through my thoughts again and again. It's a low blow, and he knows it, but maybe my inviting him to come was as well.

"We just make it worse each time," I tell him. "Our words are weapons, and our actions are grenades, and we keep aiming them at each other. I don't want to hurt you, and I can't take being hurt by you, so one of us just has to pull the pin and let it blow up before it takes us both down."

He turns, his eyes black as the dim light from the yard shines on his dark irises and anger. "And this is you pulling the pin?"

I nod, my chest heavy as I meet his stare. A myriad of emotions reflects back at me, causing a tangle of words that I don't have the energy to unravel to stick in my throat.

I push open the door before I lose my nerve, letting the chill of the night consume me as I walk toward the house, unscrewing the lid on the water bottle Poppy had shoved into my hands before leaving the restaurant. I take a long drink —the alcohol's burn a welcome discomfort as I let it clear my thoughts like a disinfectant.

18

LINCOLN

"Tell me there's more than just flat beer," I say, brushing past Pax and Arlo to get to the table where cups are stacked around puddles of beer.

"I saw Poppy tuck that bottle of booze in her purse," Pax offers, taking another drink from his red Solo cup.

"Bad night?" Arlo asks.

"Did you check their freezer?" I ask, dismissing his question.

Paxton nods. "Frozen dinners and ice."

I roll my shoulders, my skin too tight, and my thoughts too heavy. If I were at the gym, I'd crank up the fucking treadmill and run until my muscles were so fatigued I couldn't think about her anymore.

Instead, I'm stuck here because I'm a masochist and can't force myself to leave when Raegan comes into view. She notices me as well, her gaze stopping over every face except mine.

She smiles.

She laughs.

She engages in conversation and leans closer to each stranger.

She's trying to forget me.

Erase me.

Meanwhile, I'm left feeling lost in her and what we shared.

What we could have had.

I grab the glass Paxton just filled with beer and swallow its contents before refilling it and downing a second.

Pax looks at me, eyebrows raised with question. "Did I miss something?"

"I'm going to go find a distraction," I tell him.

Arlo trails me like a shadow, grabbing my arm when I don't slow down. "This is a one-eighty," he says.

I shrug him off. "She invited Derek." The words don't seem to mean anything as he stares at me blankly. "She doesn't even want to be friends. I'm done with this shit."

Arlo moves, checking me like a blocker. "That's probably for the better because this would get complicated and messy and all kinds of fucked up, but…" He levels me with a glance that lacks the usual note of humor he always possesses. "She doesn't seem like the forgiving type. If you fuck around with somebody, you're not going to stand a chance."

I nod. "She already made that choice." I drop my shoulder, but before I get the satisfaction of clipping him, Arlo moves, leaving me to my own devices.

"Have you seen Rae?"

"I'm not a babysitter," I remind Paxton, keeping my back to him as the girl in front of me presses her ass more firmly against my groin. It's been less than two hours since Raegan officially quit me, and like any bad habit, I'm already looking for a new host.

"Dude. I need to find Rae." He grips my shoulder. "Like *now*."

"I'm kind of busy here." The last chick who came to talk it up with me tried suffocating me with a kiss that tasted of throw up and was so forceful, it made my bottom lip bleed. This new girl is a huge step up, and she's clearly interested in one thing and one thing only: my dick.

I deserve this, especially since Paxton is the reason I'm going through this, thanks to this distraction of epic proportions called his little sister. In front of me, the girl runs a hand down my thigh, pulling every ounce of my attention in her direction.

"Lincoln," Pax barks my name, his patience thinning.

I spin to face him, my annoyance evolving into anger. The last thing I want to do is find Raegan. Right now, I need to release these fantasies I've been having of her with some other chick so I can go back to seeing her as an asexual being. "She's probably having fun. It's her birthday. You should try—" My words come to an abrupt stop as I notice his eyes are wide and bright, a heavy crease marring his brow as he scopes the room. I know this look, but not well. After all, Pax is usually laid back and easy going—concern isn't something we spend a lot of time with. But right now, it's apparent something has him worried.

"What's going on?" I ask. "Drugs?" We went to a party last year where someone had spiked the keg with Molly. It was a dick move that led to an investigation and later an arrest. Four girls were raped, and several couldn't remember the night. The memory of that night never veers too far from my thoughts when we go out.

He shakes his head with a tight jerk, then flicks his thumb over the screen of his phone and hands it to me.

'Dean Lawson caught with his pants down.' The headline reads below a video of Dr. Lawson getting a blowie by a woman who is most definitely not Mrs. Lawson.

The video replays several times on a loop. It's a grainy black and white image, but it's definitely Dr. Lawson. "Oh shit."

"It was emailed to the entire student body," he says. "I need to find Rae."

I quickly nod my understanding. "Okay, you go check out the front, I'll circle around the back."

The house is filled with people, everyone in denial that the weekend is coming to an end. A girl calls my name, but I keep moving, searching for Rae's gray top.

"President! Smile!" An arm wraps around the back of my neck, and a phone appears in my face, showing my reflection beside a girl with bright blonde hair. The phone flashes, and the girl smacks a kiss to my cheek before moving on. I don't watch where she retreats to or wonder who she's going to share my picture with—this is becoming my new norm.

I see her then. Blonde hair, gray shirt, a calculating expression as Derek laughs at something she's said.

Fucking hell.

I lie to myself and say obligation and friendship are what has my pace quickening, the energy in my chest growing and expanding, reminding me of what it's like to be on the field when we're down, and I know the game is resting on my shoulders. The embers in my chest start to burn brighter as well, a concoction that has my adrenaline pumping.

Derek turns as I get near, his smile falling into a frown as he pulls both shoulders back. "Beckett," he says. He's one of the few who calls me by my last name rather than my moniker. Behind him, Raegan cringes as her eyes dance across the room, returning to me before she shakes her head. Her pupils are dilated, and her cheeks are flushed, making that energy in my chest expand further. She stares at me, allowing me to briefly study the light hue of her blue eyes.

"Do you need something?" Derek asks. "Water? A ride home? Some fucking pride, maybe?"

I step closer. "Get the hell out of my way."

"That's not going to happen," he says, smiling with so much malice and intent I want to haul off and punch him. I'm ready for it—consequences be damned—but then Rae shakes her head again, this time in defeat rather than a warning, and she walks away.

"Rae," I call, but she doesn't stop.

"She doesn't want to talk to you. How obvious does she need to be?" Derek taunts.

I spin around so fast on him, he flinches, expecting my fist. "Stay the fuck away from her. I'm not going to tell you again."

"Or what?" he snarls.

Threats dance along my tongue, each one uglier than the last. "You almost got her killed. You want redemption? Move the fuck on. I beat your ass on the field every fucking game, and that's been enough, but if you push this—you keep trying to insert yourself into her life—I'll fucking ruin you."

I don't give him the chance to respond. I have nothing left to say.

I find Rae near the kitchen, sending a message to someone. "You ready to go?" I ask.

She starts to shake her head. "I thought we agreed we weren't going to do this?"

"We did, but—"

"Rae!" Poppy appears, her face split with a smile. She's definitely drunk as she stumbles to a stop and hiccups, her entire body moving from the action. Raegan laughs, reaching forward to steady her. "Are you okay?"

Poppy nods. "I'm great. Where have you been?"

Rae hitches her thumb behind her, in the wrong direction of where I just found her.

A guy appears behind Poppy. He's wearing a pair of skinny jeans pulled so high I'm not sure he has a ball sack and is wearing a black tee that's equally as tight with a backward baseball hat. He eyes me, his brows raised with a silent challenge.

I can't hide my scoff. The emo looks like a dickless tool.

"Rae, this is Ricky. Ricky, this is my best friend, Rae."

"You have a dude's name." he says, shaking her hand.

"It's short for Raegan," she tells him.

Emo shrugs. "Wasn't Raegan a dude?"

Poppy laughs. "I'm named after a narcotic."

Rae looks unsettled for half a second, but Poppy eyes me, and her smile broadens. "Lincoln! What are you doing? Are you here to talk with Rae?"

I glance at Rae as she withdraws the same damn water bottle from Poppy's purse and takes a long drink. Poppy yells what sounds like a battle cry, then reaches for the bottle.

"Lincoln, this is Ricky," Poppy gives me the same introduction. "Isn't he cute?"

I can't tell who she's posing the question to, but I offer my hand. It's not intended to be a challenge, simply manners, but douche face tries to show me he's tough by squeezing my hand as hard as he can. Dude doesn't realize I squeeze fucking tennis balls for a couple of hours every day to strengthen my grip. I constrict my hold, smiling because I could easily break a couple of fingers, and he likely doesn't have a clue. He doesn't reciprocate the smile, but he also doesn't try anacondaing my hand anymore.

"I'm going to go find something to drink? You want anything?" He looks to Poppy.

She shakes her head, smiling at him.

I consider threatening him. Warn him that he better come back and at least part ways amicably rather than make a dumbass excuse, but she's standing too close to not overhear.

"I don't think he's coming back," Rae says, standing on her toes, watching emo walk away.

"Who? Ricky?" Poppy asks. Rae nods. Poppy folds her hand with a dismissive wave. "I hope not. I told you, I'm not looking for a boyfriend, just fun."

Rae stifles a giggle. "Well, did you have some *fun*?"

"Kind of..." Poppy's nose scrunches. "Not really. We got to third base, and I learned he didn't have any idea what he was doing." She giggles again.

My eyes go wide, and I nearly choke on air. This was not the conversation I was expecting to hear. Not from Poppy, not ever.

"...but, he used his finger like a plunger. I don't think he had any idea what he was doing, and his nails were too long."

A pronounced frown covers Rae's face. "That's gross. I shook his hand!" She wipes her hand across her jeans.

"If you think about it, pretty much every person here has probably touched *something* tonight."

Rae wipes her hand again.

I have no fucking clue what to say at this point. Hearing the two discuss foreplay just depletes more of that failing screen that I've been clinging to. Plus, I'm supposed to be finding Rae and getting her the hell out of dodge because the longer we're here, the greater the chance of others watching that video and saying something becomes.

"Can we mark this night as a success then and go? I'm starving, and I have to wake up early for practice tomorrow."

Rae turns toward me, but her gaze doesn't meet mine. "Poppy drove my car. You guys can go whenever you want."

"You two are blitzed. You can't drive anywhere."

"Hardly. I'll be fine in like an hour." She turns her attention toward a group of people playing beer pong. She taps Poppy on the arm and points at the game. It's all guys. I recognize a couple from the basketball team and one from a class.

"We should—"

I don't allow her to finish the suggestion that they go play. Not with those drunk bastards who only have one idea in their brains. My shoulder hits her in the stomach like I'm going to pile drive her, but I lift her over my shoulder in one fell swoop, grabbing her arm as an anchor. "Poppy, door."

Poppy giggles. "She's going to bite you. She fights dirty."

"I was hoping she would."

19

RAEGAN

Fantasies tangle with indignation as Lincoln strolls through the crowds of people, my ass in the air and my face smothered by his T-shirt and the scent of his cologne—spicy and somehow fresh like the ocean—and laundry detergent—clean and crisp. With each of his strides, the scents hit me like a drug, pulling me deeper into previous fantasies where I imagined myself drowning in this scent and his hot skin.

A guy whoops. "Yeah, President!" Reminding me why my indignation is fighting to be heard.

"What are you doing? Put me down!" My voice is deeper, constricted because his shoulder—which feels far too broad and big—digs into my stomach, making breathing a chore. "Lincoln!"

"Go, President!" Another guy yells.

"I'm not..." I yell, trying to look for whomever just cheered Lincoln on, prepared to tell them this isn't at all what it looks like.

"Was that necessary?" I hear Paxton ask as we clear the front door.

"She wants to stay. Should I put her down?" Lincoln's voice is deeper with my ear against his back. "Pinky and the Brain are blitzed, by the way," Lincoln adds.

"I'm buzzed. There's a difference, you jackass." My voice sounds too similar to a prepubescent boy to sound threatening. "We need to discuss your choice in friends," I tell Paxton as Lincoln lowers me to the ground.

Pax doesn't even crack a smile. "Let's grab some burgers, and then you can sleep this off."

"You guys are acting like we're wasted," Poppy says, offense coating her words. "We're not even drunk." She hiccups again, lifting her thumb and forefinger to create a small gap. "Well, maybe a little. But we talked about this. You guys were in. Fun night. Let loose. Remember any of these words?"

Pax runs his hand down his face, cutting a glance at Lincoln before looking at me. "We need to go. Something's come up."

I stop, focusing on my brother's face. The way his eyes keep bounding across the yard, the crease marring his brow, the deep frown that makes him look much older. "Maggie?"

He shakes his head, and my lungs fill with air as relief soars through me.

"But we still need to go."

"Birthday?" Poppy asks, a pleading slur that confirms she's had too much to drink.

Pax's jaw grows tight as he looks across the yard where a group of people are laughing. "We need to go," he repeats.

"Okay," I concede. "But why won't you tell me what's going on?"

"I will. Let's just get to my house. Come on."

"What about the others?" I ask.

"Caleb already caught a ride home, and Arlo drove." He tips his head in the direction of the road, and I stop questioning him.

I grip Poppy's elbow, starting in the direction of where she'd parked my car.

"This was a great party," she says. "Are you sure you want to go? We could tell them we'll meet them later."

I glance at Paxton, a dozen feet behind us, his face grim as he shoves his phone into his pocket. "I think something's wrong." The words feel like a lie because I know something is wrong as the panic in me rises like a tide, washing other possibilities of what has Pax so upset out of the way.

Poppy pokes me with her elbow. "I think Lincoln's definitely not over you. I know you're probably not in the place to appreciate it yet, but him carrying you out was really hot."

I cling to my concerns in self-preservation as I glance at her, tears burning my eyes as I recall seeing him just an hour ago with a glazed expression and the girl who quickly replaced me. The significance of his previous words blowing away in the breeze. "He was making out with someone tonight."

Poppy comes to a quick stop, nearly making me trip. "What?"

"Veer left!" Pax yells before I can reply to her shock.

"I'm over this way," I tell him.

"You can't drive. You're weaving."

"I'm fine. I'm in heels on gravel." I have little doubt that I could drive us home, what little alcohol is still flowing through my system is barley keeping me warm.

"Don't be difficult," Pax says, catching up with us because we're still stopped, Poppy, trying to digest my news about Lincoln. "Just ride with us."

I pull out my phone, ready to schedule a Lyft because I can't be in a car with Lincoln. Not now. But before I can complete the request, Lincoln approaches, his gaze heavy and intentional. In one second he's grabbing my phone, and in the next, he's dropping it into his pocket.

"What are you doing?" I cry, my eyes slashing over him.

"Look," Pax says, running a hand over his jaw again. "Shit is about to hit the fan. Let's go back to my place. You guys can have my room."

I have to swallow the urge to say 'ew' because though Pax and I are close, there are limits. "I don't understand why you won't just tell me. What's going on? And why would I stay at your place when I can go home?"

"Damn, look at the dean getting his!" The words make me pause, and then lean back on my heels, working to replay the words again and again and again.

Did he say dean? Bean? Dean, like a friend named Dean?

Someone laughs, another giggles—the sound pitched and breathy. "Can you believe he had sex in his office? That has to be against the rules, right? Does that mean we get, like, a vacation or something?"

My attention sweeps to Pax, my stomach falling to my knees. My brother's poker face is as weak as my right cross, meaning it doesn't exist. "Pax? What's going on?"

He shakes his head, pursing his lips. "There's a video going 'round. A video of Dad…"

My stomach falls, taking my heart with it. "A video? Who's seen it?"

Pax shakes his head again, this time faster. "Everyone?"

"What?" I glance at Poppy, seeking clarification, but her mouth is slack, her face pale. She's as shocked as me. "We have to go check on Mom." Guilt licks at my skin like a wave, cold and unforgiving as it pulls me deeper into its tide. If I had told Mom … if I had told Paxton, would this have still happened? Maybe. But at least they wouldn't have been blindsided by it.

I feel numb as I follow to Lincoln's truck. I climb into the backseat without another objection, my childhood and innocence in this situation still back at the party as I glimpse at the video of my dad receiving oral sex from a stranger on Poppy's phone. Pax warned me not to look. I should have listened. It will be a struggle to look him in the eye ever again.

"I thought we were going home?" I cry when we pull into Paxton's driveway.

"I already texted Mom, and she didn't respond. It's after midnight. I'm sure she's asleep. Sleep this off, and we'll go over tomorrow."

Poppy takes my hand, sensing my anger. Maybe she can feel my body temperature rising. Perhaps it's because I jackknifed from the seat and am nearly through the middle console, ready to take this to the mat with him. Her grasp is warm and firm, tethering me in place. "I think he's right. If you guys go in there guns a blazing, it's just going to make it worse. I'll go with you tomorrow. I can help in any way, but once the sun is up, your thoughts will be clearer."

Maggie has always been reactive. Emotional is the term my parents use. Paxton is laid-back and calm. I can be found somewhere in the middle of the vast void that separates the two, sometimes closer to my sister, and other times closer to my brother, but right now I am channeling Maggie though I'm trying my hardest to be cool like Pax. It causes irrational tears from frustration at myself and the situation to blur my eyes.

"Okay," I concede, my throat tight. Poppy looks at me and nods, like she's agreeing with me or possibly agrees with my sudden sense. Whatever the intention, it sits heavily in my stomach as I follow the others out of the car.

Paxton's place is an old seventies house that has had few remodels. The benefit to the house is all the rooms are large, which is why they chose it—that and cheaper rent since they're fifteen minutes in the opposite direction of the party houses on campus. Even the outside screams of the seventies with the ivory paint and light green trim, a shingled roof, and an enormous picture window in the front. But, as close as Pax and I are, this place is still relatively foreign to me. Maybe if Lincoln didn't live here, it wouldn't feel so strange to stop by, but with him here, I seem to have overthought each reason, and they've always felt like excuses, keeping my visits minimal.

Caleb looks up as we come inside. Headphones tangled in his curly, red hair, the kind with a little mouthpiece, a gaming controller in his hand—it's how I always mentally picture him. "Hey!" he lowers the controller, looking over us before stopping at Pax, his eyebrows lowered. "What's goin' on?"

"Our dad's having an affair."

I thought it would be harder to say.

It wasn't.

20

LINCOLN

I learned as a kid that when you think shit is bad, it can always get worse, and today has been a reminder of this testament.

The day began with waking up to Raegan in my kitchen. Her eyes swollen and her cheeks red. I knew she'd been crying, but our tempestuous relationship hadn't taught me anything regarding how to navigate emotions and feelings like these, which made me feel like an even bigger asshole.

"Do you want to get some breakfast?" I asked.

She looked at me then, and I saw it. I saw the look of hope in her gaze that left me paralyzed for a full minute as I scrambled to decipher what that hope represented. It was a moment too long because she stood and walked over to the coffeepot, her back to me like I hadn't spoken.

"Rae," her name sounded like a plea, and even knowing that I didn't try to change the meaning by adding additional unnecessary words.

"I saw you last night." Her words were cut and dry, clearly not looking for an excuse or reason.

This conversation was likely doomed from the start. I knew she wasn't the kind of girl to accept a smile as a promise or an orgasm as an apology. I knew that, Arlo reminded me of the fact. Still, I found that girl last night who wasn't looking to know my past or my future, only a good time, and the ease of it all felt so damn good, I ignored every doubt and question that was ricocheting against my need for independence, and I kissed her.

I could've told Raegan that the other girl meant nothing or tried explaining how I'd drunk three beers in a matter of minutes, so I didn't follow her. Instead, I chose defense. "From my view, it didn't look like you had any reason to care."

I saw it then, the look of resistance, the one that said she didn't want to believe me. But in seconds, it was gone, replaced by disappointment and disgust as her nose scrunched, and her eyes turned hard.

Before I could grapple for words or a second opportunity to start the morning over again, Pax appeared.

"I just spoke with Mom," he said, rubbing his thumb and forefingers over his eyes. I'd never seen my friend look so torn down.

Raegan turned to fully face him, her eyes scouring each detail of Pax, reading him like a map. "What happened?"

"She said she was sorry, but she needed to get away. Hell, I don't blame her. I have no idea how long this has been going on or if he's going to lose his job, or what this might do to her?" He rubs a hand down his face. "She was at the airport, boarding a flight to go stay with Aunt Kayla in New York for a little while."

Raegan remained standing in place, but it was clear her thoughts were in a million places all at once.

"You can stay with me," Poppy said from behind Pax, where she was hovering by the doorway, unbeknownst to the rest of us. "I'll talk to my mom."

Raegan shook her head, her gaze static. "No. It's okay."

"You can crash here," Pax offered. "My room is yours for as long as you want it."

Arlo stepped into the kitchen then, his eyes round and his face long. Aside from the field, it was the quietest I'd ever seen him. "What can I do?" His gaze skipped across each of us like a stone thrown into the river, landing on Rae. She quickly looked away.

My chest ached, knowing she was trying to keep it all together, and that I contributed to her undoing.

"I have class," she said to no one.

"Skip it," Arlo said immediately.

"I do, too," Poppy said, stepping farther into the kitchen. "Pax, can I borrow your car?"

He nodded instantly, realizing Poppy was likely the only one who understood the right steps at that point. It prompted adrenaline to course through me, something that felt too similar to the desire to flee or fight, only I had no desire to run. I wanted to fight. I wanted a chance to break through the invisible chains that kept her stuck in the past.

"We'll go to my house. You can borrow some clothes," Poppy continued. "Are your books in your car? We can stop and get them."

"My laptop's at home."

"I'll get it," I said before reason could stop me.

Everyone's eyes moved to mine—everyone's but hers.

"I'll go with you," Arlo volunteered. "What else can we get?"

I could see it, the reality of the situation beginning to swallow her.

"We can stop there first," Poppy says. "We'll get whatever you need."

"You can stay here," Pax offered again. "We'll get it all."

She didn't nod, but she also didn't shake her head. "No. I don't even know what I need. I have to go."

Pax turned to Arlo and me. "You guys don't have to do this. I don't know what we'll be walking in to."

I shook my head, dismissing his opportunity to renege. "Let's go."

Raegan and Poppy were still wearing their clothes from last night, Pax was in a pair of shorts and him team sweatshirt, and I was in some sweats. Arlo was the only one dressed, but he hadn't showered yet. Still, we all left in our various states of disarray, matching the moment.

I PULL UP TO HER PARENTS' house, checking my rearview mirror to see Pax pull in with Rae and Poppy. I sigh when I don't see their Dad's car in the driveway.

"You think Pax is going to be okay to play Saturday?" Arlo asks.

Guilt funnels to the already building pool in my gut because apart from the brief window last night after we'd gotten home and I lied in my bed wondering how this would pull their family apart, I haven't really considered Paxton. "He'll be good."

Arlo nods. "I can't believe their mom left. Like, what is Rae going to do? She lives at home still." He runs a hand across his brow. "This is going to be a fucking shit show."

Raegan's the first one out of the car, her moves too normal and casual as she crosses the driveway and unlocks the front door. We follow, weaving through the eerie silence up the stairs and into Raegan's room, where she starts shuffling through items on her desk, shoving them into a stained backpack.

"We'll pack all of your clothes," Poppy says, placing a hand on Arlo's shoulder.

Rae stops, looking over her shoulder at them, a trace of question and objection visible in her eyes. But then she swallows, a look of resignation replacing the doubt.

Arlo scoops the contents of a drawer and drops it into a large suitcase Poppy opened and left on the bed with the instructions for him to empty the dresser while she piles shoes into a duffel bag.

"Just grab it all," Pax says, grabbing a pile Rae hasn't yet touched, shoving it into the same bag she's carefully organized.

I move beside Arlo, grabbing the articles that smell like Raegan. He opens the next drawer, revealing a line of bras and neatly folded underwear. Arlo looks at me. It's the first time I've seen him hesitate at the chance to see a girl's underwear.

Then we hear a sound that somehow is louder and more forceful than a building being leveled: the sound of a door closing.

"Paxton?" The dean's voice rings through the house. Raegan stalls, her chest falling with a deep breath as tears fill her blue eyes.

"Keep packing," Pax says, locking eyes with me. He places a hand on Rae's shoulder. "Just keep packing," he says the words softer this time, a silent assurance before he spins and stalks out of the room.

Raegan stops, though, dropping the contents in her hands before she races toward the door, running so quickly she has to grab the doorjamb to slow herself so she can change directions.

"What's she doing?" Arlo asks, but Poppy is running on her heels.

"Pax is going to lose it!" she says over one shoulder.

"Shit!" I hiss, sprinting after them with Arlo at my side.

We stop in the kitchen, where the dean stands in a wrinkled shirt near the fridge. His gaze is tired and weary as he looks at Paxton, who's on the other side of the island, his face red with anger and hands fisted with aggression. Rae is a pace in front of him, her fingers trying to encircle his wrist.

"Go pack," Pax tells her.

"Paxton," Dr. Lawson starts.

"Don't fucking talk to me," Paxton yells.

"It's not what it looked like."

His excuse is like a chemical reaction. Paxton lunges forward. Raegan yells his name, moving surprisingly fast in an attempt to be a buffer, but Arlo grabs her, hauling her back before she gets caught in the crosshairs. Paxton's fist collides with the dean's nose, sending him back several steps before he shocks the hell out of me and moves forward, his fist moving faster than my realization, slamming into the right side of Paxton's face.

"Stop!" Raegan fights against Arlo, who I think is even more shocked than me. She gets free from his loosened grip and scrambles across the kitchen, but I'm faster. I stand in front of her, unaware of what the dean's next move will be when the last one left me stupefied.

"What are you doing?" Raegan yells. "Why would you do this?"

The dean's breaths are fast and hard as he stares beyond me at his daughter. He lifts a hand, wiping at the blood starting to trickle from his nose. "Go to your room."

I can't see her reaction, but my hand at her waist confirms she isn't moving.

"You don't get to make demands. Not now," she says.

"Upstairs, Raegan. Change your clothes and get to school. I told you to mind your own goddamn business. You don't get to stand in my kitchen and judge me, especially not when you're dressed like a hooker."

Paxton yells out with rage, a sound undecipherable but one I understand clearly, a sound of bitterness and unjust.

Rae grabs my right arm, her touch grounding me and bringing awareness that I've closed half the distance between Mr. Lawson and my fist.

"Don't," she tells me. "He's not worth it. He's not worth your future."

Her words do nothing to ease the anger he unleashed. I stalk toward him, recognizing the flash in his eyes that says he wants me to come at him—he wants to fight. I'm sure it's the alcohol I smell on his breath and the fact his life is crumbling faster than a sandcastle hit by an incoming tide.

Raegan slinks in front of me, her body pressed impossibly close to mine, leaning into me. Reason tells me it's to keep her away from her dad, who's a mere foot from me, but then I wonder if she feels it too, the balances she extends to my thoughts, the ease of how she molds against me so effortlessly—so perfectly. "Lincoln." She shoves me backward, and I oblige, taking a measured step back. "Get me out of here," she says. "Please."

I stare at her dad, wanting to make him hurt, wanting to make him bleed.

"*Please*," her voice is so soft and quiet, and I know she means the word only for me. She slides her hand down my forearm, and before her touch slips away, I grip her hand.

"Let's go," I say.

She closes her eyes, relief evident as our fingers weave together. I turn to discover Arlo and Poppy on either side of Pax, his rage still heightened.

"This wasn't how it was supposed to go," the dean says.

No one responds as Arlo works to shuffle Pax back in the direction of Raegan's room. The atmosphere has changed, a rushed frenzy as we all shove things into bags with a sudden urgency.

Poppy starts to close the first suitcase while I look around, questioning what else to pack.

"Do you have your laptop? Your chargers?" Pax asks.

Raegan nods, wearing a sweatshirt she hadn't been when we'd arrived. "I've got it all."

There's still a ton of shit in the room, but I think back to my childhood room when I moved into my first apartment freshman year and how it still looked fully lived in.

"Let's go," Poppy says, closing the next suitcase.

Arlo grabs one bag, and Paxton grabs a second. Poppy grabs a duffle, and Raegan grabs her backpack. I grip the last two bags, one larger and the other a smaller bag that Rae reaches for. I shake her off and look to Arlo, silently requesting for him to lead the way.

He reads my thoughts, wheeling the suitcase across the wood floor and clearing the doorway, followed by Paxton and Poppy, who holds Raegan's hand, further proving her devotion to their friendship. "Let's go."

I follow them, making it to the living room before the dean reappears.

"What are you doing?" he asks, looking at the array of bags.

"I can't stay here," she says.

He reaches for the largest of the two bags I'm carrying, and I drop the smaller one, and shove him back. "You've already exceeded my patience," I warn him. "Get the fuck away from her."

He stares in bewilderment before moving his attention to Rae. "It was already broken. Our marriage ended years ago. Things change. We'd become friends—acquaintances," he says.

"We weren't broken," she tells him. "But we are now."

He stares at her for another second, but defeat stops him from saying anything more.

WE GET BACK to the house, and Paxton punches the school bus-yellow box that our weekly newspapers are delivered in. It partially splinters, hanging limply against the wooden post.

Caleb emerges from the house. "Everything okay?" he asks quietly.

Raegan shakes her head. "Can you help him?"

Caleb nods, moving in the direction of Paxton while the rest of us grab bags and head inside.

"Just leave them here," Rae says, dropping a bag near the front door. "I'll figure something out." She expels a shallow breath. "Do you guys mind if I take a shower?" She stops, her eyes roving across the bags. "I forgot all my bathroom stuff."

Poppy shakes her head. "It's all in the small bag. I've got it all. Your hair dryer, makeup, everything."

I grab the bag and then the one we shoved the contents of her dresser into. "Come on." I nod in the direction of the stairs, leading the way up to one of the two full bathrooms in the house.

"You can leave those in the hall," she says. "I'll be out of here tonight."

"What?"

She turns, both hands are woven into her hair. Her eyes show signs of a storm as she looks over each of my features before settling on my eyes.

"Where are you going?"

She shrugs. "I don't know yet."

"Stay here."

"I can't."

"Why?"

She parts her lips, like she's going to answer, but then stops.

"Because of me?"

"Partly."

My heart pounds objections fiercely. "Because of last night?"

"Because of everything."

"Your dad was unhinged. You should just stay here for a while."

She starts shaking her head before the final words leave my lips, her gaze falling from mine. "I don't need to see the Lincoln fan club march through here. I need some space."

Space is the very last thing I want to give her as questions race through my mind, demanding answers. Questions about her childhood, and if her dad has acted like that before. If he's raised a hand to her? If he's called her names like that previously? My strides are like a beat, steady and even as I cross to her. She looks up at me, a tear forming in her lower lashes.

"I don't want it to mean anything," she whispers. "I just want you to make me feel something else. I want to feel something that doesn't hurt."

21

LINCOLN

Her fingers fist in my sweatshirt, contradicting her need for space, as her body slams into mine with enough impact it knocks every bit of sense from me. I lean into her, catching her lips and directing her chin to the side so I can slant my lips completely over hers, stealing her air and inhibitions. Her arms go around my neck, and she lifts her chin higher, parting her lips and running her tongue along my upper lip. She growls with impatience when I don't grant her access. I pull away only a fraction, knowing we need to exchange reasons and words. She seems to recognize my thoughts because she deftly shakes her head and delves her fingers into my hair, covering my mouth with hers. She kisses me with so much need it knocks me off balance, and I respond instantly, my fingers sliding between the silky strands of her hair and grabbing her backside with the other, pressing her against my hardened cock.

She moans, the sound so pleasurable and addictive I lose what restraint I had left. I run my tongue along hers, tracing each line of her mouth. I pull back only long enough to back into the bathroom, where I flip on the lights and lock the door because I want to see every single part of her. She takes a breath, her eyes darting from the door to the lights.

"We can stop."

Raegan shakes her head. "You said that you don't date or get attached, and that's perfect. I don't want those things either. So, let's just make this simple. We use each other. We are each other's escape." She unzips her sweatshirt, letting it fall to the ground, then reaches for the hem of her shirt.

I grab the fabric before she can remove it and step closer, coming toe to toe with her. I grip the elastic holding her hair in a pony and tug it free. Her hair falls in long layers, inviting me to tangle my fingers in the strands. "What do you want to feel?" I ask, running my nose along her cheekbone, reaching her ear. I take the lobe between my teeth, grazing it before I swipe my tongue over the sensitive flesh. She leans closer, her breaths ragged.

"You," she says.

I groan softly, licking a path across her warm skin, straight to her exposed collarbone. "Where?"

She tips her chin back, her fingers tangled in my sweatshirt. "Everywhere."

I pull her shirt free, admiring the pink and gray leopard print bra that presents her breasts to me like a present waiting to be unwrapped. I take in her chest, the delicate bones around her neck, the flat planes of her ab muscles, and then back to her face and the fine layer of freckles that sprinkle her cheeks. Her eyes are shining, expressing her need and desire as she watches my gaze feast over her.

"You're fucking perfect." I place a hand on her chest, running it from her neck down past her belly button. Her skin is impossibly soft and smooth. I grip the back of my sweatshirt and tee in one fist and haul it over my head.

She bites her bottom lip, the sight so fucking sexy I have to readjust myself. She watches me, her lip turning white as she bites harder.

I groan, grasping a handful of her hair and pulling her against me. Her skin feels softer and warmer against mine, and then her open lips seal over mine, her tongue warring with mine as we duel over desires and needs. I trace the shoulder strap of her bra, and she presses up on her toes, her kisses becoming faster with excitement. I trace the strap to the clasp in the back, and she pulls my bottom lip into her mouth before freeing it and tilting her head in the opposite direction, tracing over my sides with her fingers. I release the clasp and kiss her fully before leaning back to watch the fabric slip down her arms and fall next to us. Her breasts are full, hard nipples conveying her need.

I grip her hips, pushing her securely against the far wall, a towel slipping to the ground. I lean down, tracing the pink of her nipples with my tongue. She gasps, leaning into me, a hand in my hair. I pull her breast into my mouth, flicking my tongue against the sensitive flesh until she moans. The sound is a drug, hitting my bloodstream instantly. I move to the other nipple while releasing the button on her jeans. She slides a hand along my jaw and reaches down with her other hand, tugging the fabric down.

Her eyes are closed, her lips swollen. I slow my licks, and she slowly opens her eyes, watching me as I slide her jeans down the length of her legs. Her underwear is a thin slip of pink lace that matches her bra.

"God. I want to see all of your underwear," I tell her, going down on my knees. I press my nose to her entrance, breathing in her sweet and musky scent. Her hips press back against the wall, reminding me of her inexperience. "No," I say, reaching for her hips again, pulling her back against me. "I want your legs spread over my face. I want to taste you." I take a mouthful of the fabric, making her gasp again.

I link my fingers in the lacey fabric, sliding it down her hips, down past her knees all the way to her ankles where I gently lift each of her feet and grasp the material, taking a deep breath of her scent before shoving them into my pocket.

She's bare in front of me, blue eyes wild and bright, sucking me deeper into this addiction. I lean forward, licking her seam, loving the way she loses her breath and footing, as she grasps my shoulders. I lick her again and again, my tongue flat and hard against her. She tips her chin into the air. I lap at her again, moving my hand to fully expose her. "Look at me," I growl the words.

She drops her head, her lips parted as she looks at me, the twinge of embarrassment in her tight shoulders.

"You make me so fucking hard." I fist myself. "Touch yourself."

Her eyebrows lower, shock and embarrassment coloring her cheeks.

I lean forward, tonguing her clit until she moans. I release myself and reach for her hand, pulling her fingers toward her center. "Feel that?" I ask. "You're dripping for me." I groan, watching her dark nails slide against her tender flesh, dipping a finger inside of her. Her breaths stutter, her chin falling back again. "No. I need those eyes. Watch me finger fuck you."

Her breath leaves her as she looks down at me, her cheeks flushed with more than embarrassment—desire.

I slip my finger back inside of her. Her hips jerk forward in response. "God, you're so responsive. So tight." I sigh. "So fucking perfect." I lean closer, my eyes tethered to hers as I breathe her in. She's so wet, confirming she wants me as badly as I want her. I slide a second finger into her and add my tongue, licking, tasting, and rubbing her until she's moaning and slipping down the wall, her eyes closed again. I stand, keeping the pressure with my fingers, moving my other hand to brush over her full lips, pulling her bottom lip down, and then kissing her, her taste still fresh against my tongue as I find hers.

I circle her clit and then dip my fingers back into her, creating a rhythm that she responds to with harsh breaths I silence with my mouth. She grips me, her fingers constricting, her hips slipping farther. I grasp her hip, holding her upright as I find her release and swallow her moans.

Raegan's hips jerk as I swipe along her clit again, sensitive from the orgasm. I kiss her again and then pull back, admiring the flush on her cheeks and the desire still shining bright in her eyes.

I kiss her once more. "Next time I make you come, it's going to be from fucking you."

"Aren't we...?"

I shake my head. "I have to go to practice. Shower. Take a nap. I'll be back." I steal another kiss, then reach for my shirt.

"Lincoln, this.... We're... This doesn't mean anything. It doesn't *change* anything."

I pull my hoodie over my head. "We just crossed the mother fucking Rubicon. Everything's changed." I slide my fingers across her wet lips. "Everything."

22

RAEGAN

I still feel Lincoln, even after I've showered and dressed. I attempt to distract myself by blow-drying my hair, but each time I look at a space of the narrow bathroom, I picture him on his knees, worshipping my body.

I just had a toe-curling, mind-numbing orgasm.

From my brother's best friend.

In their shared house.

In the wake of my father's publicized affair and my mom leaving for New York.

I'm totally going to Hell.

My desire to get out of the house propels me as I grab my discarded clothing. I hold them in my fist, trying not to look or think of the items he helped me remove and take the stairs two at a time, discovering Poppy on the couch, waiting for me.

"Are they gone?" I ask.

She nods. "Caleb had class, and the others left for practice."

I nod a couple of times, and then go into the kitchen, intent on finding a plastic bag I can use for my dirty clothes.

"Rae," Poppy says, following me. "What can I do?"

I pull open another drawer. "Nothing. I'm good."

"Rae." She catches my hand, stopping me. "This is me. You don't have to lie or pretend."

Her green eyes are rimmed red, her long hair pulled back into a braid. "Do you want to scream? Yell? Fly to meet your mom, so you can make sure everything's okay? Tell me."

"I don't know," I tell her, my eyes and nose burning as my throat grows tight. "I don't know anything anymore."

She reaches forward, grasping my hand. "Maybe we use this as a good excuse to get our own place. We've been talking about it for *years*. We can get an apartment, or maybe rent a house? You don't have to stay here or face this alone."

Her mother has never allowed sleepovers. Poppy wasn't allowed to sleepover, and I wasn't allowed to stay over there, it was a hard rule from her mother who spent most of her career talking to victims of sexual assault.

"I just don't want to feel," I tell her. "I don't want to feel anything."

"Next to no one at school knows he's your dad," she assures me.

I nod dismissively, the rumors at the bottom of my concern list.

"Rae," she repeats my name, her eyes falling with defeat and sadness. "Talk to me. Please. Tell me what you're thinking."

"It doesn't feel real," I tell her. "I don't know what I'm thinking." Tears blur my vision as my nostrils flare. "I can't believe he had an affair. It hurts even to consider it, to think we meant so little to him—that my mom meant so little to him. And, I can't believe he hit Paxton." My lungs compress, and it feels like I can't breathe as I choke on a sob. "And then to have my mom leave…" Poppy reaches for me, her arms a tight circle around my shoulders, holding me in place as though to force me to face my new reality.

"It was an impulse decision. I'm sure of it. She'll probably be back soon, but I know this must hurt a lot. I'm sure you're feeling betrayed and abandoned."

I shake my head, though I'm feeling each emotion she's listing off. "Don't shrink me."

Her grip tightens as I try to pull free, her cheek pressed to mine. "Want to go get something to eat?"

I shake my head again, though I haven't eaten all day, and the sun is starting to fall into the ocean.

"What would you like to do?"

"Hide."

Poppy presses her lips together, her eyes filled with sympathy that makes my chest feel tight.

"I don't know what to do. I have a class in an hour."

Poppy shakes her head. "Skip it."

"You have one, too."

"I'll skip with you."

I want to. I want to sign up for endless Saturday nights and hide from every responsibility and everyone who might know me, but right now, my thoughts are so consumed with guilt for having known my father was having an affair and not telling my mom. And for relying on Lincoln to make this pain go away, which has only made me feel worse because it just muddies the water between us.

"We should go. If I skip classes, it will just lead to those who do know to talk more."

"Screw them."

I shake my head. "It's better for me, too. If I stay here, I'm just going to obsess over everything and feel like I'm hiding from the truth, and it will make it even harder to face everyone." I expel a deep breath. "It's like ripping off a Band-Aid."

My phone buzzes with a text.

Derek: Hey. How are you holding up? If you need anything, please, let me know.

"What's wrong?" Poppy asks.

I turn my phone for her to read the message. "People are finding out."

Poppy sighs. "But, he knows you."

"Do I reply?"

"That's up to you." Poppy places her thumbnail between her teeth, chewing. It's a bad habit she broke when we were twelve by snapping a rubber band she wore around her wrist every time she went to bite, and only occurs now when she's nervous. "Do you think your dad went to school today?"

"I don't know," I tell her honestly as I slip my phone into my purse. The last thing I can think about right now is Derek. "I don't feel like I know him at all right now."

She nods. "I'll keep my phone where I can see it. If you need anything, just text me or call me—whatever. We'll get out of there."

I nod. It's the best I can do right now.

FROM THE PARKING lot to the green space, we hear no less than a dozen jokes about my dad, none of them forgiving, all of them vulgar. Poppy looks reluctant to part ways as I pivot in the direction I need to go.

"I'll be fine," I tell her. I think of telling her that the shock wave hit me a few weeks ago, that I knew, and that guilt is what's currently hitting the hardest.

"Drunken noodles tonight?" she asks.

"I have to work at the aquarium after this, but I'll call you."

She nods, hugging me again, likely realizing my need for the contact more than I do at this point.

I take a seat near the back of my physics class, realizing that if anyone might recognize my association with Dad, it will likely be my professors. I get my things out, my pulse too fast as I wait for a joke or question to be slung my way, but they don't come. Around me, people chat about their weekends, class notes, jobs—all of it familiar in my foreign headspace.

I lean back in my seat, the scar between my thumb and forefinger fading, just like my memories of that day when Lincoln and I shared a conversation that felt momentous at the time. I think of Mom's reaction, how Dad was absent, how he's been absent a lot in the past year. Slowly, my thoughts drift to that night from a few weeks ago, trying to recall what the girl my dad had brought home looked like for the hundredth time. I've been avoiding my dad and he's been avoiding me, though I still want to talk to him. I want to hear a valid excuse. I want to hear reason. Without those things, it leads me to question if I would ever be interested in someone my dad's age? Would I consider the ramifications? Am I considering them with Lincoln? How a relationship between us could impact more than his friendship with Paxton but their comradery on the field.

. . .

The ground is as sodden as the sky, which is currently a shade of gray that matches my emotions. Bare branches, an inky contrast like my memories, move across the horizon as I park downtown Seattle, ready to make a run for the aquarium. The wind pulls at the falling torrents of rain splashing across my windshield and the hood of my car, creating an ominous warning. Once the rain begins, it seems to last for months—an entire season. I zip my coat and pull up my hood. I wish I'd brought gloves, the only thing worse than dating a mouth breather is having cold hands.

Laughter pulls my eyes forward, catching a couple with their hands entwined, laughing as they race through the parking lot in clothes that do nothing to shield them from the rain. They stop at a small, white VW bug, and he reaches into his pocket, his expressions exaggerated like he's telling a story or joke. He drops the keys as he attempts to retrieve them, and they land with a splash into a puddle. The stranger leans his head back with exasperation, and the woman he's with moves closer, wrapping her arms around his middle and leaning up to kiss him.

I swallow. I breathe. I strive to ignore the niggling of thoughts that want to think about Lincoln—consider if he would ever be caught with me in a rainstorm and laugh. If he'd ever look at me like I was his axis like this man looks at the woman in front of him.

Doubtful. Guys like Lincoln Beckett want sex. Lots of sex. The dirtier, the better, which is why he didn't hesitate to peel off my panties and breathe me in like a drug.

The music dies, reminding me I've been sitting in my car too long, my mind breeding excuses. I toss my keys into my purse and zip it closed with one rough pull. The wind greets me as I push open my door. It sounds like cruel laughter as it howls, splashing my face with wet raindrops so fat they dampen my cheeks and run down my neck.

I grip my purse tighter, making a quick beeline for the crosswalk that leads me to the warmth and safety of the aquarium.

"Hey!" Cara, our aquarium's veterinarian, calls as I unlock the door on the side of the building that leads to our small and cramped break room.

"Hey," I say, unzipping my coat and shaking off the excess water.

"It's like that scene in *Forest Gump* when he was talking about the rain coming from all sides, isn't it?" she asks.

I chuckle more out of courtesy than genuineness. I don't have the mental capacity to think of Forest Gump or the scene she's referring to. I certainly don't have the aptitude for small talk—not when my thoughts are so frayed, tangled, and bitter.

Greta is near the entrance, trying to eat a muffin in two bites because she's always on the go, watching me with too much concern.

"Raegan," she says when I try to look away. "You want to help me? I need to prep some fish for the penguins."

I don't want to, but I also don't want to go out and explain for the billionth time that our Giant Pacific Octopus, Snoopy, isn't a squid. And though everything seems backward at this moment, my path here is still clear, promising an opportunity for a job in a few weeks. "Yeah. Sure." I hang my jacket and purse, changing my rain boots for my work ones, which have a permanent fish stench. I can feel her watching me, likely noticing they are all too slow and forced, my distractions eating into each task.

She smiles as I move to meet her, waiting until we clear the door before asking, "Everything okay?"

I nod. "Yeah. Just tired."

"Well, I've got some good news for you." She brushes her shoulder against mine, her eyes wide, shining with an excitement that silences the gloom I've been nursing like a bad mixed drink. "Lois called, and she saw K pod this morning," she says, referring to one of the three orca pods we track and report on.

I stop, chills racing down my arms faster than the rain falling outside. "Seriously?"

She nods, her smile growing as she wraps her arm around my shoulders, pulling me against her in a hug. "She said she saw them, and all of them were accounted for."

I lean my head back, the news spreading through me like a wave, crashing over the thoughts that have formed like lines carved on the shore, erasing some entirely and filling others, so they aren't as prominent and jagged. "That's amazing."

"And they were heading for the Sound."

My shoulders fall with relief. We've been so worried that they were going to move, forced out by the constant growth in the area.

We hit the back kitchen where the scents of fish and ice flood my nose, and though it stinks and promises a gruesome sight, it fills me with a sense of serenity that I cling to with every ounce of being.

I fall into a rhythm that calms me further, repeating the same steps I've completed a thousand times while Greta tells me about recent arrests her husband, who works for the Fish and Wildlife Department, has made. Her entire life revolves around the sea and justice, and it makes me envious in a way I wish I could stay here with her all day, hiding from my truths in her reality.

My mom swears she can sense bad news. She says before it happens, her right knee gets sore. I wish I had some strange sixth sense. It maybe would have prevented me from stepping out into the main lobby and finding Grandpa and Camilla shaking out umbrellas and arguing about having to pay to come in and see me.

Sophie, the lady at the front desk, is new and doesn't know me from a stranger on the street, her conviction for making my grandfather pay even more intense than her realization of the many staring at the scene they're causing.

I quickly make my way over to them, a bucket of penguin food in my hands. I only stepped out here because Joe asked if I'd see how Sophie was doing and ensure the line wasn't backed up after overhearing a disgruntled customer.

"Hi, Grandpa. Hi, Camilla," I say, my voice too loud and chipper in an attempt to end their conversation.

Grandpa turns to look at me and then faces Sophie again, pointing a wide and wrinkled index finger at me. "My granddaughter," he says. "You see her uniform, right? The one that says she *works here*."

I place a hand on his shoulder, urging him to step away from the growing line behind us as I try to send a peace offering to Sophie with a pleading smile. She eyes me like my smile is a Trojan Horse, looking away almost instantly.

"I can't reach your mom, or Paxton, or your dad," Grandpa tells me. "The news has been talking all day about a story, accusing him of having an affair with a student. They said there's video evidence and that two other girls have come forward, alleging they also had affairs with him." His blue eyes are stormy, a brightness shining at the edges like flashes of lightning, revealing his anger as he looks at me, waiting for me to dismantle the accusations. "What's going on?"

Leave it to Grandpa to memorize my schedule. He's the only one who knows I volunteer here every Monday, Wednesday, Thursday, and Saturday mornings, though it's the first time he's taken advantage of this knowledge.

I glance back at the crowd of patrons and then at Grandpa. "You guys want to go get some dinner?" I ask.

Grandpa's eyes grow brighter, firing more lightning. "I want some answers. That's what I want."

Camilla places a hand on his. "Cole," she says. "Let's take her to get some chowder."

He struggles to swallow back his objections, but then Camilla squeezes his hand, her perfectly shaped and painted red nails a bright contrast against my grandfather's pale and weathered skin. Slowly, he nods. "Okay." He nods again. "Let's grab a bite to eat."

I find myself nodding as well, pushing the thought past approval and into a realization but suddenly stop, the pail of creamed herring in my hand suddenly feeling like a lead brick, and my boots seeming smellier in the clean lobby. "I need to have someone feed the penguins for me and change my shoes. I'll meet you back here in just a moment, okay?"

"We'll go get the car," Camilla says, bestowing a kind smile on me. In some ways, it was hard for me to accept Camilla when Grandpa began dating her. My grandma had passed away before I was born, and Grandpa spent most of his time at our house. While I was in elementary school, he picked me up every day and took me home. We'd make snacks, watch cartoons, and he'd help me with homework or play stuffed animals. By middle school, I didn't need anyone to be home with me, but Grandpa still came, and occasionally he even helped with my homework, but he'd pepper in stories about his childhood and my grandma. When he began dating Camilla, he started to disappear from our lives, fading one day at a time until he only came around once a week. Mom insisted it was good for him—that Camilla made him happy. I was glad he was happy, but he'd never seemed unhappy before, and thus began a long sequence of internal debates about whether another human really can impact our lives and happiness.

Grandpa takes her hand still holding his, and reverses their order, then moves to hold the door open for her.

The bucket of penguin food gets heavier with each step into the back where I find another volunteer and ask them to feed the penguins. It's a job we all love because the penguins are friendly and comical, especially when it's time to be fed.

I poke my head into Greta's office, her door already propped fully open. It's one of the many details about her that makes me love having her as a boss—she's always approachable and never makes herself seem more important than anyone else. "Greta, I'm really sorry. My grandparents are here. Would you mind if I go have dinner with them? I should be back in about an hour."

"Why are you apologizing? That's great. Go. Have a good time."

I smile to keep myself to keep from apologizing for apologizing. "Thanks. I'll be back soon."

I trade my fishy rain boots for my every day rain boots and pull my jacket back on. With my purse in my hand, I make my way back out into the lobby, where Sophie waves me over. She hands me two new annual passes. "For next time," she says.

I stare at her for several beats, wondering if she heard Grandpa's tirade. I work to remember the conversation and pause when I recall him discussing having seen the story on the news.

The news.

My dad made the local news for having an affair.

The news my neighbors watch.

The news my friends and their parents watch.

The news my co-workers watch.

The news students and faculty members at Brighton watch.

That grayness that I'd woken up feeling turns a bit darker as it creeps back through me, filling all the spaces it had missed before as I get my first reminder of just how far this scandal is going to reach, and how it's only going to get bigger and worse.

I clear my throat and force a smile. "Thanks."

I make it out the doors, tears stinging the back of my eyes, and then Grandpa rolls down his window from where he's successfully blocking traffic while waiting for me. He waves to catch my attention, and I swear, my right knee starts to ache.

23

LINCOLN

I fall against the locker room bench with a heavy sigh, my breaths still labored as sweat trails from my hairline across my face. I'm too tired to wipe it away just yet. We spent the past three hours running, and running, and then running some more. I'm reasonably certain it was Coach's attempt at trying to get Paxton to focus and cease the continued whispers and jokes that kept circulating the field. With the news announcing the affair last week, it's spread like wildfire, making the first page of the student and local newspapers, even reaching national news this morning.

"Your dad fucks up, and now we have to pay for it?" Ian stops in front of Pax.

"Get out of his face," I bark.

"I'm not gonna play for a captain who's on his goddamn period and can't deal with his family issues. I'm not here for that." The challenge is clear in his tone, then he glances around the locker room, waiting for others to join forces with him.

My muscles protest as I stand, planting my palm against Ian's chest and shoving him back several inches. "Then go. If you can't put up with the hard work it takes to be the number one team in our conference—" I shrug, "—then leave. We don't want you. Winning takes hard work. It means extra practices, extra conditioning, and extra weights, and if today was too much for you, well then, there's the door."

Ian stares at me, an internal battle happening behind his eyes—one I understand. I hated today. I know we're in good enough shape that we didn't need to be pushed like it was the first couple of weeks of the season, but on the other hand, I also realize that we're only as strong as our weakest link, and with Paxton's head being everywhere but on the field, he's been our weakest link for days, something he can't continue in order to remain captain and starting quarterback. This was coach's attempt to save him, not sacrifice anyone.

Maybe Ian believes my line of bullshit. Maybe he realizes this was a final attempt to wake Paxton up before our game. Whatever his realization is, he reaches forward, his palm slapping mine with a handshake that says he's back to toeing the line.

Arlo stares at me a moment, his disbelief evident. He'd expected this reaction but from even more players when Pax showed up ten minutes late today. I purposefully turn my attention to my locker, rifling through the crap I need to clean out of it, yet delaying it for another day. I grab my shower bag and head to wash off.

TWENTY MINUTES LATER, I'm pulling into the parking lot of Beam Me Up, parking next to Rae's Honda. She's barely been at the house in the past week, slipping in and out like a ghost—a ghost who's avoiding me.

Rain cascades down my windshield like a curtain. Locals joke that we don't have a fall or a spring, just a rainy season. They're not wrong. Once the rain begins, it's a constant for months.

A man on his laptop sits in the back corner, a bulky set of headphones on his ears. Rae is near the back, restocking a display shelf. Two other baristas, one with dark hair, the other an unnatural shade of white blonde, are behind the counter, quietly giggling until they notice me. The dark-haired girl turns, cocking her head in a way that confirms she knows who I am or at least wants to.

"Welcome," she says, smiling. "What can I get you today?"

I nod in the direction of Rae. "I'm good. Thanks." At my words, Rae turns around, her expression the opposite of the brunette who was eager for my attention. Instead, I catch the scowl on her face before she turns back to the shelf she's filling with Thanksgiving-themed gifts.

I bite. I can't afford not to.

With my hands shoved into my hoodie, I walk toward her.

"I'm working," she says without turning to face me again.

"Why do you work?" The question pops out before I can filter it.

Her frown deepens as she faces me. "What are you doing here?"

"I came to talk about Paxton."

She starts to carefully align pumpkin frosted sugar cookies into a wire basket. My thought would be just to pile them in, but she's carefully lining them all up. "What about him?"

"He's distracted."

"And?"

"Does there need to be an 'and'?" She moves onto arranging turkey-shaped cookies.

The brunette at the counter continues to eye me, the end of a pen between her square white teeth and red lips. She winks at me.

Raegan sighs quietly. "I'm working, and my co-worker over there who you're exchanging googly eyes with called out last week with syphilis. I heard her talking about it tonight." She cuts through the tape of an emptied box with a razor blade, collapsing the sides before cutting open the next.

I shrug. "Penicillin kills that shit."

She balks. "That's disgusting."

"So is your assumption that I'd fuck her in the backroom."

Her eyes grow in size and color, a rebuttal surging through her thoughts but stopping at her lips. It makes me want to object and yell and lie all at once. Instead, I narrow my stare on her and make demands that we both know I'm in no position to make. "This place is dead. Let's go. I'm tired of you avoiding me like we're in the goddamn second grade." I lean forward for the next bit, her perfume invading my senses like a well-trained army, lowering my defenses, and catching me by surprise. "Don't label what we did as wrong or bad. It wasn't either one."

Raegan remains frozen, the swell of her lips so damn distracting I can't see anything else. "I'm not labeling it as anything more than an experience. You guys are always griping about girls sticking around after the fact, so you should be relieved I'm not one of them."

She starts to move, but I'm faster, grabbing her waist. Her blue eyes flash with surprise and hints of lust and anger that burns brighter as my fingers dig into the flesh beneath her black shirt. "You've never been one of them. I never compared you to anyone."

"Don't tell me you grew a conscience overnight. Call me a cynic, but I'm not buying it."

"Because it's me or because of your dad's mess?"

Anger gains ground with that question. She raises her chin, her eyes narrowing. "Because you were making out with someone else the night before we..." her words fade as she looks away.

"Jealous?"

Clearly, that was the wrong question because she attempts to push away from me, her dark blue nails a flash on my gray team sweatshirt. "Get over yourself." She rights herself, composure slipping over her like a uniform, changing her disposition and expression. "You're trying to work me out of your system," she says it like a revelation—an understanding.

I want so badly to tell her she's wrong, but the chance that this is true keeps me from replying.

I expect anger due to my silence. Revulsion. A slap across my cheek to stain my skin until morning. Instead, she calmly rakes her eyes over my face, searching for something I'm too afraid to clarify because she's silently considering something.

"Can you get off work?"

"Now?" she asks.

I glance around at the empty coffee shop. "Yeah."

"I'm supposed to work until ten. I need to finish setting this up."

"What do you have left?"

"Why?"

"Because," I tell her, "I'm tired of this, and I want to take you somewhere."

The skin between her eyes creases, like she's trying to make sense of my intentions. "Where?"

"Somewhere we don't have to talk about things or worry about anyone or anything. Just go have fun."

"I don't know..."

I spin before she can continue with a line about obligation, heading toward the two girls at the front counter who try and pretend like they haven't been watching us. I lean forward, smiling at the blonde who watches me with parted lips, intentions bright in her gaze. "Hi. I'm Lincoln." I extend my hand to her and then the girl with dark brown hair. "I'm Raegan's friend, and I really need her help with a situation. Do you think it would be all right if she took off early?"

"Yeah," the blonde says instantly without looking to her co-worker for input. "I mean, sure." She takes a fleeting look at her friend as though to confirm.

"Great." I pat the counter before they can reconsider and turn back to Rae, who's watching me, amusement shining in her eyes, though she doesn't smile. "You need help moving this stuff?"

"What are you doing?" she asks.

"Offering to help you."

Raegan shakes her head. "I mean, why are you really here?"

I study her blue eyes and the gentle lift of her lips. "Because we're friends," I tell her. The term seems nearly as honest as it does a lie. It's difficult for me to recall ever thinking of her as a friend, though this year, she's one of the few people who I can be real with. I grab the pile of cardboard she broke down. "Where do these go?"

She stares at me another moment, the skin between her eyes still bunched, but she grabs the rest of the things she was using and nods in the direction of their backroom. "Over this way."

I follow her through the door she holds open, through the mid-sized break room and out a backdoor that she props open with a brick. The alley is dark, the double light fixture over the door exposing only one of the two bulbs working. A used needle is on the ground beside the butt of a cigarette. I'm about to ask again why she works and find the least invasive way of asking her not to come out here again by herself while it's dark when she steps farther outside.

"What's going on with Paxton?" she asks, raising the lid of a large recycling bin.

I shove the cardboard inside, pushing the lid down to pack it before turning my attention back to Raegan. "He won't focus," I tell her. "We've got two games left, and we need him."

"I saw it Saturday," she admits. "There's so much going on. It feels like trying to pin down a giant tarp in a windstorm, and I don't know which corner to try and secure first. Is it because our mom left? Because our dad had an affair? Because he hit Paxton? Because he's doubting everything?" She sighs. "I appreciate you coming to me and letting me know. I'll try talking to him. Maybe I can get at least one corner nailed down."

She removes the brick holding the door, looking at me with surprise as I move to keep it open so she can go first. "Thanks," she says quietly, slipping past me. She stops in the middle of the breakroom, turning to face me. "We don't have to hang out. I don't have any expectations of you, Lincoln."

I step closer, her eyes bouncing between mine as I digest her words. Her lack of expectations is one of the most freeing things about being around her, but it's also something that concerns me far more than I would have ever assumed because, without expectations, it means she doesn't believe in me—believe in us.

"Grab your coat. We're going."

Something sparks in her gaze, then she bites her bottom lip, and for a second, I nearly forget that I'm here to convince her I want more than to be in her pants. I lean back on my heels. "You can ride with me. I'll bring you back by to pick up your car."

"Where are we going?"

"Somewhere others can't fucking interfere."

24

RAEGAN

I zip my coat up to my neck as we step outside, my co-worker's gazes heavy on us through the large windows.

Lincoln doesn't seem to notice, leading me to his black truck, where he opens the passenger side door for me, offering his hand.

It feels strange to accept it, but stranger not to, so I allow him to help me up and inside the cab of his truck where warmth is slowly fading into the November evening. "Do you have a plan, or are we winging this?"

"Are you nervous?"

A dry laugh hits my lips. "How did you manage to answer my question with a question?"

"Does it bother you?"

"Is this a contest?"

"You know I'd win if it were, right?"

I shake my head, not working to fight my grin. "Yes, because you're the stubbornest person I've ever met." I pause before adding. "You know *that*, right?"

His face lights with a smile. "Have you ever played Whirlyball?"

"I've never even heard of Whirlyball."

"How do you feel about bumper cars?"

A nervous laugh tinkers through my lips. "I don't know the last time I rode a bumper car," I admit.

"Well, that's about to change."

"What's the Whirlyball part?"

He puts his truck in gear, backing out of his parking space. "You'll see."

"As long as it isn't going to give us a black eye or broken nose for your Dad's wedding this weekend."

He laughs. "That would make it even better."

"You know," I start as he pulls onto the highway. "I was thinking about the wedding a little, and with everything happening with my dad and all the news, I didn't know if maybe you'd rather take someone else?"

His gaze cuts to me, the humor that had been there now absent. "I don't give a single fuck if one of them has a thought or opinion about your dad. Not one."

"But, it's your dad's wedding, and we told half the people at the party who my dad was. They'll all know. My grandpa found out because it made the news."

Lincoln's chin goes up like an invisible force shoved him. "It doesn't change anything."

"She was a student," I say on a sigh. "And two more students have come forward with the same accusation." It feels wrong to say the word accusation, like there's any doubt.

He looks at me, his eyes shaded by darkness. "My dad's already had five weddings. I don't doubt for a minute he'll have a dozen more. I just need to know that you're okay."

My thoughts are still fragile. A quick *'no, I'm not okay'* is screamed from somewhere deep in my heart where I work to shut the curtains on Lincoln, and my dad, and that my mom's gone on the other side of the country, and Maggie's on the other side of the world. But rather than give that scared part of me a voice, I simply nod. "I'm okay."

Lincoln stares at me for a moment allotted by a traffic light. The roads are too busy for him to pull over or remain stalled. He takes his foot off the brake, the truck sliding back into traffic as his eyes return to the road. "When you lie, you lick your lips and fidget."

"I'm not..." I instantly reply, my words falling away as he glances at my lap. I drop my gaze to my hands, where I'm rotating my phone like it's a rectangular wheel across my legs. "I knew." The admission hits my lips before I can stop it, before I can process how terrible the timing is because we're pulling into a parking lot where Lincoln has no distractions, and I'll have a dozen questions to face.

"Knew what?"

I swallow, but my throat is dry. "I knew about the affair. I'd caught him a few weeks ago. I don't know if it was the same girl or not, but I knew."

Lincoln's stare is as penetrating as it is intense, reading my thoughts like he can see my memories. "What happened?"

"I should have told my mom." Tears cloud in my eyes and clog my throat.

"*He* should have told your mom. Jesus. When did this happen?"

"Shortly after Maggie left."

"That night I took you home, after the engagement party when your dad was leaving...?"

I nod. "I think so."

"Son of a bitch." He shakes his head, taking in a harsh breath.

"This year has been so eye-opening," I admit, leaning back in the seat, so it supports my neck and shoulders completely. "In a matter of weeks, I've learned I'm not invincible, and love is like one of those really bad sheet cakes you get from the grocery store, pretty to look at but packed with regret and imitation." Memories of my dad are like bubbles, popping as they surface into a new reality. "I told you I was going to be shitty company," I say, turning to look at him.

He shakes his head. "You're more bulletproof than you think."

I don't want to debate this, not when I faced an entire firing range because of my feelings for him. "Are you going to show me what this Whirly-gig is?"

He smiles—it's weak and uneven, but it touches his eyes. "Whirly-ball," He nods. "Let's go."

The rain is light but constant drizzle that has me rushing to the front of Lincoln's truck, where he's waiting for me. Without a word, he grabs my hand, pulling me in the direction of the door. He pulls it open with his free hand, and when I try to break our connection, he holds on tighter. I glance at his knuckles looped around mine, and then at him, but his focus is on the crowded counter he's pulling me toward.

"Beckett. What's up, man." A stocky guy with auburn hair steps forward. "Glad you could make it." He reaches us, his gaze traveling between Lincoln and me, his eyebrows hitching a bit higher with each pass.

Lincoln nods. "What's up, Chris." His body is angled toward me, his feet spread like he could break into a sprint or take a hit. At the engagement party, he had positioned himself like this nearly each time someone engaged us in conversation, keeping distance, so I never felt trapped, but it also had me feeling included, though I rarely had anything to add to the conversation, similar to now. "This is my friend, Raegan. Rae, Chris," he says. "We went to high school together."

Chris grins. "You want to know anything about him, I'm your guy. I know all his dirty little secrets."

Lincoln scoffs, triggering laughter from Chris, and it grows as two other guys converge on us. "This is Petey and Juan," Lincoln says, pointing at each of them. "Guys, this is Raegan."

"Did I hear you say we're sharing Lincoln's embarrassing stories?" Juan asks, a broad smile that looks easy and as common as breathing for him. "We should start easy with her. Wait. Wait. How long have you known him?"

Lincoln chuckles. "Do your worst."

This is the side of Lincoln that makes me feel like jelly. Like my heart and feet are both levitating. Like this bond between us might be genuine and as authentic as my fears. It's the strength he exudes, how relaxed and at ease he is even when he's the target. It does something weird to my thoughts and emotions and has me believing that even in the worst situation, he'd be able to protect me from the cruelest parts of this world. In the past month, he's opened the shades, allowing me to see through windows that reveal his past, and this feels like a highway.

"My favorite story is still the grilled cheese sandwich," Petey says, shaking his head and chuckling like he's already told the punchline.

I glance at Lincoln. "Grilled cheese sandwich?"

Petey laughs harder, his cheeks growing red. "Freshman year, we raided my dad's liquor cabinet, and your boy here," he pauses to laugh again.

"Oh, I remember this," Chris says, pointing at Lincoln. "Don't try and pretend like you don't."

Lincoln shakes his head, his fraction of a smile making me grin. "I don't remember."

"You'd smoked, and were struggling with a severe case of the munchies, and you went to make a grilled cheese." Petey places an arm across his gut, as though it will prevent him from laughing. "And you were bragging to everyone about knowing the tricks to make a fast grilled cheese, so you toasted your bread and then melted the sandwich in the microwave."

Lincoln's smile grows. "It's still genius."

Petey laughs outright. "But, you used your fucking phone as one of the slices of bread and didn't realize it till you pulled it out of the microwave."

Lincoln laughs. "I think I broke the damn microwave, too."

They share in a chorus of laughter, Lincoln's eyes on me.

"What about that time he was trying to clean the pool?" Juan starts, buckling at the waist.

"Oh, God. No." Petey shakes his head. "We're not reliving that story."

Lincoln shakes his head. "We really shouldn't."

"Oh, you can't stop there. That's the equivalency of telling someone you made dessert and then not sharing," Chris says.

Juan's grin spreads. "Oh, trust me, I'm happy to share this dessert." He points at Lincoln. "So, Lincoln was supposed to be cleaning his pool, and Petey ran up behind him, trying to scare him, and so Lincoln turned around, gripping the vacuum-like it was a fucking sword, and it connected with Petey's..." he pauses, his chest vibrating with laughter. "Let's just call it his manhood region."

Laughter bubbles out of me.

"To this day, I question if I'll be able to have kids," Petey admits. "I thought that damn thing was going to castrate me."

My cheeks ache from laughing when Lincoln's grip on my fingers constricts.

"Let's go!" Someone yells from a few feet in front of us. He's older, mostly bald, wearing a black T-shirt with the name of a country band.

"Don't worry," Juan says. "We've got plenty more stories." He flashes his smile. "How long have you guys been a thing?"

I shake my head, dismissing what our tied fingers misrepresent. "We're friends."

Juan flicks his gaze to Lincoln as though to verify this fact.

"Can you believe it took me over a month to convince her?" he asks, his tone light, easy, teasing.

"I like her already," Juan says.

Lincoln chuckles as we pass through the second door that leads to a room that smells like floor polish and a lack of fresh air. "Come on. We're on this side," Lincoln says, interrupting my review of the room that reminds me of a large gymnasium, except this room has walls the same shade of yellow as the original mustard that Poppy puts on her hot dogs every home football game. It reminds me of a skating rink, a large open space in the middle, with benches partitioned by a half wall.

"How competitive is this?" I ask.

"Worried?"

"I'm trying to decide."

He grins. "I'm still debating if this was the best idea or the worst," he admits.

I laugh. "That's not very assuring."

His grin turns into a smile. "You'll do fine. You're going to kick these guys' asses." His gaze sweeps over the group, and it's then I realize I'm the only girl here.

"Have you played Whirlyball before?" Petey asks, carrying a bucket filled with what look like lacrosse sticks but without the actual stick, just a short handle.

"I've never even heard of it."

He grins. "Have you played lacrosse?"

"Does PE count?"

Lincoln's hand slides from mine, the contact a noticeable absence as I keep my hands still, each of my fingers still separated by the width of his for several seconds. "It counts. You're an athlete. You'll catch on no problem." His brown eyes connect with mine, furthering his assurance. My confidence is a dozen paces behind his as he arms me with a shortened lacrosse stick.

"What exactly are we doing?" I ask, watching as several start flooding the floor, getting into bumper cars.

"This game is like basketball meets lacrosse and has an uncle who likes hockey," Juan says. "These aren't normal bumper cars. They're faster, and you can turn quicker." He points to the far wall where a blackboard is hung with a circle in the middle. "There's a goal on each side. That's where you're trying to score."

"While riding in a bumper car?" I ask.

"A Whirlybug. And you can bump into people just not from the back. In fact, I recommend you ram people because they're going to be afraid to hit a girl. And this is your scoop." Petey says, pointing to the contraption I'm holding.

"All right, Kerosene. Give it your all." Lincoln winks—an expression as new as this experience—and my toe catches the bucket Petey had carried over to us, making me stumble just enough to draw attention to myself.

"You good?" Lincoln asks, his smile turned devious.

My cheeks grow warm with embarrassment as his knowing gaze settles on me. "Yup." I stride past him, heading for one of the red Whirlybugs.

My confidence is still trying to balance on the small iceberg in this ocean of newness when Lincoln stops at my little car and places one foot in my car as he leans forward, invading my space and air and thoughts as his hands brush my side. He grabs the seatbelt and fastens it around my waist. "Safety first." He flashes his trademark smile, the one I've seen grace newspapers and highlight reels. He's toying with me.

25

LINCOLN

Raegan's laughing.

It's the first time I've seen her laugh in weeks, and the sight and sound are so distracting, one of the players from the opposing team nearly manages to block me into the corner I was stopped in to take in the view.

The buzzer sounds, ending the game, but not the smile still spread across her face.

Several are talking, sharing highlights of the game as well as the blunders as Rae frees her seatbelt and looks across the space at me.

"You guys want to grab something to eat? We could hit up Shari's?" Juan says.

I shake my head. "Maybe next time."

He grins. "Because you guys are going to practice your friendship skills?"

One of the players from our team is talking to Raegan. It's benign and friendly, her posture expressing ease. Juan follows my gaze and then turns back to me.

"I don't think I've ever seen you give googly eyes to some chick."

"She's different, and she's definitely not some chick."

Juan shakes his head. "No, I can see she's not. So why are you guys labeling it as friendship?"

"I've done one hell of a job fucking things up. I guess we could call this my redemption period."

"By getting yourself friend-zoned?" He cocks a brow. "You know what you need to do, right?"

"Not listen to your shitty advice?"

Juan shakes his head. "Make her a nice meal—girls eat that shit up. Get her some flowers, find some shitty playlist, and then tell her you wanked off your first three years of high school because you wanted someone as special as her, but never thought she could possibly exist."

"What wizarding school of assholery are you enrolled at, dick face?"

He laughs. "I like her. She seems chill."

I nod, thinking of some of the slightly neurotic things she's said and done, then the more passionate ones, realizing that Rae continually keeps me on my toes, guessing how she's going to react to a situation.

Juan clasps my bicep. "Easy on the 'roids. She won't like you when your equipment shrinks."

Laughter hits my lips as Juan salutes me and takes several steps toward the exit. "I'll see you, Beckett."

When I turn my attention to Raegan, her eyes are already on me. "Did you have fun?" I ask, closing the distance between us.

"I'm pretty sure I'm deserving of the least valuable player award." She laughs.

"I don't know if you missed it, but nearly everyone sucks."

She closes her eyes, her laugher growing. "I couldn't believe that guy fell out of his Whirlybug." She sobers too quickly, her gaze falling from mine. "We should probably get going. You have practice in the morning, and I have class."

"Look at you knowing my schedule," I chide.

She shakes her head, the ghost of a smile sparking in her eyes. "This was fun. Thanks for bringing me."

"I'm sorry about your dad," I tell her.

"Me, too." She cuts her gaze to the side, blinking too fast.

I should leave her alone—recognize her emotions are too raw. And I don't want her to associate me with these feelings of deceit and betrayal when she likely has enough stacked against me. But, the same thoughts have distracted me, leading me to see her after practice with the excuse of Paxton as a convenient intro. "Has he done that before? Acted like that?"

Rae cuts her blue eyes to me, the humor replaced with a sheen of sadness that evokes a keen sense of aggression in me, wishing I could destroy anything that created this level of grief. "I keep wondering if I just never saw him for who he really was or if this has changed him? You know? Did being caught just make him flip some sort of switch? I don't know. I mean, he's never hit one of us, that was…" She clasps a hand to her forehead. "Maggie." She exhales. "We never called Maggie." She spins, looking at the walls, stopping when she spots the large clock that relays it's nearly nine. "Shit. It's too late. I'll wake her up."

My feelings for her are being held back by what feels like a simple piece of tape. It's flimsy, and transparent, and has no chance of holding everything back. "Call her tomorrow. She'll understand."

"I meant to call her earlier. I was trying to call my mom, so I could check in with her before I called Maggie so I could give her a better update, but my aunt said she was napping and suggested I give her a couple of days, and I forgot to call Maggie."

I place a hand on her shoulder, realizing these past ninety minutes are merely a piece of tape for her as well. I don't have the right words, I'm not sure they even exist, but I pull her toward me, wrapping my arms around her back, feeling each rigid muscle. I stroke a hand over her hair, brushing it behind her ear. "It's going to be okay. We've got this. I've got you."

The doubt remains, her muscles still bunched, but then she leans into me, setting her forehead against my shoulder. "Don't tell Pax we hung about … whatever this is. I don't want him worrying. He needs to focus on football, so do you. You guys have two games left before bowl games."

She remains in place, her breaths slowing as I continue the same path over her hair. "Pax will be fine. We just need to have a come to Jesus conversation with him to kick him in the ass. He listens to you, but we can do it together. I'll push the message, and you being there will make him listen."

She nods. "I'll be there."

The lights flash, indicating the impending closure, and Rae steps back, her lips lifting with a hesitant smile. "I have to grab my things before they shut off the lights." I follow her to the benches to grab her coat and purse before leading her back out to the darkened parking lot, the rain a fine mist. Rae doesn't duck or try and cover her hair like many girls do as they race across campus in this weather. Instead, she closes her eyes and tips her face skyward. Slowly, she lowers her chin, her gaze meeting mine before she smiles.

"Whirlyball. Maggie would love this."

Her refusal to be swallowed by this situation is proof that she fought just as hard as the doctors who worked to save her. Raegan Lawson is many things, but fighter is at the top of her list.

"What?" she asks.

I shake my head. "I was just thinking of when you were in the hospital… Your nurse called you Zenobia."

"Zenobia?"

"A woman who defied all odds and became a warrior queen a very long time ago."

Her brow creases. "I thought you weren't at the hospital?"

"Mentally, I'm not sure that I was."

Confusion pinches the outer corners of her eyes.

"I didn't know what to do. Your parents were there, your brother, Maggie. I didn't know who knew what and…" I pull in a breath of air, tracing my thoughts during those days, trying to make sense of what happened. It feels like another lifetime ago, and yet the fear feels like it was born just yesterday, still fresh in my thoughts and chest. "I came every fucking night to see you."

She stares at me, her thoughts once again racing like they so often do. I want to ask her for some insight—a glimpse at her opinions of me with the truth now laid between us. "It's late," she says.

It's not. But before I can object her phone rings, and I already know by the song that it's Poppy. Raegan doesn't hesitate, reaching for it as she walks toward my truck.

I trail her, catching her assurances to Poppy before her eyes cut to me. "Yeah, I'm actually with Lincoln." I can't hear Poppy's response, but

Rae's gaze shifts and she turns so her back is to me, and her voice drops with her next reply.

I get into the driver's side, allowing her the privacy she's seeking and turning the truck on so it can warm up.

Only a few seconds pass before she opens the passenger door and hops in.

"Everything okay?"

She nods. "Yeah. Everything's good."

The drive back to Beam Me Up to get Rae's car goes too fast, the roads nearly empty, my admission seeming like a greater regret with each second of silence stretching.

I pull into the parking lot and drive to the back where Rae's white Honda is parked. My headlights cast a beam across the hood of the car, where my full attention is pulled and then stops at the sight of a paper crane under her windshield wiper, and then her flat tires. I scan over the bare parking lot, the darkened coffee shop, the empty streets.

"What's wrong?" Raegan asks.

My knuckles are white from gripping the wheel as I pull into the spot next to her car. "Stay here."

"What?" She turns, her hand already on the seat belt retractor.

"Stay here," I repeat, cranking my door open and slamming it shut behind me before taking a few steps to her car and retrieving the note that is too dry for the current weather conditions. I walk around the car, checking out the tires that are all flat.

With another sweep over the parking lot, I climb back into my truck, pinching the offending paper between my fingers. "You're still getting these?"

Her eyes shift between mine, likely reading my anger and annoyance and trying to interpret if it's at her or the letter.

"How many?" I demand.

"They had stopped," she says. "For weeks."

"When did they start again?"

"A few weeks ago."

Her answer sends the palm of my hand colliding with my steering wheel. "Weeks?"

Her eyes narrow with defiance. "Prior to a week ago, we weren't talking. I wasn't going to come to you about this."

"Did you tell anyone? The cops? Paxton? Your parents?" I know she didn't because Pax sure as shit would have told me.

Her jaw is tense as she stares at me. "I know you're probably coming at this from a place that isn't straight out of the depths of asshole, but right now, it feels like that. So rather than me getting offended and us yelling at each other, I'm going to ask you to drive me to Poppy's."

"No. You're going to the house with me."

Her brow flattens. "Like hell I am."

"Someone slashed your fucking tires. You're not going to be by yourself."

"Did you miss me mentioning going to Poppy's?"

I put the truck into reverse and then hit drive. My foot falls heavier on the gas pedal when we hit the road.

"Is this seriously how you're going to react?"

I keep my gaze on the road, wishing I could go faster, my shoulders tense as I lose my head to the one thing that has always been my greatest vice: fearing she'll leave—whether she chooses to or otherwise.

"You can't just ignore me," she says. "We need to talk. You need to use words, Lincoln."

"You already know what I'm thinking."

"That you've lost your mind?"

A sardonic laugh cuts through my lips and the silence.

"The last notes weren't creepy. They seemed almost ... sad."

"Let's go back to your idea of not talking about this right now."

She growls with irritation. "You're infuriating. This is absolutely unnecessary and ridiculous. Poppy is expecting me, and I have no desire to sleep on your guys' couch."

My tires eat the miles until we pull into my neighborhood, where I finally slow down.

"Will you respond?" she cries.

I slide into my parking spot and turn my truck off. I track over her menacing stare, the annoyance and impatience sitting heavily on her drawn shoulders, the twist of her lips that I want to go to war with.

I shove my door open and head toward the front door, hearing her slam the passenger door before I reach the first step.

"What are you doing?" she yells.

I unlock the door and shove it open. Inside, the house is dark. Caleb is likely gaming in his room or has already gone to bed, and Arlo and Pax's cars were absent from their spots. I close the door after she stalks inside, locking it before I turn toward the stairs and take them two and three at a time, wishing I could outrun these feelings that are crashing down on me, one blow after the other, each with more impact.

"You don't get to just walk away whenever things get messy," she says, following me, albeit, at a slower, more measured pace. Maybe this is where the advantage of having siblings plays a role. Or perhaps it was having parents who previously worked through their shit rather than threw it in each other's faces and then ignored the other one like they didn't exist. "Lincoln."

I turn, facing her as she strides toward me. She stops abruptly, nearly running into me. The annoyance is still visible in her eyes, but along with it is confusion and vulnerability and something that looks way too damn similar to disappointment. It's a look that undoes me, strips me of my anger and sense. "I can't do it again."

Her blue eyes shift between mine for several seconds, attempting to read through my words. "Do what again?"

"I nearly lost you to a fucking ocean, I'm not about to let you go test the threat level of some psycho. It's not happening. You can be mad at me, you can stomp your foot, you can call me an asshole, but you're not leaving."

Raegan parts her lips, and I know before hearing her words, they're going to be of doubt. "This is insane. I don't even understand why you think you get a say in—"

I tag her around the waist, hauling her flush against me, my lips bracing her fall. Her muscles are rigid, her mouth closed. She pulls back, her eyes flashing to mine.

"I need you. I need you to stay here and have some fucking self-preservation. I need you in ways I've never needed anyone—in ways that scare the shit out of me. I need you because I don't feel like myself without you." I can't even manage to regret my admission because it's a thin shave off the surface of my feelings and thoughts.

Rae closes her eyes, her lips falling to mine, meeting in a dance that reminds me of middle school with darkened gymnasiums and our teachers filing around with rulers in their hands, everyone unsure about where to place their hands and what something so simple might mean. But those trepidations have never existed, not with her.

With our lips still clumsily trying to sort through the mess we've created, I back up into my room, closing the door with the toe of my shoe before locking the door and pressing her against it. It's nearly black in the space, a thin filter of light creeping in through the window shade because a street light is directly below. She wraps her hands around my shoulders, and I slant my head, gaining a better angle of her mouth. I slide my tongue along hers, demanding everything she has to offer while giving what's left of me that she hasn't already taken. I press against her, so close that doubt can't reach either of us as we lose ourselves in this kiss that I know will define the rest of my days.

I slide my hands to her waist, her sweatshirt and shirt bunching as I reach for her skin, needing to feel her flesh against mine. The heat of her hits my palms, and her hips tip closer, a soft moan touching her lips that I lick the traces clean from. She grabs the bottom of my sweatshirt, tugging it upward, her fingers cold as they graze my skin. I press a searing kiss to her mouth, taking her bottom lip between my teeth before I pull away to rid my sweatshirt and tee, dropping them to the floor. Her fingers brush over my chest, my stomach, my shoulders. Her eyes are hooded, heavy with lust and something I want to capture and memorize while also running away and forgetting it.

"We're complicating things," she says, her voice as soft as her touch.

"Words complicate things. Rationalizing complicates things. Expectations complicate things. This—us, this is the only thing that doesn't feel complicated."

Raegan kisses me again, the gentleness gone, replaced with the same desire that's been burning inside of me for months. We're a set of fumbling hands and limbs and jumbled kisses as we strive to free the layers separating us, neither willing to stop kissing for more than a fraction of a second as we tug on zippers and buttons and fabrics until we're both in our underwear. Her chest is rising and falling with heavy, needy breaths that make her breasts swell beneath the blue-green fabric of her bra that I'd left on in an attempt to slow things down. I trace the line where her skin meets the silky fabric with my fingers and eyes, my breaths growing short and ragged.

This moment deserves a conversation, an understanding, and a full-fledged agreement that won't be rewritten by regrets later. I kiss her, searching for that familiar hit of dopamine she offers. The moment her lips meet mine, pressing her chest against mine, our skin basking in a moment of celebration has me losing myself in our shared kiss, my tongue stroking hers, her breaths fast, hungry. She moves her hands from my shoulders, and then the nearly silent clip of metal is followed by her bra falling against my chest before she unthreads her arms and lets it fall to the floor. Her breasts are perfect and distracting as I consider all the ways I'd like to please her.

"Do you have protection?" she asks.

"Rae..." my voice expresses my internal war, knowing this probably shouldn't happen tonight and my growing desire that makes it feel inevitable.

"I want you to consume me," she says, licking her lips where my eyes are trained, hearing her words repeat in my thoughts, shredding what was left of my conscious thoughts.

I bend at the waist, swiping my tongue over her nipple, her quiet hiss of shock, feeding the inferno in my gut. I run my hand down her back, stopping where her hips swell. I lean into her, my lips tracing her ear. "Lie on my bed."

With my hand still at her waist, I lead her to my bed, pulling the comforter back as an invitation. She slips into my bed, the lacy strips of her underwear still in place. I trace over her, feasting on each perfect curve and line, stopping on her arm where the scar from that night is still a prominent reminder. I lean forward, pressing a kiss to the skin, feeling the deep groove where the cut was the worst, and follow it with my tongue. When I sit up, she's watching me, her hair fanned across my pillow in a scene I'd pay my life to repeat every day. I keep my weight on one fist, dipping my face to meet hers, caressing her tongue with mine with languid strokes, my free hand exploring her body. I memorize each line, each plane, each crevice of her blindly, learning each sensitive place by her reactions, the way her muscles constrict and her breaths pause, the way her teeth reach for my lips and the times her breaths turn into moans.

"Do we have to worry about Pax or anyone hearing us?"

I shake my head. "Pax and Arlo haven't been staying here. Caleb is at the end of the hall, and he's either asleep or has his headphones on."

She nods, reaching for the back of my neck and tugging my mouth against hers again, kissing me firmly before I reposition myself, peppering kisses across her nose, her cheeks, her neck, her chest, until I reach her breasts, where I swirl my tongue over each taut peak before taking each into my mouth, tracing the orb of her breasts with one hand while rubbing her free nipple with the other. Her short nails rake against my skin with pleasure as I trail a path of kisses down to her pubic bone. She shifts, sucking in a breath as I lace my fingers into the waist of her underwear and shimmy the fabric down her legs.

I kiss her stomach, and then the invisible line where her underwear had been. She bites her lip, squeezing her eyes shut with anticipation. I feel like I'm a fucking king as I explore her, tracing over the sensitive skin of her folds, and then sliding my finger along her clit, her breath hitching as her hips rock. I trace the line of her clit to her entrance several times, changing the pressure with each pass until her breaths are pants, and then I dip a finger inside of her, making her breath leave in a loud sigh. "You're so fucking wet," I whisper, shifting so I can trace the same line with my tongue as I continue to finger bang her. I insert a second finger and am met with approval as her hips lift from the bed. The taste of her stains my lips as I sit up, running a hand over her thighs as my fingers continue to rub inside of her, drunk on each gasp and moan that I elicit. Her hands fall from my shoulders, and she clenches the sheet in her fists, each of her breaths coming faster and harder. With her legs spread, I dip my face, tracing her again with my tongue, each swipe ending at her clit as her hips tremble until I know her most reactive and sensitive spot where I focus my attention until she cries out with pleasure, her hands tangled and her lips parted.

I breathe her in like a drug before reaching for my nightstand and grabbing a condom. She watches me silently. I fist the condom, leaning down and kissing her again. It's needy and demanding, an attempt to verify if this is what she wants. I wait for hesitance, but she greets me with a brazenness that makes me forget I'm about to take her virginity.

"Are you sure?" I whisper.

"I want you," she says, kissing me deeper, harder, longer.

Her heart beats an erotic symphony against my chest that makes me want to promise things I know the light of day will likely make appear like lust and desire. Instead, I kiss her again with a fierceness my words can't articulate until our breaths are both ragged, my erection rubbing against her entrance.

I swing my legs off the bed, dropping my underwear to the floor with the last of my reservations, and tear the condom open, rolling it over my length. She watches me, her eyes dancing over me until meeting my stare. I lay over her, hovering several inches above her as I reach down and guide my cock to her entrance. She pulls in a breath that calls my eyes back to hers. A million words are shared in a single second, half of them I can't decipher—yet I feel them. I feel all of them.

"Try and relax," I tell her, kissing her softly.

I focus on her eyes as I press inside of her, reading every flinch so I can pause and allow her to adjust to me before continuing. I feel the tightness of her virginity, watch her wince, my breaths fanning her face before I kiss her, running my hand along her waist, urging her to relax as I continue, claiming her in all the ways possible.

My breath comes out in a hiss, the desire to rock inside of her stopped by the necessity to wait for her body to acclimate to mine. "You feel so fucking good," I tell her, running my nose along her cheek, breathing more of her in, trying to steel myself as I watch her reactions again, pulling out and slowly sliding back inside, my focus on her and my control.

Rae lifts her face, watching as I slowly lower myself back into her.

"Are you watching me fuck you?" I whisper.

She nods, tipping her face to meet mine. "Don't stop."

I kiss her then, bruising her mouth as my teeth claim her and my tongue marks her, while I thrust inside of her, reaching down to rub her clit until she explodes around me, and I chase it with my own release.

26

RAEGAN

Even as my breath levels out, my senses remain heightened. Lincoln lies next to me, his fingers brushing over my arm, my hair, my face—everywhere—almost like he's memorizing me.

We're both drunk on oxytocin, basking in the high that makes the rest of the world feel a million miles away.

"What happened here?" I ask, tracing over a scar just below his collarbone.

"Water skiing accident. I hit a jump wrong, and it caught me."

I flinch. "Ouch."

He grins lazily, his fingers etching a pattern across my ribs. "It wasn't bad."

"What about this? What does it say?" I follow the script across his ribs that disappears to his side.

"Astra indlinant, sed non obligant."

"I know this is tough to imagine, but not all of us speak Latin."

His lips tip higher. "It translates to the stars incline us, they do not bind us."

My eyebrows hitch, my education feeling grossly inadequate as I try to make sense of the words. "And that roughly translates to?"

He dips his face, kissing my shoulder. "We have our own free will. That no star or god or any other power can force us to do anything."

"You really love history, don't you?"

His brows tick upward. "I'd like it more if I never had to write another essay on nineteenth-century Russia, but yeah. I feel like so much in life has very little reason, and history provides a small insight into how things have become what they are. It helps explain where we came from, how our traditions came into place, our government, our theories. It explains humanity."

I want to ask if it explains the two of us. If it provides some insight on where we go from here and the consequences I know we're going to face.

"Are we going to talk about how this changes things?" he asks, once again invading my thoughts.

My heart feels like a square wheel trying to turn as I try to keep his stare. So many conflicting emotions work to be heard, each eclipsing the last. Hope, fear, denial, and regret steep together. "Does it change things?"

Lincoln's fingers fall flush against my waist. "Let's just say your perfume has stained more than my pillow at this point."

I stare at him, hearing his words, and for some reason, the leading emotion is sadness as his face blurs from a thin layer of tears I work to blink back. "I don't want us to get into a burning car."

"That's good. I don't want that either. But just for the record, are we talking literally or philosophically at this point, because mine was intended to be both."

"You have so much going on with football, and Pax is your best friend, and you're going to leave soon, and I can't even figure you out most of the time. You like me, you don't like me, you *might* like me, you avoid me. And now with my dad and my mom and—"

"I know I've fucked up." His fingers knead into my waist as he nods, his jaw flexing. "I have. I can't make excuses. You're different—everything feels different. With other girls, I've never worried about what they think of me, what they need, or what they want. I was a selfish bastard because it scares the hell out of me to let someone in. But, with you, it matters. Everything matters. My mom ruined my dad. They've been divorced for fifteen years, and he's still in love with her. Five failed marriages later, and he doesn't give a shit because he's only loved one person, and these weddings are charades—an attempt to forget the love and anger he still holds. And I worry about that, I worry about that with you because I know you'd ruin me."

"That doesn't scare you now?"

"It scares me more to be away from you. To possibly lose you." His fingers slip from my waist, weaving with my fingers.

My fears become an infection, spreading faster than I can stop them, the rules and reasons I had committed to for avoiding Lincoln are each still valid, exacerbated by my dad's actions.

Lincoln's dark eyes drift open, his lips pressing into a firm line before his fingers squeeze mine. "I'm not him, Rae. I'm not your dad, and I'm not my dad. And you aren't either. Don't let their demons define us."

"I'm afraid they live inside of us, and we won't be able to prevent them."

He shakes his head. "Astra indlinant, sed non obligant." He repeats the words from his tattoo, of freewill and choices, and the hope he lights in my chest has me squeezing his hand even tighter.

"I should go sleep on the couch. This isn't the way Pax should find out."

Lincoln shakes his head. "He's at Candace's. He's been sleeping there for a week now."

"Candace? What? When did that happen?"

"Around Halloween."

I sigh, a new wave of disappointment hitting me for having been absent and distant from my brother. "Arlo and Caleb will tell him."

"Arlo has been staying with a girl named Kelsey, and Caleb is like you and doesn't wake up until noon." He leans up, propping his weight on his elbow as he pulls the covers higher. "Stay here, Rae, and stain it all. Stain everything."

Logically, I know I should go. Distance and space will be our only salvation when this ends. Right now, we're attempting to tether our fears with lust, and it's driving us together—leading me to question everything and the validity of it all. It also makes us both want to hold on tighter. Perhaps it goes back to expectations and control: as much as we loathe them, without them, neither of us knows how to operate fully.

The feeling of him wanting me here lures me in, but it's the way his hand finds my waist, sliding under the tee I'd put on that has me staying. It's the weight and steadiness of his grip that makes me never want to leave.

His eyes slowly open again as I'm studying his features, the darkness contouring each perfect plane and line. "I can't promise this will be easy or that I will always be rational because you have the ability to undo everything inside of me with just a single glance, but we'll figure this out."

"I'm worried you're going to regret having me here once the sun rises."

Lincoln tags me around the waist with both hands, hauling me closer with a quick jerk. "There's a lot that I regret between us, but none of those regrets involve being with you or talking with you or spending time with you. They revolve around my inability to get past the fears you'll be like my mom or that I'll lose my best friend."

"Are you still worried about that? About Pax?"

His breath fans my cheek. "I think he will want us to be happy."

"What about your mom?"

Lincoln blinks slowly, sorting through words and feelings I wish I had access to. "She tried to make things work. She tried telling him she wasn't happy. The problem was he never listened. My problem is, I never stop listening. When you talk about something, it's hard for me not to react to it—to want to fix it. I had to avoid being around you because my impulse was always to act." He nuzzles closer to me, kissing my lips, and then my cheek, and then my jaw. "You make me want to fix the whole damn world."

Kisses fan my shoulder, waking me up, though it's two hours before I need to be up. "I have to go to practice. Your car's going to be here by ten. You want me to take you to Poppy's?" Lincoln's voice is low and smooth like velvet on my skin.

I blink against the bright closet light and the opened window shade. "I need to get ready." My own voice is husky and choppy.

"I'm in no hurry."

"I'll just call Poppy. I need to arrange for my car to get fixed."

His lips fall against my cheek. "It's going to be here by ten."

I focus on his brown eyes, his still-damp hair. He looks like a daydream. "What do you mean?"

"I know somebody who works on cars. They're going to change the tires and bring it by."

"Is this you fixing stuff?"

He grins, but it teeters too close to a frown. "We need to discuss the letters."

I sigh a bit too heavily. I don't mean to sound annoyed or ungrateful, I just hate the idea of allowing something to tarnish this small piece of perfection we're huddled together on. "My dad's sister is a cop. If I tell anyone, she'll find out, and then my dad will find out, and I really don't want to deal with all of that right now."

"You said the letters sounded sad?"

"They did. It honestly felt like I was this person's diary for a few weeks."

"Have you noticed any trends?"

"Like when I receive them?" I ask.

He nods. "Or who you're with, where you're at."

I shake my head, pulling the covers a bit higher. "I thought it might be a girl who liked Derek since I started receiving them the first night I met him. But I don't know. Nothing about it makes sense, but I still think it's a she and not a he."

Lincoln shakes his head. "Caleb was right. Almost all stalkers are men." He rubs a hand over his short hair. "Coach Craig asked Paxton about you yesterday, wanted to know if you'd help watch tape. That whole situation just doesn't seem right."

"I haven't seen or heard from him since we went out to the piano bar with Maggie."

Lincoln nods. "He might have seen us?"

I shrug. "I don't think so. When I got back, he and Maggie were talking. Plus, he hasn't tried talking to me since."

He released a deep breath. "You shouldn't be alone right now. The fact that they know so much about your schedule, and that they were willing to slash your tires, says something."

"What if the girl likes you? Maybe she's your admirer, and she saw us together last night?"

Lincoln swallows but doesn't say anything, tipping me off to the realization this is a similar thought to one he has.

"I can take you to Poppy's. I'm not in a hurry."

"You're going to be late if you wait for me."

He shrugs. "I'll say I had car problems."

"You should go. Caleb's here."

Hesitation has him narrowing his eyes. "I'm not trying to own or control you, but until we figure this out, will you please make sure you're around others?"

I nod.

"And consider telling Pax and the others." He leans forward, brushing a kiss on my lips that leaves too soon.

"RAEGAN!" I turn at the sound of Derek's voice. He jogs toward me, something between a smile and a smirk tugging at his lips.

"Hey," I say, feeling a current of nerves and regret course through me as his gaze covers me.

"How are you doing?"

I nod. "I'm okay."

His brow bunches like he's uncertain of this shaky ground we've both struggled to remain on.

"I need to tell you something," I begin. "This thing between us..." I swallow, trying to find a word to describe our situation, and coming up empty. "It's just not going to work. I talked to Pax about your starting position, and he agreed not to allow this to alter the game, but beyond that, I can only be friends with you."

Derek blinks several times, his silence unsettling. "Because of your accident?"

I shake my head. "Because I have feelings for someone else—I've *had* feelings for someone else."

"Beckett," he says.

"It doesn't matter."

"You know he doesn't care about anyone but himself, right?"

I pull in a deep breath. "Coincidentally, he says the same about you."

Derek laughs mirthlessly. "He would." He takes a step back. "When he fucks this all up, let me know."

Before I can say anything to dispute his confidence, he leaves me with an entire cloud of doubt settling around me.

My head is like a firing range, my thoughts the bullets—fast and too intense. Some are strays—never making contact—others are direct targets, hitting my reality where they splinter, making each impact seem larger than the last. If Maggie were here, I know she'd tell me to go with this crazy thing that's happening between Lincoln and me. She'd tell me to forget what Derek said and to ignore the news circulating about my father, who is currently under investigation. And she'd tell me to get over my fears because they're not going to do anything but become a regret.

Expectations whiz through my head like shrapnel, dangerous and penetrating. How long will we be able to make this work? And how much will we both have given and lost?

School today was a blur as I debated how I'm feeling about everything and who might be leaving the cranes on my car. They've never done anything violent, so why now? What's changed?

The only answer is Lincoln.

My heart stutters as I pull to the curb of Paxton and Lincoln's shared house because the driveway is filled with cars. It's Wednesday, and I know they have a game on Friday. I also know there aren't enough cars here to warrant the team being here for a meeting or dinner. I pull in a deep breath and close my car door.

Math textbook.

Notes for Marine Biology.

Statistics textbook.

Warmer coat.

That's all I need before heading to Poppy's house. She's waiting for me so we can study and order pizza. It was my plan, a guise I used so I could tell her I slept with Lincoln in person.

Female voices are audible through the closed door, making each of my steps a bit heavier.

Inside, Caleb is surrounded by three girls whose attire reveals they're unaware of the near-freezing temperatures.

Caleb's cheeks are stained a light shade of pink, a frosted beer bottle wrapped in one hand. He's nervous. Caleb has only had one girlfriend, Meredith. She lived in Battle Ground, and they'd seen each other every other weekend. It was a relationship that relied on everything except convenience. She was smart and pretty in an understated and honest way. She didn't wear makeup, played videogames, and was smart and funny. We liked her, and for a while, Caleb volleyed the idea of applying to colleges where he'd be closer to her, but after eighteen months, the distance became too much, and they broke up. That was a year ago, and though he claims he's over and past it, I know he misses the comfort she provided. More than that, I think he misses how she made him feel brave —like I do when Lincoln's beside me.

Maybe one of these girls is his Lincoln—an unattainable but beautiful distraction. The thought keeps me from intervening and telling him they're not worth his time.

Snobby. I know. I'm judging them by their shrill giggles and scraps of clothes, assuming they're working to make up for what they lack in sense and ethics. But, I did live through high school. I know mean girls are prevalent—too prevalent—and that they often rely on makeup and cute clothes to hide and deceive from their ugly truths. A masquerade at its finest.

Caleb glances in my direction. Paxton claims I stare at people for too long, but as in this scenario, I'm just trying to read the situation and all the players. He grins, a silent, '*I know.*' Caleb knows the score. He isn't like Paxton, blinded by boobs and great hair. He knows they're fake.

The door opens behind me, forcing me to move aside. A girl walks in with her hair straight as a pin and as glossy as her red lips. In her arms is a laundry basket filled with folded clothes. She glances at me, reading me as I do her, taking in my skinny jeans ripped on one knee and baggy sweatshirt, stopping on my navy-blue slip-on tennis shoes which she stares at a beat too long, revealing she likes them, but then her inquiring eyes flash to my face and hair, finding my bare face because I was too distracted to get out of bed this morning, trying to relive last night. A smile forms on her lips, knowing she looks prettier and believing that will be to her benefit and my detriment.

I move my attention to the kitchen, where more voices float through the house. I spot Lincoln beside a brunette and an unnatural red-head vying for his attention. My heart falls, landing with a bang that seems loud enough to be heard all the way to Nigeria and leaves an ache in my chest. I divert my attention to where Arlo is telling an animated story to three blondes. Paxton isn't visible, and I can't remember if I saw his car. But I don't try to verify his presence, hoping I can go undetected.

I'm halfway up the stairs when the girl holding the laundry basket calls out to Lincoln, referring to him as The President. "I brought this for you," she says, lifting the basket a bit higher.

Did she wash his laundry?

Why?

Was it left at her place?

Does she stay here?

Is that what he expects?

Allows?

My thoughts overflow, slipping out in the form of tears. This isn't what I want. I don't want to buy my approval through chores and favors, by wearing short shirts and heavy makeup.

"Rae?" Caleb calls from his seat on the couch.

My blurry gaze goes to his, and through the thin veil of tears I see the concern and surprise in his expression as he gets to his feet and moves toward the stairs where my feet feel cemented in place.

Lincoln steps into the room, his small entourage at his heels. He looks across the room with one sweeping gaze, stopping on me for a second before moving to the girl holding his laundry.

I continue up the stairs, my steps too fast.

"Rae," Caleb calls again, revealing he's following close behind.

I pull in another deep breath, steeling myself and blinking the tears back as I turn to face him, a contrived smile on my lips. "Hey."

"You okay?" he asks, searching my face for each sign I'm working hard to conceal.

"Yeah. I'm fine. Are you? I saw those girls were trying to get their claws into you."

He continues his search for another beat, and I throw in a small laugh to make myself more convincing. "We haven't really had a moment to talk," he says. "I know things are kind of a mess right now."

My smile starts to slip, but I bat his words away with a quick shake of my head. "I'm good," I tell him. "I just need to grab some things."

He swallows. "You know you can stay here, right? As long as you want to, you're welcome."

His kindness disarms me, reminding me of how many of my truths he's witnessed firsthand. I nod. "I don't want to inconvenience everyone. You guys have a routine, a rhythm."

He shakes his head. "And you're a part of it."

I shake my head faster, disputing his words. I'm not. I haven't been in a long time. "Is Pax home?"

"No. He left. I think he went to go see Candace."

I wipe a hand across my face, pushing away the fine hairs that often fall across my face because my hairdresser insists framing my face is a good thing. "He's really gravitating toward her with everything going on, isn't he?"

Caleb presses his lips together, teetering between a frown and a line intended to hide his feelings. "I think he just likes feeling needed right now. You know Pax, he hates change, and after this bomb went off, I think he's afraid of more change."

He's right. So right. Paxton, like mom and me, has always hated change.

"I'll call him," I say, my tone apologetic, knowing I should have worked harder to ensure he was okay, especially with the souvenir he's worn on his face in the way of a cut and bruise from our dad, reminding me he's not.

Caleb shakes his head once, then twice. "He just needs time."

Footsteps pound behind us, and we both turn—my heart matching the bass and rhythm as hope invades the space in my chest.

"Rae Rae!" Arlo calls, a broad smile showing off his teeth. "What are you guys doing? I think that blonde thinks you guys came up here to get it on."

I roll my eyes, annoyance feels like salt in the wound disappointment created. "You can go back. I just need to shower and grab some things. I'm meeting Poppy."

"Invite her over," Arlo says.

"That depends, do I get my own fan club?"

Caleb smirks. Arlo grins. "Trust me, some of these girls would totally be into you."

I tilt my head back and laugh. "Only to get your attention."

Arlo shrugs. "Stick around, and we'll find out. I'm ordering some pizzas. You hungry?"

Caleb nods. "Cheese with extra cheese. We'll text Pax and see if he'll come by."

"If you guys keep worrying about me, those girls are going to lose interest."

"Nah. It just makes them work harder." Arlo makes his eyebrows dance.

"I feel used," I say.

His grin reappears.

"Maybe another time."

"Tell her to come over," Arlo insists.

I shake my head. "I need to study. I have a test in my statistics class next week, and I'm nowhere near ready." The reminder sets me into motion, and I move farther down the hall to where my things are clumsily organized within the small closet space.

When I turn back around, Arlo and Caleb pause their hushed conversation and look at me.

"I'm okay," I tell them.

"You should see if you can get Pax to talk to you. I'm worried he's going to lose his starting position." Arlo rubs a hand over his short hair.

Surprise has me pulling my head back. When Lincoln mentioned Pax not focusing, I had never guessed it was a dire situation. I assumed he was being an uptight asshole, and his teammates were getting fed up with conditioning. "What's going on?"

"He's late. He's missing looks he shouldn't be. He's distracted."

"Okay." I clear my throat. "I'll call him on my way to class, see if he'll meet me."

Arlo hesitates, his gaze moving to Caleb.

"What?" I ask.

"We're worried about him," Caleb answers. "He's been smoking pot every day and drinking. It's just not him."

I brush the hairs that have fallen in my face again. "I'll call him, and if he doesn't answer, I'll go over to Candace's."

Arlo nods, his shoulders slowly relaxing like my words offer an assurance that I don't feel nearly as confident about. "We'll see you later."

I gather my things and then descend the stairs with the weight of Paxton's future hanging over me like a giant shadow.

The girl with dyed red hair sizes me up, her eyes ticking over my features and then my bag. "I know you from somewhere," she says.

My heart beats too quickly. "I don't think so."

She taps her chin with a narrow index finger. "You look familiar."

Lincoln looks at me, and I stare back, silently accusing him of things that I know logically are being fabricated by my fears, but they feel too real—too raw.

27

LINCOLN

There's something in Raegan's gaze that makes it difficult for me to see or hear anything else. A glimpse of something I recall seeing in my mother's eyes before she left my dad.

She pushes her bag higher on her shoulder and then tucks some hair behind an ear. She looks tired and not just physically. With her shoulders squared, she turns, ignoring the redhead's questions and walks out the front door with a barely audible good-bye that I'm fairly certain was directed solely at Caleb, as Arlo moved back to the girl with russet-colored hair.

As I stand, Caleb and Arlo both look at me. Arlo nods a silent *'she's pissed'* confirmation. I clear the front door in time to see Raegan slam her trunk closed. I jog down the steps, placing a palm on her car door when she reaches for it.

She draws back. "What are you doing?"

"Let's talk."

"I need to go."

"Because of them?"

"Because I believed you."

That look from earlier registers in my thoughts, recognizing it was deceit. "What do you think happened?"

She reaches for her door again, and once more, I place my hand on her window, keeping the door closed.

"Nothing happened."

She narrows her eyes. "With them or us?"

"Them."

"This is a bad idea."

I shake my head. I knew things would be harder this time around. "Because some girls are hanging out at the house?"

"Because even if gonorrhea is easily treatable, I don't want to go through that."

The insult lands like a slap to my face, her certainty that I would sleep with any girl causing my temper to spike. Her blue gaze is fixed on mine, bright and determined—she's ready to go to war with me. I drop my hold on her car door and step forward, debating which urge to succumb to when I want to kiss her as much as I want to shake some sense into her. "You don't trust anyone, do you? I'm pretty damn certain you don't even trust yourself. And this excuse about your parents having kept you on a short leash is complete shit because you do that. You keep yourself tied to this two-foot diameter, unwilling to risk anything."

Her shoulders drawback, the war in her eyes dimming with every second that ticks by, my words penetrating the night air like an echo. "Everyone notices you. Everyone watches you..." she shakes her head slowly like she's debating with her thoughts. "I don't know how to compete with that."

"You don't have to."

"I can't..."

"Can't what?"

"Being a girl sucks," she says, a dry chuckle follows her words. "There's this impossible balance we're all working to find: being tough without being too masculine, being smart without being arrogant, being kind without being a pushover, being beautiful without being prissy, being successful without being too informal. It's this massive scale that is constantly in flux, and the joke is on us because everyone is judging us—constantly—and more often than not, we're our own toughest critic."

I stare at her, recognizing the several walls she's dropped. She's being vulnerable right now, whether intentionally or not, I can't tell.

"This. Us." She moves a hand between us. Her nude nails are short, and the gold band she wears around her index finger catches the sunlight, distracting me for a few beats. "I don't know that I can do this. I don't know that I can handle the scrutiny of others I know I'll receive just by being near you. I don't know if I can handle you comparing me to others."

Her nostrils flare slightly, her lips barely parted as her gaze drops.

I slide my hand over her cheek, stroking the length of her impossibly soft skin with my thumb. I tilt her chin back, but she keeps her eyes downcast. "Rae," I say her name gently, realizing how fragile this moment is.

Slowly, she lifts her blue orbs to meet mine, closing her lips into a neutral line I want to kiss and force into the curvy twist I always picture her with.

I want to tell her to fuck them. Fuck all those who think she's anything short of perfection. Fuck anyone who dares to search her for faults and shortcomings. Fuck everyone—but I know she won't accept that and definitely won't believe it's sincere. "This is the furthest thing from conventional right now, but I have a feeling we're going to need to learn to trust each other for this to work. You have to trust I have your best interest in mind and that I'm not going to do anything to try and hurt you, and I have to trust that you're not going to sell naked pictures of me to the press."

"I feel like I have a lot more to lose." Her voice hints at humor, but her eyes are sober.

I'm about to tell her she's dead wrong, but before I can, Paxton turns down the road, his music so loud it's like a siren, alerting us to his presence.

Raegan sags back, and I remove my hand, my palm meeting the air that feels icy in contrast. But even with the added space, our being out here alone has to look suspicious.

Paxton gets out of his car and lifts a bag from the passenger seat that clinks, revealing its contents: more beer. "What's up?" he says.

"Hey," Raegan says. "Where have you been? I tried calling you a few times today."

"Yeah. I was with Candace. Sorry about that. Everything okay?" He doesn't look at her or me, unaware of the obvious and only asking the question as an automatic response.

"You want to hang out? Go get something to eat?" she asks.

He shakes his head. "No offense, but not really."

She wipes her palms across her thighs. "Yeah, I know."

Her words seem to catch him off guard, and he turns, sweeping his gaze across her for the first time, likely recognizing the same things I have for the first time, the minute differences that began a few weeks ago. How it takes her smile longer to appear, the fact her arms seem like armor, constantly crossed over her body, the lack of her easy laughter. "Sorry. Yeah," he says. "Let's do something."

"We don't have to talk about anything," she promises.

Pax's shoulders shift backward, his attention shifting to me with a silent question, as though checking to see if I see the same details missing from her usual happy and fearless demeanor. "No. We should," he says, breathing out a deep sigh. "We should talk about things."

"There's a bunch of girls here," she says, shucking a thumb in the direction of the house. "You want to go grab some coffee or something?"

"Mexican?" Pax asks.

The edge of disappointment scrapes against my chest, blunt and dull.

"You want to come?" Pax turns his attention to me again, a manufactured smile that I recognize as an apology.

Raegan's eyes lock with mine, and she gives a nearly imperceptible nod. "Yeah. Yeah, let's go. We can take my truck."

I wanted Rae to take the passenger seat, wanted to rest my hand on her thigh as we drove the short distance to the Mexican restaurant we've frequented since moving here. It's farther than several other restaurants, but its short menu is authentic, and the chips are homemade—it's also Raegan's favorite. But, she gets into the backseat without a word, latching her seat belt behind Paxton.

"You smell like fish," Pax says as he kicks his feet out.

In the rearview mirror I watch her lips curl. "It's my shoes. I washed them, but they got fish stuff on them. I don't even smell it anymore." A frown tugs at her lips. "That's concerning."

Paxton and I belt out laughter, and it feels so damn good to hear him at ease, I laugh even harder.

A waitress sits us in the back, though the restaurant is nearly empty—too late for lunch and too early for dinner. Pax is seated next to Rae, and I sit across from them, sitting in the middle of the bench seat.

"How's school going?" Rae asks, stirring the Shirley temple she'd ordered with a spoon after refusing a straw.

Pax winces. "I haven't exactly been going."

She wrinkles her nose, but then nods a couple of times and takes a long drink. "I have a feeling things are going to get uglier. I saw our pictures in the paper this morning. They're questioning the validity of us being accepted into Brighton."

Paxton slams a fist against the table. Rae doesn't jump, but her eyes remain on his balled fist for several seconds before she slowly swallows.

"That's bullshit," he barks.

She nods. "It's total bullshit, but..." She shrugs.

"But what?" Paxton narrows his eyes. "Don't tell me it doesn't matter."

The tip of her tongue darts out, wetting her bottom lip. "It *doesn't* matter. You're a football god. You could've gone *anywhere*. They won't be able to contest you being there."

Paxton runs both hands down his face.

"I'm not telling you because I want you to debate the merits of the lie, I'm telling you because I don't want you to be blindsided by it." She places her hands on the table, fingers spread wide. "We need to make some decisions and then move forward. Right now, we're letting his mistakes dictate our lives, and that's going to make us all lose."

Pax sands his hands slowly, the gears in his head turning, struggling to move beyond the past couple of weeks. "I'm so fucking pissed," he says.

Rae nods. "I know." She runs her hands over her hair, narrow fingers tangling and then untangling in the strands I'd raked my fingers through just last night. I realize I've seen her do this before, when she's talked about unethical fishing and difficulties the whales face, when she was cornered at her first college party and was trying to laugh and act casual, when I'd told her nothing could happen between us because she was

Paxton's little sister. I take a drink of my water, wishing it was a straight shot of Patron because sometimes being around her makes me notice too much. Care too much. Feel too much.

Then she refuses to look at me, her gaze cast on the varnished table top checkered with colorful tiles. I don't think it's intentional or a way of forcing me to remain out of her thoughts, it's simply a condition of her impossibly stubborn and independent nature.

"I don't know what we should do. Poppy says we should talk to Dad and forgive him, not for his sake but for our own." She crooks her jaw to the side, a subtle lift of her shoulders. "I don't know if I'm ready for that yet, but I don't want it to stop you.

"You can't let him and his actions get into your head and ruin your future. You've worked too damn hard to let everything fall apart right now. You have two games left, so if you don't want to think about it until after the season, don't, but you can't let this ruin everything."

He shakes his head, a sour twist of his lips. "This is about football? Who cares about football?"

"You do," she says. "You care. This has been your dream since you were six."

He shakes his head again, this time faster. Rae reaches out, placing a hand on his arm. "I feel so fucking stupid," he says. "Thousands of families are worse off. Broken and filled with lies, and I know I'm being a fucking wimp because I can't pull my head out of my ass and this idea of a perfect family, but that's what I want. That was my security. I knew no matter what happened, I had my family."

"You still do," she tells him, her voice thick with emotions that swim in her eyes. "I will always be here, and so will mom, and so will Maggie."

Pax drops his face into one palm. It's the weakest I've ever seen him. It's also the strongest, as he continues to list his feelings without hesitation or regret before burying his face into the crook of Rae's neck. She wraps a hand around the back of his neck, the other going around his shoulders.

There are dozens of moments I've been jealous of Paxton, watching him interact with his family—they stuck by him, going above and beyond so many times, and his relationship with both Maggie and Rae has always been solid—but watching them together now has me recognizing exactly how strong their bond is. It evokes a splintering pain of jealousy and fear as I realize she will always choose him, and for his benefit, I'm grateful to know that, yet the hollow feeling in my chest where the thought continues to echo leaves me feeling empty.

28

RAEGAN

I'm supposed to be at Poppy's in fifteen minutes. Guilt beats in my chest, knowing I should be there to call her and explain what happened because, like Paxton, I owe Poppy the truth after her endless support and friendship. If I leave now, I can make it, but Pax asks if I'll watch tape with him, and my priorities realign without a second thought.

I quickly send an apology to Poppy, asking to reschedule, and because she's her, I already know she'll forgive me too easily.

"Arizona's going to be gunning for you," Pax tells Lincoln. "That guy hates you," he continues as Lincoln pulls back into the driveway that is now nearly empty.

I switch my gaze to Lincoln, who shrugs with a dismissive tip of his lips. We head inside where their robotic vacuum that Mom and Dad bought Pax as a Christmas gift is humming along, chased after by Caleb, who makes quick work of lifting a few cords that he tucks into the TV stand.

"Hey, man. You getting ready to play?" Pax asks.

Caleb shakes his head. "No. I should be doing homework." He sighs, a mutual feeling we're all starting to feel toward school as Thanksgiving break approaches.

"You mind if we put on some football?"

"I thought you were meeting Poppy?" Caleb asks, turning his attention to me, which has both Pax and Lincoln looking at me.

"I rescheduled. But, I'm wondering if I can pick your brain later. I know you took Statistics as a freshman, and I'm hoping you can explain it all to me because when my professor talks, it sounds like Latin."

Paxton chuckles and ambles to the TV, where he rifles through a stack of DVD cases.

Caleb shakes his head. "You know math isn't my strong suit, either. You should hit Linc up. He took that class. He's got, like, a computer brain where that shit makes sense to him."

As though Lincoln needed extra points toward being a superhuman. Lincoln's grin hints at something that makes my cheeks flush. "I think I've even got my textbook, still. I'll tutor you." His gaze flashes down the length of me, blatantly taking his time to scour my body.

Pax claps two of the cases together to a silent beat as he waits for the disc to load, making me jump. Lincoln remains unabashed, his lips pulling into a smile that makes my belly clench.

As Pax turns back around, I clear my throat. "Mom texted me this morning."

"Yeah? She texted me, too."

I try to smile, but even to me it doesn't feel complete. "Did she tell you she's coming home this weekend?"

Pax nods. "To stay with Gramps?"

I nod. "I didn't know whether to offer to help her move stuff or if that would upset her."

"I think she'll have to move her stuff. I don't know if he'll keep the house. I mean, since he's lost his job, I don't know if he can afford it long-term."

I pull in a deep breath through my nose, considering another massive loss, one that seems so inconsequential considering I've lost sixty percent of my family unit in a matter of weeks, and the house is mere brick and mortar, but even as I try to tell myself this, it feels like a lie. My childhood is in those walls. Indoor Easter egg hunts on years we had late springs, lazy Sunday mornings where Mom made us huckleberry pancakes, and the driveway where Dad taught me how to ride a bike. The millions of laughs, tears, and secrets those walls have shared and witnessed make it feel like it's as much a part of our family as a living person. "What's he going to do?"

Pax shakes his head, his cheeks expanding as he blows out a long breath, the game temporarily forgotten. "I have no idea. He won't be able to teach again."

"He probably can," Lincoln says. "Hell, he might even have grounds to sue Brighton."

His words pave a path of fear and doubt, and then hope. "What?"

"Most colleges only ban teacher-student relationships. Unless the policy states all faculty and undergrad students, he can't actually be in trouble."

My stomach feels sour. "That's so wrong."

Lincoln's smile is grim. "I know."

The future he mentioned his father wanting for him plays in my mind like a carousel, a future that could conceivably include defending people like my father, like those who abuse the ocean and the marine animals. It makes me feel selfish not to have spoken to him at greater lengths about his future and the multiple options that will be readily available to him.

"I'm going to grab a beer," Pax says. "You guys want anything?"

Lincoln shakes his head as I vocalize a 'no.' As Pax turns toward the kitchen, Lincoln takes a seat next to me, his hand running over my thigh. "This afternoon wasn't at all what you think it was. Arlo invited someone over, and she kept inviting friends. I went up to my room because I had no interest—none at all. I had come downstairs to grab some food literally minutes before you got home."

Home.

The word elicits contradicting emotions of both warmth and ice.

"I don't want to be this jealous and insecure part of your life. I don't want you to waste time trying to assure me when you have so much of your future to focus on right now."

"What are you saying?"

"I don't want to be a detriment to you."

"You're the only thing that makes me feel like I'm on solid ground." He shakes his head. "You're not a detriment, and this conversation isn't concluded. Before we start statistics, we're laying all this shit out. All of it."

He turns before I can respond, swiping the remote from the coffee table as Paxton reappears with a bottle of beer, Caleb at his side, opening a giant bag of chips.

"What team is this?" Caleb asks, sitting in the chair, leaving the last seat on the couch to Pax.

"Utah," Lincoln says.

"Are they good?" Caleb asks.

"Not as good as Texas," Pax says, kicking his feet up as he starts the game.

It feels like I'm expending all of my effort and energy into not moving, my focus on the game nonexistent with Lincoln's leg a breath from mine, his cologne a dare that is becoming impossible to resist now that I know the taste of it upon his skin.

"They have a strong defensive lineup," Pax says while Lincoln rewinds the same play for the third time though I haven't paid attention to a second of it.

"Rae, what do you think of fifty-two?"

I have to stare at the players for too long to even find fifty-two in the lineup. "Are you worried about him?"

"I don't know. He goes from explosive to nearly nothing. Do you think he's baiting them, or is he out of shape?" As Pax explains his thoughts, fifty-two clips the offensive lineman, slapping his helmet.

I shake my head, trying to recall the games I've watched with Grandpa this year, ones with Utah. "He's never been on my radar that I can remember," I tell him. "But, that doesn't mean I didn't miss him." I glance at Pax, making sure he doesn't misinterpret my original words as a false assurance. "I'll pay attention to him."

Paxton's phone buzzes and he nearly knocks his emptied bottle to the ground as he reaches for it. He scans the screen, entering a quick reply before he turns his attention to me. "What's your schedule tomorrow?" Pax asks.

I blink several times, trying to recall what day of the week it is. With everything going on, time has both sped up and come to a screeching halt, much like it had after my accident. "I only have three classes tomorrow. All of them in the afternoon. But I don't work tomorrow. Why? Do you have more of their games?"

He nods. "Yeah, I was going to lift weights in the morning, and then I can get some more from Craig. If you're up for it, we can watch it tomorrow night. I only have one class in the afternoon."

"I can be here around six."

Pax nods. "Okay. Let's do that. I've got to get going. Candace is waiting for me."

"I didn't realize you guys were hanging out again?" I try to keep my tone light, free of accusation, but Pax knows my question without even hearing it.

"She's not that bad."

"I'm not saying she is. I just didn't realize you guys were back together."

"Can we not do this tonight?" He rolls his neck like the subject alone elicits a mass of stress.

I nod. "Yeah. Tomorrow."

Pax extends his hand to Caleb, doing a quick handshake the two have been doing for over a decade, and then he salutes Lincoln.

I sigh, watching as he clears the door. "He's not going to make this easy."

"He didn't smoke a joint," Caleb says. "Progress."

"Unless he smokes with her," I offer.

Lincoln shakes his head. "He doesn't smoke with her because she always falls asleep."

I block out the reasons that follow that decision as I watch the beginning of the game again. But then Lincoln stands, taking my full attention.

"Ready to learn statistics?" he asks.

"I should forewarn you that my understanding and knowledge for this subject could literally fit on a notecard."

He flashes a grin, his eyes expressive for the first time that I can remember. "Then, we should probably get started."

I stand, passing the remote to Caleb before following Lincoln, already knowing this is a mistake because the confines of his room will only guarantee distractions, not to mention what Caleb is going to be thinking. It doesn't stop me or even slow me down, though.

Lincoln closes the door behind me, his arm extended, revealing each defined muscle in his forearm that makes blood rush through my body, anticipation building, making me hyperaware of his gaze on me, the heat radiating from his body. He leans closer, my breath catching in my throat. "Before we get to statistics, we need to chat about today." He moves his hand that's still loose at his side to my waist, my sweater a painful obstacle as I wish to feel him against me. "One thing I've never been proficient at is bullshit. I'm trying to let you in, and if there's anything you've learned with all the shit I've put you through, it's that I'm not good at it. But, understand this. I'm not fucking with you when I tell you I want to be the guy who's good enough. I want to be the guy you want, and I'm not going to try to fuck that up. But, this house crawls with girls at times. You know Arlo. You know Candace, and I can promise you this, I will try my absolute damndest to not fuck things up. I'll be honest with you, and I sure as shit won't cheat on you."

"I don't want you to feel obligated. Like you have to come pick up the pieces because we have this … thing between us."

He grins, closing more of the gap. "Kerosene, you're not very proficient at bullshit, either. Your vulnerability is sexy. Don't hide it from me."

"Vulnerability is one thing. I'm worried I'm going to sound like an insecure and jealous maniac because that's how I feel with you. I know how many girls watch you—how many girls want you. If someone like my dad had girls who were willing to sleep with him, and you're going to have to fend them off with a stick, it just … it scares me."

He shakes his head. "When are you going to realize that you're the only one I see?"

His words seem too big, too heavy—too much. I drop my gaze to the beige carpet of his room, but nearly as quickly, he moves his hand from my waist to my jaw, tipping my face up, waiting until I lift my eyes to his. "I'm in this. I'm all in, and I know if I'd just told you how I felt after your accident, this would be easier, but I'll do this. I'll pull your weight and mine until you're ready."

I reach for him then, wrapping both arms around the back of his neck and pulling him the last breaths to me until our chests and lips crash. It's a hungry, greedy clash of our mouths and teeth and tongues, claiming and fighting our independent wills with the realization of our shared feelings. A kiss that cancels all the ones that haven't included Lincoln, making me forget about previously bruised egos and feelings until our breaths level and our kisses become softer in the form of hopes and promises.

Lips trail over my shoulder, up my neck, and along my jaw. His hand slides over my hip and dips into my underwear. My heart runs headfirst into pleasure, the combination making me feel nearly weightless. "Do you have any idea what you do to me?" he asks, taking my ear between his teeth, and then swiping over it with his hot tongue. My love for sleeping-in ends as his fingers trail along my most sensitive parts, willing to wake before the sun every single day if it begins like this. "I need to be inside of you."

He dips a finger inside of me, humming as he ravages my mouth with his. "You're so wet." His voice is gravelly with sleep and desire, yet it coats over my skin like silk, leaving me to chase his lips because I want to make pledges and admit to him how badly I want him.

He kisses me, and I lose time, and disappointments, and expectations —I lose myself in the kiss that invades every part of me—a wave that clears every imperfection and past experience clear from my thoughts.

I cup his face with my hands, his five o'clock shadow sharp on my palms, his skin impossibly warm. "Lincoln." My voice is breathy and desperate as I move my hands to his back, tracing stacks of muscles and hot flesh.

I feel his grin on my lips as he lifts off me, reaching for his nightstand. He places the condom between his teeth, hooking my underwear on either hip and ridding them with a quick pull. His gaze settles between my legs, and though I think I should feel embarrassed by the intensity of his gaze, I don't. I feel bold, sexy, empowered. Then his fingers slide over me in a commanding and dizzying pattern that has me clutching him, riding out the ecstasy his touch produces. Before I can recover from my orgasm, he presses into me, his dark eyes skipping between my face and where he's sliding inside of me, his jaw hard as he maintains the control I desperately want him to lose. I angle my hips up, and he swears. "You can't do that. You feel too good."

I do it again, moving our bodies closer. He drops his head, a groan vibrating through his chest. "Stop being gentle with me," I warn.

Lincoln's dark gaze cuts to mine. "Trust me. That will come, but not yet. I want you to feel good, not pain."

I consider his words, paying attention to my body. The heat of him, the pressure of him, the high of him all feel good, but there is still the whisper of soreness I can't deny. Lincoln seems to read my thoughts, recognizing my own admission. His lips curve with a grin, and then he leans more of his weight on me, kissing me until I forget to be nervous or self-conscious about the exchange. He resumes his controlled rhythm, his gaze tracing over my body and my face, kissing me with a tenderness I wish I could translate into words. Then, Lincoln sits up, propping my knees open, as he changes the speed and rhythm, placing his fingers exactly where I need them until I'm moaning his name, and he's saying mine like a plea.

Lincoln wraps the blankets around himself like a cape, inviting me into the throws. He holds me flush against his chest, his strong arms bound around my arms and waist. "Your first class is at one?" His lips graze along my neck, disappearing into my hair. My entire body feels relaxed, humming with the energy of his touch, and for the first time in a long time, my entire body feels warm.

I close my eyes, ready to sleep until lunch. "Yeah."

"Good. Go take a shower and get dressed. We have somewhere to go."

My eyes remain shut. "Where?"

Lincoln shift, his heat falling away from me. "You get a ten-minute power nap while I shower. But then, you have to get up." He trails a line of kisses down my shoulder blade.

"You don't want to get up," I protest, reaching for him as he settles the blankets over me.

He leans over me, his lips scoring my skin. "Ten minutes," he repeats.

29

LINCOLN

"**A**re you going to give me any hints?" Raegan turns, clipping her seatbelt in the passenger seat of my truck.

"Not yet."

"Ominous. I feel like you're encouraging me to create a bell curve for how often you come out and tell me what you think versus the times you hint at something."

I grin. "Just helping you with your statistics class."

She pulls in a deep breath, leaning back as I drive forward. "How are you feeling about the game tomorrow?"

"This season has gone by so fast. It's weird because I hate the idea of football being over, but at the same time, we're so close to going undefeated, that I just want it to be over, so we don't continue to have this hanging over us—the doubters talking about how we'll lose, the fans holding unrealistic expectations."

"I'm sure that gets to be a lot," she says, finishing my thoughts.

"Not justly. The game is beautiful. The field is where I feel the freest. I dread the idea I'll only have one more year to play."

"You won't," her response is automatic, and so sure, it's difficult not to believe her.

I turn, and Rae's gaze checks the sign and then me, accusation so heavy in her unspoken words that I can feel it on my skin. "Where are we going, Lincoln?"

"You don't have to go any farther than the parking lot," I promise her. "Not unless you want to."

"I don't want to go."

I breathe out a sigh, my convictions for bringing her out here weakening, succumbing to fear that she's going to be angry with me and pull back when she already has an entire set of dominos stacked against this working, and I might be the one who tips the stack. I steal a glance at her, noticing how wide her blue eyes are, how rigid her shoulders are. "I know."

"Then why are we going?"

I glance at her again, working to lower my defenses that tunnel past vulnerabilities into a territory I loathe because I've spent too much time here in the past few months: weakness. "Last year after I blew out my shoulder, I was so determined to get back out on the field, but then my first game back, I was legit hyperventilating on the field. Even now, it will flare up and get tight and ache and it fucks with my head. I worry I'm going to hurt it, that I'll be forced to quit. But, the doctors have assured me it's fine, that tendons just take so damn long to heal. Most of my pain is likely mental. Psychosomatic because I'm so damn worried about getting hurt that I delude myself into thinking it does." I clear my throat, trying to bridge this situation to one of the many subjects we've skated over. "Kind of like what I did with us."

I make the right turn that leads into the marina, the gravel lot she'd fled to after Maggie had left and has since avoided. My tires crunch over the gravel as I pull into a spot, keeping the engine running in an attempt to comfort her.

The water is dark this morning, a shade of blue that is so black it reminds me of a painting in my father's art collection where the waves are reaching for a boat like arms, ripping it apart. Rain falls against the windshield like tiny taps, encouraging us to step outside.

"Sometimes I feel like I'm drowning again," her voice is quiet, but clear.

Her words gut me, making the regret that lives at the hearth of the fire that's been burning in me for so many weeks expand. "You can't allow that moment to define your future."

She faces the windshield. "My fear of drowning keeps me from going out on the water, but things between my parents has had me thinking for weeks. Marine biologists aren't exactly a booming market. It's tough to get jobs in the field and tougher to get one with cetology. I don't want to have to rely on someone else to support me."

"Fuck that. Fuck him. Don't lose your dreams over your dad and his mistakes. You can't let that dictate your future. This is your dream, Rae. You can't put a price on that."

"It's not that easy. My parents never had money. This lifestyle of catered events and trips to Europe is not what we grew up knowing, and it terrifies me that I'll have to decide which bill to pay even if I'm successful."

"You can't think like that. You have to focus only on what you can control, and what you can control is overcoming this fear and doing what makes you want to get out of bed every morning."

Still, she doesn't look at me, her blinks slow. "They'll never allow me to be on a team once they learn what I did. I endangered so many that night."

"Someone once told me making my own obstacles was stupid."

Her gaze kicks to me, the ghost of a smile on her lips. "I'm pretty sure I said something more insightful than that."

I grin. "Fuck the rules. We make our own rules."

"Is that your motivational speech that segues to us getting out and facing my fear? Or are you going to tell me about some historical figure who nearly drowned and then faced their fears and became something significant?"

I chuckle, shaking my head as I reach for her fingers to tie with mine. "That's the end of my speech."

She releases a long sigh. "Let's go."

"Do you remember all of it?" I ask her as our feet cross the gravel, our strides short as her gaze remains on the dark Pacific.

"I think so. I guess it's hard to know for sure, though, right? I mean, I don't remember getting out or the helicopter or any of that."

Likely because she had one foot on each side of that fragile line.

"I remember hearing your voice," she says, taking her first step onto the floating dock. "I remember how my muscles were so cold they ached and then stopped feeling anything. I didn't feel anything when I'd cut myself." She glances at her forearm, though it's covered by her jacket. She moves her blue gaze to me. "Are you still angry with me for that night?"

I swallow the immediate yes that is both instinctual and instant because it's the selfish response, and I've already realized that. "No. We should all be willing to fight for things that are important to us—for what matters."

We stop several feet from the end of the pier. Rae's chin is raised, her eyes closed. She looks like she's having a silent conversation with the sea breeze and waves licking at the dock, a truce with the current and her fears.

Several minutes pass, and my sneakers and jeans growing wet, but I remain silent, waiting for her to find the peace that's been missing in this vital relationship of her life. Then, she opens her eyes, her eyes glittering with tears. "Thank you for bringing me out here."

"When you're ready, we'll take a boat out."

She smiles, and though it's faint and her eyes still hold tears, there's something in it that makes me feel whole. "This was what I needed. I needed to just be here."

Rae doesn't expand, doesn't mention if her confidence is restored or if she's ready to be back out on the water, and after pushing her this far, I respect her space, not pushing her any further—not yet, anyway.

"This is what we've been working toward. We have two games left," Coach Harris smacks his gum, pacing in front of us in a pair of slacks and his customary red Brighton sweatshirt. "I want to see focus. I want to see hustle, and I want to see you sending motherfucking Utah home with their tails tucked between their goddamn legs."

Arlo's leg bobs, knocking against mine before he stands. I pull in a breath, my thoughts tracing over the hours of tape we poured over last night. Each risk and opportunity for tonight running through my head like they're already a memory.

Pax stands, angling toward the bathroom. I pat his shoulder before he moves away from us.

A clip to my shoulder has me snapping my attention forward as Derek passes.

"What the fuck?" I demand, shoving him.

He propels himself off the wall, getting in my face, his eyes burning with anger and resentment, void of the fear he ought to be feeling. "You need to stop meddling," he warns.

I shove him back again, gaining a solid foot of space, enough for me to rotate my hips before driving my fist into his face, but before I can connect, Coach Harris appears, confusion and annoyance marring his silver brow. "Jones, what in the hell are you doing? If you derail my team tonight, son, you're going to wish you never left Texas."

Derek shrugs off his invisible grip, moving toward the tunnel. I stare after him, every cell in my body wishing to follow him and seek a revenge that's been like a tide in my head, consuming too many of my thoughts and regrets. Coach Harris stares after him, waiting to ensure he doesn't return before looking back at me. "You want to share what that was all about?"

"Beats the hell out me," I say, though I know it must be about Rae. Thoughts of the cranes and their cryptic words infiltrate my mind, filling me with a rage that places a bullseye on his back.

"Hey," Coach Harris barks, grabbing the front of my jersey. I slowly move my gaze to meet his. "Not here. Not tonight. This is your team. You carry them to another win or you carry them to a loss. It's on your shoulders, President. Be their leader. Show these assholes what you're made of."

I roll my shoulders, but my muscles are still tight with the realization that for the first time. Something matters more than the game—more than the win.

"Beckett," Coach Harris growls my name, a warning that's mere decibels from a threat because as much as he attributes this winning season to our futures, his own stands to benefit heavily as well.

"He's good. He's good, Coach," Arlo says, patting my shoulder before slinging his arm around me. "He's just ready for the game."

Coach Harris stares at me, a silent threat of the hell he could make reign on my life.

I nod, turning to follow Arlo, who remains at my side. "What the fuck was that?"

A single look, and he knows. "I was wondering how that was going…"

"He's pissing me off."

Arlo nods. "He's trying to get into your head. He wants you to fuck up. Don't give him that." He pounds an opened palm against my chest. "Rae doesn't give a shit about him. You know that."

I can't get into how my fears are spiraling, hitting far beyond the possibility of Rae liking him and straight into what type of threat he could potentially pose to her safety—again.

"Focus on Utah now. We'll deal with asswipe tonight."

We hit the field, and the lights, the noise, the adrenaline take over the second I step onto the grass.

Arlo pats me a couple more times. "We've got this. Don't sweat it."

Pax catches up to us, a sports drink in his hand. "What'd I miss?" he looks across the field.

"Nothing," I say automatically, knowing if I tell Pax about my assumptions, he'll lose all sense of sanity.

30

RAEGAN

"Wait. Rewind." Poppy says, her feet dancing as her smile spreads, pausing with her half-opened bag of cotton candy still in one hand. "You slept with him, and you didn't call me?"

"I tried calling you a million times yesterday."

"I know, but this is newsworthy of you hiring one of those airplane guys who write words in the sky."

"I'm not addicted to pain. In fact, I'm trying to avoid it. Can you imagine the crowd of pitchforks coming at me? Paxton in the lead."

Poppy flinches, but her face relaxes before my concerns. "I think he's going to be fine with it."

"I think you've had too much sugar."

She laughs. "Seriously. Pax loves you. Your happiness matters to him. If you tell him Lincoln makes you happy, he's not going to get in the way of that."

My thoughts take off on their own, considering the different responses Paxton might have to the news and how my words might impact his reaction.

"When are you guys going to tell him?"

"I don't know."

"Well, since you're not going slowly anymore, you guys should consider doing it soon because I don't think he'll take the news very well if it comes from an outside source."

"It's only been a few days. We don't even know what is going on between us. There have been no labels or expectations."

Poppy stops herself from saying something more by pressing her lips together. I know she doesn't agree—that she wants to shrink talk me in hopes of getting all my emotions to the surface so we can neatly sort and label them and thus Marie Kondo'ing my thoughts and make everything better.

"Have you tried calling your mom again?"

I give a single nod. "She didn't answer, but my aunt said she's still planning to fly home on Monday. Maggie called me today."

Poppy's face scrunches. "That couldn't have been an easy conversation."

"It wasn't. There were a lot of tears. I think that's the hardest part of this whole situation—none of us saw this coming. It's like we're all paralyzed and don't know how to react or move forward."

She nods thoughtfully. "But you will. It's going to be hard, but you guys will figure this out."

"Is it strange that I worry about him? I worry he's all alone and will do something awful. I mean, he lost all of us, even Grandpa, and his job… But, then I think of how he reacted that day we packed up my stuff, and it makes me wonder if I even know who he is and if I want him to be in my life?"

"That's a decision you'll have to make. But, there's no timer on it. You don't have to decide today or tomorrow or even next week. Focus on these things that are bringing you happiness now, and the other things will find a way of working themselves out."

I nod, hating the nervous energy that still exists in my chest when I think of all the unfinished pieces of my life at this time. "Lincoln invited us to a party tonight," I tell her. "He said most of the rugby team will be there."

She fishes out a large handful of cotton candy, hesitation clear in her green eyes.

"You're afraid to run into Chase?"

"Not afraid… I just don't want to make a bad decision if I start drinking, and he's there."

"I'll be your wing girl. Pax is going to be out, so I was planning to spend the night with you, anyway."

Thankfully the teams both take the field to start the third quarter. Paxton started the first quarter slow, his strides unsure and his vision tunneled, but Lincoln cornered him two minutes into the game, bringing their facemasks together, and since that moment, Pax has looked like himself, being the natural leader and breaking down all the barriers set forth by the opposing team.

"How's Pax doing?" Poppy asks, nodding toward the field.

I shake my head. "He could probably use some of your EQ." I bump her knee with mine. My voice is teasing, but I'm truly considering if it might help him. Paxton has always struggled to face his emotions, but once he does, he's always been good about discussing them. Meanwhile, I have a penchant for avoiding both.

"What about Derek?" Poppy asks, her voice a little quieter, more serious.

I glance at her. "You mean, have I told him about Lincoln?"

"Just that you're not interested in him…"

I shake my head. "He texted me this weekend, and I ignored it."

"Maybe that's the best course of action. I mean, it's not like you guys were actually together, together. But, if he keeps trying, you should just tell him you're not interested. You don't want him to get too invested and leave a wasteland of hearts at your feet."

Her words haunt me, drawing my attention over the field, watching Pax, then Lincoln, and finally, Derek.

"Maybe we should swing by my house and change," Poppy suggests as I help her gather the wrappers from her concession stand dinner.

I glance at my purple coat concealing my red Brighton U sweatshirt and black matchstick jeans. "That sounded more like a suggestion than a question."

She nods. "It was."

"Of course, it was."

My phone vibrates in my palm, and though I was expecting a text from Lincoln, actually seeing it sends a shiver of anticipation down my spine.

Lincoln: Meet me in an hour at the house. Poppy optional.

Me: Where are we going?

Lincoln: An athlete-themed party. Costumes required.

Me: You hate me, don't you?

Lincoln: Don't forget, my number's 44.

"What?" Poppy asks, reading my flustered expression.
"It's a themed party."
"What's the theme?"
"Sports?"
Poppy laughs and then begins to giggle, bending at the waist because she can't catch her breath.
"I really don't see the humor in this."
She stands, wiping a tear caused by her laughter. "I'm dying to see how you make an excuse to Pax about wearing Lincoln's number."
I groan. "Yeah. I can't. I need to at least let this season wrap up, so I don't mess that up for him."
She's still hiccupping with laughter as we arrive at her house, digging through her closet.
"What do I wear?" I ask.
"You have to dress like a football player. If you were a dude, you'd be on the team."
I shake my head. "No. I'm more of the mathlete these days."
Poppy throws her head back, a fresh wave of laughter tickling her. "Oh. That's perfect. We'll make you a sexy nerd."
I should have said no.
I should have messaged Lincoln and canceled.
But should have and I are starting to cross boundaries a lot, and so

here I am, dressed in a short plaid skirt, a black pushup bra visible with my low white blouse tied at my waist and the necklace Lincoln bought me around my neck.

"I should have been a mathlete," Poppy says as we park at the address Lincoln had texted me after I told him we were running late and would meet him at the party. The cold air promising rain has me regretting my decision as it licks at all my uncovered skin, reminding me of how exposed I am.

"This is going to be so weird." I scrunch my nose. "Seeing my brother in this violates, like, a dozen sibling codes."

Poppy takes another swig from the invisible laughter bottle she's clung to all night. "I'm so intrigued to watch tonight play out." With her midriff exposed and a tiny pair of black shorts she used to wear under her tennis skirt, she climbs the driveway, our hands linked.

My heart thunders in my chest, making me feel lightheaded. "I have no idea how I'm going to talk to Lincoln with Pax around."

Laughter teases Poppy's lips. "You've been doing it for days. You'll be fine."

A guy opens the door as we reach the porch, his intentions diverted as he takes a long look down me and then up Poppy, a grin splitting his face. "Wow." He nods, his attention split between us—mostly our breasts, his face vaguely familiar. "I'm Johnny," he says, reminding me of my first college party and meeting him then.

A guy with shaggy brown hair appears behind Johnny, slapping a hand to his shoulder. "Where's the keg?"

"I got distracted," Johnny admits. "My definition of perfection just arrived."

I exchange a look with Poppy, but she's beaming, a sucker for flirting, even the worst and cheesiest lines.

"Maybe we'll see you later," I say, gripping Poppy's fingers a bit tighter and tugging her toward the opened front door, regretting I hadn't waited to see if they'd go in search of the keg when they nail themselves to the doorway, requiring us to brush past them.

"God, and you smell good," Johnny says, taking an exaggerated breath through his nose. I continue past them into the shadowed house where red is splashed across nearly every person, white and black numbers written across faces and chests.

"I'm pretty sure you're going to get an A for originality," Poppy says.

I'm regretting allowing her to talk me into wearing a pair of black stilettos as I pass another group of guys, feeling like I'm in a display case as their eyes follow us.

Poppy pulls out her new favorite concoction of orange juice and vodka and takes a long pull before passing me the bottle. My nerves are desperate to dim the multitude of second-guessing. I take a drink and then a second one before returning it to her.

"No going upstairs with anyone," I tell her. "And if things aren't going well, find me. We'll get out of here."

She grins. "Are you giving me this pep talk or yourself?"

"Both," I admit.

Poppy grips my arms with both hands and gently shakes me. "Have fun, Rae. Don't think about anything tonight. Just ... have fun."

I try on a smile, hoping it looks more genuine than it feels. "You're right."

"I'm always right. I don't know why you haven't figured this out yet." She flashes a wide grin that I don't doubt will cause several guys to start approaching because my best friend is gorgeous, and when she smiles, she's downright breathtaking.

I glance up to confirm my point, catching sight of Chase making his way toward us. "He's coming," I whisper. "Chase."

"Shit," she mutters.

"Want to ditch him?"

She sighs. "No. I should talk to him. Clear the air. I'll never be able to date one of his teammates if we have bad blood."

I swallow my laugh, knowing she's mostly full of hot air at this moment.

"Do I look okay?" she whispers as he gets closer.

I nod. "I'd offer at least three c-notes if I saw you on a corner."

She laughs again, her beauty radiating and drawing attention to some guys standing even closer, creating a competition Chase wastes no time to close, sliding a hand possessively around Poppy's waist.

"Remind me to work on convincing the student body to only throw athlete parties from here on forward," he says, taking Poppy in with a long and slow glance.

"I'm going to get something to drink," I say. "But I'll be close." I eye Chase, a frown heavy on my lips. "Really close."

"Rae!" Poppy calls as I start in the opposite direction.

I turn to look over my shoulder, ignoring a scrupulous set of eyes traveling over my midsection.

"I love you!" she yells.

I blow her a kiss that she catches in her palm and presses to her lips. Then her eyes grow bright, and her smile turns devious seconds before a hand meets the bare flesh at my side.

"Tell me you're here to tutor me," the voice is rough and playful and too familiar.

I spin around and discover Arlo, whose eyes grow three sizes as recognition dawns on him. He throws a hand across his eyes, tipping his face toward the ceiling. "Rae Rae," he says. "Do not tell Pax I just said that."

"Deal."

He groans, wiping his hand from his face and looking at me again. "Or the President. He'd kill me."

I laugh, my cheeks burning with a flush I know is staining my cheeks. "I'll forget about it if you do."

Arlo nods. "Already done." He takes a long drink, though he already looks a little unsteady, likely contributing to his delayed recognition. "When are you planning on telling me about you and Lincoln?"

My cheeks flush, and he laughs, taking another gulp. "I have no qualms. He likes you. You're good for him. But, you guys need to tell Pax because if I could figure it out, you damn well know he will."

"Next week, after your last game."

He shrugs. "Not a bad plan. But, we still have bowl games. There's really no reason to wait." Before I can consider his words, he lifts his chin. "Pres!" he calls.

I turn, seeing Lincoln. He pauses, his eyes traveling over me in one quick pass. He pivots, making his way toward us, his attention on Arlo. "Hey." He's wearing his practice jersey over a pair of jeans, his dark hair mussed in a sexy way that makes me want to mess it up further. He discreetly glances at me, his eyebrows lowering a fraction before looking back at Arlo. "I don't know how long I'm going to stick around," he says.

"What? Dude, your expectations are getting too inflated. This is the best party of the year. You basically have a buffet of woman to choose from, all of them tattooed with your jersey."

I take a fleeting glance around the red jerseys and shirts, realizing how many display his number. I wonder if he's offended I didn't wear his number?

Lincoln nods dismissively like he doesn't feel the need to explain his reasoning.

Arlo winks at me. "Yeah, I get it. Well, I'm off to find someone to celebrate with." He cuts into the crowd, leaving me with Lincoln in a sea of people.

"What sport are you representing?" he asks, his gaze dropping down my front too fast.

"A mathlete."

The ghost of a pirate smile appears but is gone before I can appreciate it.

"Poppy with you?" Lincoln asks.

I nod. "Yeah, Chase showed up. They're talking."

He nods. "I'm going to get a drink. If you need anything, call me." He walks away, making my heart sink faster than a popped balloon.

I should take advantage of tonight and spend this time with Poppy, dance and drink too much and have fun, but no matter how many times I try to tell myself how I should feel and act, a trace of bitterness creeps into my thoughts, tainting the moment.

I slide between two guys making their appraisals of me obvious as I follow Lincoln to where he stops at a table cluttered with clear and brown bottles and reaches for the nearest one to him. I catch it in my hand before it meets his lips.

"Lawson," he says.

"Really?"

"What?" His tone is innocent, his eyes wide, making me believe I'm fabricating the situation and making something out of nothing.

"Are you really going to act like this?"

"Like what?"

"Like I'm not here."

He pulls the bottle from my grip and takes a long swig, wiping his mouth with the back of his hand. "Before you say anything, alcohol kills the germs."

"I wasn't going to."

His eyes taunt me, knowing I'm lying.

"Forget it," I say. "I thought we—"

"Thought we what?" his words are a demand.

"Why are you mad?" My tone reflects the anger visible in his darkened eyes.

He tips the bottle back, taking another pull.

I blow out a sigh, glancing in the direction of where I left Poppy when Lincoln's fingers slide against my skin, his nose skims my shoulder, and then my neck, stealing my breath. "You walked in here, and I wanted to fight everybody in here." His voice is quiet and ragged and utterly intoxicating. "Everyone's watching you."

"Except you," I whisper.

His fingers slip farther across my skin, pressing into me, leaving the memory of his touch like a branding. "Especially me," he says, pulling me closer to him.

"You've barely looked at me," I remind him, hoping he doesn't hear my breath hitch as his fingers span across my stomach, his touch too light.

"I can't see a goddamn thing tonight except for you."

"And anger, apparently."

"Like a red fucking lens," he agrees, his free hand trailing the back of my thigh, his touch varying between an intense and direct route to a light trace I have to focus my attention on.

"Is Chase a nice guy?" I ask him.

"Define nice."

"Should I intervene?"

"Isn't that her decision to make?"

"Sometimes, we all need saving from ourselves."

His lips graze my neck, his grip tightening, pressing harder against my skin, revealing each callus on his hands. He breathes me in, and it knocks me unsteady, leaving me drunk on his touch. "Sometimes it's not the before you have to consider, it's the after. Regardless of what he's done or acted like, what is he like now with her."

I work to keep my footing and prevent myself from leaning into him and letting him swallow me whole. "Are you going to work me out of your system tonight?"

He dips two fingers below the waist of my mini skirt, tangling in the hem of my underwear. "I'm going to try," he says.

I eye the door of a bathroom open. "Meet me in there," I say, pointing to the opened door.

He shakes his head. "My idea involves tying you to my bed."

I blink through the mental images, the idea paints in my head, a thrill racing through my veins.

I grab the bottle he'd drunk from and take a long drink. "I'll see you in two minutes."

31

LINCOLN

The bottle dangles from her fingers, her hips swaying to an intoxicating beat. Her long legs command my attention, watching her go to the bathroom where she closes the door behind her.

My heart pounds in my chest, desire and lust making me feel untouchable as I weave through the crowds, my focus never veering from the door she's locked behind.

I scrape a knuckle against the white door, and when the handle starts to give, I push it open, pushing it closed and flicking the lock into place before facing her.

She takes another drink, then sets the bottle on the large counter, licking her lips as she stares too long at my mouth. She wants me to kiss her. I can tell by the way she's looking at me, the way her body bows toward mine, and the slight gap between her lips.

I close in on her, her blue gaze falling between my eyes and my lips with her intentions clear.

"Public bathroom?" I ask. "This surprises me."

"I have this ... fantasy," she says, her voice huskier as I run a hand across her chest.

"What's your fantasy, Raegan?"

"I want to do something sexy in a crowded place, where no one knows what's going on, but would if they paid attention."

Her chest rises at my touch, the black lace staining my thoughts. I dip my mouth, pressing a kiss to the soft flesh of her cleavage. "What kind of sexy thing do you want to be caught doing?"

She shakes her head, her cheeks turning a light shade of pink that reminds me of her innocence. "I have no idea."

"I'll give you some ideas," I tell her, righting myself and focusing on those pools of blue that pull me in and drown me, smoothing each concern and reason we shouldn't be here doing this, making me forget everything except for the promise of pleasure. I seal my mouth over hers, and her hands wrap around my neck, hot against my skin. I grip her hips, lifting her up to the vanity where I plunge my tongue into her mouth and part her thighs. She moans, and I practically come undone, ready to shred the tiny skirt that has had enough glances tonight I'm amazed it's survived the weight of the attention, and move inside of her, marking her so deeply and thoroughly she won't be able to forget me.

Her lips crush against mine, her legs wrapping around me, making the desire to fuck her here and now against the counter a near requirement.

She slants her head to one side, deepening the kiss, and my hands fumble, tugging and pulling at the fabric around her waist, warring with her skin, demanding it expose each inch to me.

Rae kisses me, pulling back with lust shining in her eyes. "The zipper's on the side," she says, smiling as she peppers kisses against my mouth before pulling my lower lip between her teeth and gently biting the flesh.

My heart bangs erratically in my chest, chasing my desires in tireless circles. I reach for her skirt, forgetting about the zipper as I push the fabric up around her waist, revealing black underwear that conceals every part of her I want so badly to invade. I glance at her face for approval and find her eyes round with surprise, her breaths coming in shorter bursts as her nerves build. "You okay?" I ask.

She swallows, and then nods, her blonde hair hanging in wide curls down her back. "Do you have protection?"

I run my finger down her slit, loving the hiss she breathes in as her hips shift with the slight pressure. I blow out a breath, trying to steady myself and the weight of desire.

Rae reaches for the bottle and takes another quick pull.

"Are you nervous?" I ask.

She nods. "And a little .... Embarrassed."

"Embarrassed?"

"I've felt uncomfortable since I got here, like I've been on display, but this brings that to an entirely new meaning."

A near-silent laugh breaks through me like a sigh.

"What?" she asks.

I shake my head. "Your sexiness and confidence are so fucking beautiful, but your vulnerability..." I shake my head, searching for this feeling in my chest. "It makes me feel like a god."

A smile curves her lips, and then she laughs, a sound that is so carefree and beautiful, it makes me feel nearly weak. "Like you needed an inflated ego." She reaches forward, tagging my jersey and knotting her fingers in the cheap polyester fabric. She pulls me closer, her soft lips brushing mine as soft as I'd touched her, like she's testing my reaction or possibly her place in this exchange. I remain close, opening my eyes when she doesn't move to kiss me again. She's inches from me, her eyelids heavy with her own desires—desires I wish to learn so I can give them all to her.

I slide my hand along her jaw, grazing her cheeks, flipping a switch that carries this moment from sexy directly to intimate as we keep each other's gazes, exposing our desires and the energy that builds between us —something so strong we'd be able to produce power to the entire Pacific Northwest if they could find a way to channel it. I lean closer, the first to close my eyes as I capture her lips with mine, demanding she kiss me. Her hand falls from my jersey, going around to the back of my neck, her kiss severe and intense, feeling like an answer to a question I didn't know I'd been asking. We kiss until we can't breathe, our breaths labored and eyes feral as we stare at each other.

I hook my fingers around each thin strip of her underwear covering her hips and tug them down past her knees and ankles, dropping them to the cream-colored tiles, exposing her. I grip one of her ankles and bend her knee, pressing a kiss to the silky skin stretched over her kneecap as I plant her foot on the counter, her bright red toenails a stark contrast to the white marble counter. Her eyes trace over herself and then me too fast, revealing her nerves. I grab her other ankle, bending that knee and pressing a kiss there as I set this foot on the counter as well. "Stop," I tell her. "Stop thinking. You're fucking gorgeous."

I watch her as I run a finger over her, catching her wetness on my fingers.

She's soaked.

I groan, running another finger down over her folds and using my other hand to spread her apart. Keeping her parted, I stick my thumb into her mouth. I see her pulse in her neck, beating faster than a clock as she thinks too long.

"Suck," I tell her.

Her eyes flick to mine, and then her tongue fits around the bottom of my thumb, tracing a pattern that makes my jeans feel too tight. She pulls my thumb farther into the warm, wet confines of her mouth, making me forget her inexperience for a few moments as I war with the idea of undoing my pants.

I pull my thumb free from her mouth, and then strum it against her clit, making her hips immediately rock against my hand as she closes her eyes. I run my thumb along her clit and then lower, dipping it inside of her. She gasps. I groan. She's so fucking wet I could slide inside of her so easily.

"You're so fucking wet. So responsive." I groan as she bites on her lip, swallowing a moan. "I want to make you so damn dirty. Mark you so you can't remember anything but my cock inside of you."

I run my thumb gently over her clit once again and enjoy watching her hips push forward to increase the pressure. Then, her hips relax, waiting for me to return back over the same area now buzzing with anticipation and alive with nerves. Instead, I run my thumb farther down, parting her again as I slide my middle finger inside and feel just how soaking wet and warm she is for me.

She grinds against my finger, the movement making her already tight pussy become even tighter, and I stroke the inside of her as a form of reward. "That's right, baby. Grip my finger. Show me exactly what you want, and I'll give it to you."

I slide out, running my fingers along her clit, moving slowly, but increasing the pressure with each pass over the sensitive flesh until her thighs begin to tremble, and her legs struggle between spreading wider and closing with the last of her inhibitions that are keeping her from climaxing. "Stop thinking, Rae," I coach her. "Just feel it. Absorb just how good I can make your body feel."

She gasps.

"Your pussy loves this. Your pussy never wants me to stop. I bet I could even make you squirt if I kept this up long enough. Do you want to find out, baby? Do you want to find out exactly what I can make your body do?"

She pants in fast and hard breaths that I move forward to swallow, catching every part of her as she starts to scream her release.

Her knees fall together, leaning back against the mirror as I kiss her mouth and then her nose. She slides her feet forward so they drop off the counter. "I feel really tingly and warm," she admits.

"That's the alcohol."

She shakes her head, then leans forward. "It's your turn."

I shake my head. While I love the idea of her on her knees, her hand and lips wrapped around my cock, it's not here on the cold tile floor. "I just needed to see you come." I bend, grabbing her panties from the floor, and holding them out to her.

She pushes off the counter, threading her feet into her underwear, and pulling them into place before righting her skirt. "Are you not... Are you afraid of..."

"I thought we were past filtering yourself?"

"I don't understand? I thought guys always wanted to get off? Do I not make you...?" She trails off, her cheeks tinged pink.

I grab her hand, pressing it against my hard on. "This. This is what you do to me."

Her eyes drop to my groin, where the slight heat of her hand through my jeans makes me ready to propose we go back to the house, find refuge with everyone gone. "I don't understand," she says. "Why don't you want to sleep with me?"

I scoff. "I've thought of how I'd like to bend you over, hitch you up against a wall, watch you straddle me..." I shake my head, "I've thought about fucking you so many times I could write a book. I have an entire list of positions I need to fulfill with you, but not here. Not like this. Not when you're sad and angry, not in a dirty bathroom." I reach forward, smoothing a strand of her hair. Her eyes are still wild, exposing her release that I can still smell on my fingers.

32

RAEGAN

I glance at the bathroom counter a final time before exiting, wondering what I looked like from his angle. I pray I looked sexier than I feel thinking about it. Lincoln left a few moments ago to ensure no one sees us leaving together. I already looked for something to wipe down the counter with, but there was nothing except a half-filled bottle of ibuprofen and about a dozen bottles of hairspray.

A fleeting glance in the mirror confirms my hair is still in place, my makeup carefully applied. My skin still feels too hot, and my muscles too loose, but all in all, I look like me—correction, I look like me with a heavy hand of eyeliner and several layers of clothes subtracted.

I pull the door open, greeted by the noise of the party increasing tenfold. Cigarette smoke taints the air that smells too sweet from the multitude of girls here, all dressed like me in minimal clothing and hope—the hope the guy they've been vying for notices them tonight and chooses them. As Arlo had pointed out, the guys seem to have their choice tonight as girls place their bids with the jersey number from the guy they like prominently displayed across their faces and chests.

A guy stops mid-stride, roaming my body with his eyes, crossing the fine line of flattery to predatory. When Lincoln stared at me, it made me feel beautiful and wanted. This guy makes me feel violated in a way that makes me regret having agreed to wear this outfit. I turn and am about to head for the first sea of people I can disappear into when an arm wraps around my shoulders, and a familiar scent anchors me back to a safe and secure feeling.

Lincoln stares at the guy, his threat clear.

"Sorry," the guy manages before continuing through the house, craning his neck around after going a safe distance.

A part of me feels embarrassed to see him again, especially after having tried to picture myself propped on the counter and considering what he did to me, but then Lincoln's eyes dance over my face, silently asking a dozen questions that all have to do with my safety and security, and my previous thoughts scatter.

"Do you have a T-shirt on under your jersey?" I ask, remaining huddled close to him.

Lincoln nods.

"Would it be weird if I wore your jersey?"

A smile hits his eyes, but not his lips, which remain in a neutral line. He takes a short step back and reaches behind him, pulling his jersey off with one quick tug. A white V-neck tee slides back into place. His bare arms are tanned, roped with thick muscles and corded with veins that are possibly sexier than his smile. Rather than handing it to me, he rolls the fabric on each side like he's prepared to dress me. His hands are another of my favorite features, wide fingers and squared nail beds, calluses and each slight imperfection making a tally on my list of favorites. I'm pretty sure my eye twitches as I look at him with speculation at the idea of him helping me get it on.

"Your independence might be a higher peak than Everest." He steps forward, gently pulling it over my head. He continues holding it while I stick my arms through, watching as it falls below the hem of my skirt.

"This might be worse," I admit, noting how it looks like I'm not wearing anything underneath.

Lincoln shakes his head, his fingers tracing down my lower back, stopping on my behind. "You wearing only that while astride me has just added to the growing list."

Shock hits me like a glass of iced water. He talks about sex with so much ease and confidence.

The smile finally hits his lips as he shakes his head. "Why does that embarrass you?"

"Does talking about it ever embarrass you?"

"It?" He cocks an eyebrow, making me feel childish and even more inexperienced.

"Sex."

His grin grows. "You had no problem talking about it while you were turned on."

"Vodka might have played a part."

His dark eyes shine with disbelief, but he doesn't voice his doubts. He steps closer, his presence sucking the air out of the room and making my temperature ratchet up. His eyes glitter with the reflection of the dim lights and something that appears like a promise. "I plan to corrupt you. Dirty your thoughts so everything you think and hear reminds you of sex." His breath fans my face, his gaze so sharp I swear it's penetrating my thoughts.

My heart feels like a butterfly whose wings have gotten wet and can't take flight—stalled and too heavy. It would be so easy to get lost in this labyrinth we've created. I fear taking one too many wrong turns could easily displace not only my feelings but my understanding of who and what we are. I shuck off his jersey, realizing the last thing I want to be is another fangirl who proudly displays my hopeful intentions. "I think this creates the opposite effect. Thanks for playing interference with the creep, though."

This time his smile is on his lips but doesn't touch his eyes. He pulls his jersey back on, filling it out in a way that enunciates his masculinity and makes me want to reach out and touch each plane of muscle it conceals.

"You want to play beer pong?" he asks.

"With you?"

"That was the idea."

"Are you worried someone will see us together?"

His eyebrows lift just enough to make me feel stupid once more. "Have I ever worried about anyone seeing us together?"

"I don't know," I answer lamely. "We don't really hang out."

"Because you avoid me."

My jaw falls, and like a fish out of water, I move my mouth in attempt to refute his words, but nothing comes because he's right, I just had no idea he knew.

His smile grows cocky. "Told you I know you."

"I don't avoid you. I just... You're Paxton's friend."

He nods. "So's Caleb and Arlo."

That's different. They're different. But explaining those differences would be connecting too many dots for both of us, so I roll my eyes and plaster a smug grin on my face. "Yes, but they're cool."

He chuckles, the sound soft and deep, suddenly transferring against my shoulder as he presses me to his side and moves us in the direction of the long dining room table that's been converted to a beer pong table.

"Pax looked good tonight," I say, hating the silence though the room is filled with noise. "Whatever you said to him, it really seemed to register and get him out of his head."

"It got him back in his head," he corrects me. "Paxton is a great quarterback because he sees the field so well. He knows how people move and can predict things most can't. When he loses that, he's relying simply on his athleticism, which is good, but it's not what sets him apart."

I want to ask what he said to him on the field, but several guys greet him as we approach the table. His hand falls from my arm, a new smile on his face—one I recognize from newspapers and the local tabloids that follow Brighton and college football—it's his stage smile, well-rehearsed and perfect. He blows off a multitude of compliments, laughing at jokes, hugging people, and shaking hands like they're all personal friends, though I've never seen any of them.

I'm a second thought for them—a fixture that will be replaced tomorrow and the day after and the day after that. Still, a tall and lanky guy with straight blond hair that hangs close to his eyes looks me up and down a couple of times, each pass slower than the last. "Do I know you?"

I shake my head. "I don't think so."

"She's with me. This is Raegan." I can't decide if I prefer the order of those two sentences or wish they'd been reversed.

"Raegan," the guy repeats my name as though trying it out for size. He nods. "What's your costume supposed to be?"

"A mathlete," I say.

A lopsided grin appears on his face as several others repeat the word. "You don't like sports?"

"I'm pretty sure sexy is her sport with those tits," a guy with a buzzed head and bulbous nose says, his gray eyes narrowing in on my chest. "They're pretty nice."

Lincoln swings his head toward the guy whose smile is cruel and lewd, his fists ball, and I feel his body lean forward, ready to tackle. I link my arm with his, holding onto his bicep with a hold that hopefully appears more casual than it is. "Actually, my real sport is being smart, sexy is just an extracurricular. But, if you're going to be an asshole, at least be an accurate asshole. I have fantastic tits."

Several call out their agreeance, others howl with laughter. The guy with the buzzed hair mashes his lips together, wanting to fire back but smart enough not to with Lincoln at my side. Lincoln's weight shifts back on his heels, his lips a playful smirk as he shakes his head. "Fantastic is the understatement of the year."

I wink, playing the role like the Academy is going to vote on my performance. "Who are we going to beat, first?"

FOUR GAMES LATER, we're undefeated, a large crowd gathered around the table like we're in Vegas at a table with stacks of money being bet. Instead, Lincoln is the main attraction, the opposing teams and their gulps of beer our winnings.

"You need to start charging people a fee to watch," Jamal says, coming up and bumping fists with Lincoln before wrapping him in a man-half-hug. Jamal is also on the team, but I've only seen him at the house a couple of times for team dinners, and I've never spoken with him. He glosses over me but again doesn't say a thing. It's ridiculous and stupid, but it leaves me feeling more objectified than the guy who openly gawked at me. Like he only sees me as a placeholder who isn't worth addressing.

"I'm going to go check in with Poppy," I say as Lincoln glances at me.

"It's getting pretty packed. You want me to go with you?"

I shake my head. "It's okay. I'll be back."

"You better! I have next game!" Arlo yells from a few feet behind us.

I turn without stealing another look at Lincoln, knowing girls are already replacing me in multiples. As time has passed, so have the drinks. A girl with bottle-blonde hair staggers past, yelling something unintelligible. I wait for two of her friends to chase after her, giggling before continuing past a group of guys in their speedos, thinking about Maggie and her idea of rating man bumps. I conceal a grin and continue, spotting the rugby team and Chase, Poppy at his side. She's smiling, holding his hand that's draped over her shoulders. It's ridiculously cute, and I pray he realizes she's the best thing he could potentially hope for.

I turn my attention toward the crowd dancing, searching for Paxton or Candace. He stopped by shortly after Lincoln and I started our first game and was shockingly calm about my costume, only wincing once when I had to bend over to retrieve the ball after it fell and several guys cheered. He told me he was going to get a drink and some air, but that was well over an hour ago.

The French doors off the dining room are pitched open, and I follow the slight breeze like a moth to the fire, conflicted about the cold rush that feels both better and worse with each step I take. The backyard is dark, filled with overgrown weeds that are starting to crumple with the nearness of fall.

Pax is nowhere to be seen, causing a niggling that makes me feel a little guilty for having spent so much of the night with Lincoln when Pax likely needed him more.

I head back inside, circling the house twice to discover Paxton isn't the only one missing—Lincoln is as well.

33

RAEGAN

"Wow! Look at you." Victoria greets me at her door. We've been friends since grade school, our relationship one of convenience, spending time together when alternatives aren't available. My being here amplifies that reality, allowing the guilt to seep into my chest. Without being able to reach Lincoln, I don't know if Paxton is with him or not, leading me here for the night.

"Yeah, there was this themed party," I try to explain, slinging my bag higher on my shoulder.

She steps back, allowing me inside her small apartment with bare white walls and sparse furniture that promises a crick in my neck and broken sleep. "So…" she says, closing the door behind us. "Things seem kind of crazy lately. How are things with your parents?"

"About as good as expected, I guess."

She laughs, her gaze too inquisitive and prying, assuring me this is only the beginning of her list of questions. "What does that mean?"

I shrug. "If you're following the news, you likely know more than me."

"What?" Her question is pointed, my unease at being here growing rapidly. "I mean, who did he even have the affair with?"

It's the question so many have speculated about, and the thing that has kept me up for countless nights.

"Does it matter?"

"I mean, you're probably having a really hard time. The news was saying your GPA didn't really qualify you to be accepted to Brighton."

We had a weighted GPA system, where I earned above a four-point GPA because of the numerous honors classes I worked tirelessly to excel at. Still, her question stings, hitting the question that's been loosely bouncing around in my thoughts like a car rattle you can't quite ignore. "Yeah. You know the tabloids. They're always looking for new angles to make a story worse."

Her raised eyebrows refute my words. I already knew people wouldn't believe I was accepted into Brighton on my own merits—maybe I wasn't, but I jumped through the same hoops every other student did, my grades and excessive hours of extracurriculars and volunteering making me believe I might have.

"How's Paxton?" she continues her line of inquiry to her favorite subject—my older brother. She harbored a blatant crush on him for years, making excuses to see him each time she used to come over.

"Um, he's well. This has been hard on him, but he has a good support system."

My phone beeps with a text from Poppy.

Poppy: Did you get there safely?

I hate the disappointment that taints my appreciation for it being from Poppy, who loves me so completely she checks on me even though I know her feelings are buzzing about Chase.

Me: Yes. And you were totally right. Victoria hasn't changed a bit.

"Sorry," I say in way of explanation for paying attention to my phone. "How are things going with you?" I attempt to change the conversation to what has always been Victoria's second favorite subject: herself.

. . .

My time at Victoria's is thankfully brief, due to an outing with the aquarium that has me leaving with a scribbled 'thank you' note left on her fridge before she wakes up.

I think of Lincoln's words as I make my way to the visitor's spot I'd parked in last night, his warning for me to not be alone. The sentiment hasn't left me, causing me to look over my shoulder at every sound.

Once again, nothing seems amiss. There's nothing on my car, nothing tainting the day—except Lincoln's unexplained absence.

I make my way to the marina, my chest growing tighter until it's hard to breathe as I park in the large gravel lot.

I've been mentally preparing for this moment since the first day I woke up in the hospital, and though I'm healed, and my thoughts are beginning to settle, I still feel a sense of unease as I stare across the dark, choppy ocean.

I unlatch my seat belt and grab my coat, locking my car. I walk toward the dock, one foot in front of the other. I think of Maggie and the countless fears she's faced, of my mom flying home to face her fears, of Lincoln taking the field again after blowing out his shoulder.

The floating dock shakes under my weight, stirring additional fears to life.

"Raegan!" Lois calls to me from a dozen feet ahead. She turns around, walking toward me in her puffy, black coat. "How are you?" she asks.

I smile, pulling in a deep breath through my nose. "I'm good. A little uneasy, but mostly good."

She nods. "We're glad you're here."

Greg smiles at me in greeting as we reach the end of the dock, my hands tucked into my pockets, my hood up because all my hats and gloves are still at home.

"You look cold," he says.

"Well, that's good. Cause I'm actually freezing."

He laughs, offering his hand to help me come aboard. This feels substantial and equal parts foreign and familiar.

Breathe. Count. Breathe. Smile.

Aside from my nerves that leave my hands and legs feeling unsteady, I know my co-workers are aware of my personal situation. My name isn't a secret, and they're all well read, keeping apprised of details and news that I rarely make time for. No one has said a word about the situation to me, however.

The wind blows harshly against my skin, and though it stings, I'm pretty sure I'd be shivering even if it were hot out.

"That's my girl," Lois says, her eyes too heavy with sympathy for me to believe she doesn't know about my dad. Her black coat falls nearly to her knees, a black beanie covering most of her hair. Wide silver rings cover most of her fingers that dig into my arms with a security that feels maternal, making my eyes grow wet. "You still feeling okay?" she asks, handing me a lifejacket that I cling to a moment before being able to move to put it on. I force another smile as my breath leaves me like a short stack of smoke.

Lois nods like she understands the words I'm not able to vocalize. "You know, you're always welcome to stay with me if you ever need anything."

The invitation might be a welcomed reprieve if it didn't threaten to break all the carefully placed lies I've constructed to remind myself things are going to improve. I don't want anything to feel too permanent because I'm not ready for there to be a next because that implies there's an after, which forces me to consider the before.

"Thanks," I tell her. "I appreciate it."

She nods again, reading my answer and biting her lip. She's always been able to read people so well. She once told me it was because she's an empath, able to pick up on other's emotions and feelings—sometimes, even when the people experiencing them aren't able to recognize them. There have been too many instances where I've witnessed her do this first hand not to believe her. I also think that Poppy has the same ability, which is likely why helping people has always been a draw to her.

We go through the checklist, the order offering a sense of comfort as we get everything prepped.

The salty air cleans my lungs and mind, making everything seem father away and smaller as the turquoise water laps at the boat, and though I once found the sound to be soothing like a familiar lullaby, I have to remind myself more than once to breathe, keeping far from the edge.

"Raegan, look!" Lois calls once the engine has been cut and the others begin moving around, gathering tools to run tests and recordings.

I look out where she's pointing in time to see Blue crest the surface. Tears blur my vision and make my entire body feel too warm. I knew he was okay, but I didn't realize until now how badly I needed to see him.

I stay several feet back, too far for him to likely see me, but he and the other three members of his pod restore another piece inside of me that I know I'd never be able to fix alone.

"He sees you," Lois says confidentially, perched at the opposing corner of the boat. "Look at him showing off. He's missed you."

I don't know if there's any truth to what she says, but something in my heart prays it is.

When we arrive back at the docks, we're all soggy and cold, and Kenny is making references to "soggy bottoms" with a thick British accent because each staffer seems to spend their evenings watching The Great British Bakeoff. The joke is often used, yet we still laugh, cleaning the boat and completing the checklist of items we complete with each outing—the rhythm and routine feeling more familiar.

"You want to grab a bite to eat?" Lois asks as we step onto the slick dock.

"I would, but I have a shift at the coffee shop soon." Soon being relative since I technically have three hours, but with the way Lois is so fluent at reading my thoughts and feelings, sitting across from her without an ocean full of distractions would leave me without a single defense. "Raincheck?"

She nods. "Definitely. My offer stands. Always." She hugs me, tightening her grip rather than loosening it like so many do.

We take short, careful steps to keep from sliding until we hit the concrete where we avoid the puddles forming throughout the parking lot.

"Is that a friend?" Lois asks, her gaze directed in the distance though mine's still on where to step. I glance up to see a black truck parked beside my Honda. The driver's side door opens, and Lincoln unfolds from the seat, stepping into the fine mist that seems to be hanging in the air rather than actually falling. He's wearing a gray sweatshirt covered in a lightweight black jacket and a pair of jeans that look like they were made for him cover his long legs.

"My brother's best friend," I explain.

"Is he doing okay?"

I shrug. "This has been hard on him."

She presses her lips into a thin line, her eyes reflecting the painful words she hears with my silence. "I'll see you next weekend?"

I nod, and she reaches to hug me again.

I wish she'd continue walking me to my car, buying me an easy excuse to avoid Lincoln as well. I tuck my hands back into my pockets, making a mental note to stop and pick up some gloves tonight after my shift. Lincoln kicks forward, his gaze sweeping across me. "Are you okay?"

I stare at him, considering how stupid his question is.

"Your phone's off," he says.

Lois rolls her window down as she drives by, waving.

I wave back, calling a good-bye. "My battery died." My voice is so neutral; I'm impressed and shocked at the same time.

"You didn't come back to the house last night."

I shake my head. "I stayed with a friend."

"I'm sorry about last night. Pax and Ian got wasted and could barely walk. I helped Arlo get them into his SUV, and he was worried they'd throw up, so I rode home with them. But, when I came back, you were gone."

I glance around the parking lot, hoping his presence doesn't create more hushed rumors about me. I've worked at the aquarium for years, successfully keeping my personal life and drama far from it. "I didn't know where you went, and you weren't answering your phone," I admit.

He nods. "I lost it. I spent the morning at the store, getting a new one."

Hans, the leader of our outreach time, drives by, honking and waving as he passes.

"I'm not trying to create doubt or make you chase after me. I was planning for us to talk, I just didn't know what was going on last night and figured it was best if we slept it off. Was everything okay with Pax and Ian?"

He shakes his head. "It was nothing. They slept it off, and Poppy probably hates me because I borrowed Paxton's phone last night to call you, and when you didn't answer, I called her to make sure you were okay. I should have let you know what was going on. I told you not to be alone, and then I left you inside."

"Technically, I was surrounded by a ton of people."

He grins, running a hand over his eyes that reveal his exhaustion.

"Are you trying to apologize?" I ask, kicking a loose rock with the toe of my boot. "Because you kind of suck at it."

His arms drop to his sides, humor sparking in his dark eyes. "I left you."

"I noticed."

"I didn't mean to. I've never been good at this stuff."

"You don't have to," I tell him. "You had every right to leave."

His lips look fuller as he clenches his teeth, making his jaw become so defined it looks nearly sharp, giving Charlie Hunnam a run for most gorgeous jawline. "Why didn't you go back to the house?"

"I didn't know if you'd be there," my reply tumbles out too quickly, sounding more like an argument.

"Was that a lie? Because you kind of suck at it," he uses my own words against me.

"It's weird," I admit.

"Why?"

"Because you guys have your own routines, and I don't want to ruin that."

"You won't."

My shoulders rise, my muscles still tightly wound from the boat ride as I work to find the right words so it doesn't sound half as lame as it does in my mind.

Lincoln steps forward, his hand gripping me above my elbow. "Stop censoring yourself."

I shrug him off, taking a step back from the energy that floats through me when he's too near. "I have to."

"That's bullshit. You say you can't be yourself around me, but that's only because you refuse to."

"Because you make me feel ... messy." I shake my head once, swallowing the word vomit that I feel like I'm choking on. "I care what you think. I care more about what you think than I think I've ever cared about what anyone has thought about me. Poppy calls me fearless and claims that I have all this confidence, but when I'm around you, I lose it. I lose it all."

The mask I've become so accustomed to seeing him wearing slips, and his eyes flare. "Was that so hard?"

I throw my head back, growling at the sky and him and at the multitude of emotions that are turning so fast, I'm sure I'm about to drown in them.

Lincoln steps closer, humor and warmth pooling in his eyes. "I like that you care."

I shake my head. "Then stop telling me to stop censoring myself."

He laughs softly, then licks his bottom lip, his gaze catching on my mouth, making me wish he'd step closer and kiss me. "I wanted to make you feel dirty, but I can live with messy."

"I already regret telling you that."

Lincoln rubs his lips together, then smiles. "I know." He takes the slowest step on earth, closing the space between us, and I feel like it's the day we first met when I was a mess as I push wet strands of my hair back with my red, freezing fingers. "Does this mean you're done with Derek?"

"Derek, who?"

Confidence shines in his eyes as he smells the victory, licking his lips again.

"No, I'm serious. Which Derek? I was dating like five of them."

I'm trying to study the flash that appears in his eyes, but before I can label it, his lips crash upon mine, equal parts punishing and victorious as he swipes his tongue across my lips, coaxing them to allow him access. I breathe him in, the fine drops of rain dancing across my cheeks and forehead, tickling my nose. His tongue expertly slides against mine, an invitation into the current I've experienced and know will turn my world upside down. And I jump with both feet.

He pulls back before I'm done, his gaze traveling past my shoulder. "You went out on the water?"

I nod, looking back across the ocean that still seems so unfamiliar.

"How was it?"

I swallow. "Harder than I expected. I thought I'd feel more comfortable once we got out there, but it all felt very raw still. But, I saw Blue."

His eyes turn soft, and his hands tighten at my waist. "But you did it. You took a big leap. You should be proud of yourself. I'm hella proud of you."

"I didn't help them with anything. I was literally a boat ornament."

He shakes his head. "You went out there. That's huge. Don't discount this accomplishment. We all have to start somewhere. Trust me. After I was cleared to play this summer, I didn't start off with hardly anything. It takes time to build back up."

I pull in a deep breath, wanting to believe his words so badly I nearly ask him to repeat them so I can create a new playlist of words in my mind to drown out the doubt. But, then he looks down as he links our fingers and pulls me in the direction of his truck.

"I'm soaked," I tell him, watching the water from my coat run across the leather seat.

He glances at me from the driver's seat where he starts the engine. "I was hoping you would be." He grins mischievously, closing the doors, blue lights illuminating the space as he sits beside me.

"Is everything sexual with you?"

"When you're involved." He leans closer, reaching for my jacket. "We have three hours until you work, and probably one until you get hypothermia."

"How do you know when I work?"

"I stopped at the coffee shop first."

"Stalker."

He grins, reaching for my coat, tugging the zipper down to reveal my red Brighton U sweatshirt. He peels it off, tossing my jacket to the front passenger floorboard with a thwack of wet fabric. "Have you had breakfast?"

My head spins, trying to account for the darkness in his eyes and the calmness in his tone. Then the blue lights time out and go dark, the hum of the engine making the space turn warm.

Lincoln grins. "That was my easy question, Kerosene." He rubs his thumb along my bottom lip, the touch equal parts casual and intimate.

"If I stay at the house, every line will be blurred."

"That happened when we crossed the Rubicon."

"What about the other girls? Football? Pax? This is easy now, but me being there complicates everything."

"Maybe, but right now, I lose my fucking mind wondering where you are. And, football is football—if anyone understands what that entails, it's you. And if you'd pay attention," his gives me a pointed look, "you'd realize there haven't been any other girls."

"One did your laundry the other day."

He winces. "I know this won't make it sound better, but I didn't ask her to. Sometimes girls just come and do that kind of shit."

I wipe a hand down my face. He catches it as my fingers splay across my eyes. Pulling my fingers free in his rough, warm hand, he dips his mouth, kissing the still chilled skin over my knuckles.

"I need to watch you come again."

His words sling my heart so far outside of my body, I'm left staring at him, my breath caught in my throat.

That darkness in his eyes spreads to his lips, curving into a smile before reaching for me, tangling his fingers into my hair before he steals my breath.

34

LINCOLN

My ego might have undermined her independence as her words confirmed what I'd hoped but had been too afraid to believe. I spent an hour confirming I still have self-control as I locked Rae and me up in the back of my truck. My ego inflated and my dick hard and throbbing as I finger fucked her until I watched her come on my fingers. I hit the pause button again, knowing her second time shouldn't be in the back of a vehicle. Thoughts and questions were being stitched together as she followed me out into the cold mist to her car, but after hearing the reason she runs her thoughts through extra filters, I struggled to force the words out.

"Breakfast," I say. "Let's get something to eat."

Her eyebrows rise with question. "Is something... Is there a reason you only focus on me?" Concern is etched across her forehead. I press a kiss to the creased skin, and then another to the corner of her lips, then the other corner.

"I'm still waiting for you to change your mind," I tell her.

She shakes her head in short, confused twists. "What?"

"You waited for nineteen years before you had sex. Obviously, there was a reason."

Rae's cheeks flare pink. "It's called having a family of stop signs. My mom was our principal. My aunt's a police chief. Pax was a legacy. The only guys who wanted to have sex with me were looking to place a notch in their belts. It was never about me."

This theory seems as plausible as Kennedy being hit by a stray bullet. Raegan's sexy as hell and smart as a whip. She's funny, she's kind, and those figures in her life would only make the journey greater. "I don't believe you."

She scoffs. "Well, it's true."

I shake my head. "It can't be. I've been trying to ignore you for almost two years."

"I've been trying to ignore you for longer."

That new spark hits my chest. "So, you've been wanting me for three years?"

She rolls her eyes, the movement exaggerated and pronounced before placing a hand on my chest and trying to shove me. It causes her to stumble, but I grab her before too much space can build between us. "I'm not changing my mind," she says, confidence rounding her eyes as I follow the curve of her body with my hand, stopping on her ass.

"I don't want you to feel pressured."

"You sound like such a girl. Next, I'm going to start thinking you have feelings for me." Her smile is a fragile curve, and for a second, I'm suspended in time, memorizing every detail I can absorb like it's an order from a higher power, telling me I will want to remember this moment years from now.

"There's a breakfast place over on Second. I checked out their menu while I was waiting for you, and they have, like, forty drinks available at breakfast."

"You're never going to let me live that down, are you?"

I grin. "Not anytime soon, no."

She only argues twice when I suggest we drive my truck, but I kiss her and remind her it's only a couple of miles away, and she complies, following me to the passenger side, where I prop open the door, the scent of her orgasm mixing with the leather scent of my truck. It's euphoric.

. . .

"Is this weird?" she asks, brushing either side of the laminated menu with her thumbs.

"What?"

"This. Us, being here so casually. I feel like we just skipped twelve steps."

"Why?"

"I don't know. I think we hit all the stages, but they were all in a weird order." She slouches in her seat, folding her lips against her bottom teeth and diverting her attention to her menu as our waitress stops at the table. I take the few seconds to study her, recognizing the pull of her lips in a southern turn as a similar expression to the one Paxton makes when he's frustrated, hers is just so much milder it's easy to miss.

"What can I get you kids this morning?" the waitress asks, flipping to an empty page in her small pad of paper.

"Could we actually get a few minutes?" I ask.

"Do you want me to start with drinks?" she asks.

"Sure. Could we get two coffees, a hot chocolate with whipped cream, and an orange juice? No straws."

She jots our drink order with a smile. "Sure thing."

I focus my attention back on Raegan, waiting until she looks up at me. "What are you thinking over there, Kerosene?"

Blonde hairs tangle in her eyelashes before she swipes them away. "I just..." she pulls in a deep breath. "I don't know. I had an entire list of rules why I should avoid you..."

"Rules?"

She nods. "Rules. I just never thought I'd need to actually apply them because you have a line of girls who follow you around, doing your laundry and painting your jersey number on their faces..."

"Rae," I say when she doesn't continue.

Her eyes slowly meet mine, bluer with the light blue fabric stretched across the booth behind her.

"I won't do what your dad did." The moment I say the words, her eyes shine with emotions I know she won't recite, regardless of how much time I allow because that's the fucked-up thing about the relationship we have between our parents: we want them to be gods among men, we expect that and provide the platform for them to live out that lie. We feed that image lies, excuses, and dreams, and some parents abuse that, taking advantage of the unconditional love while others strive to meet it, and some fuck it up so royally, it's difficult to remember the moments when we saw them as anything except regrets.

The waitress arrives with our drinks, placing the orange juice, hot chocolate, and one coffee in front of me. "You ready to order?"

Rae blinks all the emotions away, then lifts her chin, her gaze clear as she looks at me for confirmation.

"Go ahead," I tell her.

She grins. "He'll have the crepes, extra strawberries with a side of hash browns, extra crispy. And I'll have the eggs benedict, extra hollandaise sauce."

The waitress turns her silent speculation to me, and I have to work to hold back my laughter as I nod. She gives a silent look of judgment, then spins around.

Rae shrugs. "Since you ordered for me, I figured I'd order for you."

"Crepes?"

"Those are actually for me. That was just my perverse joke because I knew she'd expect them to be for me like she expected all these drinks were for you."

I chuckle, entertained by the rationale behind her decision as I slide the hot chocolate and orange juice to her. "How'd you know I always order eggs benedict?"

"With extra hollandaise," she tags on, straightening her silverware before her blue eyes flash to mine, playful with a touch of something that makes my heart pound in my chest, recognizing it without understanding it. "I've also paid attention."

"You can stay in my room. I'll take the couch."

She shakes her head. "That would qualify as interrupting your routine."

"If you want this to be the topic of our first fight, I'm cool with that."

Her chin draws up. "I don't understand why you're being so stubborn about this. I can stay with friends and be safe and not make our relationship go from dating to living together."

"Your stuff is all at our place. There are four of us living there, so you'll never be alone. I have the most comfortable bed on the planet—a fact shared by no other than one Raegan Eileen Lawson. And because I can't fucking sleep when you're not there," I tick the reasons off on my fingers, staring at her, daring her to challenge any of my points.

Her lips fall closed, and she blinks once. Twice. Three times, her response missing.

"Paxton's still staying over at Candace's. She lives alone, so it works. You can stay in his room, the living room, or my room. Your choice, Kerosene."

"Are you going to stop calling me that?"

I grin, tucking my menu between the condiments and the window. "No. Are you ready to admit I won our first fight?"

"That wasn't a fight."

"Like I said, Everest."

"I'm going to smother you in your sleep."

"Hopefully with those fantastic breasts. That would be a great way to die."

She shakes her head, pressing her lips together as she fights laughter.

"By the way, that was quite literally the hottest moment. I was ready to pull you back into the bathroom after you said that."

"I was worried you were going to hit him."

"Why did that make you worry? He deserved it."

"Because you would get in trouble."

"My dad's a lawyer."

She scoffs. "The guy was just trying to show off in front of his friends."

"Maybe I was trying to show off for you?"

"You should try by ordering one of these smoothies. They look really good. I'd be totally impressed."

"Totally impressed?"

That grin of hers flashes. "Strawberry-banana or wild berry. Your choice."

"My bed. Decision made."

35

RAEGAN

I stand in Poppy's room, her full-length mirror a reminder of my own, except hers is surrounded in a thick black frame, the only accent color in her room.

"You look beautiful," she says, standing beside me. My dress is a deep shade of amethyst with a sweetheart neckline, so long it brushes the floor. My nails are a nude tone, my eyes heavily shaded with eyeshadow and eyeliner that made me feel bold and beautiful when Poppy had applied it and has left me second-guessing everything since.

"I look really intense."

Poppy clutches her stomach and throws her head back, belting out a laugh.

"Why are you laughing?"

"Only you would overthink this. You look gorgeous. Lincoln's going to want to do it with you in the bathroom and the coat closet and every other room he can sneak you into."

"What do I say if someone asks about my dad?"

Poppy's smile slips fractionally as the question sinks in. "If someone asks about your dad, then they're an asshole."

"I don't dispute that, but I feel like I need to be ready for this question. I mean, what if someone knows him or knows *her*." I sigh. "She was young. It's possible her parents could actually be there tonight. Can you imagine?" I told Poppy about having seen the girl a few weeks ago, a secret that still felt heavy, though significantly lighter after telling Lincoln. Admitting it to Poppy made it even lighter until the idea of telling any of my family members populated my thoughts, then it felt like an anvil.

She nods. "I doubt it. She might not even be from here. For all we know, she's from some small town in Missouri." Brighton has been silent about who she is, and I've dutifully ignored the news and haven't heard anything from my dad. Maybe he knows I'm not ready to forgive him? Maybe he's still trying to clean up his mess? Or maybe he just doesn't care anymore now that he doesn't have to hide anything?

I pull in a deep breath, the dress constricting around my waist and chest. "Hopefully, no one will say anything. They'll probably just whisper behind my back."

Poppy frowns. "Honestly, that sounds more likely to me, and in those cases, just ignore them. Focus on Lincoln and meeting Dr. Swanson."

I nod, working to prepare myself for this public appearance that I'm selfishly making all about myself, when likely few will be paying attention to me. "You're right."

"Of course, I'm right. And, if anyone asks about your dad, just ignore them and find another glass of champagne."

I laugh off her suggestion. "Do you have a handbag I can borrow? Black maybe? That's something I didn't even consider packing."

Poppy nods, opening her closet, which is meticulously organized, going to the area where her handbags and purses are all neatly aligned. She returns a second later, a small black clutch with a leather bow on the front in her hand.

"Thank you." I take it to her bed, where I open my purse to transfer the few items I'm going to need for the night.

"What is this?" Poppy grips a folded crane hooked on my wallet. "Rae?" Her eyes are wide with a silent accusation because, in Poppy's eyes, omissions are lies, and this is another in the long line of my omissions from this fall.

"I didn't want you to worry," I tell her lamely.

"Does Lincoln know?"

I know better than to reach for the offending letter, knowing it will only make her react. "It was on my car Friday after class."

"Raegan, whoever this is, he's following you. He knows your schedule."

"But he doesn't call. He doesn't try talking to me. He doesn't even write threatening words. This one had song lyrics on it—bad song lyrics at that."

Her green eyes flash to mine, cutting past the bullshit. "Why are you joking about this?"

"I don't want everyone to make this into a big deal and worry about it. What if I'm right and it's just a joke? I mean, it makes sense that it's a joke because they stopped after my accident and then when they started up again, they took a sharp right and just became goofy and random. Maybe it's someone I know who's just trying to make light of things?"

"What about your tires?"

I cringe. "We're not sure that was the same person. What if that was just some random jerk?"

"Or maybe it's someone who's freaking stalking you. Do you understand the potential threat here? You're so smart, and yet you're being so dumb about this. I want to shake you."

"I've spent hours upon hours reading about stalkers. None of these behaviors fit into any of the profiles. But I've stopped social media altogether. I never post where I'm at. I went from living with my parents to staying with friends or a house with four guys, and I'm rarely alone. I've received no gifts, no calls, no nothing. I feel like me blowing this up would just exacerbate everything and make it into something it isn't."

Poppy ignores my reasoning and proceeds to read the letter. Her eyes scan over the text twice before she looks at me. "Are you reading these?"

"I've read all the others."

"Raegan," she says my name like she's exhausted by my ignorance. One I know is deserved, yet still struggle to accept.

"Can we just deal with it next week?"

"How many have you received recently?"

"Define recently."

"Raegan," she groans.

"Ten? A dozen, maybe?"

"A dozen! He's telling you he watches you. This is scary. I'm worried. You need to tell people. You need to tell Paxton and your parents and the police."

"I will."

"Like you told everyone about your dad's affair?"

It's a low blow, one that leaves a gash in my sanity and conscience. Every day the line between right and wrong seems to thin and blur.

"I'm sorry," she says, reaching for me. "That wasn't fair. I get it. I get that too much is going on, and it's hard to know where to focus your time and energy."

"School alone is drowning me," I tell her. "And then I have the aquarium and the coffee shop, and my parents, and Pax is struggling, and..."

"And you want to enjoy this time with Lincoln while everything is new and fun and sexy. I get it. But, you're selling yourself short. You've got this, Rae. You only have a couple of weeks before finals, and you can afford to take less shifts at the coffee shop, and once you guys tell Paxton, you won't feel like you have to sneak around to see each other. But you can't ignore this," she holds up the unfolded crane. "This needs to be at the top of your priorities right now."

"Can I have one more night off before facing the music?"

"One," she says. "Tomorrow, we rip off the Band-Aid."

I pull in another deep breath, already dreading the moment.

The doorbell rings, breaking into the dread I'm imagining that will come with dissecting these letters and my next step. Poppy's eyes meet mine. "Stop thinking this is all temporary. He likes you. You guys will figure all of this out. And I'll be here for you, every step of the way." I thread my fingers with hers, feeling the same weight, the same warmth, the same comfort I've always found in my best friend.

"I'm sorry I didn't tell you."

She shakes off my apology. "I'm sorry I've been so focused on moving on. I know I've been distracted this year."

My throat grows tight as tears slip down her cheeks, proof that she's still trying to recover from her heartbreak. "Don't apologize. You've always been here for me. Sometimes I just feel bad for depending so heavily on you."

Poppy laughs, but it's garbled. "You spent every day of our summer coming over and trying to cheer me up. Every. Single. Day. You're the reason I was able to finally get out of bed and go to class and laugh this fall."

"I just helped. That was all you."

She shakes her head again. "It was you. This is what friendship is—we help each other, rely on each other to help us through the bad times, and celebrate the great times. I'm here for you, and I won't let this crap pull you down. I swear. We'll get past your dad, and this creep of a loser, and Pax, and all of it. I promise. Go enjoy your night and celebrate looking like a freaking princess with your prince charming."

She blurs as tears build in my eyes.

"No. No. No. I was giving a happy speech. Girls rule, and we'll persevere, rah, rah, rah!" She pumps a fist into the air, her hand still holding mine clutching tighter.

"This feels like a terrible idea. Every time I'm with him, I feel more—so much it feels impossible and too big and too great, and it just feels like I'm setting myself up for heartbreak."

Poppy's lips slide into a smile that teeters into a frown as she fights back her own tears. "You can't look at it like that. If you expect every relationship to fail before it even starts, you're not even trying."

"But this isn't just some relationship…"

She nods. "I know. I get it. It's Lincoln." She purses her lips. "You have to fight for it. Let all those feelings you've had for three years out, and let him in. Trust me, he's not going to go anywhere. You guys have something. I see it—hell, I feel it. There's an energy between you guys that is palpable. It makes me excited and so damn happy for you and hopeful and jealous because I want that. I want someone who looks at me like he'd part the sea and knock down mountains if he had to—the way Lincoln looks at you."

I work to silence the fears and doubts that conflict with her assurance, the fact we've barely begun and how lust can be so misleading, but I focus on her words and the feeling that is so much deeper than just in my heart where the butterflies swarm whenever I see him or hear his name or think about him.

Poppy keeps my gaze, waiting for me to take another deep breath before she nods. "Everything's going to be okay. We've got this." She hugs me, her grip tight like she's trying to keep my thoughts and confidence together. "My mom is likely grilling Lincoln. We should save him." She studies my makeup, brushing a single finger below my left eye. "You look perfect."

We find Lincoln in the living room, Poppy's mom across from him. "You know, Rae's like a daughter to me."

It's hard to believe her words, considering Poppy's mom has always been so stern and cold, but the realization she's like that even with Poppy has several walls of assumptions falling.

Lincoln nods. "I have no doubt. It's hard not to care for her." His attention cuts to the stairs, hearing our shoes, and his jaw falls, his gaze following each of my movements.

"Be sure to drive safely. No drinking. Make sure she's home safe," she continues.

Poppy giggles quietly at my side. "Can we modify my list to include a guy who falls speechless at the sight of me?"

We clear the last few stairs, and Poppy's mom smiles at me. Lincoln slowly approaches, his dark eyes dancing across my face, the hint of a smile warming each of his handsome features before he leans forward and kisses my cheek. "You're stunning."

"You guys have fun," Poppy says. "I'll call you in the morning. We'll do lunch or something. Get together..." I know what her trailed off sentence implies—discussing the cranes with everyone.

I nod, knowing it's another part of the picture I have to acknowledge.

Poppy's smile grows as Lincoln holds the door open, offering his hand to me.

We walk to the passenger side of his truck, where he opens the door. "Think they're watching us?"

"Poppy, definitely."

His smile flashes. "So, I need to make this kiss PG?"

I grin, the unsteadiness I'd felt upstairs disappearing as I breathe him in and absorb the strength that translates through his touch. "Only for now." He leans forward, that pirate smile stealing my heart as his lips brush against mine before he steps back and helps me into his truck before going around to the driver's side.

"I went out again today," I tell him. "Onto the ocean."

His grin steals my breath. "How was it?"

"Easier. Blue was there, too."

His grip steals my inhibitions. "Did he show off for you?"

"Is it crazy to think he knows who I am?"

"You're the one who keeps telling us how brilliant they are."

"I know he's brilliant, it just seems kind of selfish to think I matter to a creature as brilliant as Blue."

His gaze steals my thoughts and fears. "Do you realize how many people's lives stopped the day you got hurt? You're the furthest thing from insignificant. You matter to Blue because you matter, you matter to all of us."

"Are you saying all of this because of the dress? Because you're getting a little sappy."

He chuckles. "Just wait until I'm taking the dress off of you. I won't be able to censor my words then."

Thankfully, I don't have to think of anything witty or sexy to say in response because Lincoln's pulling into the valet of the hotel where the wedding is being held. An attendant opens my door, his smile instant as he takes in our attire. "Welcome, are you guests?"

"We're here for the Beckett wedding," Lincoln says, accepting the ticket and passing a bill to him. He offers his arm to me, and I slide my arm through, wishing I'd worn a dress with long sleeves that covered my scar that looks nearly purple against my skin without the shawl I had to help camouflage it at the engagement party.

"Why are you frowning?" Lincoln asks as we pass through the doors, the sweet scent of eucalyptus greeting us.

"I should have worn a jacket with long sleeves. As I get pastier, my scar seems to be getting darker."

Lincoln smiles, rotating my arm to look at the jagged line. He raises my elbow, kissing the spot where my skin puckers and is the ugliest. "Eventually, I'm going to convince you when I tell you to fuck the rules and expectations. Besides, no one's going to be looking at your scar. Trust me."

"My fantastic boobs will distract them?" I ask, eyeing the massive lobby. I've never been in this hotel, and while my family has definitely moved up in what we can afford, we've never stayed at a hotel with indoor water features and elaborate bouquets on every table.

"I was going to lie and say it was your winning personality, but..." Lincoln stops, his eyes dropping to my chest as I laugh. "Seriously. Don't worry about your scar or your dad or anything else. We're going to have fun, dance, you're going to wow this marine biologist, and then I'm taking you home where I'm going to worship every"—he kisses my lips, and then my neck—"square inch"—he kisses my ear, and my exposed shoulder—"of your body."

The desire to find a restroom or other closed-off space to hide and live out these promises has my stomach clenching, and each of my cells hyper-aware of every breath and touch.

He leans closer, his lips grazing my ear. "Hold those thoughts. We need ninety minutes for this wedding to wrap and to find Dr. Swanson." He kisses me, his lips a tease between pleasure and desire. Then, as I'm ready to differentiate the notes, his lips fall away, and he weaves his fingers with mine, leading me across the elegant lobby.

36

LINCOLN

She smells like summer and Christmas morning and fresh blueberry pie—all my favorite things in one, though it's something floral and sweet rather than piney or fruity or woodsy.

She releases a quiet gasp as we walk down the aisle, the white runner leading to a large arch where a podium has been placed. "I think that's him." Her gaze is lasered in on a man with white hair, wearing a gray suit that would make my soon-to-be stepmother cringe—Dr. Swanson.

"Want to sit by him?" I ask.

She quickly shakes her head. "No. I need to think about what I'm going to say."

"That you're a badass."

Her laughter is too quiet to gain attention, but her smile is so fucking bright, I swear half the room notices her. "I should sit in the back. This means a lot to the others who are here. I'm just here for you."

I continue down the aisle, stopping where Dr. Swanson is seated alone. She looks at me, her eyes wide with silent objections. "Dr. Swanson, I'd like to introduce you to my girlfriend, Raegan Lawson. I think you guys will have lots to talk about. She's actually studying to be a cetologist."

His brows raise with an obvious appraisal. "You don't say?" He stands, extending his hand to her. "It's a pleasure to meet you, Raegan."

She smiles, and just like everyone else on the receiving end of her smile, he grins.

"You know, you look familiar," he says, scrunching his forehead as he stares at her. "I saw you in some articles. You jumped into the Sound to cut a fishing net."

"To save a dolphin," I interject.

Dr. Swanson looks at me and then her again. "At the price of her own life. Tell me, do you regret your decision?"

Raegan blinks, that highway of thoughts surprisingly calm as she maintains his stare then shakes her head. "I regret hurting people who I care about, and I regret not having packed a dry suit, but I don't regret my decision. I think humanity loses itself and its value when we think our lives are more significant than the lives of other species."

He stares at her, assessing the words that make so many things seem suddenly trivial in life. The wins, the losses, my impending future, and the choices that I've resented for so long. It doesn't matter because while I love the game, the adrenaline, and the rush I get each time I step out onto the field, it still pales in comparison to what I feel for her. I would live in a one-bedroom shack as long as she was there with me.

Dr. Swanson grins. "Please, sit. I'd like to hear about your future ambitions."

She looks at me, her blue eyes clear from the doubt she'd had earlier as she smiles. "Thank you," she says. "I'll see you soon."

"Badass," I whisper into her ear before kissing her cheek.

I head back down the aisle, smiling when someone waves at me before ducking into the room where my dad's preparing to say 'I do' for the sixth time. He's wearing the same suit as me, but his tie is a lighter shade of blue—chosen by Carol.

He clears his throat, tightening his tie.

"Looking for a getaway car?" I ask. "My truck's valeted, but I've got the ticket." I start to reach for his ticket, smiling as I do it.

He grins, reaching for a tumbler filled with amber liquid.

"I'm only kind of joking," I tell him.

Dad straightens, swallowing the alcohol as he stares at me—possibly trying to find his words or trying to decipher if I'm joking. "I thought we discussed this."

"Discussed what?"

"*Her* dad is in every newspaper in town because of the scandal."

"A scandal she played no part in."

"Do you think anyone cares if she played a part in it? It's her dad. It's going to reflect on her."

I shake my head. "Well, that's too bad for them because if someone wants to stir up shit, they're going to be dealing with me."

"Think about this, Lincoln. Think about your future. My associates aren't going to want to see you dating a girl whose father had a public affair with a student."

"And in a few months, the news of your sixth divorce will be plastered across the front pages."

"Lincoln," he quips, brows creasing with a frown that barely touches his lips. "What's that supposed to mean?"

"It means I've watched you date, marry, and divorce five women in ten years. Rather than marry her, maybe you want to stop and figure out what is going to actually make you happy because she's not coming back."

He takes another drink, draining half the glass. "This is my wedding," he snaps, his jaw tensing. He doesn't move toward me, his anger a completely different beat than Raegan's father's. Although he's lacked at parenting in many regards, I don't have a single doubt my dad loves me, and he's a man of respect, and for him, that means you never strike another person—not with your fist at least.

"Why couldn't you just try harder? Why'd you miss every dinner, every anniversary, every birthday?"

He slams the glass onto the table, the alcohol sloshing across the surface. "Dammit, Lincoln. What's wrong with you? Why in the hell are you dragging this all up today—now?"

"Because we should have talked about this shit years ago. Because I've nearly walked away from the girl I know makes me a better person because I'm so fucking afraid I'm going to turn out like you."

He pulls his head back, feeling my words and the anger and resentment filling them. "You should want to be like me. I was able to provide you with the best education money can buy. Tutors, coaches, trainers, vacations on private islands, every toy and game you could ever imagine—I gave it all to you."

"I know, Dad. And I know you did it because you loved me, but what I needed was my parents, not to be shipped across country because you didn't know what to do with me."

"She's who left," he yells.

I nod. "But you let her. Every time you missed a weekend, a vacation, a dinner—you opened that door for her, she just decided to walk out."

"What am I supposed to do? I can't change what happened. I can't go back in time. I did the best I could."

I think of the stories Pax and his siblings have shared. The family history they share and the way it's now shattered just like mine had all those years ago. "I know, but, Dad, Mom and I never cared about the gifts or the fancy vacations—we just needed you, your time."

He runs a hand over his hair, his shoulders falling as my words seem to register to him a decade too late. "I always wanted to give you what I didn't have."

I nod. "I know. But you've missed so much, and it scares the hell out of me to be honest with you because you don't hear what I tell you. She's the only person who actually sees me for something more than a football player or a life of privilege. She sees me. She gets me."

"I get you, son."

"Then, you'd stop trying to force me into a future I don't want."

Dad pauses, releasing a long sigh. "I've built it for you."

"Dad, I love football. I love history. If I can't make it to the NFL, I want to do something that allows me to do something I'm passionate about—something I give a shit about. And I need something that allows me to spend as much time as I can with her rather than something that will always be pulling me away from her."

"If you get drafted next year..."

I nod, both of us knowing what he's saying. "I know. But that's a couple of years, not a lifetime."

"You can't change your life for her. You have to both follow your passions or you'll resent each other."

"I've never wanted to be a lawyer, not even when I was a kid. And to be honest, the only thing I feel passionate about right now is her. She makes me feel alive. She makes me feel whole."

His lips pull into a grim line, a silent threat of the pain he's endured because he tried following his heart, and it led him to a life filled with empty relationships and promises. "She must be pretty special."

I shake my head. "I love her."

Dad pats my shoulder. "Maybe after everything settles down, we could discuss this some more." He lifts both palms. "I'm not saying you have to, but we could even consider adding a new specialty at the firm, something with history."

I lift my chin, ready to refuse even the idea, but he shakes his head.

"Let's just talk," he says. "Man-to-man. Maybe I can even give you a few tips on your game."

I tap my fist against his bicep, making him chuckle. "Come on, your old man's got some game."

"Yeah. Luckily you write a really good prenup, too."

"I like her."

"I know. I'd feel better about this if you loved her."

He swallows. "It's hard to find someone who's willing to love a broken man."

I place my hand on his shoulder. "Maybe you just need to find the person who makes you feel less broken."

"Maybe that will be wife seven?" He winks, and for a second, I consider going out and calling the wedding off on his behalf because he clearly needs some intervention. "She's a good woman. I have a good feeling about this," he says. "She learns about my job, takes an interest in what I do. I've even stopped working on Saturdays."

I rotate my wrist, glancing at my watch. "Well, if you're ready, this is your final chance. You can take my truck or give this a shot."

He grins. "If someone gives Raegan shit, let Torrie know. She'll escort them out."

"Does that include you?"

His grin spreads into a smile. "If she makes you happy, she makes me happy. But her dad seems like a real tool."

I sigh, shaking my head. "I didn't see it coming. I thought he was a good guy."

"He might be. We all make mistakes, and sometimes those lead to even worse mistakes. Or, he might just be an asshole."

"Jury's still out."

Dad laughs. "You're a natural."

"Let's go get you hitched, old man."

Guests have been seated, and a harpist sits off to the right side, playing a song that sounds nothing like my dad's taste in music. But I don't focus on that for long because my attention is focused on Rae. She's mid-conversation with Dr. Swanson, her hands moving around animatedly like she does when she gets excited about something.

"He doesn't like anybody," Dad says, following my gaze.

"I'm fairly positive it's impossible not to fall for Raegan. Plus, she's studying marine biology. Cetology, to be exact."

"Cetology?"

"Dolphins and whales."

"Smart girl."

I nod.

Raegan turns in her seat, our gazes tangling. Her smile hits me like a sucker punch, my admission to my father ringing in my ears as I realize how much love I have for her.

We walk toward the officiant and take our places, and I see her eyes following me, a smile staining her lips and my memories.

The music changes and the guests stand, turning to face the back where Carol appears in a white gown. Her sister is her only bridesmaid, and like Dad and me, they walk together. I still don't know if she'll be in our lives for long, but for the first time that I can recall, I feel hopeful for my dad that she is.

As the ceremony ends, Dad and Carol walk past a line of applause and cheers, their hands clasped. I turn my attention to Raegan. She's clapping and laughing at something Dr. Swanson tells her before her eyes turn to find me, then her smile grows. I cross the distance, extending my arm for her to take.

She threads her arm through mine, stepping beside me. "I'll see you at the reception?" Raegan asks him.

He grins. "I'm hoping to see your resume this summer for my summer program. Maybe I'll have to come pick it up so I can meet your dolphin. Blue?"

Her blue eyes grow round, and she nods. "You're welcome anytime."

Dr. Swanson nods, turning his attention to me. "Hold on to this one. She's a special young lady." With the tip of his head, he follows the crowd toward the reception hall.

She watches him disappear around the corner, and then her attention shifts to me, her eyes still bright and round as she smiles at me. It's blinding and perfect and endless. I want to say a thousand words, all directed toward promises and declarations, but they all tangle together into three simple words that seem nearly too big. Instead, I pull her flush against me and kiss her. She places her hands on either side of my face, drawing me closer as she kisses me without abandon, her high translated into the kiss that has me wishing to leave here and now. She pulls away slowly, her smile still intact, calling for a reciprocation.

"I'm sorry I missed the conversation," I tell her honestly.

She shakes her head. "I don't feel like I said any of the right things."

I kiss her again, a chaste brush of our lips that I can tell she regrets as her eyes open slowly like she was waiting for more.

"We should go in there," she says.

"We can leave."

"We can't leave. It's your dad's wedding. Plus, there's cake. I have rules about cake."

Laughter hits my lips. "I thought you preferred ice cream."

She shakes her head. "My grandpa prefers ice cream, but I've never discriminated when it comes to sugar." She slides her hand down my arm, joining our hands. "Plus, I've never danced with you, and I've heard you can tell a lot about a guy by how he dances."

"Oh, yeah?"

"Yeah." Her tone is a challenge, but her eyes are bright with laughter. "Plus, this dress deserves to be worn for more than an hour."

"My floor would love to wear it."

She tries to hide her laugh as she shakes her head. "Poppy is way better at compliments."

I tug her back against my chest, her eyes dancing between mine. "You look beautiful in the dress, but Raegan Lawson, you could wear my jersey, sweatpants, or nothing at all and still be just as sexy." Her cheeks color as she grins, leaving another stain on my thoughts.

37

RAEGAN

I take a seat at the assigned table, Lincoln at my side. He's talking to the other three couples at our table, answering questions about Brighton's win last night. My lips are tipped into a smile I can't seem to fight, my shoulders relaxed with his hand on my thigh—and even with the slight chill in the air, I feel comfortable, my breaths easier.

As the table breaks into a gentle laughter as Lincoln makes a joke about the weather, I lean close to him. "I'll be right back."

"I'll come with you."

I grin. "No. They're loving your attention. Practice your interview skills. I'm just going to run to the ladies' room and see if Mom's texted."

He stands, helping me up. "Don't leave me for too long. You're not the only one who isn't cut out for small talk."

I press a chaste kiss on his cheek. "Maybe we can find a restroom together on our way out." I reach for my small clutch, smiling at the table as I excuse myself. Lincoln's eyes are on me, heavy and intent with lust and desire—the concoction that always spikes my bloodstream and makes me feel beautiful and bold.

I make my way through the maze of tables, the intricate and colorful topiaries constructed of greenery and flowers set in the middle of each table has my gaze skipping across each candle and person and ribbon, still shocked by the utter elegance and grandiose of it all. The bathrooms are even fancy, the doors going all the way to the floor and don't have gapes at each side, a real handle that locks on the door.

I wash my hands, memorizing the fancy details that I plan to tell Poppy about tomorrow like the neatly folded hand towels in place of an air dryer and the multiple bottles of soaps, hair spray, even perfumes that are neatly set on the counter beside an attendant who smiles at me.

"What a small world. You're Lincoln's friend's sister, right?" I look up, catching the familiar sight of Nikki in the mirror.

I toss my used towel into the hole of the counter and turn to face her, guilt swimming in a tall glass of inferiority as I take in her perfect figure, flawless skin, shiny hair, and movie-star smile. I nod. "Or you can just call me Raegan," I say, trying to laugh. "It's a little shorter."

She smiles. "You really like him, don't you?"

My response is delayed, caught between honesty and remorse for having hurt her. I want to tell her it wasn't intentional—that I would never have consciously kissed another girl's date, that we'd tried fighting our feelings for each other, and unfortunately allowed others to get hurt in the crossfire that came with the battle of our wills and desires. "I'm sorry," I tell her finally.

Nikki shakes her head, smiling grimly. "Don't. I hurt him, and now he's just trying to..." she shrugs, a tight smile on her lips, once again reminding me how much I hate trailed off sentences.

"Trying to what?"

She giggles. It's a sweet, tinkering sound—a giggle I hear a million times each night I go to a frat party that lacks authenticity at every level. "He's Lincoln Beckett. The President." She does a semi eye roll like I'm missing such an obvious point. "And our dads work together. They've been friends *forever*. Lincoln and I used to take baths together." She giggles again, only this time the sound feels like warning bells. "We've basically been betrothed since birth. He just needs to blow off steam, get back at me."

Nothing about her words matches any of what Lincoln has said to me —or how he's acted—yet for some ugly reason, it's easier to believe her theory when it makes so much more sense than Lincoln suddenly liking me after knowing me for three years and barely even having spoken to me in that time.

Maggie's voice is a quiet whisper at the back of my thoughts, telling me how it's never okay for a woman to tear down another woman when we have enough obstacles in our way—that when a woman does, it hurts most because it's always vicious, intentional, and often pragmatic, hitting us the hardest. I'm about to blow her off and focus on the facts, the reality that Lincoln's never been dishonest with me, but then I catch sight of her necklace and freeze, my breath stolen as I recognize the gold chain and pearl necklace.

Nikki brushes her fingers over the elegant piece of jewelry. "Beautiful, isn't it? Every year for my birthday, Lincoln gets me a piece of jewelry with a pearl on it."

I feel nauseated and betrayed and angry and so much—too much. My eyes fill with tears and before they fall in her presence. I turn, catching the attendant's drawn shoulders and pity smile as I pass through the door she holds open for me.

I pass by the reception, hearing the emcee announcing something over the microphone, my gaze blurry as tears fall so fast I can't manage to swipe them free before more replace them. My lungs feel tight, my chest as well, and it makes me feel a wave of panic as I try to compare the feeling to how I'd felt in the hospital.

I step through the automatic doors, the cool November air swallowing me, making the trail of tears on my cheeks burn.

The valet attendant looks at me, his actions unhurried as he walks toward me like he's hoping someone might help me if he goes slowly enough. "Miss?"

"Could you call a cab or Uber or anything?"

Relief washes over his face, his shoulders visibly falling under the red sport coat he's wearing. "Absolutely. Right this way." He places a hand on my back and extends an arm, directing me through the few cars still running as people unload their bags, and some get into their cars for dinner. He leads me to a black SUV and opens the back door.

As I slide into the leather seat, my phone rings.

Lincoln.

I ignore it, reaching for my seat belt. I nearly recite my parent's address before catching myself, dreading each number of Pax and Lincoln's street address. I need my car, clothes, and school things.

The driver remains still for a moment, his dark eyes watching me in the rearview mirror though he's already entered the address. "You're sure?"

Not even a little.

"Yeah."

My phone rings again, rattling nearly as hard as my heart is.

The driver takes a final glance at me, then puts the SUV in gear, driving forward, past the cement cover. Raindrops splat against the windshield, angry and loud, splintering with each hit, just like my heart.

38

LINCOLN

I call her again, my unease growing like a damn tide, pushing me well over my breaking point. I push open the women's restroom door, surprising the attendant who quickly waves her hands and shakes her head, shooing me back out the door.

"I'm looking for my date," I tell her.

The woman follows me out into the hallway. "You're going to need to wait out here."

I look over her shoulder, craning my neck to see beyond the woman I recognize as the wife of one of my father's partners. "Her name's Raegan Lawson. She's wearing a purple dress. Blonde hair, blue eyes. Looks like a freaking runway model. Can you ask if she's inside? Call her name?"

The attendant pulls her chin back, her gaze dropping to the polished ivory tiles.

"Did you see her?"

She crosses her arms over her chest, lifting her chin with a universal look that screams at me to fuck off.

"Please," I ask her, reaching for my wallet. "She's been gone a while, and I don't know where she went. She's not answering her phone." I grab the largest bill in my wallet.

She takes it, sliding it into her pocket as she lands a glare on me that is as icy as it is haunted. "She left."

"Left? Left the restroom? When? Did you see which direction she went?"

"She *left*. Most girls don't stick around when they learn their date bought another woman jewelry."

Her words are worse than any blow could deliver, hitting me with a force and might that leave me speechless.

The attendant nods, then slips back into the restroom. The cake hasn't been cut, and I know Carol is going to throw a shit fit if I'm not there to dance with her, but those thoughts are forgotten as I race down the hall and through the lobby, my valet ticket already in hand as I hit the doors. "Hundred bucks if you can get my car in less than five minutes," I tell the skinny blond who takes my ticket.

He gives me a single pass, stopping on my watch before turning and sprinting out of sight.

I scroll down to Rae's name again, hitting 'send' for the fifth time. "Come on," I mutter. "Answer."

She sends me to voicemail again, that fire in my chest becoming an inferno that burns each security that makes up our relationship. I consider calling for help. Asking Poppy or Arlo or Caleb to check on her and make sure she's okay while I wait for my car, but before I can consider if it's a good idea, my truck pulls into view.

"Thank fuck," I say, reaching for another bill and opening the door. I shove the money into his hand, closing the door before he can say anything and tear out of the driveway.

I blow through a yellow light that turns red when I'm halfway through and speed up, cutting across double yellow lines to pass the cars in front of me, waving through each obstacle like it's the field, and they're keeping me from the end zone—keeping me from her.

Raegan's in the driveway, wearing a pair of jeans and a gray sweatshirt that looks two-toned with half of it soaked from the rain, shoving things into her trunk. I pull in, barely turning my engine off before hopping out of my truck, the door still open as I cross to her.

"Don't," she says.

"We need to talk." I glance at the contents of her trunk, which is nearly filled. She's trying to pack it all, preventing her from having to return. I know this, just like I know she sleeps on her stomach and doesn't talk until she drinks a full cup of coffee in the morning, and that she can't recite a joke because she laughs too hard before the punchline.

"No. We needed to be honest, and you weren't. I don't have the time or the heart space to do this."

"Rae, it wasn't what you're thinking."

She stops. Her hair is soaked and sticking to her face, and her makeup has been washed off, her eyes and cheeks both red. "So, you didn't give her the pearl necklace that was in your truck?"

"It doesn't mean anything."

"Jesus," she drops her head back, her hands going to her head. "Of course, it means something. It means something to her, and it means you guys have a history far greater than what you tried to pass off as nothing." She reaches for her trunk, slamming it shut and keeping her hands on it. "And it means something to me."

"I'd bought it months ago, and I was late for her stupid birthday, and I didn't even think about it, Rae. It wasn't supposed to mean anything. I couldn't return it and there was no way I was going to give you a gift I'd bought for her."

She sighs. "Why couldn't you just be honest and admit you like her. That you've liked her for years?"

"Because it didn't matter. She didn't matter. Don't you understand? None of it matters anymore because you're the only one I care about. I love you, Raegan."

She shakes her head, her brow creased. "Don't. Don't say that. Not now. Not after I find out about this." She blows out a breath, tears falling in wide paths down her cheeks.

"Can we just talk about this? Let's go inside, and I'll tell you every last detail."

She shakes her head in short bursts, her tears falling faster as she leans back on her car, arms folded across her chest. "I'm sorry. I can't. Not right now. I need some time and space."

"Rae," I say, taking a step closer to her, wanting to hold her, to assure her of everything I know is true—of the clarity I found in telling my dad words I've needed to tell him for a decade. She twists, taking steps toward the front of her car.

"I can't. After what my dad did, I don't know what to think or what to believe, and I'm sorry. I don't want you to have to clean up and make up for his mistakes, but I just can't do this right now."

I nod. "You can stay here. We don't have to talk—"

She shakes her head again. "I need to go."

Pax pulls into the driveway, his music too loud, but I don't look at him. My world is split in two parts: Raegan and not Raegan, and right now she's the only thing I care about. "Please. I know you're upset. I know I've hurt you, and I'm sorry—I'm so damn sorry. If I could take it all back, I would. I'd take back that lost time after you got hurt. I'd take back trying to convince myself we could only be friends. I'd take back every fucking moment of knowing her if it meant you'd understand how much I care about you, how much it kills me when you're away."

Her lips are parted, her attention on me. "For how long? How long are you going to be interested in me before someone else catches your attention? How long until another girl is doing your laundry or wearing a necklace you bought them? You scare the hell out of me because you wouldn't leave just a bruise, you'd leave a crater." She slips into her car before I can assure her how many cards she holds, how Nikki could make me consider wanting to try, but it was her who committed me to the fact.

"What's going on?" Pax looks at me, his gaze critical and unsteady, tugging at the very thread of our friendship. I know I need to tell him the truth—be honest with him finally and tell him I've fallen in love with his sister—and if this was anyone else, I'd stop and try to ensure this final thread doesn't break since he's the closest thing I've known to family in the past decade, but I can't because my heart is already out of my body and speeding out of sight.

"I have to go."

"Stay away from her," he warns, stalking toward me as I rush to my truck. "Don't!" he yells.

"I can't," I tell him, wrenching my door open.

"The fuck you can't." He grabs a handful of my tuxedo, trying to haul me back.

I shake him off with one vicious pull that knocks him unsteady. "Don't do this, man."

He comes at me again, anger contorting his face into a stranger. "Stay away from her."

"I can't," I tell him, shaking my head. "Don't you understand? I can't. I wish I could."

"She's not a short-term addiction," he yells. "She's my fucking sister."

"Do you think I don't know that? Do you think I don't know she deserves better than me? More than me? I know."

Paxton's chest heaves with heavy breaths. "You're the one causing this mess. Just stay away from her. Time apart. That's what you need."

I yell, the sound a pain my soul can't translate into words that has Paxton staring at me. "Can't you see that's what I've been doing? What I've been trying to do all fucking year? You're like a brother to me, and so I tried. I tried staying away from her out of respect for you, but I can't anymore. I just can't. You can hate me, you can bench me, you can do whatever the hell you need to, but I've got to do this for me. For her because I know she needs me just as badly as I fucking need her."

He swings his head, looking to where her car was parked and then back at me. "This has been going on all year?" The anger in his voice ebbs with the addition of confusion and what I think is a note of realization.

I nod once. "I've tried my damndest to stay away from her. I swear to you, I tried so fucking hard to stay away from her and forget it all because I knew it could fuck things up between you and me—because you're the closest thing to a brother I have, but I can't do it anymore. I can't fucking think when she's not around—I can't even breathe."

Paxton sighs heavily, scrubbing a hand down his face. "I knew something was up, I just…" Another heavy sigh. "How the fuck am I supposed to take this? She's my sister. If you mess with her, I'm going to hate you. And if she fucks things up, I'm going to be pissed at her. You guys have me in a lose-lose situation where I'm fucked no matter what happens."

I nod. "I know. I'm sorry, man. I'm sorry you're in this position, but I have to go. I fucked up again, and I have talk to her."

Reluctance has him dropping his head back again, rolling his shoulders like it might help ease the idea of me being with his sister. "No," he says. "I forbid it."

39

RAEGAN

The skies are growing dark, the rain hitting my windshield like a strategic attack, making it difficult to see even with my wipers on full blast. My sweatshirt drips, a constant *plop, plop, plop* against my floorboards, and my jeans are so wet they're plastered uncomfortably to my skin, cutting into me and wrapping me in a familiar coldness. My knee aches, and I question if it's psychosomatic or if I'm channeling my mom? If my knee hurt earlier?

Thoughts and reason are at war, each objection met with an assurance, and each guarantee met with a new resistance that rolls down my cheeks and makes my nose grow stuffy and my head throb.

I press the 'call' button on my steering wheel. "Call Poppy," I say.

Her phone rings twice. "If you're calling me to brag about delicious wedding cake and more delicious sex, I'm hanging up."

My throat grows tight as I try to laugh, but it makes me cough, the sensation too familiar, reminding me even more of those days following the accident.

"Rae?" she says, her voice changing in an instant, concern and dread deepening her voice and canceling the cheer. "What's wrong?"

"Do you mind if I stay with you?"

"What? Yes. I mean no. Come over, or I can meet you."

I pull in a shaky breath, wiping my eyes because the rain has everything blurred without the addition of my tears. "I'm like fifteen minutes out."

"What happened?"

"I don't know," I admit. "I don't know if I'm just sabotaging things or if I'm finally facing reality. Do you remember Nikki?"

"Yeah…"

"She was there tonight. Apparently, Lincoln's dad and her dad are business partners, and they've known each other forever. Like taking baths and family vacations together, forever. And she cornered me in the bathroom. I know she was trying to get to me. She was trying to get into my head and make me doubt things because she likes him. Because as girls, we have a way of finding the greatest vulnerabilities and then picking at them like a loose thread, and she didn't delay in ripping that thread. He gave her a necklace."

"A necklace?"

"A pearl necklace."

"She told you he did?"

I shake my head, though she can't see me. "I know he bought it. I saw it in his truck weeks ago, and he admitted to it."

"What?" She sounds as angry and confused as I do, and I can picture my best friend pushing both hands into her red hair like she does when she's stunned. "Why? Why would he do that?"

"She said he gets her a piece of jewelry with a pearl every year for her birthday."

Poppy releases a gentle growl. "Okay. It's all right. He's a guy. Guys are dense. To him, it probably means next to nothing. He probably doesn't realize it even means anything to *her*."

"It's jewelry, and so, if that is the case, then the necklace he gave me means nothing." My admission is quiet, a painful reality I've been trying to ignore since I recognized the offending piece of jewelry.

She sighs heavily. "I don't know. I feel like after everything you guys have been through—after all, that he's done to prove his feelings—this has to be a mistake. I think you're right. I think she was trying to get under your skin, and she hit you right where you're the weakest because you still refuse to believe you're good enough for him, which you are. He chose you. He wants you, and she knows that, and she was bitter. Come over. We'll order pizza and share a good cry, and then I'm going to make you write 'I'm good enough' twelve thousand times or until Lincoln comes over, whichever comes first. My money's on Lincoln, though."

"There are so many things against us."

"I know. I get it. I understand how debilitating that fear is. How scary the idea of taking a bullet to the heart is, but you have to stop being your own worst enemy."

My thoughts dash to another night, the first night Lincoln kissed me when he'd lit a cigarette and I'd told him he was creating an obstacle for himself, and he'd said it was because he was at least able to have a say in the matter.

If I want a say in the matter, why am I running when I should be fighting?

A fresh round of tears spring to my eyes as I think of his words while I packed to leave, him telling me he loved me, and how I didn't reciprocate the words though I've felt them and thought them no less than a million times.

"You're right," I tell her.

"Which part? Because I've said a lot."

I laugh, wiping my nose with the back of my hand. "All of it."

"It's okay to feel overwhelmed. Love has a way of making even simple things seem overwhelming if you try to dissect it, rather than just live in the moment—and then when you find that balance, everything feels easy."

My thoughts flip to times we've been alone, to him meeting me after Maggie left, and the past week where each moment has felt easy and natural and too good. A lead weight presses against my stomach. "I think Pax figured it out. He was confronting Lincoln, and I left." I groan. "I left him to face it alone."

"It's probably better that way, honestly. They need to have it out and clear the air."

"Yeah, but I should be there."

"Actually, you shouldn't," Poppy says. "They've been best friends for three years. You and Pax will need to have a conversation, sure, but so do they."

I consider Poppy's words, thinking about the bond she and I share—how when she started dating Mike, our solid relationship suddenly felt flimsy because, like our egos and our hopes, relationships can be severely damaged with our own negative thoughts.

"If Dylan doesn't like my eyeliner, he's in for a show when he sees my current look."

Poppy chuckles. "Pizza? Chinese? Thai? What do you want?"

"I'm not hungry. I just need to sort out my feelings and try calling Lincoln so I can apologize. But, you're right. They need their time, and I don't want to interrupt."

"My mom's working late, so I'm getting pizza and Thai. Once you smell it, you'll be hungry."

The last thing on my mind is food as I glance at my dash to see if I've received any texts from Lincoln. There's none.

Ahead is the exit for the Sound. It feels like a beckon—kismet of sorts, and I'm already pulling the wheel to take it.

"I'm going to stop at the marina. I just need to gather my thoughts for a few."

"It's raining."

"I know."

"It's getting dark," she says.

"I know. I just need to go there for a little while. The ocean and I, we're still trying to make peace ourselves."

"I know. I get it. Have you talked to your mom? She's getting home tomorrow, right?"

I release a sigh. "Yeah. She called this morning. She asked if I wanted to move in with her or stay living with my dad."

"What did you tell her?"

"I didn't know what to say. I mean, I don't know if she wants me to be with her and I can make it easier for her to go through this transition or if she asked out of obligation?"

"Your mom loves you. You know if she had her way, all three of you would be living with her still."

I think of Mom's reaction when Paxton had started talking about moving out, how she'd made all his favorite meals and bought a larger TV in the living room in hopes he'd change his mind. Even then, it didn't feel like she was trying to bribe him—it still doesn't. She was just trying to fight for him to stay longer without actually saying the words, knowing she'd put him in a tough place.

"You're right. I think part of it is I always imagined that when I moved out, it would be because you and I were moving out into an apartment together—not because my parents were getting a divorce and my dad had a girlfriend who was one year older than me."

"Technically, two. She's Paxton's age."

I groan. "Don't tell me the details. I don't want to know."

"I know. But you're going to have to face them, eventually. Not now, not tonight, but soon you're going to have to talk to your dad and at least figure out where you guys stand. He's going to be back at school soon."

"What? But, he resigned?"

"I guess, he withdrew it."

"Can that even happen?"

"I guess so," Poppy says.

I sigh deeply. "I heard it on the news yesterday while I was working. He made a public apology, and I guess it's with a review board or something? I didn't catch the end because the phone was ringing off the hook."

"It still feels like he's a stranger."

"I know—I get that. Maybe if you guys met somewhere on neutral ground, like, to get breakfast or something, it would be better?"

"But what do I even say? Hey, Dad, how's your girlfriend? Was it worth losing the family over?"

"Probably not the best opening line..."

I chuckle—it's a dry and mirthless sound. "Probably not. We'll see. I should probably see him before I run into him on campus."

"Exactly my thought."

I pull into the familiar gravel parking lot, my thoughts racing in more unwanted directions.

"You've got this, Rae. It's going to suck, but you're going to get through it, and you won't have to do it alone. We're all here for you."

Her affection makes my eyes burn with tears. "You're the best, and I really appreciate you going through all of this with me. I don't know where I'd be this year without you."

"I'm pretty sure my debt is still greater. While I try to block out most of last summer, I vividly remember you showing up every single day, sitting with me while I played Tracy Chapman on repeat and ate my weight in frosting."

"You were dealing with a broken heart."

"And so are you," she tells me. "Not all broken hearts come in the same shape and size—just like not every broken heart is due to a boyfriend. In your case, it's your dad. And that's okay. You deserve to be sad and mad and grieve. And when you're ready to start, I'll be there with the tubs of frosting and movies, and Oreos, just like you were there for me."

I swallow the denials that start to bubble up like a geyser, wishing to be heard.

I start to open my door, not ready to end our conversation, but anxious to get closer to the water. The moment I open my door, the cold air leaches through my damp clothes, heckling me for leaving. If I hadn't overreacted—if I'd stayed and asked Lincoln about the necklace—I'd likely be dancing with him and eating what appeared to have been the best wedding cake in the history of cakes.

"Should I call Lincoln and see how things are going? Or text him?"

"Raegan," A woman's voice calls, making me jump.

I turn, chills coursing down my arms. A woman is a few steps behind me, a purple coat with sleeves too short. Her proximity makes my heart accelerate, but then she pulls her hood back, allowing me to see her face.

Lindsay Meyer.

My muscles all feel weighted and sluggish, like my bones are made of uranium, too heavy to move as I stare at her, considering all the millions of silent questions I've wanted to ask her. The information I've worked to avoid with every paper that has had her name and face strewn across the front.

Her hands are together, her thumbs brushing over something white between her fingers.

"Why are you holding that?" I ask, recognizing the crane as one of more than a dozen that I've found over the past few months.

Lindsay's eyes grow dark as she sneers, yelling a sound that makes my heart feel both fearful and sad—a pit of emotions I can tell she can't translate into words. She throws the crane at me, hitting me in the chest.

"It's all your fault." She pulls back, and I'm frozen, attempting to digest this moment: her presence, the cranes, her involvement and knowing so much about me when I've questioned so much about her. "You took him away from me." Her hands pull from her pockets, and the sadness in her voice is cut by the sight of a gun that looks heavy and clunky in her hands.

"Rae!" Poppy says in my ear. "What are you doing? Is everything okay?"

"Lindsay's here," I say, my voice rushed and too quiet.

"What? Lindsay? Lindsay who?"

"Hang up," she demands. Her anger is intense like the sun, burning me just by our nearness, scaring me further because I can tell she's not acting on a plan but emotions. "Poppy, I have to go."

"Rae, is that her? Oh my God. Rae. Get in your car. Rae? Get in your car. Now. Lock the doors."

"Turn it off!" Lindsay shrieks.

"Poppy, I have to go."

"Raegan, get in your goddamn car!"

Before I can reply, Lindsay reaches forward and rips my phone away. I don't try and stop her as a familiar feeling floods back into my body—I spent weeks obsessing over the moments I spent underwater, remembering the details to a painful extent—yet this part, the surge of emotions and energy that makes everything seem more intense: louder, brighter, slower—I'd somehow forgotten this part.

40

LINCOLN

"How in the hell am I supposed to trust you?" Pax asks, pausing when his phone rings, playing a tune for several seconds before he reaches for it. "Yeah?" His brow creases. "Poppy, what?" He shakes his head in tight jerks, his brow furrowing. "Slow down. What are you talking about? What do you mean?"

I swing my door open, ready to climb in when Paxton yanks me backward, his eyes round, and his lips agape. "Call the cops, and tell them what you just told me. We're leaving now."

My heart feels like a firecracker exploding, each blast a fresh fear as Pax goes silent, his brow stitching as he listens to something more that Poppy says. Paxton swallows, then looks at me, his face pale and his eyes too round. "Shit. Shit. Shit," he chants. "Call the cops. We're coming." He ends the call and looks at me again. "We have to go. Let's go." Paxton moves around to the passenger side of my truck and climbs in.

"What's going on?"

"Rae's in trouble. Our dad's girlfriend followed her... She's at the marina. She's there with her."

My blood turns to ice, crystalizing as the idea percolates, making my skin prickle. My knuckles turn white as I grip the steering wheel, reversing and coming to an abrupt halt that makes my tires squeal before

I peel out, resuming my earlier race. "What do you mean she's there? Like, she's talking to her?"

Pax shakes his head, working on dialing a number that I presume is Rae's. "I don't know. I don't ... I don't know." His throat clears, and then he punches the dash of my truck with his phone. "Fuck!" He returns to his phone too fast as I turn my windshield wipers up even higher. "Poppy said she's who sent the cranes. That Rae's still been getting the fucking cranes..." He lands an accusing glare on me before hitting more buttons on his phone. His words settle against my nerves, raking against me like a vegetable peeler, making me feel raw and exposed in the most painful ways.

Paxton puts his phone to his ear again, impatience has him tapping a beat on the dash. "What's going on?" he demands. "What have you done?" There's a rush of words I can't hear, and then Paxton slams his knuckles against the door. "Your girlfriend's been stalking Raegan for months. She fucking followed her to the goddamn marina. Don't tell me you have it under control."

My thoughts are consumed with images of Raegan in the ocean, imagining her face down, floating across the surface. It's a nightmare that's plagued me since the night of her accident and took her sleeping beside me to end. I blare the horn, riding someone's bumper like a royal asshole until they move out of my way.

"You haven't handled it. This isn't handled." He hangs up, running a hand over his hair. "I'm going to kill him if something happens."

More cars honk and flip me off as I pull to the shoulder and drive like it's an added lane, but I don't give a single fuck as I listen to these foreign words process with the impossible situation at hand.

"What are we going to do?" I ask.

Paxton shakes his head. "Caleb," he says. He fumbles with his phone once more, cursing before his phone starts to ring on speakerphone.

"Dude. How do you always know when I'm getting food?" Caleb answers.

"Caleb," Pax shakes his head like the words are impossible to find to describe the current situation. In truth, they are.

"The person who was leaving the cranes for Raegan," I say, "It was the dean's girlfriend. She's left more, and now she followed Raegan, and she's with her at the marina."

There's silence. "What?"

"What do we do?" Pax asks.

"You call the fucking police. Don't get involved. You don't know what you're doing. You could make it worse."

"It's Raegan," Pax yells, his frustration vibrating around the cab of my truck, landing on me like the rain falls on my windshield, soaking into my fears and pooling with my own anger.

Caleb sighs. "When you get there, talk to the girl. Calmly. Don't try and get too close, and just buy time until the police arrive."

I shake my head, hating his words nearly as much at the situation. Being told I once again can't interfere is like sitting on the sidelines of a losing game, like watching Raegan walk away and not working harder to fight for her.

"What if she's not close to Rae?" Pax asks. "What if we just take her down? Tackle her."

"You don't know if she has a weapon or if she's going to hurt herself or Raegan," Caleb warns. "You don't want to spook her or make her feel worried. That will lead to a bad scenario."

We reach the gates that are permanently propped open, my tires spraying gravel against the metal post. I slow down, my headlights bouncing off the ground with the sudden dip in the road.

"Be calm. Keep your distance and try to find some middle ground with her. Get her talking to you. Make her see Raegan as a person rather than a hindrance," Caleb continues.

"There!" Pax says, shooting his arm up and pointing near the dock.

I pull as close as we can get, leaving the engine running and the headlight on for additional light as we pile out, trying to slow our speed as we make our way down the dock that sways with our added weight.

They're standing near the end, under the single lamp post. The ocean a black backdrop that crashes, trying to meet the heavy rain that continues to splatter against every surface. Raegan's body is tense, her hands on her head as a girl dressed in a purple coat stands next to her, a gun in her hand moving toward us as we near.

"What is this?" the girl yells. "What did you do?" She swings her attention to Raegan, her voice and motions unsteady.

The sky is growing darker, trying to meet the heavy rain that continues to splatter against every surface. As we get closer, I inspect Raegan, tracing her pale face, her hair which is soaked like her clothes. She flicks her attention to me, her eyes wild, but her body still.

"We just want to help," Paxton says, raising both hands in the air as he steps next to me. "We aren't going to hurt you. We aren't here to blame you. We just want to make sure everyone's safe." This is a one-eighty from the side of Paxton, who was ready to throw down in the driveway fifteen minutes ago.

"Why are you here?" Lindsay yells. "How did you find us? What did you do?" She yells the accusation again, turning the gun back on Rae, who meets her gaze.

"You don't want to do this," Paxton says. "Let's just talk. Tell us what we can do."

She shrieks. "It's her fault!" She moves closer to Raegan, who grits her teeth as Lindsay waves the gun over her. "She made him choose between her and me, and he chose her. He's *always* chosen her."

"He didn't choose either of us," Raegan says. "He chose himself."

Lindsay stares at her, a heavy frown marring her face.

"She's right," Paxton says. "He's who did this."

"No. No. No!" Lindsay shakes her head in rapid jerks. "After she was hospitalized, he started to pull away, and then after she walked in that night, she ruined everything."

Raegan watches her, and I recognize the rapt attention, the way she's reading her body and movements like she reads the screen while watching tape.

"If he loved you, he'd make it happen. Trust me. When a person loves someone, they aren't afraid to go through hell," I say, distracting the girl, hoping her anger and attention will shift to me because I'm the farthest from Rae.

"You have no idea what love is!" Lindsay shrieks, her attention snapping to me, moving the gun to follow suit. "You guys barely know each other. You've been together for a second, and we've known each other for two years! *Two years!*" she yells the words. "She was supposed to move out, and then he was going to get a divorce." Her attention starts to redirect back to Raegan too quickly.

I step forward, the action immediate and unmeasured, a reaction because I can't sit back any longer. It has her swinging the gun back at me, her eyes hard and narrowed. "Why does everyone want to save her?"

"It was me," Pax says, taking a step closer as well. "I told our dad I'd never speak to him again if he left our mom for you. It was my fault. If you want to blame someone, blame me."

"He's lying," Raegan says as the gun turns to Paxton. "He didn't even know until the video came out. It was me. But, it wasn't to hurt you. It was to protect my family—my mom. He made this mess, and we'll help you. We'll help you figure everything out."

"How?" she yells. "I was kicked out of school. My parents won't speak to me. My friends call me a homewrecker, and he's not even here to help or stand by me after everything I've lost—everything I gave up for him." Tears choke her up, and for a second, I almost feel sorry for her, realizing she drew the short straw.

"My dad can help you," I volunteer. "He's a lawyer, and he can get you back into school. He'll take it on pro bono. It won't cost you a cent."

Lindsay starts shaking her head. "I won't be able to come back from this. I'll be arrested. I want to hurt her. I want to make her hurt like I hurt. I want her dead." Her tears increase, flooding my fears as her words repeat.

"You don't," I tell her. "You don't want to live with that. You don't want someone else to hurt. You haven't done anything that you can't come back from. Let's keep it that way, okay? Let's just take a deep breath, and put the gun down."

She looks from me to Raegan. "How do I know this isn't a trap?"

"Because he's the most honest person you'll ever meet," Rae says. "And because I love them, both of them, and they won't do anything to hurt you or me."

Lindsay looks haunted and defeated—a concoction that scares me more than the anger that had been so visible because one doesn't see reason or the potential loss when they already feel like they've lost everything. She moves, time slowing like so many movies have portrayed, like you know the moment is coming, allowing you to memorize every detail so you can appreciate it all one final time.

Raegan's face falls, her arms dropping to her sides as she recognizes the same reality—my reality. Raegan screams, the sound masked by the gun firing.

41

RAEGAN

I slam into her, my weight taking her down easily. We fall fast and hard, her head hitting the lamppost, the sound eerily like that of a melon cracking and making my stomach churn before my knees and hands hit the slick wooden dock. The gun clangs against the boards near me. I reach for it, losing my grip as I do, my chest hitting the dock and knocking the air out of me before her legs slip from mine, and there's a loud splash.

My attention shoots to Lincoln who's crouched, his eyes impossibly wide. "Are you okay?" he asks, moving to stand.

I nod, my heart beating so fast, I'm dizzy. "I'm fine. Are you okay?"

He nods, climbing to his knees and then his feet.

"We have to help her." I tear my attention away from Lincoln, though my entire body wants to reach for him, feel his heat, the security of his touch, the assurance of his kiss.

"She tried to shoot us," Pax says, moving to Lincoln when I take too long.

"I know, but it's his fault, not hers." I glance back at the dark water, knowing she's sinking farther into the depths with each second.

"Raegan!" Lincoln yells. "Don't."

I glance at him. "I won't leave you. I promise. But, I can't let her die. Our dad did this to her."

Lincoln starts toward me. "If you jump in there, you're crazy."

I grin. It feels reckless and irrational, similar to my mood. "Fifteen seconds," I tell him. "Also, I love you, too," I say, and then I jump.

The contrast of the cold water flooding every inch of my body has my thoughts flashing back to that night I jumped in to save Blue. I feel imaginary tugs on my clothes, making my heart pound in my chest with fear as I thrash my arms to rid the invisible attack I know is only in my mind.

The water laps at my skin, a silent countdown in my head, echoing the dangers of being under for too long as I dive down, praying I have some chance to catch up with her.

I kick and push the water, swimming so deep I can barely see, my eyes burning with the tiny debris floating around and the salt.

Then, my hand brushes against something soft, making me cringe. Nightmares of the stories people have told for centuries about monsters that lurk in the depths of the Pacific make me nearly suck in a breath of the icy salt water, but then I feel the warmth of skin and fabric. I wrap my arms around her, everything weighing me down: my clothes, her, her clothes. I kick and push, clutching her dead weight as the time starts to speed up. Then, warm hands tap my arm, and through the dark and murky water, I see Lincoln, and beside him is Pax, here for me like he's always been there for me. Lincoln grabs my hand, and Paxton takes her weight before shoving me upward. I follow Lincoln, kicking as my lungs start to burn, and my muscles start to ache. I clear the surface with a gasp, my breaths coming out in fast bursts as I suck in the night air, rain falling across my hair and face as I look for Lincoln.

He swims toward me, his hair pushed back, and his eyes still wild and wide. "Are you okay?" He cups my face, his eyes following the path of his fingers as he traces over me.

I nod, still shivering. "Are you okay? Did she hit you?" I ask, scouring the details of his face and expression.

Lincoln leans forward, his lips crashing against mine in a clumsy and cold kiss. "She missed. She hit the water." He kisses me again, gentler this time. "God, you scared me."

Tears pool in my eyes, but before I can answer, Pax surfaces several feet away, Lindsay still in his arms as he heaves a deep breath.

I tread water, attempting to ascertain the best way to help get her out, my arms and legs cutting through the water, the freezing temperatures feeling so different than they had that night with Blue, the fear inside of me nearly forgotten as the same comfort the ocean's always provided returns. There's no way I should have been able to reach Lindsay, not with how long it took me to dive in and the lack of visibility. The ocean helped me, I know it did, and I don't question the how or why, I simply revel in the fact that my purpose and place feels renewed.

"I can't tell if she's breathing," Pax says.

"We need to get her out."

Lincoln appears beside me. "Let's get her to the ladder. I'll climb out, and I can pull her up. Time's not going to be our friend."

Lights start twisting in the air as we swim toward the dock, and then I hear Poppy yelling my name, and a man arguing with her to stay back. A police officer appears, shining his flashlight on us and blinding me. Then another officer appears, this one shorter.

"What's going on?" the shorter officer asks.

Paxton shakes his head, all of us speechless for a moment as we digest the last few moments. Then, Dad appears, his brow furrowed, and his beard gone. "Raegan. Paxton." He places a hand on his chest, his head tipping skyward, making my emotions feel weighted with a constant train of conflicting thoughts. "Thank God you're both all right." He looks at us and then Lindsay. "Is she okay?"

"I don't think she's breathing," I tell him.

The officers each take a knee, helping to lift Lindsay out of the water before we follow, climbing up the rickety ladder.

The second our feet are on the dock, I catch sight of an officer doing chest compressions on Lindsay while another officer lays a blanket over her legs. A frantic chain of words are spoken, and then I see Dad. He hovers over her, watching and listening as intently as we do.

Responsibility and fear press on my lungs as I wait with bated breath. It's a confounding and overwhelming sense of emotions that pass through me as I watch Lindsay lying there, knowing it was my dad and their list of broken promises and lies that led to this moment. And though I know I didn't intentionally hurt her, I'm already thinking about how I could have done something—anything—differently so it didn't end like this.

"We've got a pulse. Turn her!" They move her to her side in time for her to throw up a stomach-full of seawater.

"Medics should be here in less than five," one of the officers says.

I shiver, the combination of the cold water and icy wind and receding adrenaline creating a tenseness that makes my entire body hurt, though my mind feels a new sense of ease and calm.

"Raegan!" Poppy yells, her feet falling loud and fast across the dock. She doesn't hesitate, wrapping her arms around me even though I'm sopping wet. Her grip is tight, her embrace warm for a full second before she pulls back and looks at me with a scrutinizing glance. "Are you okay?"

I'm barely able to confirm with a nod before she's hugging me.

A fire truck arrives, closely followed by an ambulance, and we watch in silence as they assist Lindsay. My ease grows as she moves her legs and arms, and then plummets when she motions to the back of her head.

"She's fine. She's going to be just fine," Lincoln says, placing a hand on my shoulder. "You saved my life."

Before his words can sink in, Dad walks toward us, pushing a hand through his hair. He looks ten years older than he did a few weeks ago. He stops several feet in front of us. "Are you guys okay?" His gaze crosses between us, guilt furrowing his brow. "I swear, I had no idea she'd do this."

"But you should've," Pax says. "You ruined that girl's life, and in the process, you nearly took Raegan's. That's on you."

Dad nods. "I know. I understand." He turns his gaze to me, silent apologies creasing his brow. "I'm sorry. I'm so sorry. I never meant for this to happen. I never meant to hurt anyone."

Poppy keeps hold of my arm but turns to face him. "You can't expect them to accept your apology. Not now, not after this. You're going to have to clean this monumental mess you've made, and then after you do that, you can offer another apology, but you can't expect an acceptance. That's not how apologies work. It's her choice. It's his choice."

"I didn't—" Dad starts.

Poppy shakes her head. "It doesn't matter. Actions speak louder than words. Prove that you're sorry, and don't make them feel guilty for not being ready to accept your lousy apology after everything you've done."

Dad nods. "I will. I'll fix this."

Memories of him promising to fix things that night I found him with Lindsay make my eyes sting and betrayal to creep into my thoughts. Still, I want to believe him. I want to think of the man I knew when I was little, the one whose toes I stood on as he spun me around the kitchen, and sat patiently with me while I stared out at the ocean, waiting to catch a glimpse of a whale. The one who attended every football game of Paxton's and cried openly when Maggie left.

"Dad," I say, taking a step.

He stops from turning around, the same hope I'm feeling apparent in his eyes. "It's not just us who need you to clean things up. You need to talk to Maggie and to Mom. And you need to help Lindsay without taking more from her. You've hurt her so much."

Dad presses his lips together, running a hand over his shaven jaw. He slowly nods. "I understand."

Pax blows out a long, slow breath as Dad turns, speaking to an officer who approaches him. "You're out of your mind, you know that, right?" He asks. "I can't believe you jumped in there."

"Yes, you can," I tell him.

He fights a smile, running a hand over his face as water drips from his hair. "You're still crazy."

"I fell in love with your best friend. If that isn't proof that I'm crazy, then I don't know what is."

Pax shakes his head, a near-silent scoff. "I told you to date a book nerd."

"I did," I argue. "Have you seen how many books he owns?" I ask, glancing at Lincoln.

He smirks, his brown eyes bright with humor. "This is true," he says.

"If that wasn't bending the rules, then I don't know what is," Pax says with a smirk.

"I'm pretty sure they broke the rules," Poppy says, turning her attention to me, bestowing me with a wide and familiar smile. "Finally."

I move my attention to Pax. "I'm sorry I didn't tell you," I say. "I know this sounds like an excuse, but I just didn't want to interfere when you already had so much going on. I swear, I was going to tell you, after your last game, I was going to tell you everything."

Pax links his arm around my shoulder, his touch cold for several seconds before turning warm. "You should have told me about the cranes, and Dad, and Lincoln."

I nod. "I know."

"But, I get it. And while it's strange as fuck, I get it. I see it, now. It's going to take some time to get used to this, but," his gaze cuts to Lincoln, "I'm not going to get in the way. You guys need each other, and I'm not going to mess it up." He pulls in a breath. "So, kiss and make up while I go buy you five minutes from all these cops." His hand slips from my shoulder, and he walks up the dock with Poppy at his side.

I turn to Lincoln. His wet dress shirt is plastered to his chest, and his lips are starting to turn a light shade of blue. "I'm sorry I left. I should have stayed and talked to you about everything. I should have explained to you how I felt and why it bothered me so much, and I should have trusted you instead of her."

He shakes his head. "I wasn't even thinking. That stupid necklace I gave her meant nothing to me, but I can see how it would mean something to her, and more importantly, to you. I didn't mean to hurt you. I swear, I will do anything—*everything*—to make sure you're safe and that you're happy and feel heard—feel seen because I see you, Raegan Lawson. I see every part of you, and I love you."

I reach forward, trailing my fingers over his cheek. "I was so scared when she aimed the gun at you," I admit.

The column of his throat moves as he swallows. Then, he lowers his forehead to mine. "I swear to God, I'm building you a bubble."

I laugh, closing my eyes as his hand comes to my waist, anchoring me.

"I need to hear you say it again. Tell me you love me without following it by diving into the fucking ocean again."

My lips curve into a smile, my laughter catching in my throat as he takes a step back, his dark eyes more intense and intent than I've ever seen them—his vulnerability fully exposed as he stares at me.

"I love you, Lincoln. I love you so much. I've loved you—"

He silences me with a kiss that is demanding and impatient, much like Lincoln is. We kiss urgently in the borrowed time, knowing later we'll be making time for slower kisses where we can appreciate these words and their truths.

EPILOGUE
LINCOLN

Coach Harris chews his gum so furiously his jaw pops with protest. He leans back on his heels. "This is it. This is what you've all been working for." He peers at our team, stopping when he reaches me. "Let's get back out there and show this team what you're made of. You hear me?" The team whoops and claps and then turns back around. Coach Harris stalks to me, his hand on my shoulder. "You all right, son?"

I nod, drying my hands on the towel. "Never been better."

He grins. "I see that. You're not just playing like you've got something to prove—tonight you're playing like you've got something to lose."

I think about his words as I drift back to my place on the field, soaking up the sounds, the lights, the energy that still feeds me like a physical substance. I glance higher into the stands, and though I can't find her with the thousands crowding the bleachers, I can feel her presence.

Pax makes a beeline for me, his gaze intense. "Stop hunting for my little sister, and get your head in the game."

I flash an immediate grin. "You have your game habits, I've got mine."

His lips tip upward. After that night on the dock a month ago, something changed for all of us, something individually as well as collectively.

A price was put on friendship and love. A reality we'd already met once that reminded us nothing is guaranteed and everything should be savored. "You feeling okay?"

We've worked diligently to keep the details from that night out of the press in hopes of saving what was left of Lindsay Meyer's reputation. Last we heard, she transferred to a school down in Oregon, and her parents moved with her.

Pax nods, then glances up into the stands. "She's in there somewhere. Don't let her down," he pats my shoulder, the same one that has felt weaker all year and still hints at the idea.

We're at our final bowl game of the year, Christmas having passed just two days before, a Christmas that was different in nearly every aspect from years past. Things between my dad and I didn't magically resolve with that single conversation at his wedding. He's still in denial that my future won't include a plaque on a door at his law office, and though he spends more time at home with Carol than he has with his ex-wives who came before, he still has a long way to go toward reaching any husband of the year awards. Still, Raegan and I went to brunch at their house, where Dad asked too many questions about her dad and her future, and not enough getting to know her. Then Raegan gave him a book about Andy Warhol and the history of modern artists, and it was as though a switch was flipped and the side of my dad that so commonly focusses on business dealings seemed to fade as the lesser-known personal side of him peeked out. They began discussing life and how she had visited Italy as a freshman, my dad's love for the museums in Italy, her adoration for the culture and food, and before I knew what was happening, they were laughing, and Raegan pulled me into the conversation with both hands, talking about me and our undefeated season, how school was going, and my continued love for history that had us debating modern-day culture and the impacts of past civilizations and which brought us the greatest rewards and cost us the greatest detriments.

After that, we spent the afternoon and evening with Paxton and their mom, grandpa, and Camilla in the new house their mom bought a couple weeks before. It's a small brownstone, built in the early 1920s. Raegan's still struggling to know where things lie between her and her dad, and I don't blame her. At times I want to give my unsolicited advice and tell her to keep him out of her life—especially after everything I saw he was capable of and the destruction he caused others, but Raegan isn't like me. She has the ability to forgive, and considering I've been on the receiving end of that quality, I don't dare hinder it, only learn from it.

We line up, and I watch the field for the markers Raegan warned us about. I take a final fleeting glance at the crowd before my focus falls solely on the field and each player.

"WHY AREN'T WE CELEBRATING?" Raegan asks, pushing against my shoulder with hers.

"We are."

"We ditched everyone and came out to eat tacos."

I grin. "You said they were the best tacos of your life."

"They were. When in California, baby." She leans her head against my shoulder, a breeze blowing her hair and perfume to greet me. I smile, pressing a kiss to the top of her head as I stare at the ocean. The waves crash with a natural rhythm dictated by the moon that sits two-hundred-and-thirty-eight thousand and nine-hundred miles away.

"Dr. Swanson accepted me," she tells me quietly.

I shift, moving to see her. "I told you he would. He didn't stand a chance after meeting you."

Raegan grins. "I get to swim with Blue, and it's all thanks to you."

"That was all you, Kerosene."

In one quick move, she closes her eyes and leans into me, her lips warm and impossibly soft as they meet mine, a confidence there that has strengthened over the past month. I place my free hand on her waist, pulling her closer to me as I claim her mouth while she claims the space in my chest that's solely devoted to her. Her body relaxes against mine, wanting me—trusting me. My fingers at her waist slide beneath her sweatshirt, connecting with her flesh as I swipe my tongue against her lips, parting them. She moans. It's gentle and quiet, yet I feel it in my chest as I swallow the taste of her. Everything about her makes me feel empowered and emboldened in a way that is more powerful than any win on the field I've ever experienced.

I slide my tongue along hers, demanding everything she has to offer while giving what's left of me that she hasn't already taken. I move my hands to her thighs, and she knows what I'm going to do before I lift her, making her tense and pull back. I lean closer, silencing her objections as I lower myself to the ground with her on my lap, my hands on her ass, pulling her so close doubt can't reach either of us as we lose ourselves in this kiss that I know will define the rest of my days.

When she pulls away, we're both out of breath, our chests heaving as I wish I could transform this beach into anywhere else that would allow me to strip her of her clothes and inhibitions and consume every last part of her.

She leans her forehead against mine, our breath mingling in quick bursts that make my lips dry. "Let's go. I want you to consume me."

I swallow her breaths, my forehead still pressed against hers. "I don't just want to consume you, I want to own you—possess every part of you. Make your heart beat like mine does for you."

"It already does."

ACKNOWLEDGMENTS

First off, I have to thank my family. I disappeared for hours and sometimes days while I wrote Raegan and Lincoln's story, and then re-wrote them, and then re-wrote them again. A special thanks to my husband for taking on the painful job of teaching me about football and football lingo and football schedules, and everything else I didn't know and sometimes didn't want to know.

A very special thanks to Arielle Brubaker for finding the time and patience to fit these books into her schedule and help me through so many concerns and doubts I harbored. Also, you are a genius mind reader, and I'm never letting you go!

A huge thanks to Terri Peterson, who is always my fearless Guinea pig, who received chapters of Bending the Rules over a year ago and has patiently been waiting all this time.

Thank you to Lisa Greenwood for being such a wonderful friend and forgetful sounding board. I'm glad you were still shocked by Raegan's accident, though we discussed it at great lengths! Ha!

And a GIANT thank you to all the readers and bloggers who have picked up these books and read them. I know the world is a bit crazy right now, and I sure hope these stories gave you a small reprieve. I appreciate you reading these books and wish I could give you all a giant squeeze!

ABOUT THE AUTHOR

Mariah Dietz is a USA Today Bestselling Author and self proclaimed nerd. She lives with her husband and sons in North Carolina.

Mariah grew up in a tiny town outside of Portland, Oregon where she spent most of her time immersed in the pages of books that she both read and created.

She has a love for all things that include her family, good coffee, books, traveling, and dark chocolate. She's also been known to laugh at her own jokes.

www.mariahdietz.com
mariah@mariahdietz.com
Subscribe to her newsletter, here